WILD HORSES

Reality is, at best, an illusion between two lies.
— LLUÏSA CABELLERA

NATURAL OVERDOSE

Faith has been broken, tears must be cried,
Let's do some living, after we die
'Wild Horses', THE ROLLING STONES

It isn't the least bit strange – in fact I'd say it was only natural –
that the first of these stories begins at a funeral. But rather than
the archetypal wet winter morning, it was a sweaty, torrid affair
at the height of summer.

Things inside were pleasant enough, at least temperature-wise
because churches, as we all know, are natural fridges but when
(*'Brothers, go now in peace…'*) we went back to our vehicles
to wait for the coffin before following it to the cemetery, the
concentrated heat inside our car burned so oppressively that
it threatened to suffocate us there and then. Sitting inside my
beloved but air con-less Marlene as she trailed the corpsedelivery-
van were: Eulàlia (in those days still playing the role of my lover);
Lídia (ditto, but for Fermí); Fermí (oh, the inevitable Mín) and
me (Alexandre Oscà i Punyol, sat behind the wheel).

Nine or ten years earlier, the recently departed Lluïsa Cabellera
i Enbosc (today mourned by parents, sibling and friends), Fermí
and I had formed a tightknit family much more tightly knit than
conventional ones. In fact, we shared everything. And when I
say everything, I mean absolutely everything: flats, food, cars,
parties, drugs. On some occasions, casualovers and on many
more – like good little brothers and sisters – a bed. I, on the other
hand, had shared both bread and bed with her in Ibiza back in
'75 as well as after our arcadian adventures in Lo Pont de Suert
during the *annus horribilis* of '82. That's why, despite the sun's
silent savagery, we felt obliged to go to the cemetery and endure
our own slice of impotent nostalgia. If only we'd punctured all

four tyres and the engine had burst into flames on our way there.

Not even the slightest whiff of a breeze breached the walls to the city of the dead and the few spots of shade next to the open niche had been taken up by the family. And so we had to stand rooted to the spot under an implacable downpour of forty degree heat in our tragic 'trying not to be outcasts' outfits. I remember how I unwillingly began to picture the morbid biochemical processes already underway inside that very box. And no matter how much I tried to think about something else, all I could see was Lluïsa, wrapped in an exquisite blue dress she'd never worn before, turning into mould and maggots and nothingness.

It's funny, for lack of a better word, but I didn't picture the Lluïsa of recent times, teetering over the abyss of physical collapse due to the body blows dealt by AIDS and methadone abuse, but rather the graceful Lluïsa, the intelligent, sublime woman I'd met in Ibiza twelve or thirteen years back. The cogs and gears in the subconscious portion of my brain, machinery I'd long lost control of, subjected me to the terrible torture of recalling that brief taste of nirvana: how remote our teenage island happiness seemed! Within my devastated soul, rather than twelve years it felt more as if twelve centuries had passed.

I would've happily sacrificed a couple of fingers from my right hand to have been able to take off my suit jacket and unbutton my shirt, and every single last one from my left to have been sat outside some-bar-some-where with an ice-cold-double-dry-martini slipping down the hatch. The soaking sweat suffocating my armpits, crotch, feet, hands and head made me feel dirty, so to speak, as though to blame.

But ultimately, as usual, nothing good came of anything: neither the sacrifice of having attended that re-enactment of Hell nor having had the tact to come in conventional clothes. Someone, somewhere, at some point, had decided that we were in fact guilty, and after half an hour of the tip tapping trowel sealing her rite of passage, and under waves of heat capable of drowning Poseidon's horses, just as we'd crossed the sacred threshold, Lluïsa's brother, Pep, sprinted up behind us, slapped a hand on Fermí's left shoulder and spun him around.

'You've got some fuckin' nerve coming here! Billy big balls, huh?! One day they'll get so inflated you'll float away!'

We all knew what he was talking about. And we knew it wasn't a joke either, but a full-on-full-frontal assault.

'What's wrong, Pep? What are you getting at?' I hit back in a conciliatory tone.

'You can shut your fuckin' mouth for starters, you sonova-bitch! You're the guiltiest of the lot!'

Pepsin, as Lluïsa liked to call him, had completely lost control: a rabid impotence – in reality, one that I shared – had taken hold of his grief and if he'd been able to, he would've crushed the pair of us like someone stepping on a cockroach. I was already acquainted with him to a point from when Lluïsa and I spent a few months living with him in Blanes, back in the horrible year of '82, to be exact.

'I don't know what the hell you're getting at. Nor do I think it's the right place for a Pep talk.' I answered without modifying my tone.

'Don't get funny with me, sonovabitch, or I'll make you understand another way!'

'Get in the car,' Lali ordered us, blocking Pep in an attempt to avoid the threats spilling over into punches.

The mo(u)rning procession, emerging from the cemetery in a large huddle of farewells and final condolences, were met by our pathetic scene straight up ahead.

'Let's do as she says, Lex,' said Fermí as he turned towards the car.

'Yeah, let's do as she says…' I muttered, following behind him, feeling both angry and ashamed, 'because if he calls me a sonovabitch one more time…'

And that's when Peptic Pep went completely apeshit.

'What did you mean by that?' he screamed, hurling Lali to the ground with his left arm before launching himself at me just as I was turning around.

Now, I'm not a violent person, I assure you, but if there's one thing that makes me lose my cool it's seeing a fully grown man (that bastard Pep was forty years old and six foot tall) physically harm a woman. Even more so if the woman weighs barely nine stone and happens to be my girlfriend. So, taking advantage of my momentum, I spun onto my left foot and thrust my right one up and out as fast as I could: Pep slammed into it at a hulking speed and we both fell on our arses in the cemetery car park. In a flash Mín and three or four figurines from the funeral cortege came to re-establish the peace. But the war was already over: Pep was curled up in spasms of pain, gasping for breath, his arms wrapped around some point between his pubic bone and navel, while I limped to my feet to help Lali just as she was limping to her feet with Lídia's help. Oh, and with ten centimetres of gravel rash on her thigh as a fine memory of the day.

I recall Mín pushing me towards the car as I turned to see if that fucktard wanted another kick with the other boot on behalf of his sorely missed sister but he was still sprawled out on the ground surrounded by family and friends. The look on their faces convinced me to get hopping away on my good foot and behind the steering wheel: just as on so many other occasions, we escaped the scene with a screech of the wheels and more than a few scratches.

Apart from beating a hasty retreat out of town without stopping to put diesel in either our tanks or the car's, I can't establish any sort of sequential order regarding the rest of the day. The subsequent scene impressed on the subdivided memory of the subdivided self that I was back then – precise despite the heroin haze – is of Fermí in his boxer shorts, sweat pouring off him, under the swaying night time shadow of the magnolia tree in the golden girls' garden (Carrer de les Acàcies, Barcelona), body deep in the night time needle but his mind as clear as day, asking me if deep down we weren't to blame after all. If my memory hasn't distorted the experience like on so many other occasions, I answered him by saying, no, we weren't, but I sure as hell felt like I was. What I can't be sure of – not even if my life depended on it – is if that conversation took place the night of the funeral or a month later.

AUTOBIOGRAPHICAL LLUÏSA: EXHIBIT 'A'

Don't discover the last twenty-five years,
Honey, just in one night
'Kozmic Blues', JANIS JOPLIN

More than anything, it's the smells. Smells are what mark my psychophysical pleasure levels. A thousand years ago, when I still lived in Arenys, *chez mes viellards*, I couldn't bear the stench of feet spilling out of my brother Pepsin's room to flood the corridor and any other room without its door firmly closed. I also loathed the stink of Dad's cheap Canary Islands cigarettes and Mum's homemade tomato sauces, which she was always cooking when the last thing I felt like was eating. Some days, as soon as I was up, I had to flee the house (always down to the sea) to avoid feeling sick. Mama Angelina looked at me one day and thought I was pregnant. But, no, it wasn't that; not that day, at least.

During the first escape (aged sixteen and taking advantage of a school trip to the Science Museum, Martina, Raquel and I got 'lost' at a guy I'd met the previous summer's house) a range of aromas guided me along the path to liberation over the five days that the adventure lasted.

I can still smell the velvety emanations of my sweat in transit and the bittersweet exhalation of my virginal sex pulsating with desire. I can still smell the aftertaste of soap on his armpits and the salty scent of his sperm. In fact, the boy in question smelt very good in general. At least until the Civil Guard turned up accusing him of kidnap and the sexual perversion of minors. That's when his distinct olfactory stamp suddenly shifted to the cowardly reek of regret. I got him out of a tight spot by testifying that I'd sworn to him we were all eighteen but I immediately erased his name from my list, instantly consigning him to oblivion.

The second adventure the following summer was much more succulent and fulfilling. Strolling along the beach one day, Martina found a handbag containing one Spanish passport and three cards (I.D., driver's licence and Barcelona Boat Club membership) in the name of one A. B. de la C.: twenty years old, dark hair and eyes, student, living in Sant Cugat. What's more, there was twenty-three thousand eight hundred and forty-six pessetes which, for us, was a lot of perfume. As much as she didn't want to hand it in, the whole thing smelt too fishy to Martina to be legit. But as they say, opportunity makes the thief, and I immediately began devising a truly criminal plan, the first part of which was, naturally, to ditch the bag and pocket the cash and documents.

'With a nice hairdo and a bit of makeup any one of us could pass for A. B. de la C.! I betcha I could get to New York on this passport.'

'Send us a postcard when you get there,' replied Martina sarcastically.

But the essence of freedom was too alluring and all three of us succumbed to it.

Still lurking deep in the sinuses of my soul are the rich bouquets blowing along Les Rambles the day when, making the most of another highschoolgetaway, we obtained our second I.D. The idea, a true masterstroke, was Martina's but it was Raquel and I who wrote the script. The plot was simple: playing on the innocence and ignorance of Men regarding the strategies and vocabulary of Girls, we presented ourselves at the Lost Property Office, No. 1, Plaça Catalunya to ask, with the frenetic anguish that the role of three guileless girls in trouble demanded, if anyone had handed in a dark, leather bag. The words had been careful chosen by Martina: bag, so as not to limit it to any one size; leather, because everything looks like leather to men; and dark, in order to cover all browns, blacks, purples, greys and blues.

The assistant who attended us was an affable man with silver hair and moustache who gave off the whiff of living in Gràcia, between a eucalyptus and an acacia. While I explained in detail how my friend had lost her bag on the metro, '… because you *knooow* how it is, *ruuushing* about everywhere, this way and that, boy, what a day!, and now all this mess with the bag, you just never can tell, huh?, *you just never can tell*, because…' the man opened his eyes wide and furrowed his brow. When I finally stemmed my torrent of banalities and feigned embarrassment, a smile blossomed beneath the tips of his moustache, so soft that, just for a minute, it made me feel guilty.

For a minute and not a second longer because as soon as the man turned and looked down at the bottom shelf I caught the overwhelming scent of impending victory. If the name of the game is deceit, then so be it. After another outpouring of puerile guff and speculative fibs, we left with a small, synthetic leather handbag the colour of christknowswhat containing an I.D. card and six thousand one hundred and ninety pessetes. It was a paltry pot, but our pride at having pulled it off was a prize in itself: Ciutadella Park, where we went to celebrate with a bottle of moscatell, was a euphoric kaleidoscope of fragrances and emanations even sweeter than the cheap liqueur.

Now I'm approaching thirty and nearing the end of the line, I understand that these were the caprices of our pubescent bodies and spirits, opening like wildflowers amid the hazardous winds of adulthood.

The best thing, despite the defection of Martina, the brains of the operation (who'd in fact always reeked of Hamletian intellectualism), was that the dream of obtaining my first taste of true freedom materialised in an arena as intensely perfumed as Roussillon. The coach trip to Narbonne and the sixty-seven days and twenty-five hours that the adventure lasted are still impregnated with southern breezes and the aroma of mown fields, pressed grapes and ripe fruit.

On monsieur Pipot's farm, a second generation immigrant and uncle of some friend of Raquel's, we picked, collected and sorted the aromas of white and red grapes, peaches and plums, pumpkins and pulses, in addition to soaking up every animal stench going: pigs, rabbits, mares, dogs, ducks and hens. And then there was our own private kaleidoscope of aromas back in our living quarters where we washed off (or not) ten hours of joyful country labour.

When we phoned home and monsieur Pipot told them we were fine and working well they let us stay until September: ten or twelve years have passed since then and I still don't have the words to describe it! Each time we touched, even if only a hand, our surroundings exploded into fragrances, and even fetidness and firebrands distilled the bittersweet breath of perfect nature: whether it was in the morning when we got up at the break of dawn to go out into the fields, or at night after our tender evening performance as we'd lay down on the bed, stretch out our arms together and touch the sky. Looking back, it doesn't seem at all strange to me that the two of us, Raquel and Lluïsa, Lluïsa and Raquel, chose that nirvana to calibrate our homosexual potential. We shared realities and dreams, food and chores, walls and ceilings, and it only seemed logical to also share that bed of adventure and our florescent desire.

It goes without saying that when I got back, *chez mes viellards*, the same old nauseating pestilences almost made me go out of my mind because mixed in with it like a bubbling, burning acid, was a psychological persecution levelled directly at me. I've felt too much nausea in life to ever go back to mudtown.

Luckily for me, a week and a day later I'd be turning eighteen (finally!) and would be running off to Ibiza to live as one with Raquel and the galaxy.

Or at least that's what I thought, because at the moment of truth, at the port terminal with two tickets in my hand, Raquel spewed up some traumatic sob story and, as they say, abandoned ship. But the flow of ferries was much saltier than my tears of rage and compassion so, after getting my money back for her ticket, I set sail, my roots sighing a long farewell but with the buds of future flowers on my lips.

SEA, SEX AND PSYCHEDELIA

Here Odysseus charmed for dark Circe fell,
Still her perfume lingers still her spell
'Formentera Lady', PETER SINFIELD, KING CRIMSON

my stony stare creeps its one thousand yards and reaches the bird
of prey perched on the speaker in the corner. it contemplates the
half dozen anonymous beings contorting on the tiny dance floor
as if analysing the proteinic composition of its meal.

it leaps, elegant to the point of indolence, and clean rips off
the crewcuthead of some slimfitgirl dancing with fragmented
movements, nefertiti style. headless subnefertiti continues to dance
amid her entourage, none of whom show any signs of grief and
go on grooving.

the Eagle has seized its prey in its talons, swooping solemn
and ennuied, and continues its flight towards the speaker above
the booth: i see it, above my head, devouring with indifference
slimfitnerfertiti's crewcuthead. as it methodically pecks at its prize
(now the eyes and nose, now the lips and ears) the Eagle gradually
transforms into a sphinx carved from ancient stone: first its talons
and legs, then its torso and wings, all the way up to its head, eyes
and crest. like a cinematic dreamscape à la René Magritte.

as it gulps down the last piece of brain, its beak also turns to
stone, and the monument tumbles and explodes against the hazy
glass of my eyes.

Oh right, yeah: my name's Alexandre Oscà i Punyol and I'm in
the DJ booth at the hippyhangout that Californian Martha and
Glaswegian Bob opened two years ago as Woodstock's. I wonder
whether I have enough time to roll some Lebanese (to enhance
the rhythm of the rising pyramid) before mixing the tracks (one

coming up, the other coming down) in an unrepeatable moment. It's three in the morning and on the right turntable I'm playing 'Remember the Future' by Nektar while on the left, to celebrate three days of thunder 'n' lightning on the island, I'm lining up 'Riders on the Storm' by Jim.

Without me seeing her, She enters the booth. Without asking permission. She enters the booth barefoot and silent without asking permission and touches my back, almost making me scratch the record, and asks me, buzzing in my ear, what track I'm about to play. I'm pretty certain if I hadn't had it lined up already that I would've played a different one, just to teach her some manners and to maintain my musicman aura. But coincidence and, let's just say, her adolescent beauty compel me to celebrate with an impassioned kiss the fact that we'd chosen the exact same song in the exact same moment. It's worth saying that in those days, though dead and buried, Jim was still Jim.

She invites me to a Brazilian blunt (which she rolls and lights so adeptly it's almost comical) and I, returning the favour, offer her the rest of the green pyramid that's been spinning for the last sixteen minutes on the Nektar label. I'll never know for certain if it was true or not because, while yet to excel in the dark arts of deceit, She already knew how to hide her intentions when She wanted, but according to her She'd already dropped a whole tab after dinner, as it so happens, of the exact same type. What I can say though is that Ibiza was awash with it and our hippyhideaway was no exception.

We lit the Catherine wheel amid laughter, kisses and caresses which, though not lascivious, were certainly uninhibited. But we were young and everyone at Woodstock's had their hands full with something or someone. We continued to drink, smoke and caress each other's limbs and lips behind the hazy glass of the booth for a few or a few hundred minutes and that's when

She bit my earlobe until it hurt and told me She wanted to make love, there and then.

'Are you sure you're old enough?' I asked with a mocking but defensive tone.

Laughing, She turned around to face me, and with a fluid movement undid the five buttons on her dress. The dress, a type of pink slip that looked like something out of the 1920s Berlin cabaret, opened to reveal two revolutionary peaks whose slopes plunged into the heavenhell valley of her pubis.

'I don't know, you tell me,' She replied, dragging out each syllable.

After a couple of seconds of heavenly general inspection which, shone through the acid prism, lasted an eternity, I decided (with the power of Poseidon, god of the seas) that her shoulders and ankles were absolutely aquatic: a mermaid: a nereid: a water nymph.

'Do you always go around without any knickers on?' I commented, leaving the lack of a bra and shoes for another time.

'In Ibiza, yes. Unless I have my period.'

Then She sat on my open lap and continued to turn up the temperature to the point that, taking advantage of side two of Pink Floyd's 'More', we registered our first fuck. (I don't know if you've ever had the pleasure of making love completely unexpectedly with a total stranger while coming up on acid, but I assure you it's an absolutely unforgettable experience. Or maybe it isn't. Because I've experienced a whole bunch of similar stories that have evanesced after an immortal orgasm. Looking back, in all likelihood it was her: the splendid, the sensational Lluïsa Cabellera, with her spontaneous, sincere way of approaching people and things, who helped file that fuck under unforgettable.)

After that first encounter, after Martha kicked us out of the booth with that awkward, embarrassed laughter so typical of

Yanks, we ended up boarding Fisherboy's boat (one of the countless friends Siren Girl had all over the world) to watch dawn break over Formentera. Oh, Formentera! When I say the words Formentera and Lluïsa, I can feel the first novel of *The Alexandria Quartet* coursing through my veins. That must be why I later got accustomed to calling her Justine, the nickname meaning so much to her that, as a passionate disciple of Master Durrell, she used it instead of her real name where nobody knew her. And now I'm on the subject, I just have to mention our second fuck: on the dew-covered beach when we returned to shore.

But then the loathsome tunnel reappears, lined with images and feelings as chronologically unclassifiable as they are sensorially alive. The flavours of my private universes were turned upside down in the space of twenty-four little hours: instead of sea, hangovers or ripe fruit, my mornings smelt of Lluïsa. And at night, her fragrance, like the forest floor soaked with animal perspiration, was yet more intense: more than eucalyptus, kief or fried fish. Coffee, spliffs, rum & coke (the more innocent of the two), everything, absolutely everything, had a joyful dense spicy Siren aftertaste. And in a more intimate way, so did the music, the beaches, the waves, the clouds and the stars: it was as if Formentera existed only for us, and everyone in Ibiza knew it and was an accomplice.

The nirvana lasted until one dreadful day when she didn't appear at Woodstock's (nothing strange about that) only for me to spot her later, in the bar next door, fused in body and spirit to some Dutch guy. I don't think I've ever been especially jealous, but that summer Lluïsa was much more than a companion: she was me. That body I saw, held between the arms of that Dutch boy (blonde paunchy six foot three), was mine. I ran like a man possessed because it felt like they were sodomising my spirit but I knew I couldn't breathe half a word of complaint to anyone so I ended up getting the sloppydrunkblues so bad that the following day, shamefaced as hell, I was forced to confess to Lluïsa that I'd seen them.

'Jesus, Lex, if I got as wasted as you did each time you had your hands full in the bar I'd be an alcoholic in two weeks!'

Afterwards came her dignified, calm response: her life and her genitals were hers, and it pleased her (or had pleased her) to share them with me. I understood, I even downright defended it on a rational level but then in the evening if she didn't turn up at our grotty island grotto, a tapeworm the colour of mucus would slide through my guts in the DJ booth. First, I tried making her jealous but seeing it only made things worse I attempted to reach a pact regarding a certain level of fidelity.

'No way,' she answered while sucking me off with the tonguing technique of a concert clarinettist. 'I love you a lot and I enjoy fooling around with you but life has only one path and I'll keep following mine, playing with whomever I chose. The sooner you get it into your head, the better for the both of us.'

We were on the beach underneath the lighthouse, naked and adrift from the rest of the world; if the world even existed, of course. She finished a blowjob that, in addition to causing supreme pleasure, caused a supreme tear in the most intimate fabric of my being: I saw suddenly that she'd never be Mine, that she never had been.

Our separation, which I couldn't do anything to prevent, happened more or less gradually three or four weeks later. It started by her disappearing from our home and the hangout for one or two nights. Later, packing underwear, sandals and nothing else, she went to live at Ester and Ton's house. I say house: in their mini-loft above the garage behind the bar they owned. Needless to say, that was less painful than if she'd gone to live with Dutchboy but the anguish it caused me was equally acute and it came out in waves of hysteria and a sea of tears.

Though not being on any of my usual routes, I passed Bar Eston a couple of times a day to grab a coffee and offer her a smile. I once plucked up the courage to ask her to come back to the flat, even if it meant sleeping in the other bedroom but she, uniquely capable of reading my wounds of jealous passion like a mirror, said she was fine for the moment, that she needed space to be who she was and wanted to be (let's not forget: the loft was 30 m² max). Oh, and by the way, Ton would be bringing her over in the jeep in the afternoon to pick up her guitar and plant pots, if that was good for me.

After that I only very, very occasionally dared go to Eston, instead strolling around the area until the point of exhaustion in the hope that fate would put us in one another's path again. And often, too often, I'd think I'd see her jet black head of hair entering a shop or her stylish, slim silhouette turning the corner. Quite what I would've got from a chance meeting hadn't crossed my mind. I remember having one fixed idea slap bang in the centre of my brain and I told and retold myself that if I'd met that woman in that way it wasn't to lose her only three months later.

Two months had gone by since she'd left me but I was convinced that any day now, in some miraculous way, we'd fix everything. Over the years I've seen this happen to almost all men and an awful lot of women when a relationship ends unilaterally. I've seen it in marriages of fifty years and in relationships of five. I've seen people who have digested it in ten days and others who haven't shit it out in ten years. There are (fortunately rare) cases of people developing a genuine psychoemotional wound, what specialists call 'trauma', and it can mortgage and bankrupt an entire life. I'm not trying to say my case was anywhere near that serious because the only price I paid when she finally left for Amsterdam with one of Dutchboy's friends was three months of daily drug, alcohol and sex orgies. Weeks after her farewell, I received a letter telling me she'd found work washing dishes and that she was doing well. She trusted me enough to send me her telephone number and address in case, you know… one day… but no monkey business or hot pursuits, okay? I have no idea how many times I've cursed losing that half a page; too many to count. Luckily, I still have the poem that came with it.

White is the mark of the morning mist
when I'm awoken by a jasmine kiss.
The ringlet waves crash a kind of blue
as I breakfast cocoa, mint tea and dew.
A shot of coffee under a diamond sky
as Lucy breathes her bored poppy sigh.
The afternoon treads on pink salmon skin
and spreads the stench of seacunt and sin.
Its death drips down as harvestable sap
as the breeze blows bold warming lilac
capable of sedating both time and space.
The flower fragrances fuck out of reach.
The astral body burns down on the beach
And I float through mists of opium and spice.

(EsTon, Ibiza, 2nd December, 1975)

I can see clearly now (as clear as dawn under the Formentera lighthouse) that She was a hundred times stronger and more courageous than I was. She knew what she wanted, much more than I did, and She was willing to pay whatever price it took. I hadn't got there yet. And that's not forgetting She had only just turned eighteen, and I was almost twenty.

Looking back, Mín and Lex, Lex and Mín, instead of her

executioners, were her victims. But victims as guilty as executioners and just as much to blame as the ultimate guilty victim: LLUÏSA. Racing like a rock along the rapids of this degenerate world, I've known people who've become hooked on a certain type of 'wild' lifestyle or a certain type of hard drug, with everything that that implies, including death and even worse things, purely for the sake of someone else. But this, fortunately and unequivocally, wasn't the case with Lily, Mín and Lex. I've rationalised and repeated it to myself a hundred times a day then re-rationalised and re-repeated it the following day but in emotional terms I wasn't able to absolve myself of anything: I thought one thing and felt another.

For years I've preferred to think it was this terrifying feeling of failure (that hounded me for a thousand nights after Lluïsa's death and the scenes at the cemetery) – The Big Event – that made me decide, idealistically and impulsively, to quit heroin and the worlds that orbit it for the second and penultimate time. But that's a different, longer and much more complicated story.

LOST AND FOUND, OR NEITHER OF THE TWO
1. *Voodoo Child Back Home*

Herein are Photos of Ghosts
PREMIATA FORNERIA MARCONI

Within the growing evanescence of my days of youth, more vaporous with each passing day, I conserve some utterly unaltered moments in my sub-memory. I say 'sub' because it's vital to view it as a partisan, highly subjective guide distorted by time and one's own defences to godknowswhat extent. One of these clear-cut images – the meeting point of numerous plotlines and the point of departure for countless others – is the first time I tried heroin.

One ominous Sunday in July of the Summer of '76, I took a tumble in the DJ booth at Woodstock's, causing a titanic thud. The reason for the tumble was a trip but the reason for the trip was that at seven o'clock in the evening I was already locked and loaded on acid and maria. Bob, who'd been as bitter as a lemon with me for days, came and scooped me up off the floor like a rotten piece of fruit.

The truth is I remember very little about it due to the fact that when I nosedived, in addition to breaking two records and a tonearm, I smashed my head against the corner of the sound table and was left curled up on the floor seeing stars. But Bob paid me what I was owed, plus a little bonus, and advised me to take a long period of abstinence, especially when it came to LSD, but I wasn't having any of that. The long and the short: I beachbummed around for two weeks and afterwards, sick of the Lluïsa-infected air, packed two pairs of underpants, four t-shirts and five hundred records and hightailed it to Barcelona. Back in Barcelona after fourteen or fifteen months of Pityusic life, I was like a fish out of the Balearic waters, and so I potted the easy red by wasting a small fortune on a taxi to Sallent. But in Sallent, or rather, at my folks' house, only my sweet little sis Dolors, aka *Loleta*, actually seemed pleased to see me. Kiddo, my big brother and primogeniture of the clan, who normally acted as friend and shield, was going through one of his psychoemotional downward spirals and treated words as if they were pure gold. Mum, as usual, met me with a list of rules and a stinking mood after the initial hello:

a. smoking outside of your own bedroom or bringing illegal drugs into the house: prohibited;
b. arriving late to meals or not turning up without prior warning: prohibited;
c. listening to music or making any noise after ten o'clock or coming home after midnight: prohibited;
d. and if you're thinking of staying a while, you better start looking now for a barber and a job!

I didn't say anything because my options had been downsized to shut up or leave and I wanted to see my old man Agustí, who was having a check-up at the Vall d'Hebron Hospital. The mood lightened slightly over lunch thanks to little sis and when we stepped out for coffee, Kiddo, as if commenting on the weather, mentioned that Dad had been diagnosed with leukaemia and that he wouldn't see his next birthday.

At dinnertime (nine o'clock sharp) and set to the sound of the intolerable tick-tock of the dining room pendulum clock, I was finally able to greet and contemplate him: in fourteen months he'd aged ten years. He was almost completely bald, despite being in his mid-fifties, but bald in the sickliest way imaginable: one clump of hair here, as thin as silk, another clump there, and patches and more patches all over. His skin was an oily yellow and he had the sunken, staring eyes of a cadaver. But what pained me more than anything was that even though he ate as twice as much as us as always, he was little more than a lanky bag of bones. After dessert, and choking back a tear thicker than his own neck, he gave me a kiss so tender it would've warmed even Mum's heart before disappearing into the bedroom.

I felt very old and very sad, so sad that my post-dinner coffeecognac and nocturnal traipsing around Manresa lasted until four in the morning. Fortunately, at the last dive of them all I bumped into Sílvia Gómez, a former sixth-form semi-girlfriend of sorts, waiting for her boyfriend, Ignasi Llorés, to close the stall for the night. I admitted more to her about the stuff going on with my folks than I meant to but to my surprise she knew a hell of a lot more than I did about it: Dad basically lived at the peak of affliction and Kiddo had had a nervous meltdown over some tragic event at the mountain refuge he'd been stationed at (six deaths apparently in just one night), and was still undergoing treatment: 'It's understandable then why your mum's teetering on the edge of hysteria and the little one's started drinking cider and smoking hash with her mates.'

'*Loleta*? You must be getting your wires crossed: she's only twelve.'

'You're the one getting your wires crossed: last week she turned fourteen. Anyway, Lex, if you don't mind sleeping in a big girl's room, you can spend the night in my bed. I haven't slept there for two weeks.'

'Full-board at Hotel Llorés, are we?'

'Only half.'

When I went home the following afternoon, or rather, to my folks' house, I already had Sílvia's permission to stay a while at her flat so it was just a question of putting up with my long-suffering mum's inevitable ten-minute torrent, greeting my ghostly begetter with a hug and a couple of monosyllables, and grabbing my still unpacked backpacks. Seeing that I didn't have a car or any more money to blow on taxis, Kiddo helped me with my record cases as far as the bus stop.

'She has to put up with a dying husband and an idiot son, and she takes it out on you. Don't take it to heart.'

But when I asked why (why she took it out on me, I mean), he just nodded and said he didn't know.

At the bus stop bar, with a beer and tonic water between us, I tried to turn the conversation onto him. He quickly clammed up like an oyster before then getting as angry as a wasp: if they'd already told me then I already knew but if I wanted his version I'd have to wait a while because right now he wasn't in the mood for storytelling. It was as if I'd accused him of being a serial killer. But while I was recovering from the shock and mulling over how best to frame an apology, he went over to the bar, paid for the drinks and left without saying goodbye. He must've also been under terrible strain so don't take it heart, right? Fortunately, after a sour swig of bitter-tasting beer, the bus arrived.

There can't be more than twenty kilometres between the little house my folks had built in the southern part of Sallent with the savings of six lives and the basement flat Sílvia was renting in Manresa's La Balconada, but for me they were worlds apart because in Manresa I immediately found a life of my own. But I couldn't help sometimes feeling sorry for little-not-so-little Loleta.

But I'm straying slightly from the story I originally set out to tell or I've at least turned it into an exhaustive prologue because there's no real connection between all of this and what comes next, other than my 'lived experience'…

With my personal pvc collection and Sílvia's recommendation as warranties, I found work as a dirt n disc jockey (that is, a disc jockey slash dogsbody) in a Catalan version of an English pub with a shiny new American nine-ball table instead of a dance floor (undoubtedly the first in central Catalonia). Sílvia took her sheets to hotel Llorés and transferred her rights and responsibilities for the Balconada basement over to me, which I'd be sharing with a half actress-half nymph called Mercè, the girlfriend of a guy called Fermí, who I'd met in passing before passing out one fledgling drunken night the last year of sixth form.

The long and the short: a regular working day like a thousand others, let's say the last Thursday in March or the third Tuesday in April, after a coffee and two spliffs for breakfast at five-fifteen in the afternoon, the aforementioned Fermí accompanied me to the bar – back then a Hard Rock Café – for a game of English pool. I can state without fear of fabrication that my perception of light, volume and velocity was already altering in a progressively irrational way on the way there. Once inside the bar and having switched on the lights and poured two large dry martinis, things seemed to improve, but it was enough for me to put the red and yellow balls on the green cloth to realise that, despite it being five or six days since I'd dropped any acid, I was tripping. Just as I was starting to get a grip on things, two large packs of baying students bundled in through the door, the same ones that came once a week to get drunk on sangria and play cards. Luckily for me Fermí was on hand to help because everything was slipping through my fingers like water.

When I told him what was going on, he found it fucking hilarious and, amid laughter, jokes and moral lessons, began telling me all sorts of things from the encouraging '*relaaaax, enjooooy* yourself, it's free after all!' to the mindfucking 'beware of the shrew for the shrew is shrewd!' And he laughed and smiled like a mean kid with an easy target. If I'd had more time to trivialise the scene his good humour might've rubbed off on me but right then Marta, my boss' wet blanket of a wife, walked in: Josep Maria was ill and she'd be covering for him. That was a genuine catalyst because at least I could've conned Josep Maria, even if it meant admitting that I'd smoked one too many and needed ten minutes of fresh air, but with weedy Marta, a nice enough person but with as much get up and go as a bowl of boiled spinach, I had no idea what I was going to do. I didn't know how to look at her or talk to her, or to make her understand or hide from her that she was the colour of purple sapphire, jagged like quartz, and had walrus skin and hair like moss.

I put on a record and mumbled to her that I was starving and would be popping out to buy a pastry, which instead of annoying her seemed to soften her up. Fermí paid for his drinks, which were more than on the house, and followed me outside with a half-smile-half-hug.

'Not going down?' he asked, no longer joking around.

'Anything but.'

'Let's go to my car: I'll rack you up a little line that'll cure you in no time.'

'A little line of what?

'Of gear. What else?'

He always called heroin 'gear' or 'smack'.

'I've never tried it before,' I replied, as if that were a stumbling block.

'Suit yourself,' he said with a slightly bemused smile.

'It won't make me any worse, I hope…'

'No, man, of course not! Mark my words: a little snapshot of smack is the perfect antidote to flashbacks.'

It's worth saying that, in addition to Fermí and Mercè, I knew loads of people on the islands who took it and who even used needles, so it'd long since stopped being a taboo. Surely one little line wouldn't get me hooked in any sense of the word.

What's more, the acid I hadn't dropped, inexplicable but real, instead of tapering off was taking off again, and as we walked towards the glory of his greenminiminor I had to lean on his liquid back, as if we were two intimate friends, because the pavement was swimming and swirling, ready to submerge me. If I hadn't been so shocked and ever so slightly scared, I would've stopped to watch it because the hallucination was something special. We went down a stairway and he had to help me even more because I couldn't work out which foot had to go where and when: the steps swelled before me like a Pityusic hangover.

By this point I'd already surpassed a hundred tabs and on only two or three occasions had I experienced a comparable aftereffect. Fortunately, the car was right up ahead and nobody was any the wiser thanks to Fermí's wizardry, ever smiling that cheap whore's smile I came to love so much: oh, my sorely missed sonovagun!

I must confess – because it's the truth and nothing but – that a small line and a short smoke made me a man again in six minutes flat. When I got back to the bar, back in control and determined to get along with Marta for once in my life, she asked me with a grin why I hadn't saved her a bite. After changing the record, serving three tables and washing ten glasses, I snuck out to the bakery opposite and bought her one with lots of pine nuts and cream.

2. *A Taste of Honey*

'Stairway To Heaven', LED ZEPPLIN

'It's been years since Jim, Joplin and Jimi set sail for the paradise of visionary musicians. The Beatles fell out, over paper or personal pride, and probably forever more. Whether or not Bob Dylan and

Syd Barrett have gone mad only their psychiatrists can tell us, but what seems certain is that The Band and Pink Floyd will be the next to join the Stones, the Eagles and the Who in the billionaire dinosaurs club. But just because death and corporations have buried a few prophets and their music doesn't mean Utopia has died with them. And it is precisely because Utopia is alive and well, and because we want to keep it that way, that we proudly present the first lesson in the Hippymusic Teachings: dedicated, naturally, to Jim Morrison.'

I read the speech from the DJ booth, officially inaugurating the Hard Rock Café Teachings with tears in my eyes, God knows why, God knows for who, and turn up 'When the Music's Over', which I had playing in the background during the intro: for a Thursday the turnout is spectacular. If this gets reflected in the takings and continues this way, Josep Maria will give me a pay rise for sure.

Soon it'll be two years that I've been slogging it here and I'm finally getting to work as a disc jockey. I'd had the idea for monographic DJ sets since last summer but Marta had always found a reason to pick holes in it. But one night last January when Josep Maria was in Barcelona, after mopping and stocking the fridges, we went at it hammer and tongs on the pool table. I had the feeling that the following day she'd find an easy excuse to fire me but the opposite happened: I've never had to be with her for more than ten minutes on our own and her husband treats me better than ever.

At home, I mean, my folks' house, a whole feast of things has gone on, both big and small. Old Agustí confirmed Kiddo's forecast and died last August. In fact, the few times I went to see him he himself told and retold me that it was "the only good thing" that could happen. I shed more tears over his passing than I thought I would and even now, one year on, it doesn't take much for me to cry if I think of him. But maybe it's because

I'm going through a bit of a rough patch, despite life generally going pretty well for me.

I'm sharing the flat with Sílvia now, who ditched Llorés after telling me about how she'd dream of me in her bed, alone or with other women, night after night. I'm not the hot-blooded type, let me make that clear, but feeling yourself desired like that is enough to tempt anyone. Mercè moseyed off to Barcelona and has since wormed her way into none other than the *Comediants* theatre company. And Mister Fermín Guzmán, aka *The Libertine*, aka *El Malo*, still has a bed here and comes over to crash when it suits him. On the subject of Mín, how he lives, what he does, when he eats and where he sleeps is an unsolvable enigma. And on top of that and the flat, there's our business partnership in narcotics: I look after hashish and acid, he takes care of heroin and cocaine. That way, between the two of us, we're almost always fully stocked. Obviously, my deejay job suits us snugasabug when it comes to moving the merch on neutral ground, although the day someone grasses me up to Josep Maria I'll be out on my arse again. But for the time being, and that's already a lot, the vibe at the bar is good and the pigs only fly by if we shut up shop too late.

And now Gus has just entered the booth and I immediately clock the strong cravings and weak arguments in his eyes.

'Listen, Lex...' he mumbles. 'You got anything?'

'No. I've told you a hundred times that *here* I don't have anything. *Ever.*'

We both know that's a lie but That's Life.

'Come on, man.'

I look at the clock between the decks.

'In half an hour Mín will be here.'

'And he's got some?'

'I think so.'

'But it's not definite.'

'Yes, yes, he's got some.'

'Half an hour?'

'Maybe less.'

I forget about Gus and pick up the mic because I have to read my translation of 'Indian Summer'. When I'm done I switch it off again, feeling satisfied, but when I look at the set list I realise the spectre is still standing there.

'Listen, Lex...'

'What?!'

'You couldn't spot me half a gram from your stash?'

'Jesus, Gus! Always the same! I don't know if you're capable of getting your tiny brain around this, but I work here! And on top of that tonight I'm doing something I really enjoy and which happens to be very complicated... If you want to wait for Mín, wait for him, if not, get a move on, you don't need mama's permission!'

'Alright, man: I'll remember this when the shoe's on the other foot.'

'And now threats! Get out of the booth, Gus, and leave me alone!'

'Alright, mate, see you next Tuesday...'

'Fuck off!'

I change the record, set up the link and go to the bar to fix myself a rum&coke. I see that Josep Maria is rushed off his feet so I serve a few customers for him at the bottom of the bar. Way at the back, at a table full of kids, I clock Loleta, but just as I'm about to march over there my mental alarm clock goes off and I bolt back towards the booth. And there I find none other than Fermí, sat behind the decks, mixing the tracks.

'If I'm sick one day, you can fill in for me,' I smile.

'Whenever you like,' he smiles back.

'You've got style...! A goddam pro.'

'You guys are doing alright, huh?' he says, looking out over the bar: almost full and it's not even eleven.

'Not too bad. Did you find any marzipan?'

He nods, lays down out a pack of twenty and takes out a cigarette.

'You've got four eighths and two quarters in there. I'll leave it here for you,' he says, placing the pack next to the speaker and lighting his cigarette as if it were the most appetising thing in the world. 'See you later.'

'You not having anything?'

'Got work to see to.'

'Talking of work… Gus came to see me and I was about to scratch one of his eyes out.'

'You scratch what's between your legs. I'll go have a little word in his ear when I've got time.'

'You've seen him already?'

'I don't need to. He owes us thirty thousand pessetes and only comes looking for us when he hasn't got two to rub together. End of.'

'OK.'

He passes me the heroin-laced cigarette – or what we called a 'smoking gun' – and I suck on it avidly because it's the first of the day.

'You sure you don't want anything?'

'Water.'

'The last of the big spenders!'

'Water and a walnut.'

A 'walnut' in our private slang was a shot of scotch over a single ice cube. I prepare the next track according to the set list and take two more drags before giving him the cigarette and telling him to mix the track if I'm not back in time: I know he loves doing it. He smiles with the tip of an eyebrow, gazes out across the room and makes a perfect 'o' with a single exhalation of smoke.

'Sweet as a nut.'

3. *(Business) Partners in crime*

There's a rose in the fisted glove
And the eagle flies with the dove
'Love The One You're With', STEPHEN STILLS

That continuous present continued present long into the future, for that night and the thousand more Arabian nights to follow were all similar in content but specially unique and intense in form. And though already knee-deep in the dark arts, back then we still had that spark of excitement capable of transforming any Monday or Wednesday morning, 3 a.m., into an unrepeatable experience. And that's without even mentioning weekends, which sometimes started on Thursday evening and didn't end until Tuesday afternoon.

There were nights when we'd have lock-ins at the bar, (with or without Josep Maria, as by then he trusted us) and others when we'd get into Mín's mini, more beaten up than a Chinatown whore, and head to Barcelona, Terrassa, Sitges... Fed up with her job at the atelier, Sílvia gradually infiltrated both our business and pleasure, and by the time we realised it we were already three partners in crime.

I don't know which night it happened because they were all so alike but one morning, all three of us arriving home worn out and wasted, she mentioned to me as we got undressed that she'd like to call Mín and for us to do it together one day. If the idea didn't rub me up the wrong way, of course. I chewed it over as we synchronised our respective bodily temperatures under the sheets, and concluded that if I had to risk a love triangle then those angles were fine by me. We called Mín, who took it with one of his trademark smiles, and as he racked up three H (night) caps, Sílvia and I made love with a possessive lust we probably hadn't felt since our first fuck. Fortunately or unfortunately, the rest is a blur, a mix of dreamlike images and nocturnal visions of other Pythagorean adventures down the years, with different protagonists and different angles.

The inflexion point of that bombardment of experiences was our trip to Amsterdam. In those days, any druggy who took him or herself remotely seriously travelled either to Amsterdam (junkies, daytrippers and speedfreaks) or Morocco (stoners, mystics and variations on the theme). The project, cultivated over time by Mister Guzmán, was to get three hundred thousand pessetes together and invest half in gear, half in acid. According to his calculations we could earn half a million net without too much effort. Then, with more money to play with, we'd be able to step up our day-to-day workings here.

It's worth mentioning, in honour of the truth, that we painstakingly prepared the whole thing down to the last millimetre. Before we got started I rang Lluïsa to get some intelligence. I couldn't be too explicit, not that it was necessary: a clinic is a clinic and a supermarket is a supermarket. Then Mín and I got passports, and while he traded his Morris Minor for a Seat 1800 built like a hearse and fixed it up piece by piece at the garage of a notorious cousin of his, Don Alberto Delpez Guzmán, aka *Dixi*, I devoted myself to convincing Josep Maria to give me a week's holiday and month's wages in advance. The week's holiday was no problem because we hadn't closed over the summer and I'd been there twentyplus months working six or seven days a week ten or twelve hours a day, but I must confess that I probably wouldn't have got the cash without Marta's help.

The initial aim was to do the trip at the end of November

in order to earn the lion's share during the local festivals when the demand for drugs – legal and illegal – goes through the roof, as though they were nothing but trinkets adults hand out to one another.

Mín, in addition to the car, which for godknowswhat reason to do with fines was put in my name, contributed detailed maps of half of Europe and one hundred and ninety thousand pessetes in godblessamerican dollars. After a colossal effort, I managed to get one hundred and seventy together, and Sílvia, who knew a dishwashing-summer's worth of English and would justify our trip at the borders if necessary, scraped together fifty, which would at least pay for the abortion as the crotch of the matter was that the girl was ten weeks into a pregnancy that no one wanted or could afford. It was this incongruity that in the end made us bring the expedition forward two weeks as an abortion in Barcelona was still incredibly complicated and expensive, not to mention illegal. And Sílvia, poor thing, couldn't wait much longer.

So, the second Sunday in November, after closing at three-thirty, we each knocked back a double whiskeyespresso and departed in the direction of Terrassa and the motorway up to La Jonquera and the French border. Before leaving Manresa, we made a short pit stop by the basilica to take our respective doses and didn't stop again until the service station before the border, where we filled her up and each swallowed a ham and cheese toasty and another whiskeyespresso, before taking a leak and tending to our habit with a fat line.

Mín was driving and I was up front with him, pouring over a map of what to us isn't southern France but Northern Catalonia, and counting the kilometres between cities. I calculated that between seven and eight we could be in Montpellier and proposed losing half an hour by breakfasting on the seafront. The proposal was accepted to great acclaim. We crossed the border sweet as pie, and set off into an unfamiliar, foreign land. To this day I can still feel the delirious excitement of that trip...

While it's true that all three of us had our sights set further inland, France was virgin soil and we had fun reading the road signs and the names of cities we knew in Catalan now written in French – Perpignan, Narbonne, Béziers, Montpellier – and the kilometres between them. The car, after Mín's modifications, could get up to two hundred km/h but because it was such a lengthy trip we decided not to pass one thirty. I wish I knew how to even begin to describe the sheer sense of freedom I felt that first night, during those first hours, as we hungrily devoured kilometre upon kilometre of open road.

In Béziers we stopped in a rest area to stretch our legs and take a swig from the thermos. Sílvia had equipped the boot with an ice box and all the food and drink we would need for a week: cured meats, cheeses, canned fish, fruit, water, wine, beers, coca colas, whisky and, naturally, lots of hot black coffee. And Mín had also done a beautiful job with his artisan pack of cigarettes travelling in the glove compartment, hidden behind an open pack. He'd unwrapped it, filled it with smoking guns and closed it again with the silver paper, cellophane and everything, with such dexterity that not even Monsieur Dupin would've discovered it. What's more, he'd installed a fifty by twenty-five table that hooked to the passenger seat head rest (an invention as useful as it was simple) so, after clambering into the back, he promised us three lines of what the Doctor ordered. But the icing on the cake were the lateral cup holders and a small light that connected to the cigarette lighter socket. A work of art: man, Mín was a resourceful sonovabitch when he put his mind to it.

Radio Montecarlo, which we'd tuned into after pulling up, was giving the seven a.m. news report: if we wanted our seafront sunrise, we'd have to look lively. With Sílvia sat beside me, I got behind the wheel to cover the sixty kilometres between us and breakfast.

Ah, I forgot to mention that while we pissed and drank coffee she went to the toilet to remove and clean one of the two one gram bags she was carrying inside a condom hidden in her vagina. We didn't take much of the stuff yet but Mín had been shooting up for a few months already so, after we'd unequivocally banned him from smuggling any needles on board, together with the cigarettes he snorted a generous quarter gram every five or six hours. Some might think we were being disproportionately paranoid; others that no precaution is ever too much but the truth is that in those days, between the three of us, we still did things with a bit of forethought.

We left the motorway at Frontignan (I think) and wasted five minutes looking for a view that caught our fancy. It wasn't difficult because it's a stunning spot and dawn was already breaking. While very chilly, the cold awoke the senses and relaxed the nerves. Bread and tomato, ham, cured sausage from Berga and chorizo omelette; then a round of dry white to toast the dawning of our Dutch adventure and the undisputed whiskeyespressos and lines of H: two small snorts for Sílvia and me and one fat fix for Mín, who then curled up on the backseat and fell asleep just as we re-joined the motorway, ours noses pointing towards Nimes, Orange, Lyon. From this leg of the journey I recall, with special fondness, the blowjob Sílvia was adamant on giving me, until a difficult ejaculation (or rather, delayed because of the effects of the horse), despite the risk of doing ninety in the slow lane in the golden glow of the rising sun.

At around ten-thirty on a bright morning, under a sky full of shimmering cumuli, we stopped for twenty minutes' r&r and a few other things on the outskirts of Valence. I remember because it was where Mín lost Sílvia's heart forever more.

With a yawn and one of his famous half smiles, he says: 'Hey, you wanna know something? While I was sleeping I dreamt Sílvia got in the back and sucked me off.'

'If you're horny, go to the toilet and use your imagination. But don't be too long because we have to make Dijon by lunchtime,' I shot back at him, peeved at the crassness of the joke, just as I was stepping out to go fight with the first self-service petrol pump I'd likely ever seen in my life, rounding off the sentence by slamming the car door.

'Yes. I think that's a good idea,' I heard Sílvia tell him in an irritated tone. 'Buy yourself a dirty mag and wank yourself to death in the toilet because, I assure you, all these mountains will be a thousand metres under the sea before I suck you off again, as you put it!'

And then she got out too, in the direction of the bar, finishing her sentence by slamming the door at least three times as hard as I had. But the whole thing didn't escalate any further, in part thanks to my telling Fermí that he apologise and explain to Sílvia that it'd been a regrettable joke and nothing else (because we still had well over two thousand kilometres to ride together) and by lunchtime (beef steaks with locally sourced mustard) the large Pernods had already re-established harmony. At least on the surface. Because as far as Sílvia was concerned the threesomes and familiarities were finished. I'd even go as far as saying that, when it comes to Mín, she's never since offered or accepted anything more than a polite peck on the cheek.

Women, or some women at least, can be like that. That doesn't mean I don't understand why she was angry but nor does it mean I wasn't pleased to have her all to myself again. Sexism? Possibly. I'd sooner call it basic vanity and egoism… but who can ever really know the who and why of every what and when?

4. *Comings, goings and returns, and escapes back and forth*

For if we don't find the whisky bar
I tell you, I tell you, we must die!!
BERTOLD BRECHT, KURT VEIL

I'll close this chapter by saying that the purchase was as straight-forward as the abortion, as Lluïsa was also developing a horse-hobby and had friends in all the right places. As always.

To avoid a mild heart attack at each border crossing, Mín wrapped forty-six grams of highgradegear, which looked like colourless cement, in thick plastic, placed it in a black metal tube and superglued the lid in two places. He emptied the oil can, placed the tube inside, filled the can back up with oil and put it back under the bonnet. The five one hundred sheets of acid tabs, prewrapped in plastic just in case, ended up at the bottom of the ice box, now full of French cheeses and German wines.

The little I remember of Holland in general, and Amsterdam in particular, is hazy. We arrived in the middle of the night and left at sunset, which in winter in those latitudes comes on early, quickly and is completely grey. Four canals, two coffee shops and one chaotic Dam Square is all I retain of it, along with the small-scale sampling and wholesale eating of both horse and acid, and the purple walls of a pristine clinic where Sílvia and I spent six hours that lasted sixty. In other words, half a dozen windmills, silhouetted against the darkness or beyond the halogen lights of the highway, and not even a whiff of a tulip.

In terms of our return trip, it's important to mention that Lluïsa asked us for a piggyback ride (a two-week holiday, she said, even though she had no job or plans to go back to), and everything went like clockwork, apart from Sílvia: she wasn't feeling at all well, either in body or spirit; she felt nauseous every one hundred kilometres and wept in silence for five minutes straight every twenty-five. At dawn I finally convinced her to snort a good line of skag and she fell asleep in the foetal position, her thumb in her mouth and her head on my lap.

Once back in Bages we went directly to Dixi's garage in Sant Fruitós because we'd decided not to go anywhere near the flat with a full horsebox, just in case. The oil can, ice box and Mín stayed there, along with Lluïsa, who was planning on going to Arenys to see her family. The car, Sílvia and yours truly went back to La Balconada where, surprise surprise, the fuzz were waiting for us (two narcs from the Civil Guard, to be precise). But they were looking for one Fermín Guzmán driving a green Morris Minor so when they were greeted by a red Seat registered in my name they decided to leave it for another day. I can still hear Sílvia sniffling like a kidnapped child as I closed the front door behind us:

'Take me home, Lex.'

'You are home, Sílvia.'

'I mean to Santpedor.'

Santpedor is where her dad had built a small residential complex and bought himself a luxury villa with the profits. But, of course, this wasn't the right time and she wasn't in the right state.

'Get into bed and sleep for two days if you need to. When you get up, I'll take you straight there, if you want.'

It must've been a premonition because by the end of the week our entire Manresa microcosm had faded forever more into the ether: Sílvia went to sleep off the abortion, drugs and rock & roll at Daddy's mansion, I was let go from work with apologetic pats on the back and a full month's pay, and Fermí and Lluïsa, sleeping and living together from day one, decided that the Balconada basement was boring, packed their few possessions and headed off to a decrepit farmhouse halfway between Solsona

49

and Oliana. Apparently, one of Dixi's pals down in Viladecans was renting it but never went up there in winter. And I, dazed and confused by the acrobatics of events and the quicksilvers of addiction, hooked both on the substance and the lifestyle that followed it, followed them there. But if anyone thinks this is an attempt to reduce my own personal responsibility and lay the blame at their feet, they are, quite simply, wrong. I followed them because I wanted to and because I had nothing better to do. What I can't deny, however, is that Sílvia was right when she told me as we said goodbye on the villa terrace, that I was still in love with Lluïsa and that I always would be because I'd mythologised her. In any case, she was completely wrong when she told me that, sooner or later, Fermí and I would come to blows over her.

3-7-96

Cal Fumall, Malanyeu (Alt Berguedà)
From: Alexandre Oscà i Punyol
To: Enric Costales Grausec

Dear Enric,
exiled within this exquisite wooden cage where you keep me
protected from evil, i've finally managed to organise a few notes
on those moribund memories, so utterly tragic and risible, and
which seem, for reasons beyond me, to interest you so much. for
better or worse, i've managed to overcome the deep disgust at
putting them into words. nevertheless, i must confess, if i didn't
feel so indebted to you, over the money and the trust you've
invested in me, i wouldn't have got beyond the title. though the
tone at times may seem superficial, each line has cost me a tear
or three and more than a few paragraphs a drinking bout. in
terms of coherence and style, neither of which are scholarly by
any stretch of the imagination, i'd appreciate it if you refrained
from overediting the text, if at all possible, in the event that they
conjure up some image of lived realities. come what may, i'd
prefer you to wait until my death, which i doubt will be long
coming, before publishing. if that proves commercially unviable,
i beg you, above all, to safeguard everyone's anonymity under
their character's name.

From your grateful apprentice writer,
Alexoscat

CLÀUDIA: ONE CHARACTER, TWO SCENARIOS
1. *Night of disasters*

Oh my Lady Fantasy,
I love you!
CAMEL

Lluís was in the kitchen frying up dinner and I, Agustí Oscà, known by everyone everywhere as Kiddo, was wielding an axe out front making sure of the firewood. We were at the backend of March but a full foot of snow had fallen just three days ago and tonight it would freeze over again.

Catching my breath, I looked up at the sky, deep blue like a whale's hide, and just as I was about to get back to work I thought I'd glimpsed a coloured spot near the Aurora summit. I searched for it with my gaze, shielding my eyes, but the last rays of the setting sun were shining directly at me.

'*Lluíííííss!*' I shouted towards the kitchen.

'What's up?' he answered, opening the window.

'I think there's someone up there,' I mumbled, nodding in the direction of the ridge.

'This late? You're kidding me!'

'I just saw an orange blob, about the size of a plum.'

'Don't smoke anymore maria.'

'Twice I've seen it.'

'Don't drink anymore absinth then.'

But just as he was closing the window, we both heard a remote yet wretched scream.

'Shit!' exploded Lluís.

Ten seconds later he was coming through the front door dragging the rescue rucksack in one hand and the stretcher in the other.

'Have you switched off the stove?' I asked, already heaving the rucksack onto my back.

'Shit, shit, shit, shit...' he muttered as he turned and shot back inside.

I set off up the mountainside: the slope was southwest facing and although there was half a foot of half melted snow, it held up fine underfoot. I saw the tiny blob again, coming downhill fast. It was most definitely a person. When I saw Lluís coming up fast behind me, I picked up the pace. We heard another scream of unadulterated desperation and, without stopping, Lluís responded with a shout of encouragement. I could hear him muttering: 'shit, shit, shit' between clenched teeth the whole damn time. Then the curious orange shape appeared no more than five hundred metres away: it started to run in our direction until stumbling and continuing its roly-poly descent. We also began to run and after a marathon minute we reached where it had collapsed: it was the ghost of a girl. Nevertheless, frozen panic attack to one side, she hadn't broken anything. She was conscious and spoke very quickly, without rhyme or reason. Lluís blew softly on her cheeks while I took the brandy out of the rucksack. We forced her to glug from the bottle, making her splutter.

'Prepare the stretcher,' Lluís instructed me.

'I don't need zat,' she interrupted with a delicious French-accented Catalan as she slumped to the ground and inspected her legs. 'I'm fine. But Pierre and Gaston are up zer...! You gotta go look for zem!'

'Drink some more, sweetheart.' She took another obedient swig. 'And now tell me everything, but *s-low-ly*. Where were you coming from?'

'From ze other side of ze Bars peak. Over ze Nou Fonts pass.'

'And you're saying there are two guys up there?'

'Zey fell over ze edge. But zey're not dead... because I heard zem shouting.'

'And what did zey, *they*, say?'

'Zat I didn't try and come down. Zat I ran to get help.'

'How long ago did you leave them?'

'Two, maybe, zree hours.'

'You've got to take her back right away, Kiddo,' muttered Lluís. 'Sit her three metres from the fire, take her clothes off, and massage her with alcohol. But before you do anything, call the helicopter and the volunteers down in the village.'

Then, saddling himself with the rucksack, he looked at the sky and noted the time while I got the girl onto the stretcher and begged him not to leave on his own at nightfall.

'One last question, sweetheart... What's your name?'

'Clàudia.'

'OK. Clàudia, do you have any idea where you were when your friends fell?'

'Zey're not my friends. Zey're my brothers.'

'Your brothers, then... Don't cry, now. Do you know where you were?'

'We had just passed Fontblava... near ze Lladres cave.'

'Get back down the hill and call the helicopters, Kiddo. But, above all, she mustn't go near the fire for a full hour,' he repeated, already with his back to me, already heading off alone.

'Good luck, pal.'

I headed back to the hut with stretcher and passenger without once looking back. Once there, I poked at the fire and sat the girl in the armchair in the corner with a blanket and two cushions. I took her shoes off to see if her feet were blue: they were an utterly bloodless blue, like her nose, ears and hands. Not at all surprising seeing she wasn't wearing any gloves (she said she'd lost them) and that her boots weren't at all adequate for crossing the high Pyrenees in the depths of winter.

I brought her dry clothes and told her to get changed before turning my attention to the radio, a piece of equipment I'm far from an expert in. About ten minutes later (the sun had disappeared and a thick grey had flooded the sky), I was ending an unbelievable adventure over the airwaves: the captain in Barcelona shouted down the line at me that they were in the middle of a thunderstorm and couldn't get up in the air, and that I should ask the French for help; I repeated, howling back at him, that it was already a miracle that I'd got through to them, and that *he* inform the French directly, or the Swiss, or the Italians, because to me and to those stuck up there the nationality of the rescuers didn't mean shit.

'Shit,' the fashionable word that day, seemed to solve the controversy and after making him directly responsible for what might happen, I hung up. Having switched on the gas stove, I poked my head into the sitting room and muttered 'shit' once again when I saw that Clàudia was in the exact same position I'd left her in. No, that's not true: she was listening to the walkman she had in her coat pocket and mumbling along to the melodies. I got back on the radio to speak to the boys down in the village, who always had our backs when there was a genuine emergency. I caught Andreu in the Red Cross clinic and explained the crisis to him.

'Let me get a couple of jeeps together and we'll be up there right away,' he promised me.

I went back into the sitting room and began taking the girl's clothes off. She let me do it with total indifference and it embarrasses me to admit that my libido wasn't quite as blasé about it as she was. One thing you've got to understand is that Clàudia was a beautiful little French girl. I put a pair of knickers on her from the six or seven pairs that were always in Lluís' sock drawer and the t-shirt that Àlex had sent me from Ibiza – the only clean one I had. I remember the whole tender, tragic scene, as though it were a film: I told her to move her fingers, she stroked my ear with her right hand, I studied her feet. I told her to move her toes, she repeated the caress with both hands. We kissed each other fleetingly, I don't know why, just as the old radio receiver began to crackle and splutter something. It was the French helicopter asking for information. I explained the little I knew and told them to come to the hut but they insisted on inspecting the area first, telling me to take special care of their compatriot. It filled them with solidarity, the poor sods, that the three castaways were French.

Lluís, expert among masters, would always classify high-altitude rescues according to three categories: the downright bad, when after hours, days and weeks of searching you manage to save the lives of those stranded; the inherently tragic, when after risking ten or fifteen lives in the rescue it's not possible to save all the castaways; and the absolutely infernal, when in addition to losing the lives of those already lost, those of a few rescuers are lost too. The case of Pierre and Gaston was one of the worst examples of the worst category:

we'll never know why, but the French helicopter crashed at the bottom of Cigonya cliff, behind the Llampecs mountains. There was no storm, no fog, no high winds reported. Nevertheless, the helicopter plunged to the bottom and exploded with its two souls onboard; one of the three vehicles that drove up from the village skid on a frozen part of the roadside, slid over the edge and kept on rolling until it hit an electricity pylon: out of the four travelling in the back, only old Tines' son got hit bad: he broke his third lumbar vertebrate. But the two up front weren't so lucky: the driver lost an arm, and the co-pilot, Andreu from the Red Cross, his life. All we're left with is the uneasy consolation that if the pylon had given way then the electric current would've likely fried all six of them;

and, finally, to fill the crapper to the brim, there's Lluís.

What happened to Lluís is even more incomprehensible than the awful rest. As ranger and mountaineer, he'd spent ten years going from one cabin to another and he knew the Pyrenees, especially the Catalan side, as if he'd given birth to them. In all likelihood the avalanche spotted by the two helicopter pilots on the western slope of Bars peak in the light of the flares minutes before dying had encased him in its frozen belly forever more. Two French rescue teams and two Catalan rescue teams, the lads from the village, a stricken Kiddo, and a shedload of lost Lluís' elite mountaineer friends from across Europe searched for him, obsessively, for three weeks. When officials called off the search, a number of mountaineers, a few friends from the village and yours truly persisted for another two months. But nothing: absolutely nothing. Not even the rucksack. With regard to Pierre and Gaston, Clàudia's brothers, we found them the following day, around noon, four or five hundred metres from where she'd told us. Two frozen stiffs.

Getting back to the chronological course of events, I spent the rest of the night hanging on the radio, swallowing down one piece of bad news after another, while the girl, stock-still and stupefied, wept dry tears onto even drier cheeks, the whole while listening to the same cassette once, twice, a hundred times. It provokes a deep sense of shame in me, I don't know why, to recall that night: despite the terrible circumstances, we made love, naked and silent, possessed by an extreme tenderness, in the armchair in the corner. The room glowed fluorescent orange on account of the fireplace and the three candles, a colour that will remain forever associated with Clàudia. Of course, it may well be the second part of the story that makes me say that.

The morning after that strange and terrifying night, while I was out searching for Lluís, the father of the ill-fated family came to collect the girl and the two bodies which the helicopters had since transported to the hospital in town. Clàudia left me a poetic thank-you note together with her phone number and address. I promised myself I'd call her and pay her a visit but the search for Lluís, eternal and futile, left me broken so when I finally left 'his' cabin I went to stay a while at my parents' place in an attempt to forget those all-too-tragic events.

2. *An orange in Orange*

Picture yourself in a boat on a river
With tangerine trees and marmalade skies
'Lucy In The Sky With Diamonds', THE BEATLES

Five and a half years later, in August of '81, a casualover from those times called Nati suggested going to an open air rock festival in Orange, Occitania: three full days of concerts with the best international artists. I wasn't really up for it, partly because Nati wasn't my idea of someone to take to a psychedelic rock concert, and partly owing to the fact that all those people and hours of partying seemed tedious to me. But, glancing at the festival programme, I saw that the largely unknown group that Clàudia was listening to the whole tragic night would be playing on the first day. I mean, that we were both listening to, because she'd told me to put the cassette on our – I mean, lost Lluís' – stereo while we made love.

Advisable or not in psychological terms, that's what clinched it for me. I knew it would be hard, I knew I would suffer, I knew I would have a bad time. But I also believed that I might be able to exorcise the old neurosis embedded in my soul. Despite her living in Montpellier and being a fan of the group in question, it didn't ever enter my head that I might bump into Clàudia. But that's exactly how it went.

We (Nati and me, and Joan and Joana, who came with a tent to stay for the whole three days) were sitting on a flowery terrace enjoying a few late afternoon beers before entering the arena when a slim, elegant but ghostly girl left the bar licking an orange flavoured ice cream. I have a remarkable ability to remember faces but I sometimes struggle to recall the relationship, so when I grasped just who she was, she was already on her way down the path in the arms of the oestrogenic phantom who'd been waiting for her next to the marquee. I got up like a shot and caught up with them: it wasn't Clàudia. Well, I mean, yes, it really was Clàudia, but she didn't look anything like the one I'd known: pale, with an almost saffron tone, thin in the extreme and with a curling of the lips and a deep frown that I wasn't able to classify. At first, I didn't think she remembered how we knew one another but then she changed abruptly and became extemporaneously coy. Taking the plunge, I sheepishly invited them to join us over at our table but her friend declined saying they were in a hurry.

'If you want, we can catch each other later at the concert,' Clàudia offered with a lustful smile.

'I'd love to. But where?'

'Don't worry, I'll find you.'

And they walked off down the path, arms wrapped around waists, Clàudia with her ice cream, her friend with the Afghan she'd just skinned up. I'd have sworn I'd never see her ever again but, true to her word, she found me by one of the sixty-nine beer tents inside an open air arena where, according to the organisers, there were more than fifteen thousand people. If I'm going to be completely honest I should mention that, despite my scepticism, I'd given Nati the slip just in case, leaving her with Joana and Joan. Whether I found Clàudia or not, I wanted to experience that concert with an unburdened soul, free from

Natis and Joana-Joans.

Clàudia said hello with a straight kiss on the mouth (lip service, as my brother Alexandre calls it). Afterwards came the caresses, slow but incisive, and more and more kisses, now in true French spirit. While they poured us two double Pernods over ice, I remember asking if she really wanted to make love on the bar top. Yes, she answered, with a lascivious laugh, and took me off towards a nearby slice of secrecy sheltering between olives trees and tents. She made love to me with such intensity that at times I was disorientated. It was the finest, most absolute heterosexual experience of my life: under the olive tree with its witchlike silhouette, amid two or two thousand orange tents, because in Orange, orange was the fashion that year. I repeat: it was sublime. Peals of laughter and waves of music inhabited and swirled in the shadows; snippets of conversation and snake-bodyshrieks slithered towards the lights; and us, in the Beautiful centre, loving, possessing, melting into one another: one body within our bubble of passion! More than just sublime, it was slightly terrifying.

We stayed there amid sex, Pernod and Afghan blunts for two, maybe three hours. Just as I was beginning to fully savour the Moment of All Time and Wholeness, the speakers introduced the group both of us had separately come to see. She said she didn't want to move, that she'd hear them just as well from where we were, that she'd dropped acid, an 'orange' to be exact, and didn't want to be shoved around. It was clear we were too far away to experience all the magic of the live show, but the magic I was sharing with her was already enough.

I'll never ever get the idea out of my head – no matter how many psychiatrists rummage around in there – that I could've done something; that I could've suspected, imagined, *done* something. But the three or four times I tried to talk to her once the fateful concert was underway, she got annoyed at me, commenting and repeating with the utmost seriousness that she was an adoring slave of Empty Silence, each time with greater praise and conviction. I was sufficiently drunk and euphoric to not let a bad vibe spoil my night so I went to the bar closest to the stage, thinking it might be better for each of us to fly a little while on our own rocket ship.

I can't have been away from the Wiccan olive tree for more than ninety minutes. But it was enough. She was sat with her back to the trunk, her arms resting on her knees and her head in her open hands. Perfect equilibrium. I spoke to her, first in a whisper then with smiles and interjections. The only movement came from a few rebel hairs. Then I touched her shoulder while searching for her lips with mine: she was as stiff as a board and fell to one side. I was scared but I tried to remember everything Lluís had taught me: look for a pulse, chest compressions, mouth-to-mouth resuscitation.

I screamed 'help' in all the languages I know while discovering, to my disbelief, that she was dead and frozen. Yes, yes: not merely cold but frozen. I touched her hands, face, chest and underarms: ice. A security guard turned up with two medical assistants. The girl was dead. Frozen, said one of the medics, with a bewildered voice, and that the judge would have to be notified.

'Wot d'ya mean *dead*? Wot d'ya mean *frozen*?' shouted the security guard, angry and suspicious.

'As frozen as a flatfish!' the frightened medic hollered back. 'See for yourself if you want!'

I had major problems convincing the knucklehead that I had no idea what had happened to her. Thank goodness for the medics: if not, I'd have taken a pounding for sure. Finally, French law officials arrived (the judge in question, his assistant, a police captain, a hundred officers and forensics and photographers and godknowswhatelse), and sealed off the area and started combing for clues. Needless to say, as suspect and/or accused and/or culprit, I ended up in handcuffs and down the local fucking police station. They treated me very well. Apart from holding me in a cell for eight hours before finally putting me in front of the judge and slapping me with a ten thousand franc fine for the seven grams of 'hashish resin' they found in my pocket, they treated me very well. However, if I hadn't made the right call by telephoning Senyor Cercós, Dad's lawyer friend from Manresa, I might still be there, because they all seemed certain I was the sole sorcerer capable of decoding that enigma.

No doubt I put my fat foot firmly in it by telling the judge (a beautiful, sophisticated Madam Bovary) the whole incredible story, drugs and sex included, beginning with the night at the refuge. She listened to me with perilous patience bordering on academic before consenting to a blood test in order to confirm that I'd consumed nothing more than hash and alcohol the night of the concert. The forensics confirmed that the girl had frozen to death. But considering it didn't make any scientific sense, in August, in Orange, with a minimum temperature of seventeen Celsius, they sought the answer in the high quantities of LSD they'd found in Clàudiacorpse's body. I'm aware that her case is still the source of clinical research and specialised controversy and that students of psychiatry, pharmacology, toxicology and/or etcetera continue to base their doctoral theses on it.

I, in any case, had to go back to my parents' house to rest a while because my psychosomatic togetherness had shattered for the umpteenth time, and that was when I began preparing my first trip to Nepal.

But I've always asked myself how things would've turned out if Clàudia, tinkertampering, had slipped an orange into my drink without telling me.

ONE BRIDGE, TWO BRIDGES, A THOUSAND BRIDGES

'Bridge Over Troubled Water', SIMON & GARFUNKEL

Fermín Guzmán, aka *El Malo*, son of business owners of Phoenician mien, discovered the panacea for our structural ills by leasing a large, gloomy, abandoned cafébar tucked away in an arcadian corner of Alta Ribagorça called Lo Pont de Suert (five hundred thousand pessetes up front and eight hundred thousand more over eighteen months). The original idea was Lluïsa's and she'd been gnawing our ear off night and day about it ever since our trip to Amsterdam half a year ago: establish a base of operations that served as a front so we could work cool-calm-collected and learn to save. The substratum of the project – already bang on the money, it must be said – was that we couldn't keep starting afresh each and every morning, adapting to whatever the dawning day had in store for us, constantly putting ourselves in the hands of Lady Luck like existential tightrope walkers balancing blindly over the abyss.

I still believe that at the outset of our addiction we were hooked not just on the drugs but also on the lifestyle that came with them. The insolence they implied on a social level, the financial independence, the indifference towards any type of future that wasn't immediate and, above all, the groove, as artists and execs call it, of being busy all day long, up, down, left, right, in, out, like someone with a non-transferrable, transcendental task. It was Sílvia, when saying goodbye as both business-partner and partner-partner, who told me that we lived perpetually in a film halfway between docudrama and road movie, writing the script as we went along, according to the circumstances. And she added that she was getting away from me, and especially Mín, who ever since the Amsterdam trip repulsed her to the point of enmity, because she was convinced that the story would have a young and tragic ending and that she, instead of living at two hundred kilometres per hour and dying childless at thirty, wanted to live to ninety and grandmother sixty kids.

But that's how life often goes: Sílvia chose to stay in Manresa and patch things up with little Llorés, while we packed the present into a few boxes and set up shop in Lo Pont de Suert. The original plan to fix up the top floor like a real home (we called it our lil' house on the prairie) was limited to a bathtub and a second-hand washing machine because the television set and sound system went down in the bar. We mended a few leaks in the loft, repaired the chimney, and painted the walls of the café, kitchen, downstairs toilets and two upstairs bedrooms white, leaving the rest for forevernever.

We opened around eleven thirty half twelve to serve the local slacker kids a few beers and the old timers who came in for a couple of rounds of whiskeyespresso and ginrummy, and closed at four a.m. for the penultimate scotch on the rocks and any burning bizniz that couldn't be put on ice. But the bar supplied us with only about half of what the three of us needed in terms of money and madness, and neither did our local and provincial contacts offer much of a solution. And that's how we got used to leaving town; one, two, at times all three of us, for dealings and debauchery in places as near or far as Vielha, Lleida, La Seu d'Urgell, Berga, Puigcerdà, Barcelona, Zaragoza, Valencia, Madriz or Bilbao Baggins. The astral anecdotes of those forty months that our perfect three-way anarchy lasted amount to almost all the stars in the Milky Way. Lluïsa whispered it to me our first night alone and together in bed in six years, with both the bar and Fermí locked up by court order. Now that the two of them form part of the night sky, I will risk revisiting one or two.

1. *Bridge of fortune: Breaking (down) and entering*

And Louise holds a handful of rain,
Temptin' you to defy it.
'Visions of Johanna', BOB DYLAN

The first starstory I wish to tell, as tall as it is true, took place in the dead of a December night, one thousand years ago on this day. I – Lex, or Àlex, to local acquaintances – had taken the red 1800 first thing in the morning, that is, around eleven fifteen, and left town to stock up on marzipan. Marzipan, coconut and chocolate, if I'm not mistaken.

Lily and Mín stayed at the bar, which we'd christened Barcadia, but as the afternoon rolled by they got more and more nervous because they knew the biscuit tin was empty and come closing time they'd be yawning and salivating like monkeys. My phone call from Sabadell telling them not to expect me until godknowswhen made Mín's mind up, and Mín, scared stiff by just the thought of ten minutes of the agonies, talked Lluïsa into going to some local dealer's house ten kilometres up the road. The price would be scandalous, accustomed as we were to buying in bulk, but half a gram would do them. They closed early, raided the till and, as I'd taken the Seat, put all their hopes and fears into a beat-up 2CV that some bright spark from Lluçanès had left as down payment.

'Ten there and ten back: you can do twenty miserable little kilometres,' is what she told me Mín was muttering as he turned the ignition.

After some petulant protest at its neglect, decay and frozen insides, the moribund motor started up and accepted clutch and first gear. Lily locked the patio door and got in the passenger seat. With a bit more smoke, noise and time, as they drove away he declared, doubly prophetically, that they'd make it as far as they had to.

They were passing through some anonymous town and were more or less halfway there when... cough, cough, cough... the car stopped dead. Mín, who knows his fair share on the subject, took one look at the engine and repeated his original slur: 'Fuck the patron saint of petrol!' It was a ghostown: there wasn't a single whorehouse or petrol station in sight, and the only bar, a hundred metres further down, was chained up. But opposite to where the car had breathed its last was a small bank branch with its fluorescent lights still on inside.

Swinging between rage and desperation, Mín muttered about perhaps trying their luck with the bar while Lily, ever the more decisive of the two, banged the palm of her hand against the bank window. And that's when Mín had one of his unstoppable impulses: taking out the mini pocketknife he always carried on him, he slipped it into the middle of the circular lock on the front door and, after a flick of the wrist and an echoless click, opened it. He already had one foot inside when Lily grabbed him by the arm, took hold of the knife and hid it in her pocket.

'Is anybody there?' he said slowly and softly.

Silence.

'Hi, yeah, sorry... is anybody there?'

More silence. To be more precise: a radio playing in an unlit backroom. But no human response. Guzmán *El Malo*, ready for anything (for a change...) walked towards the radio and repeated the same question for the third time, this time in a normal voice. Then, with one finger pressed to his radiant, excited smile, he looked at Lily and pointed questioningly over to the giant safe against the back wall. She cried no with her head and arms and indicated with two eyes and two forefingers the cash drawer behind the counter. He begrudgingly obeyed and darted behind the desk to prise it open.

'I was sure that at least three or four alarms would go off. But nothing: just the radio playing. 'Horse with No Name' by America, to be exact,' Lluïsa used to tell me, smiling from every pore.

Five packs of five thousand, seven packs of two and eight of one: nine hundred and forty thousand extremely welcome pessetes that Mín (good job it was winter) stuffed into each and every pocket, while Lily kept her eyes and ears on the nocturnal desert outside. Giddy over the find and the risk, they walked out of the bank without having seen a soul: she told me that Mín automatically headed back towards the car but Lily, as crafty and as cunning as an entire family of foxes, dragged him downhill: she already had a plan in mind. They walked two hundred metres south and left the town along the riverbank. There were no lights and at night only couples ventured down there, and in the middle of winter only the hottest under the collar – 'nuff said. They looked around for a plastic bag that wasn't too dirty and hid the money in a rubbish bin.

'And what if they come to empty the bins, what then?' asked Mín as they walked away.

'What? At two o'clock in the morning?'

'No, but in six or seven hours?'

'In six or seven hours they're free to do whatever they want. Let's go back to the car…'

'The car? But it's out of petrol!'

'We need to move it, you numpty…'

'You're right. Let's push it down the road and call a cab.'

They went back into town and moved the 2CV three streets down, wearing their balls for bowties, it must be said, because if anyone saw them they'd be up to their necks in porridge for a good while. Afterwards, instead of calling anyone, much less a taxi, they stuck to golden girl's golden plan by following the footpath that connected the ghostown to that of the small-time dealer's at a slow, steady pace. Fortunately, a big slice of moon shone overhead. According to Lluïsa, Mín was a sight to behold: ecstatic over the nine hundred thousand tucked under his wing but sweating feathers because he was already clucking pretty hard.

After seventy-five minutes of effort, complaints and stifled laughter, they arrived at the house they'd originally set out for, having already agreed not to breathe a word about the adventure because, as everyone knows, you can't spill the beans from an empty can. If anyone commented on the car, or lack of, they'd simply say that they'd left it down in the square so as not to attract any attention. Naturally, they bought a whole gram instead of half, investing the entire day's takings and owing three thousand on top, before asking if they could take their cold syrup there and then, despite the practice being almost always frowned upon. But the small-scale dealer, over the moon at having such distinguished customers who consumed twice and handled three times as much as he did, made an exception – even if they had showed up out of the blue night at four in the morning.

After gunning half a gram together and preparing an eighth in smokes for the road, Lluïsa and Fermí, Fermí and Lluïsa, rode the thrilling wave of drugs and larceny back into town. But not back to the anonymous town where car and bounty awaited, but directly (exactly seven kilometres following footpaths and the main road) to Lo Pont de Suert. Lucky buggers.

Bridge of fortune (B-side)

in the winter daytime never comes. even a spittle of dawn would do me cos i'm falling asleep and i'm falling asleep cos in the winter dawn doesn't break until midday and cos i'm whacked on white lady and weariness and cos the cassette player's eaten my tape. but i don't want to stop cos i'm almost there.

it's been one of those long, sleazy trips when you can't find nothing nowhere. in Manresa: zero out of three and no one where they was meant to be. Sabadell same shit: no one there and no one knew where the people were who were meant to be there. and finally Barna even worse: sure no problem! but in half an hour…

half hour waits are the worst form of anathema for any (un) accustomed customer-consumer. they don't operate within the parameters of ordinary procedures and can drag on until who*knows*when. i know of cases when some hook up's half hour especially if he's a tout has ended up lasting three ten even thirty calendar days.

on the other hand it's normal at christmas or easter or at the start of summer for there to be a slump in supply. basically it's on account of an organic rise in demand, bent coppers doing a spot of p.r. and straight dealers being half on holiday. that's when you have to cross your heart and hope not to die and trust down at the heel hustlers who keep promising you half an hour half an hour while moving heaven and hell to cram it all into a day's work: if they're not working out some way to walk off with a month's wage, of course.

i'm falling asleep with both eyes and i should stop but i've only got six kilometres to go and i'll cover them in one fell swoop (tomorrow i'll buy some toothpicks to hold my eyelids up).

just as i was beginning to despair i got introduced to a short monoblock of a man with a slight hump on his left shoulder and a Canary Islands accent and now i'm hauling three kilos of chocolate at the bottom of a case of champagne and twenty grams of turkish delight in my shirt pocket just in case i have to ditch it. so this is no time for pitstopicnics cos the police aren't half as stupid as they like to make out at times. no matter. now i'm feeling good: it was tough going but in the end it came off. give my love to Lanzarote!

i'm pulling into town (eyelids suddenly lighter), i'm heading up to the bridge (working my lats), i'm turning off (indicator absentmindedly on, indicator absentmindedly off): barely a hundred metres more hollow huff n puff and brake down, handbrake up, silent stop in front of Barcadia. i inhale deeply, curse my eyes but tell myself before anything as always: unload.

i get out and open the boot. out of the six or seven different packages i grab the bag of cheeses and the case of champagne. i wind up the windows, lock the doors and walk to the front door with the case under my left arm and the keys in my right hand. the dawn sky is dirtdim still and the temperature (which i don't feel) sub-zero.

i open, enter, close, place the case and bag on table 6 and head upstairs. but upstairs, unexpectedly, inexplicably, there's no one. i go back downstairs, store the champagne and chocolate in the cellar, leave the still bagged cheese in the fridge (above all, a place for everything and everything in its place, as Lluïsa Cabellera *semper dixit*, referring to sex and drugs), poke my head into the back garden and see, to my surprise, that the 2CV isn't there. they've gone. perhaps for a party. perhaps forever. but not far, that's for sure, not with the 2CV.

i plug in the coffee machine, i switch on the electric heater, i take a shower: they'll be back: there's no hurry, i think, standing under the steaming water.

wrapped in three towels and two dressing gowns, i cook up the penultimate fix of the day, which is just beginning for the rest of the world but is already twenty hours old for me, cos i don't trust the price-quality relationship i've obtained. when it comes to drugs, without a done deal, you're drawing fucking lots.

then, bursting through the back door, out of use in the winter, i hear two whispering voices. my instinctive reaction is fear: fear they might be burglars or nutjobs. but soon enough i recognise that sonovabitch's giggle and her tiger lily tears: business partners having a ball, i see. she says they're crying from holding their laughter in so much, now they've finally made it home.

lily pad Lluïsa explains to me the joyful serendipitous nocturnal happening while Mín, with the corresponding discretion, moves the Seat onto the back patio to siphon a can's amount of juice. when he's finished we all get in to go rescue the 2CV. and the hidden treasure from the rubbish bin, of course.

All that remains to say is that when morning broke over our state of pure panic the success of the operation was absolute, and our sudden capacity for capital investment led us, one month later, to repeat the Amsterdam trip, this time using a coach full of football fans as a front. But on this occasion, they convinced me to play left back in the bar, enjoying trip and match alone (at the end of the day the kitty was shared but the dough was their find). Oh, I mustn't forget to mention that the traffick-tripping was accompanied by another abortion – such a well-kept secret that not even Fermí knew anything about it. According to Lluïsa, it would've only made things worse.

2. *Bridge of snow and ice: Mad Max*

She don't lie, she don't lie
She don't lie, Cocaine
'Cocaine', J.J. CALE

Unnecessary lineages to one side, Maximilià was hands down the maddest Andorran I've ever met. I guess that's why everyone called him Mad Max. Going on what he himself explained, mainly to Lily, the great trauma of his life, the last and most alarming in a long line of them, was on account of a sister who'd helped him out of more than one stinkhole, even securing him a cushy number as concierge in a comfy hotel in Pas de la Casa. He'd been there a year and a half, perhaps because his sister was director and not his brother-in- law (who had a car dealership in the centre of La Vella as his main line of business) when tragedy struck like an earth-shattering streak of lightning. On their way to Barcelona one morning, with Max behind the wheel of his brother-in-law's BMW, they smashed into an oncoming bus at one hundred and forty km/h; he got away with a broken leg and wrist, but his sister, oh!, his sister left her life there on the roadside. And Max, within and without, decided that he was to blame. Forever and ever, amen.

When we met him, Mad Max wasn't just a junkie of the highest order but also consumed a whole range of other substances, especially alcohol and cocaine. But the worst thing of all was that he injected coke. I really believe, all things considered, it was the only way for him to escape his schizophrenic reality, however much (i.e. all the time and every day more) it led him into an even worse one.

According to my personal and painful portfolio of hard drugs and the different ways of doing them, the most dangerous and damaging, the most destructive and alienating, the most absolute in every sense of the word, is injecting cocaine. Snorting it is no joke, believe me, but slamming it elevates all the symptoms to crisis point and tends to turn an addict's life into an unimaginable kaleidoscopic chaos of anxiety-hysteria-paranoia-neurosis.

Whatever the backstory, the character in question showed up at the bar one early afternoon prepared to finish every last drop of Pernod in the house. Seeing it coming, at six-thirty Lluïsa took the trouble to go out and buy three more bottles. The individual, an intriguing stranger to us, departed at nine with six large Pernods between belly and brain, only to reappear Around Midnight with a local userabuser. That first hook up was through this middleman but the second one the following day, and the rest over a three- or four-month period were direct.

Max had quite clearly lost his grip: on the one hand, he had a highly sophisticated level of education and culture which, when put to good use, made him irresistibly charming; but on the other, his unbalanced emotional constitution often pushed him to the limit. To ridiculous, grotesque, absurd limits. To the limits of rationality and of life. And that was when things got frankly frightening. Fermí was adamant he was a walking overdose, signed and sealed the very moment his sister died. He even suggested that we bar him, for the sake of everyone's health. But Lluïsa, beyond whether or not they'd screwed a couple of times, had grown fond of him and the idea upset her. I recall, vividly in fact, one of the last times he was at a Barcadian lock-in: he'd already banged enough racehorse to lose sight of the world, only to go and cover the table in French francs and demand we sell him more. We told, retold, and subsequently re-retold him that we didn't have any more, which was a lie. Lluïsa tried to convince him to snort a bit of skag but he was no longer listening: he fixed his demented eyes on the toilet door before springing to his feet and darting off to holler at creatures only he could see.

'Get out! Out! You cowards!'

Fermí fixed him with a homicidal glare and I closed my eyes, cringing inside, while Lluïsa went over to open the doors, turn on the lights and show him that no one was there:

'Nothing. Not even a dormouse,' she sang softy, as if to a child.

That calmed the fella down slightly, perhaps for a whole minute, before he became fixated by the stairs leading up to our flat: he kept getting up, silent and shaking, jumping towards the first step and pressing his back against the wall, a finger on his lips and on maximum alert. I was getting genuinely scared but Mín was already seeing a few tones beyond red. In the end Lluïsa found the solution by telling him she'd cook him up a speedball: Max let the wool be pulled over his mad eyes and injected a cocktail that was 80% potent heroin and 20% cut cocaine: after a couple of minutes, when the two drugs had taken their respective effect, he went back to being mild-mannered Maximilià who knew how to behave and even offer an apology. But Fermí had seen enough and, grasping the opportunity, calmly but firmly packed him off to his car and goodnight take care.

There had been similar scenes prior to that one and, despite deciding there and then to never sell him anything stronger than wine ever again, it wasn't the last. That came one September afternoon. Mín and I had just got back from Lleida, and Lily and Madman were both sat in the beer garden we'd set up on the back patio. Max sat facing the other way, his back almost completely turned towards golden girl, while whispering confidentially to an interlocutor invisible to our eyes.

'Who's he talking to?' I asked her in an aside.

'He goes between his brother-in-law and his sister. But I think his sister sometimes turns into his mum.'

'His poor mum...'

'His poor mum? Poor Max, more like!'

Dénouement: the fella gulped down five large Pernods in ninety minutes and left like it was nothing. Well, not quite: perhaps he was a bit dejected on account of the fact that the three times he mentioned blow Lluïsa swore we didn't touch it anymore, something he knew perfectly well was a lie. I can still see him, looking spick and span in his pecan brown cotton outfit, French glasses and Italian boat shoes, getting into his immaculate

VW for forever the last time. We've never been able to ascertain, not where the money that he threw around came from, because everyone knew that his sister, for better or worse, had left him a large capital sum, but rather who pressed and polished that impeccable wardrobe. Sometime in February, around carnival time, the kid from town who'd played middlefiddle that first night came in with the news that he'd been found in a coke freeze with a dozen needles on his lap in the car park of some nearby ski slope: Fermí was right yet again.

At the risk of making an even greater hash of things than I no doubt already am, Max crossed this final frozen bridge two or three months after Mín and Lily crossed their previous bridge of good fortune. Life, or at least that kind of life, is usually a two-faced coin, without any amount of consciousness. Not even a shred.

3. *Bridge of goodbyes: Search warrant*

'L'Oucomballa', COMPANYIA ELÈCTRICA DHARMA

I've already said that they were years – three and a half in total – of absolute abandon and excess. But back then we still gloried in the frenzy of living in and for the moment at the expense of our health and hopes for the future. But like everything that's alive in this universe, our bar/arcadia was destined to die one day or another. The first serious warning – if only we'd taken more notice of it – came in October '81. Truth be told, we'd already been debating for days the pros and cons of extending the lease, due to expire on 15th of January. The business, or rather the bar, was beginning to feel the effects of the reputation it had gradually earned, and Vielha's finest, as diligent and steadfast as worker ants, made sure of it by coming every other Saturday to scrutinise our licences or reprimand us over the latenightnoise. Deep down, and I say this with utter sincerity, we should have been grateful to them. If only we'd known how to give the gesture the merit it deserved.

One Friday Around Midnight, the whole squadron landed: two jeeps, two squad cars, seven uniformed policemen, two plain clothes officers, two sniffer dogs. They blocked all doors (front, back, kitchen, toilets, cellar and stairs) and demanded I.Ds from all the patrons, something I doubt they had the right to do. They superficially searched anyone without papers and the three or four they knew by sight, finding a couple of buds that didn't even add up to ten grams and a parachute with less than a quarter gram of gear. They let the others leave, while the two officers stepped outside with the little piggy with the parachute. The three of us remained inside with the seven policemen. They wouldn't even let us take a piss. And by God did we need it.

The two officers, sergeant major Esteban and sergeant Paezo, came back in and kicked off the usual intimidation tactics and threats: the kid talked, he's signed a confession that we sold him the dope, that they already had enough to yeahyeahyeah. Lluïsa, however, stopped them dead in their tracks: if they had come to search the premises and they had a warrant to do so, surely it was time to get started. But if they already had enough with what they'd found and could save us all the bother, even better. Either way, she wanted to phone our lawyer. The sergeant produced a document signed by some Vielha magistrate and gave the order to begin. As expected (because there's always someone with too many eyes, too many ears, too much of a mouth), they went straight for the cellar. Fortunately for us, we'd recently moved the priest-hole.

For starters, the big pack, on that day containing fifteen grams of smack and twenty something of sniff, was under a ten-kilo stone in an empty lot a mile out of town. Sure, at weekends, we had to make two or three roundtrips a day, but we had our two cars: the Seat 1800 and a yellow R5 that Lily had exchanged for the 2CV plus one hundred thousand pessetes: or we'd randomly borrow some customer's car.

In any case, it was now crystal clear that these precautions were well justified: they didn't find any drugs in the cellar because it had been more than a month since we had last stored any drugs there. Illegal drugs, you understand, because under a tile in the loft was half a quarter piece of hashish and in my bedroom they'd find a further half ounce. For more than a year we'd only bought chocolate for personal consumption, trying to keep to truly profitable transactions in order to limit our circle of customers in a grotesque attempt to improve our image in the town's eyes.

But what was troubling me (Lily and Mín looked relaxed enough) was the bag I'd left in the second kitchen drawer down after serving the half gram the cops had found and a whole gram that had luckily already trotted off into the night. It didn't add up to even two grams, but it'd be enough to close the bar a while and give us a few headaches. I remember repeating to myself that I'd have to be a cold bastard and invent a way of getting in there and swallowing it, but not a single convincing pretext came to me, so I kept as quiet as a corpse, as I tend to do when racked by doubt.

Although the sergeant major told us we weren't under arrest ('*por lo menos aún no*' – not yet at least), Lluïsa got permission to phone her friend Marc Tejida, who sat on the Pont de Suert council and was a bit of a big fish in local waters. And from that precise moment, our lawyer. She was accompanied by a uniform to the kitchen door where the telephone was and went inside to make the call. She had the drawer (and the baggy!) just inches from her hip but she didn't know and there was no way for me to get the message to her. I got up in I-don't-know-what direction but the sergeant minor howled at me to stop.

'I'm only going to the toilet,' I improvised.

'Not fucking likely, sunshine. Now sit down, shut up and start praying,' he said, but in Spanish, naturally.

Fermí was about to jump him but I stopped him with a stare before going over to the beer taps and, one foot inside the bar, filled three drip trays. Mr Tejida had luckily got married two months beforehand and was sat on the sofa in his large house consuming hours of television (and who knows what else). Eight nail-biting minutes later he came rushing through the door.

Men and dogs came out of the cellar the same way they'd gone in and afterwards poked their noses around the beer garden, where they found a handful of roaches but nothing else. Then a dog and two officers went upstairs while the other led his handler into the kitchen. I had the overwhelming urge to intervene somehow, to try to distract their attention, but I was frightened of only making things worse. Luckily our lawyer stated that it would be better if he could witness the search and that way if they found something no one would be able to suggest that the agents had planted it. That made the sergeant heave two heavy sighs. We were one thing but Mr Tejida, lawyer and elected councillor, was very much another.

I couldn't fathom how any of that would solve the problem of the kitchen drawer, but they went in and after an eternal couple of minutes came out and went upstairs. Maybe the dog had a cold. In the firstfloorflat they inevitably found my shitty stash on the bedside table. And as if that justified the spectacle, they didn't even bother going up to the loft.

They made me sign a couple of forms with our lawyer's consent, condemning me to the kafkaesque archives of posterity as a perverse user of hashish, forever and ever, amen before then rattling off a few unconvincing threats and summoning me to appear the following morning at Vielha police station. Then they grabbed the dogs, their tails between their legs, boarded their motorised fleet and disappeared into the autumnal fog like spirits from the vasty deep. I leapt like a shot into the kitchen but the bag wasn't in the drawer. Lily came in full of giggles while pulling up her miniskirt and pulling down her knickers, a manoeuvre that was as exciting as it was clumsy, and before I knew how to react, beyond just staring with my mouth and eyes open wide, she put two fingers up her vagina and pulled out the motherfucking baggy.

'What do you say? Should I clean it or no need?'

'No need! I'll swallow it just the way it is!'

Then the two of us were all hugs and kisses while I told and retold her that she was the smartest, most skilful midwife this side of the Pyrenees. As we opened a bottle of good cava (which we still called champagne in those days), Marc asserted that a shitty half ounce was nothing to sweat over. When Lily laughed and said that we owed him a payment, he smiled back and said a good line of golden wouldn't go amiss. I seem to remember, at Marc's request, us listening to Jeff Beck as we settled the bill on the bar top but they could be meshes of a different afternoon because Marc came in a lot before getting married. In fact, it was he who made us see how we were sowing the wind, warning us as our friend of what he wouldn't be able to save us from as our lawyer:

'Today you got lucky but when a pitcher goes too often to the well it ends up cracking. I don't know whether you get the metaphor or if you need me to draw you a prison.'

We got it and even assured him that we'd look for a way to take a couple of month's holiday from general dealing. But we all knew that was only the lie the situation demanded.

In any case, Barcadia had already taken its first step towards the tomb; a tomb that was sealed shut a few months later, one January evening, when they were lying in wait for us on the edge of town. It was Mín's run, just like it could have been Lily's or Lex's. And he paid for it with a year of porridge in Lleida, which he would no doubt have saved himself the trouble of doing if we'd listened to our lawyer's wisdom. But back then we – Mín and Lily and Lex – were so busy hurtling along our helter-skelter addiction that we wouldn't have allowed ourselves the option of getting off, even if we'd truly wanted to. In all likelihood, we still had much further to slide.

4. *Bridge of no return: Tailor-made epitaphs*

White bird must fly
Or she will die
IT'S A BEAUTIFUL DAY

Despite Mín's inevitable rage, Lily and I – naturally, automatically – resumed our relationship, and over the next twelve months of that year befouled by an omnipresent nausea named the '1982 Football World Cup' we learnt to feel, to feel and to suffer, deep deep down, the desire and the need, the need and the powerlessness to quit heroin. For my part, I already knew that I loved Lluïsa Cabellera as much as it was possible to love a person other than myself and that if I wanted to continue loving her beyond the habitual banging and balling, we had to destroy the prison we'd condemned ourselves to. I've always thought – and back then was no different – that she didn't love me to the same degree. But that could be simple narcissism or, even worse, recalcitrant sexism.

Whatever the case, what we did share was the determination

to learn to live smack-free. We discussed it with those closest to us, i.e. her brother, Pep Pepsin, and my brother, Sphinx Kid, even with a doctor and, as was fashionable in those days, a handful of psychologists. Everyone, absolutely everyone except for my inestimable brother, agreed on two things: getting clean for good would be much harder than we thought, and that the only chance we had at that moment was doing it separately. We tirelessly sailed, sailed and sank (within the raging storm of craving and enduring, of being and non-being) for more than three hundred days, starting at a small house on the outskirts of Granollers where, once Pont de Suert had been liquidated, we shared a roof with the model Raquel, an excasualover of adolescent Lluïsa, ending at the refurbished farmhouse Kiddo offered us up in deep Ripollès country, with a couple of stays along the way at Pepsin's flat by the beach in Blanes. It was a kind of excruciating, absurd wheel: we stifled the monkey on our back with eight days' abstinence, twenty pills and a Herculean effort, stayed on the straight and narrow for a few *weak*ends but then, with one excuse or another, whether it was owing to my impotence or her depression, we were back to the beginning. Just a few weeks later and we'd find ourselves on the edge of, or within, daily use once more. And so we'd go searching for the help of twenty pills and another dose of Herculean willpower. Big wheel keeps on turning.

One of the many theories on trauma preaches the importance of finding uncontaminated spaces, which is why we rolled from one place to another. Another theory, already touched upon above, eventually convinced Lluïsa to leave for Belgium and a 'Detox and Personal Recovery Farm Stay' led by a bizarre sect the name of which I won't even whisper for fear of summoning the Devil. Meanwhile, I sought shelter under Kiddo's wing at the woodland restaurant-inn he'd leased near Sant Llorenç de Morunys. I have to admit that out there it was relatively simple for me to forget about skag, perhaps because of the majestic way my ineffable brother relished routine. Kiddo knew how to give the moonlight and a bit of maria more meaning than I was able to find in the entire universe and ten kicks of the horse. Shame he sold his share to his business partner a few months later and ran off to Nepal to exorcise himself of christknowswhat imaginary sin. The place was no longer the same and I went to look for another job. In any case, though, it was there and then, thanks to the sacred muses one breathes there, where I became enamoured (as the dictionary puts it) with reading and with writing poems, short stories and novels.

If I'm being honest, I felt so joyfully liberated from my previous 'pathos' (oh, destiny! oh, chance!) that not even in my wildest dreams could I have imagined that we'd barely passed the halfway point of our monumental classical tragedy. None of the three theoretical protagonists – neither Lluïsa, nor Fermí, nor Lex – were able to perceive it, but it was much better that way: if we had we'd have undoubtedly topped ourselves and curtains down.

From those days and months after the great Barcadian comedown, Mín's imprisonment and the impotence of addiction, I still conserve a few pages penned by them both. From Mín, I have one of the three letters he sent me, written with secret sarcasm in a moment of rare lucidity in which he explains – all the while mocking himself, the deceased and the entire funeral – that the funniest thing of all is how he went six months without writing to us after

"...paying for my lawyers and solicitors and sending me pocket money each month. I admit I got worked up in the worst possible way but I thought it was unfair you two were in bed, free and together, while I was inside with nothing but micromanagement and masturbation.

"But I also admit, even if my cellmate doesn't agree, that it's normal you got back together because you've always been hers and what's more you met her before me and anyway it's not exactly the first time across our shared time and space that she's shared us. And as far as she's concerned, heavenly Lily, well, I think in her own way she loves the two of us. Anyway I know that I love the two of you because I know I can count on you, even if you do have your own problems.

"I'm also happy to hear (having overcome the purely egotistical question) that you've both decided to get off the bucking bronco because after everything we've been through (and I'm not just saying this because of my 'sojourn') it would be stupid to stay in the saddle. I truly hope you get clean like I am. That way all three of us will be able to go dine on oysters and laugh at the lemon aftertaste and all the bread we dipped in gravy.

With love and envy,

Guzmán (who's trying to be Goodman)
Lleida Gaol, 9-9-82"

AUTOBIOGRAPHICAL LLUÏSA: EXHIBIT 'B'

'No Exit', BLIND FAITH

GAME OVER
The Lord of Riches had been trapped
in an ambush by the Venomous Goblins,
while the Optimystic Princess
harboured within the unlikely Second Part
the Confused Spirits belonging to
the beautiful Prince of Percussion.
But His Love could no longer flow
for the Duke of Dykes ruled cruelly over
the Prince's liquids and the Princess' sea,
obstructing the art of Copulation in the deep cunt of the Void.
The Castle of Dreams was
inevitably cordoned off with tape
by order of a Governing Nostalgia
leaving the Goblins to capture the
ineffable Lord of Riches.
The Game's protagonist no
longer accepted a beginning or an end,
but they were obliged to keep playing
and therefore to keep losing,
while they still had something to forfeit.

Lluca, Blanes, 3-3-82

I am in a nightmarish facility with the appearance of a farm but the reality of a prison, where they've cured me of the physical agonies through a programme based on baths, massages, infusions and whispers, leaving me to slowly digest the full taste of my torment. Of course, I'd love to go back to choosing what I do when I get up but I'm in a KafKaesqueKult with a military structure and a mystical but sadistic spirit where they aspire to cure the mental and emotional withdrawal with a programme based on unbending discipline, an overdose of unpaid hard labour and perpetual public confessions of my most intrinsic sins. I'll eat my own cunt if I last more than two weeks.

I am on a Belgian train without a ticket or passport with the aim of getting to Amsterdam. In Belgium today it's so foggy and opaque that even the snow won't congeal. Outward image of my inner landscape.

I am at the border police station: although it's fucknowswhat past five in the morning and the border crossing has the rep of being like a sieve, they were wide awake and sucked me in like a magnet. As I only spoke about Amsterdam in doubledutch, the Belgians have fortunately handed me over to the Dutch and the Dutch, after the standard phone check, have had no other option but to believe that: my bag along with passport plus money plus ticket was stolen on the train and my habitual place of residence is Johan's house, who I haven't seen since the bus(trafficking)trip three years ago but was tipped off by telephone in Brussels before I boarded the train thanks to a few francs begged in the name of Christian charity.

I am on an identical Dutch train after Johan paid for my onward journey at the general bank: if the winter storm which, according-to-the-english-language-paper-belonging-to-the-man-opposite, is battering Scandinavia doesn't get us first we'll be arriving in Amsterdam at noon: in contrast to the fabulous Flemish heating inside, outside it's snowing cats and dogs. Oh poetic reflection of my pathetic image.

I am (after Magda picked me up and packed me off) at Johan's house, my third and last Amsterdamn boyfriend, who's still married to his plasticfantasticlovers day and night but now sharing with someone who spends all her waking hours in a sloping loft because the workshop never stops expanding and devouring more and more space. I am listening, while crying convulsive tears of impotence and solitude, to an album of late-romantic Russian music that I used to listen to a lot when I shared life with Lex on the Pityuses and also last year in Blanes at Pepsin's apartment.

I am a lament that would like to laugh but is condemned to cry, a fountain unable to drain itself and dry out, wind that always blows, speech that never stops. I am a nightingale that has flown across France but misses its roots and the mother that gave birth to them, or at least the places of those past ages when the mirage of free will was still believable. Oh Arenys! Oh Ibiza!

I am a fiery desert in the eye of the storm, a four-dimensional crossroads devoid of directions, signposts or paths: if it weren't for the cross stuck in my vein that I drag beside me, I'd buy myself an Arabic translation of *The Quartet* and go live in Alexandria, even if it's only to die of a venereal disease contracted during a priceless loveless fuck: any martyrdom would be better than the martyr I currently am, far from home and far from myself, far from the days when smoking and even shooting up was a sign of life and happiness. Far, so very far, from the dreams of love and sex and the Utopia of day after day choosing my own dawns and dusks. Farsofar from everything I'd imagined when I was young what my life would be when I could decide it for myself.

I am, in short, private sharp-edged suffering because I am, no more no less, an x-ray of what I hoped to be.

I am, without any more metaphors, the contradiction of wanting to live freely, and buying and dealing and using heroin every day. All that remains to add is that it's a devastating agony that empties existence of all euphoria. Even that of drugs. And if it's true that heroin addiction is forever,

I am a corpse that accepts this illness as a shroud and Amsterdam as a tomb.

Lluca, Amsterdam, jnry83

MÍN'S WORLDS
1. *The everyday day*

You know that Satan sometimes
appears as a man of peace
'Aniversari teujà', BOCANEGRA

It's five past ten on a hellhole of a morning and I've been waiting half an hour. It's rainy and sunny; rainy and sunny and windy, off and on, and it's half an hour past the agreed time. I light a cigarette (the second to last) and I'm hit by a hammer blow of nausea just smelling the smoke. I can't control my shaking hands and the cigarette falls to the floor. The sickness rebounds against my stomach and liver, and I vomit the last swig of milky coffee and the first painful slop of bile. I've swallowed dozens of monkeys, gibbons, chimps and orangutans in my time, and more than one adult gorilla, but this here today is a bona fide King Kong. If she doesn't get a move on, Ruth is going to find a stiff. I crush the sicksoggy cigarette against the car mat and use my elbows and knee to clean the steering wheel. Then, in the left hand side wing mirror, I see it: a white R5 with a mass of black hair behind the wheel, its indicator flashing. It turns. It comes up the street where I'm sat, parked near the corner we agreed to meet on. It comes up level to me. And calmly passes by. I beep my horn for three seconds until I suddenly remember the fucking cops. But a quick glance at the licence plate tells me this car isn't *the* car that I'm waiting for and therefore it isn't the girl either, the one I've been waiting for and am still waiting for, while the whipping wind brings two long lashes of rain. Ten twenty-five: three quarters of an hour. She's had problems, she won't be coming. I study the dashboard clock as if trying to memorise something. In the meantime, so as not to die of boredom, or simply not to die, I think about the nearest place to buy a monkeywrenching fix. Just when I decide to take a look around the cathedral square, where there's usually someone passing-the-parcel, I catch sight of another white R5. Yes, yes! Finally!!

Untrue to type she parks up carefully on the corner and, also untrue to type, gets out the car and walks over to mine. She sits in the passenger seat (finally! finally!!) and says 'let's go' above the sound of the slamming door.

'Where?'

'Get moving. I need you to give me a taxi ride.'

'I'll do anything you want, Ruth… but give me five minutes. If I don't get something in me right now, I'm gonna croak…'

'Alright, listen, here's what we're going to do: this is yours and *this* is a gram for the teacher in Torelló. She's expecting you at eleven. That means you've got half an hour to stop clucking about and get yourself over there. I'll leave the car here in case they're looking for it and we'll meet at twelve on the dot in the square below the apartment. And if you behave yourself there'll be a little something in it for you, o-*kay*?

'Okay. How much is the teacher s'posed to give me?'

'Twenty-three for today plus twelve from the day before yesterday makes thirty-five. And charge her the full amount 'cos I need the dough.'

'Loud and clear.'

Ruth got going on foot, a shopping bag in her right hand, an umbrella and the gear in her left, and I headed straight to the bar on the corner, checking – one pocket, two pockets, three pockets, four – that I had my full works on me. As I lit a cigarette (last one), I ordered a beer to keep things above board. After pecking at it, more out of disgust than thirst, I slithered, literally, off to the toilet. The short time I was in there is a genuine horror story. For starters, I hadn't thought to grab any water so, not to have to go out again, I took it directly from the toilet bowl. Then, having automatically and stupidly lit up at the bar, I realised I'd left myself without a filter, meaning I'd have to collect the water without the needle. Lucky, the syringe was detachable because if it were one of those American or Italian jobs doing the rounds I don't know how the hell I'd have managed it. And to top it all off, the merchandise in question was what they call 'marble', owing precisely to its hardness and that working it requires a certain technique and a lot of patience. Two things that, dribbling and shaking like a cold, epileptic turkey, I felt claustrophobically lacking in.

I vividly remember – so much so that my spine still tingles just thinking about it – how petrified I was that piece of substance in solid state wouldn't enter my vein because someone somewhere had told me it could be lethal, and despite the urge to shoot up once and for all, after backtracking a bit of blood I waited two or three megaseconds, sure that same someone somewhere had also told me that blood temperature aided, to some degree, dilution. But right then a loud thud on the door and the owner's voice yelling whocareswhat about the cops brought me back to raw reality and, bang!, gunning it quick, I scoop up my kit, emerge from there like a tornado, everything a vertiginous sequence of screenshots, like the one of me telling the owner to shove his fucking hissy fit as I blow through the bar and out through the in door.

I also remember being behind the wheel of a moving car and having passed two sets of lights when the stuff started to kick in for real. About time! Let's see if that teaches me, once and forever, not to be a dipshit after hours and to keep some in reserve for breakfast. After all, the all-night vigil back at the Manresa flat with Lex and Silvi was already animated enough, amid spliffs and music and sex, and one more rail or one less fix was all the same. But, you – shit, I really don't understand what you're playing at sometimes – go all in at three in the morning, gambling it'll last you until midday, but then five or six hours later, in bed, you're like a possessed pig sweating on a spit roast. That'll teach you.

I'd hazard a guess this marble bullshit hooks you quick but the rush is short-lived. Then again, it could just be what doctors call 'tolerance'. Every day I take a bit more and every day it has a little less effect. But that's the way the cookie crumbles, however much I hate to accept it.

Warm inside and with that aftertaste on the palate of the soul that makes you forget all the pain, be it physical or mental, I headed towards Torelló, and at eleven-o-two pulled up in front of a 'no parking' sign next to the apartment block of the afore-mentioned teacher, someone I must've met about half a dozen times, either accompanying Ruth or going solo like today. Normally she stood by the window that looked out onto the street and came down when she saw the car. But she wasn't, of course, expecting a green mini, so I got out and rang.

'Yes?' came a muffled voice.

'It's Fermí. I'm here for Ruth.'

The electric buzz of the front door answered for her, which wasn't something I was expecting. But bearing in mind that intercoms are all ears, into the lift and up to the fourth floor it was. Between second and third I began to worry about that 'no parking' sign.

The teacher, a short, freckled redhead from Boston, greeted me in a dressing gown and woollen scarf over cotton pyjamas, and told me 'come in, come in' in her purring Catalan before pussyfooting back to the bedroom. It was March maybe April already, and the teacher in question had been living in the apartment in question for at least six months but, with the exception of the bedroom, where only a wardrobe, dressing table and large desk appeared alive and in working order despite the chaos encircling them, the apartment – bathroom and kitchen included – was a series of cold damp white rooms with a few bits of furniture scattered around, lost in some corner or randomly cut adrift amid piles, stacks and mounds of suitcases, boxes and bags full of books, notebooks, shoes, candles, maps, letters, postcards, dolls, ashtrays, cutlery, glasses, trays, coffee mugs, tea sets, and an unclassifiable, unending etcetera, etcetera.

I say that the apartment was cold, but could also easily have said it was glacial, chilling, frozen over. The bedroom, on the other hand, was like a smelting furnace, *a hundred in the shade!*, as Lex would say, thanks to a kilowattguzzling monster with four giant bars going at full throttle. After jumping back into bed, dressing gown and all, the nouvelleanglaise said:

'I need you to give me a helping hand.'

You could be forgiven, on account of her American accent, for thinking it was a sexual favour she was after but, in light of the situation, I preferred to play dumdum.

'If this is about money then you're woofing up the wrong tree. I'm just the errand boy and even that's saying a lot.'

'That's exactly what it is: a little errand. I've had one hell of a night, diarrhoea, vomiting, tremors, the works, and half an hour ago, to top it off, I got my period... God, I feel skanky.'

She paused to emphasise her unbearable psychomenstrual predicament with a large slice of withdrawal weaved into it, and gave me a cheque while asking, *begging*, me to hurry down to the bank. I looked at the figure with a Buster Keaton face and read one hundred and fifty thousand pessetes (which was a hell of a lot of dough back in '77).

'If he's got doubts, tell him to call me.'

'If he's got doubts, better he calls his priest.'

'Huh?'

'What's your number?'

'Local code plus the year Cervantes died.'

'Never heard of him.'

'Cervantes? You're kidding me.'

'What year did he die?'

'1616,' she smiled, before seasoning it with a sarcastic wink: 'Jot it down, just in case.'

'If I *really* try, perhaps I'll be able to remember it: sixteen sixteen, sixteen sixteen…'

Then she sat up with a start, rested her back against the headboard and, stretching a shaky and most likely fevered hand towards me, asked if I trusted her enough to give her the gear while I went to the bank; p'raps a good line would help her to shift her stinking cold and be able to go to work in the afternoon with her head on the right way round. When I was back, as payment for services rendered, she'd cut me a slice of something nice. From the way things were looking, everything was on the house that day. I've no idea why but this only happens when you don't really need it. When you're starving without a cookie crumb, the Toot Fairy never comes a-calling.

I gave her the bag Ruth had given me as she emerged from under the blankets and placed an enormous book with a laminated cover between her knees and thighs, cursing and damning to hell that solid material which there was no way of crumbling if not with a tonne of patience and a coffee grinder. A coffee grinder, Lilliput version, is exactly what she grabbed from under the bed and where she placed the lump of marble once freed from the plastic. All the while, her hands, feet, knees, lips, eyelids and breasts shook without let up with the small and not so small tremors of an illness I knew all too well.

'If I'm not back in an hour, phone the old bill and tell them you've been robbed,' I said with a Kirk Douglas smile.

'Okay… What's your name?'

But in reality she was no longer listening, immersed as she was in the preparation of the only thing that really mattered in her life at that moment: her fix. And, just like that, I walked out without even saying goodbye, closing all the doors so not to see any more mirrors, thinking how that scene deserved to be in some hyperrealist short film. One of those that Mercè the Playactor likes so much.

Running off with Ruthella's gram was killing the goose that laid the golden-brown eggs, of course, but disappearing up north or way down south with one hundred and fifty thousand green beans belonging to a newenglishteacher from Boston who probably wouldn't dare report it was a temptation I was more than aware of. If it had happened half a year before who knows how it would've panned out because back then I was blindly crossing a desert as blind as it was blinding, when I would commit any cruel act without considering its complications or consequences in any way. It was during one of these reckless moments, just before my 'reunion' with Lex, gambling everything on one card as usual, that Cousin Dixie, a certain Ramon (M.I.A.) and I collected eight hundred thousand *peles* from the office of a Sabadell supermarket by kicking in, at night time and with premeditation, just a single door. I made the solemn promise that my share would serve to set things up so never again would I have to steal to survive. Or rather, to shoot up. It's too dangerous and too much of a moral minefield. Especially when it's no longer a supermarket but an individual just as if not more deadbeat than me. P'raps it will make one or two laugh but according to my code of conduct, abusing a person's trust, in this case Caroline's, was a much worse crime than robbing some rich company.

When I stepped out of the lift all these ephemeral, insignificant concerns were no more than a rueful smile which a car horn, repetitive and imperative, immediately wiped off my face.

Untrue to form, I didn't have the energy or the minutes to spare with squaring off with anyone. And that's in spite of the man asking for it (pure fermenting turd curd on legs), as he continued to complain about not being able to get out of his garage, repeating and repeating, parrot-like, the same three phrases: twenty minutes, an outrage, the police! I weakly claimed it was more like five, max, and fled in the direction of the bank.

A quarter of an hour later, happy to have found a place to park (and having bought a litre of purified water and a pack of pretty-looking sharpshooters), I went back to the lift, the flat and the skankydoodle. But Caroline had changed considerably: she moved and spoke with singular grace and was active, attentive and attractive to the point of excess. Only her eyes, normally soft and catlike, had transformed into two cloudy blue-grey glass balls. While she was bringing me a slice of pie and a beer into the bedroom, I forced myself to go to the toilet, not because I particularly needed to, but to check if my pupils were like two deadened marbles as well. And as I calmly cooked myself up a generous shot from the gram I'd delivered her, she performed the minor miracle of catching Ruth at home and told her, in no uncertain terms, that I'd be held up for half an hour.

Half an hour isn't enough to fuck your brains out, I thought, already getting hard. But I'd got the wrong end of the stick, for what she really wanted me to stick in her was the needle. I refused for a while, I really did, arguing that after snorting diesel, sticking more into a vein could kill her but I admit I didn't resist anywhere near enough. Perhaps because I sensed that if I gave in to her desire then she'd give in to mine, of course. The most fascinating thing from that pathetic labyrinth of pleasures and agonies is how our unspoken conversation, with its intimate and painful personal reflections on my own drugdependency, affected me. We outlined it with a few gestures and phrases before sublimating it into a hit and a half-hearted orgasm without consistency or passion. We didn't formalise it with phonemes or sentences or syntax because inside we deemed it entirely unnecessary. At least I didn't because the questions I would've impulsively asked (for example: why was she punishing herself in that way and why that inhospitable domestic destitution and why risk losing a well-paid job on easy street), these and many more similar questions referring to the different levels of liberty and slavery of the inner entity that governs our will, all or almost all of them, were being instinctively answered in a mirror where an irrational reflection of my ego asserted them in the voice the rushing east coaster reserved for her stupidest students.

I never saw mainline-Caroline again, not even to deliver her the morning paper, because just a few days later the bad guys, or more precisely a drug squad corporal and native of Jaen better known as *El Niño*, finally nabbed Ruth with six one gram and four half gram baggies and they threw her in the clink for nine months and a day. My poor canary!

I say I never saw sweet Caroline again and in one sense it's true but in another it's a lie. A lie because for some strange reason, even to this day, some ten or twelve years later, I often dream about her, sometimes sexually but normally she's giving me pedagogical speeches full of anglo-saxon morality on the advantages of quitting hard drugs, the hopes and expectations of recent years plotted on graphs, and the path towards inner discipline and definition (such as reading, walking, swimming, exercise, enjoying sex or learning Russian) which, without the need for naltrexones, methadones and psychologists, develop and achieve the oh so controversial yet desired freedom. Other times, we go shopping for hard drugs together, up to our eyeballs in gorillas, but the dream disintegrates into a frenzy of fear and panic and anxiety, and comings and goings and returns without any other coherence than the abyss, overflowing with bloody syringes and hopeless waits without reward in increasingly reduced spaces.

Many years ago, during my Caroline dreaming, a teacher from when I was ten appeared who for no other reason than a pencil moustache personified my dad, the distinguished commander Fernando, killed in active service against cirrhosis of the liver, just after forcing me to take my First (and last) Communion. But his speech, transcendent and peremptory during the dream, evaporated the moment I woke up, of course.

I didn't obtain anything tangible from bookworming the works of Doctor Freud, despite throwing myself into them heart and psyche during the fifteen months I spent in the Lleida slammer after our Pont de Suert adventures. But that's a different rabbit hole entirely because the day to day of the title of this story took place on planet Vic and its natural satellites, many moons ago in the spring of '77.

2. *Immortal presents and eleven thousand second hours*

Who or what I am escapes me,
Every changing minute shapes me
'The Confessions of Doctor Dream', KEVIN AYERS

At twelve-fifty, twenty minutes over the half hour delay, I parked up by the aforesaid square, leapt out of the car and ran to the bar: I wanted a piss and to buy a can of the cold stuff because Ruth babe would be arriving very soon and very sour, of course. Two minutes later, in fact, she was already in the mini, sat in the passenger seat with a don't-you-*ever*-do-that-to-me-again scowl on her face. But she was in such a rush she didn't bother to give me a rock n rollicking.

I started her up and she started explaining that yesterday, around half nine on the night run, she'd played leading lady in a slapstick film that could've ended up a tragedy, slipping and sliding through the old town alleys with a drug squad car on her tail, its siren blaring and tyres screeching around every corner, until she finally managed to hide in a car park, hide the contraband and phone a friend.

'That's why I can't risk the Renault. At least not with cargo on-board.'

Meanwhile, we did half a dozen hook-ups in the city, following a route that she'd devised with mathematical precision according to the place and time we had to meet each customer, while also avoiding certain buildings and lights. First, we picked up someone known to everyone as Slim, perhaps because not even junk had been able to completely eliminate his tendency towards obesity, and while Ruth counted the paper and gave him the baggy, I drove three blocks down in the direction of the supermarket. After spitting out Slim, we picked up the bakery girl by the supermarket side entrance. The bakery girl was twenty years old and had a flexible, athletic body. But that particular day everyone was monkeymad and my heel dragging hadn't helped. Madeleine, I think she was called, who was certainly a couple of slices short of a full loaf, begged, blagged and beseeched us to drop her on the corner near the bakery, where they were no doubt effin' n blindin' because it was already a quarter of an hour since she said she'd be two minutes. Ruth made a rare exception and we took her a few blocks closer, making the most of it to head back into the centre and serve Jordi, a pretty kid from a pretty rich family who worked at a building society. Afterwards we picked up the umpteenth desperate junkie, a guy called Stew, who was not only completely stewed but had been waiting for seventy minutes at the train station (a gram and a half, and half a problem with a bad credit rating), and we dumped him five hundred metres up the road and left the old town to go see Gyppo. Now, Gyppo was a Roma of around fifty years old waywardly married to María, a gypsy girl of seventeen, who he treated like a dog. He'd set himself up as a faux farmer in a farmhouse half in ruins where he peddled anything that might earn him a buck: drugs, tools, jewellery of all type and value, car radios, televisions, stereos... He even touted the teen who, when pickings were lean-fleshed, which was almost always, worked for next to nothing at the dirtiest tumbleweed whorehouse in the county. We even went to Torelló to serve Joanot, a Menorcan albino who owned a honky tonk for local junkies, and then a kid with short ginger hair and a redtomatonose, whose name I've never known. Ruth called him Ripoll Two'clock because every afternoon, come rain or shine, Christmas Day or Easter Monday, he came down from Ripoll at two o'clock on the dot to pick up his habit. And if she couldn't be there she had to find someone else to go and serve him, every day, at exactly two o'clock, so he wouldn't be left in the lurch, of course: Ripoll Two'clock.

I don't know how many more characters I'm leaving out because we went from Sant Joan to Sant Roc, crossing squares, down streets, up to apartments and into the odd bar or three, according to a schedule that was even starting to square up. By half four we'd finally finished the noontime run, today longer than ever because of last night's adventure and this morning's diversion, and took the N-152 direction Barcelona. We stopped to inject some diesel into the tank and to put a little something in our stomachs (she had spanishomelette, I had a croquemonsieur) to cushion the diesel we'd inject ourselves with at one of the many outdoor shooting galleries along the habitual corridors of our habit. Or that's what I thought because when we were back on the dual carriageway, to punish me, little babe Ruth had the bright idea, bearing in mind at nine we had to be back in Vic, to man the phones and plan the inevitable night run, that it'd be better if she cooked up in the car and I kept clocking up the kilometres. To not lose time with a pitstop, she injected me in my right hand with the resulting danger for road safety. But watcha gonna do?

At five forty-five, we entered the burning beehive of a housing estate (to remain anonymous) on the outskirts of Tarragona, similar to the ones that encircled Barcelona at the time, such as Sant Cosme or Can Tunis or Sant Roc or etcetera: rows of symmetrical blocks four or five stories high made with the cheapest material possible, normally exposed tiles or unpainted plaster; a subodega or infrabar every couple of blocks; a police van every few metres; the inevitable dustdirt square with a broken slide in the middle where scores of kids more dangerous than a hailstorm played at smashing cars and mugging passers-by.

Fresh in my retina is a series of screenshots from the tender-loving neighbourhood of La Mina one diabolical day when, after picking up a little something, I found eight to ten of the monster midgets kicking the living daylights out of my car door trying to pop the lock. If anyone thinks that when they saw me running towards them and shouting that they got scared and scarpered then they are sadly mistaken. On the contrary: two of them, like a pair of savage Shetland ponies, kept on kicking my poor car in an attempt to open the door while the others tried to keep me at arm's length with back kicks, insults, spitting and stones. I had the urge to charge at them with open palms, spinning my arms like a windmill, to see how far the devil dwarves would fly but I had to swallow them down because those miniature criminals were from the neighbourhood and knee-deep in mothers, fathers, sisters, brothers, cousins, neighbours, friends and friends of friends who'd have me strung up in a second if I had so much as touched one of them. Happens in the best of families. Using my arms to protect myself from their projectiles, I leapt towards the passenger door before diving behind the wheel. As I started her up, they continuing pursuing, insulting, pelting me... but the radio was still in its place, hidden under the seat, and I was in a hurry to get the hell out of there and feel the happiness of a warm gun.

Another characteristic of these sad estates condemned, like me, if not more, to scrape by on the meagre returns offered by crime and violence, are the corpsecars. You find a few burnt out, some smashed up, and many more simply dumped. There used to be a van on the outskirts of El Prat, situated on a sunny, deserted plot behind an equally deserted warehouse where three or four people lived for an entire year. The last few months they even set up a onestopshop selling small amounts of a whole catalogue of drugs. If it hadn't been for that, which in the end led to the intervention of the cops and the disappearance of the van, someone might well still be living there now. One day, years later, in a parallel world one thousand two hundred kilometres away, deep in the Neapolitan underbelly, I – walking by in a hurry and without uttering a word – saw some poor bed bug who'd been shooting up in one of these corpsecars being repeatedly punched by a mob of local dealers, ratifying an unwritten but sanguinary law clearly stating that you come to the *neighbourhood* to buy but never to inject. Of course, Naples is another galaxy, even more ferocious than Catalonia, and there, in those sorts of ends, the police tend to drive through – and only when it's absolutely unavoidable – at sixty km/h and with the sirens off. And the days they have to pretend to be doing a ministroke of work, they *almost* always give prior warning. I know because one day they caught me like a sitting duck and the first thing I did when I got out (three days later and after paying half a bribe not to get kicked out of the country) was to make sure *someone* always gave me the right info at the right time.

Returning to that remote day with Ruth, we were back in Vic without any hiccups and on time by nine. The evening is etched on my memory because the very same girl who'd always been so sexually standoffish after the night run, invited me to dinner and to spend the night with her. Sex, in the same way as drugs, is always badly spread out. Either you get so much of it you're almost fed up by it, or you can't get as much as a sniff. Of course, in those days, happily married to the needle, sex had nowhere near the urgency for me that it has for any normal human being. Perhaps that's exactly why it came about without having to go looking for it.

I stuck around babe Ruth, as friend and buyer, beyond her imprisonment and beyond her relationship with a certain Fabià – Bián to friends and customers – a musician whose breadandbutter was stealing and dealing; but the first night we had a genuine opportunity we ended up in bed again. But only one night because she didn't want Bián to find out, not while he was in La Model, not with the stretch he was staring in the face, and neither had it crossed my mind to break things off with tiger Lily.

At times I think women, in a generic sense of the word, feel an unconscious, or not so unconscious, aversion towards overt male sexual desire but, paradoxically, they become impassioned and will do anything to create and stimulate it when they meet someone who doesn't openly manifest any. In other words, they can't bear being an object of sexual desire, but they can bear sexual indifference even less. This easy judgement is no doubt influenced by the fact that, seven or eight years later, in Big Barna and amid the randomness of a night when Pere the Painter dragged us to a luxury brothel to celebrate the fact he'd exchanged three paintings for forty grams of columbo, I ran into gypsy girl

María earning a living behind the bar; the same María I knew as Gyppo's slave, transformed into a fully-grown woman going by the name of Susana.

Oh, Vic! Oh, Gyppo! Luckily, it was all water under the bridge. Unfortunately, she remembered enough to explain it all drip by drip: Gyppo, who passed himself off as her husbandlover but was in fact her own flesh and blood father, was found one midsummer night with a switchblade buried deep in his spleen. No, she hadn't knifed him, despite having wanted to on more than one occasion, and most likely one of her uncles or brothers from Bonavista had done it, mortified at how he treated her. Only her mum went to the funeral, afterwards offering her the chance to come home. But Susana had no home and she never would, not until she had one of her Own: she knew how they were looked at and what life they led in the large, respectable family engendered by Uncle Andrés, the women who'd worked as whores, you understand. So she got married, even worse than the mediocre majority, to a pimp peachy on the outside but putrid on the inside, and in that present moment, aged twenty-five, she was a widow and mother to two-year-old Jordi, the apple of her eye. For the kid's sake, she'd decided to get out of sex work asap, just like she'd got out of hard drugs, and dedicate herself to business. Man, she was impressive. And highly communicative; as though in a previous life we'd known each other as intimate, freely-chosen friends instead of through random drugbusiness or bartoptoplessness.

That big Barnacle night, after the childish rituals at the whorehouse were over, we ended up together again, in a holy trinity with Lex at the apartment he shared with a girl called Eulàlia on Plaça Padró. It still resonates with me because it was the first night I got back in the horse saddle after two years of almost complete abstinence and it knocked me for six, of course. And also because months later Lex hooked up with the aforementioned Eulàlia, as much as she considered herself an unswerving lesbian, and the apartment on Plaça Padró turned into a sort of second home for me.

Nevertheless, the most remarkable thing from those pre-historic times, when I learnt about the graces and disgraces of the trade inside the Vic-Sabadell-Manresa triangle, is that, paradoxically, between hits, I would often tell myself I was better quitting. But the truth is I never really made an effort anywhere near deserving of that word until the 4th of January 1982 when Sergeant Paezo from the Vielha Civil Guard caught me on the road into town with twenty-five grams of blow and ten of smack. It cost me fifteen months, in accordance with incorruptible judge justice. I know plenty who've paid more for lesser crimes and others who've paid a lot less for more to much more serious offenses. The scales of justice, as the symbol shows, are blind and therefore subjective. Nevertheless, objectively speaking, everyone knows that the paper you put on your plate plays, to a degree or two or more and depending on their number and value, a part in the decision made by the creditor charged with determining what and how much you are to pay in prison. Personally speaking, and without wanting to justify in any way a neo-feudal penitentiary system that shames our famous Western Democracy™, in a purely subjective and personal sense, I believe that isolation was productive for me. I understood one must perfect oneself, whether wishing to live within or without the law, and that the best option is usually keeping your nose clean and looking out for number one. I also realised that shooting anything and everything was dumb and that drugs should be business and entertainment but never again habit and self-destruction. And the truth is that when I got out on the 9th of April 1983, though still an habitual user because chasing the tiger was fashionable inside, I was no longer, mentally or physically, what doctoring doctors understand as an addict. A few months later, working at the garage Cousin Dixie had just opened in Olesa, I even learnt how to enjoy a blunt, a beer, a bottle of cava or a black coffee. I'm sure I would've been completely cured, at least from brown, if it hadn't been for meeting Lex and María Susana again. And above all and everything... if not for that dirty trick called AIDS.

But Lex and Susana aren't to blame; they're only guilty in the same way that I am. The ones that invented or propagated the virus, because I firmly believe it's an artificial invention that has gotten out of control, designed to destroy certain segments of the non-submissive population, *they* are the ones that I blame for my second stretch of junkdependence. Anyway, what's done is done: no point crying over spilt milk, even if you're up to your neck in it.

On the other hand, in prison and at other times in my Life as an Addict, I have felt, enjoyed and cried over the peculiar beating of the everyday day and the eleven thousand second hours driving it: a concept of time unique to lovers and junkies, nowhere near as outrageous as it may first appear, that doesn't adhere to any known clock. Although it's possibly because my memory that actually corresponds to it has been embellished by similar days and blended to the point of universalising the sensation of these experiences of the single infinite day. But this final reflection and, by extension, the rest of these absurd words without meat or message are theoretical probabilities taken from a notebook that María Susana left in Lex's car. A notebook that I (being the fetishist that I am) keep as a stolen relic.

ON HOURS AND THEIR SECONDS

Then John said that Luke had attested to the Master halting the Sun's movement for a full minute during the twilight hour on the wedding day to eternalise his teaching on the versatility of time. 'All your presents shall be, by my voice, immortal, and your hours shall have, by my word, three times more seconds than one hour.'

Yet, in that very moment, the atoms of sand that measure the elapsing corpus were damp on account of the Calvary premonition thus no one knew how to establish with certainty what miracle was revealed by the concept of 'one second'.

I never had the occasion to meet John, who departed for Alexandria one lustrum ago, or Luke, who had already been in Heaven for two, and much less the Master, who celebrated his martyrdom the very day of my birth, thirty-three years ago this very dawning day. Even so, I, Jacob Andreas of Bethlehem, also known as the Mathematician, do humbly claim to have discovered the essence of the concept of a 'second'. One second, for example, am I.

Apocryphal Gospels
Jacob Andreas of Bethlehem
1st April, 32 B.C.

Regard your days as railroads.
Think of your past selves
as the wagons of a train
whose locomotive is your voice.
Mumble,
mutter,
cough,

shout:
the future embraces you with your own arms.

Once more the sky menaces me
with meaningless clouds.
Just in case, I grab my old pen
and throw my dice once more.

Image of Perfection:
human toads
licking the anus
of their bloody larva:
oh God.

Give me your breath:
I'll weave a gondola of
pure carbon to cut any canal.

Like the dead,
you're blue blooded:
sad monarch of the forbidden kingdom!
your heart melts,
blue, because of your wounded gaze.

On the dark side of the void,
bellowing blood,
lacerating life,
the concept of light
is born, grows and explodes
at the same rate that the concept of
depth rises up and dives deep.

On a thin edge spins
the two-tailed coin,
tossed towards X
as if veiling a first principle.
My being growls with savage laughter
to hide the emptiness
that fills both faces.

1-8-96

From: Fabià R. Juncadella (Ap. Co. nº 20, Barna 08029)
To: Lex Oscà i Punyol (Cal Fumall, Malanyeu, Barna 08699)

What's up, you junkie bastard? You're still alive I see! You know, with all the cars and drugs I didn't think you'd make it to thirty. I really enjoyed getting your letter: it kept me entertained for a whole day, which means a lot in here.

I didn't know Fermí had died. Rest In Peace. Though fifteen years ago (actually fourteen and nine months), given the chance I'd have killed him myself, egoist that I am, because in the terrible loneliness of my cell I couldn't bear thinking that he at that precise moment could be Next to her body. Or Inside her soul. Often, like a cardboardcutout Othello, I imagined them making love this way or that, and then cried with rage, frustration and pure impotence. In those moments I'd have pummelled him to a pulp given half the chance, possibly her as well, and then committed suicide immediately afterwards.

Now I know for certain it was only once and that Ruth continued to help me for seven or eight years, even after she left for Basel to live with her Swiss watchmaker. It still has me half in stitches when I think about it because for the life of me I can't picture her neatly tucked into the rigid right angles of Helvetic society, married to an upstanding millionaire shop owner and playing queen consort in the home, the business and the marriage bed. No doubt for Fabià Jr., who turned sixteen the day before yesterday, it means an education I could never dream of giving him.

But the long and short of it is that I took all that stuff with Mín and Ruth real bad when it happened. In hindsight, perhaps it was a stroke of luck because afterwards I sank into a mammoth depression and, as a result, the prison psychiatrist took notice of me. I don't understand these men who don't want women in the workplace: I assure you, for us in here it's a massive deal to go to the psychiatrist and find a chick of twenty-five with an Olympic swimmer's body and a Hollywood actress' smile! Her name was Glòria and I swear to you, for me, she was pure glory: first she cured my depression, then she set me up with music classes (the rehabilitation programme pays me a wage, too, yes sirreeee!), and in the end she made me understand that inside or out, up top or down low, without heroin one lives much better. And normally longer.

Believe it or not it's ten years since I stopped using, except for a thin rail to see in the new year. To be honest, I wouldn't have the money to do it anyway: in here robberies are a hundred times poorer and a thousand times riskier. It's years since I last went to the psychiatrist because God knows where Glòria is now but I continue giving guitar, voice, harmony, drum and percussion lessons every morning and the remainder of the day I continue praying that my irreproachable conduct convinces the irreproachable judge that I'm no longer a danger to our society of a hundred thousand dangers.

In all honesty (but don't tell anyone 'cos it's embarrassing), I feel a bit like Raskolnikov (I'm sure you've read it), a character that's capable of comprehending that his crime against a human life deserves, no, demands, an exemplary physical punishment in order to avoid a much worse psychological sentence.

Apropos of the memory morsels you asked me to send, I've sullied a few sheets of paper, situated in the Paris of '68 and London of '69, about a character who doesn't want to be me but looks pretty similar. Let me know what you think. At first I wanted to recount my banking adventures but I'm afraid, things being the way they are, you'll have to go solo. That went on for two or three years anyhow, and I reckon you know all there is to know already, and then some.

Health, literature and stardust!
Fabià.
(P.S. Write soon!)

FROM BONANOVA TO THE LONDON-SYMPHO-NIC-BAND VIA RED PARIS

'Set the Controls for the Heart of the Sun', PINK FLOYD

I was born and bred in Bonanova and schooled at the Lycée Français. My pitiable progenitor was a nomadic consul in the Franco regime and I learnt geography at the same rate that I forgot his face: Marseille, Bratislava, Dubrovnik, Dortmund, Rotterdam, Edinburgh... I'd see him for a week at Christmas and ten days in summer if we happened to be in the same city. It's no wonder then that when poor Antònia – my long-suffering mother – died we ended our relationship with one another in ten minutes flat: I was twenty years old, an active member of the Trotskyist wing of PAU (Partit d'Acció Universitària) and a committed Communist from sweet sixteen.

My pitiable progenitor, Don Ignacio de Robles Capmañs, no doubt had the group under surveillance and, quietly, out of respect for my mother, his second wife, got me out of a couple of sticky situations that otherwise would've turned me into a political prisoner in two seconds flat (something I was no doubt desirous of in my unconscious substratum). Ten days after her funeral and he was leaving for Oslo, where they'd just named him – finally! – ambassador but before departing he wanted to 'straighten me out' as he used to say (even sometimes deigning to say it in Catalan at home).

All that sociocultural agitation, not to mention the implicit political subversion, had to stop immediately if I was planning on continuing to be his son. His career (yes!, even his precious career, that had led him to make so many sacrifices) was in danger because of me. And it just had to be now, just as he'd achieved the dream of an entire lifetime...! Of an entire family! It ends here!!

It was the same old speech, indisputable to the point of despotism, crowned with 'it ends here', just to ram it home. I told him not to worry, that being the son of an active representative of Spanish Fascism sickened and ashamed me, and that he could henceforth add me to the list of dead relatives, under my mother's name. He swung an open palm at me so hard that it put me on my backside and it was one of those slaps that sting for a lifetime. The following day, without a single further word having been uttered between us, I left a note and packed my bags so as to avoid any further persecution: 'I'm going to Paris, to Laura's. I trust you'll forget me as quickly as I've forgotten you.'

Since that day, we've only seen each other once, when little Fabià was born, aka his Grandson, on the 30th of July 1980, and we ended up coming to blows again. Though I don't accept any moral blame over it because Don Ignacio Robles Capmañs was an intolerable, intractable dictator, I'm embarrassed to recall how that day, in the hospital café, after seeing mother and baby, I paid him back in full.

I'm losing sight of what I really wanted to say but, you must understand, it's very hard for me to place events. Right now, for example, I feel submerged within the frenetic Paris of my first months. With terrible attendance but excellent grades, I enrolled at the music academy and was earning a few francs playing blues at all manner of bottom dollar boho dives. In the morning, on the university campus, where I practically lived despite not being enrolled there, we formed committees and formulated strategies; the afternoon, if not rehearsing, was usually dedicated to lovemaking (with her, or him and her, or her and her...); at night, we lost ourselves like worker ants in the subterranean labyrinth of the velvety underground, through tunnels and caves awash with music, alcohol and intoxicating fumes.

A summer went by, and then an autumn, and my personal

situation, and the geopolitical situation in general, was heating up day by day. It was clear it would soon reach boiling point and explode. One November Monday morning *ma tante* Laura, who saw me a couple of times a week or a lot less, made one last secondtolast attempt. I've invented, as if it were a game, an imitation of the conversation between us:

'Your father phoned.'

'My father…? Let me see, let me see… hang on a sec. No, doesn't ring any bells, sorry.'

'Don't play dumb with me.'

'I'm sorry, Laura, but you're the one playing dumb. If you want to tell me something, go ahead, nothing's off limits, but don't mention the Shadow's name in front of me! At least not while Franco is still alive.'

'Don't speak with such resentment!'

'It's the resentment the Shadow and his Franco want to leave me as a legacy. I'll only be cured when they're both dead.'

'Alright, forget about it. What I'd like is to ask a few questions and to get a few answers.'

'That stinks of fascism, too. Intellectual, at least.'

'Didn't you say there was nothing off limits?'

'*Vas-y alors!*'

'Where do you sleep?'

'Wherever. Lately, at a girl called Madeleine's place, in Montmartre.'

'Where do you eat?'

'You're joking, right?'

'What drugs do you take?'

'You mean beyond absinth and pot?'

'Yes.'

'Now and again I drop a trip.'

'A what?'

'Acid.'

'LSD?'

'That's what they call it.'

'You're going to get hurt, Fabien. And it's a shame because you have a big future ahead of you as a musician.'

'Big or small, it's my future.'

'It's so hard to believe you're only twenty.'

'Twenty-one in thirty-two days.'

'And legally an adult.'

'Finally.'

'And free to mess up in whatever way you choose.'

'*Épatant!*'

Laura – Antònia's little sister – has always had outstanding psychological aptitudes and from that moment onwards, and to this very day, she's respected all of my decisions and helped me whenever necessary (in other words, a thousand times). Just last week I received her bimonthly letter with the bimonthly three thousand francs that allow me to pay my Hotel bills without having to ask the watchmaker ticktocking my wife for money or complicate things for myself on the black market.

Back in Paris it's Christmas 1967: I'm celebrating like never before, still in battle with the city and waging war on the world. I discover that, in addition to music, I have a good ear for languages and I make the effort to learn and speak them whenever possible: an English side salad, a few slices of Dutch cheese, an Italian pastry, a German dessert, etc.

Later, Paris is aflame with workers' strikes and student marches. Fortunately (or unfortunately), I take little part in them because at that time Madeleine, myself and a dozen *camarades* were in the middle of forming a 'psychedelic rock' band, possibly the first in what the amphibians call *La République* and we lived and worked on what's often called and miscalled a commune, in a farmhouse one hundred kilometres from the Sorbonne. A hundred physical kilometres that on a mental scale represented a hundred thousand. It's worth also mentioning that my dyedin-thewool P.A.U. Barcelona HQ Trotskyism had begun to despair at dialectics on the basis of seeing how base leaders basically used it to overrule the base. Or maybe it was also because the endless cocktail of psychedelic drugs and electronic music had already begun to transport my thinking towards a philosophical vision of politics that radicalised my approach in favour of a nebulous anarchy full of roses, rock ballads and, above all, free love. Now it seems to me that we didn't know where we were going, but it's a lie. I know it's a lie because we knew perfectly well Where we wanted to go and also, instinctively at least, that we'd never ever get There.

I'm writing these sketches from inside a prison cell which, to this day, after fourteen years and nine months, I still don't know when I'll leave, but that doesn't mean I regret those fossilised dinosaur days. If it did any good, perhaps I'd regret a couple of later decisions, first in Amsterdam in the early '70s and then in Barcelona in the '80s over stuff to do with drugs but never music or thinking or living in general. But that's a darker, much more gothic story.

Either way it's upon leaving Paris, July 1968, when the fantastic adventure that would lead me to joining the London-Symphonic-banD as drummer and percussionist begins. But I'm getting ahead of myself as usual: I did two concerts with the Frenchies somewhere along the Seine, three in Brussels and fifteen to twenty between Bruges, Amsterdam, The Hague and Rotterdam. Afterwards, when we were at a loose end over what to do or where to go next, magnificent Madeleine, who had got with a Brummie pianist after I started going with Louise, called to say they had a tour signed and set up but had fallen out with the supporting act. I promptly bought three hundred tabs, glued them deep inside an old Spanish guitar that had sung better days and we hopped the channel splitting the continent. Needless to say, I had to smash the instrument to pieces to get the Lucy out again but the effort earned me five hundred pounds to pay the tavern-bills.

The tour lasted seven weeks, not bad by anyone's standards, and then we got ourselves a month long contract at some Hammersmith dive. The third Saturday I get a call: the drummer in Maddy and her boyfriend's band has had his brain fried by too much Californian Kool-Aid and she wants to know if I'd like to change outfit and instrument. I was equally as handy, if not more, on drums as I was on guitar, rhythm or lead, and playing with Syd and knowing Syd excited me more than a verdant forest of *sinsemilla*. I presented my group with the dilemma: the two remaining members of the Paris line up Hit the Road, Jacques that very night in true French style, that is, without coming back *plus jamais* to pay the hotel bill, and Parisstardust died of an embolism there and then. I picked up a cheque for the week we were owed in Hammersmith and went to form part of the London-Symphonic-banD, a group that now forms part of music mythology.

I have to say, because it's the pure, unadulterated truth, despite the human and musical might and character of David More, lead guitar, Nicholas Writ, bass, and marvellous Madeleine, who sang and played flute and sax, the authentic tribal leader by virtue of capacity and conviction was Maddy's partner: the unreal Syd Lyserd, born Roger Syd Wines, pianist, lyricist, composer and much, much more.

That man, if he really was a man, spoke to God every day before breakfast, usually Around Midafternoon. Not with a pre-ordained God or anything overtly religious, but merely the religion of comprehending existence within the great, kozmic Oneness. I know it'll sound like cheap-science fiction to you but when He spoke, when He 'transmitted' his non-transferable truths and experiences through his cosmoriginal musical languages, I promise you it was full of rich, fertile content. And not only did we, his privileged bandmates, receive it but also the audience, larger every day and mythologising him more with each show: Syd Lyserd! No doubt (now it's easy to draw this conclusion) that was one of the factors forcing him to maintain an increasingly accelerated rhythm of consumption – basically LSD of all colour and creed – that no human brain could bear, not even his mind-blowing endogalactic specimen.

All that's left to add is that the group's name, 'London-Symphonic-banD', was always written that way in honour of the substance known as lysergic acid, revisiting The Beatles' idea of 'Lucy in the Sky with Diamonds'. I can still recite a couple of Syd's lyrics with LoSybanD. Man, they're still as fresh in my memory as though we'd played them yesterday.

COSMIC TUNE
Time is the bass
that plays our dear red god
to strengthen the background
of energies and vacuums.
I look for the harp
of frozen gasworlds
where no sun reaches,
where Depth is
the Only measure.
Time is the sharp flute
echoing in the guts of Old Fat Saturn
with the soft stink of

his last eaten descendants.
I have One endogalactic soul
plugged into the heart of that
happy happy universe.
And I'm sharing it with you
in swollen time.
I'm sharing it with you
with these flat, idle words
within without a ring of rhyme

THERE'S
There's a wild pulse beyond
our bloody pressures
rhythmically bouncing in the heart
of Everywhere and its Not,
where Nobody begets any beginning.
There's music too,
beyond our hearings and their sounds,
coming straight from
these cosmic cymbals that
star-systems play in tune.
There's more minds in That Sea
than tree in all winds:
let's sing deep silences everywhere
and lewdly listen to those Huge
Endogalactic Souls.

Lyserd, as his closest friends called him, was a fanatic of this Truth but, as I've already mentioned, he aspired to be in far too constant contact with it. And he paid the price when one night he collapsed onstage in the middle of a show. We were at the one and only Marquee Club, opening for an all but forgotten band called Soft Machine, and Lyserd was in the midst of a full-blown mind mutation, left hand on the piano, right hand on the synthesiser. Suddenly (and not for the first time) he got stuck on one chord. Everyone abandoned ship as best they could until it was just Him and me: Him with his chord, always the same tone and length and accent, and me marking the beat, increasingly feebler and more concerned, on the splash symbol. After one of those minutes that seem to last a thousand seconds came the first catcall and Lyserd, drooling like an epileptic, stood up with fire in his eyes. If he could've I'm sure he would've launched himself into the crowd but he didn't even get the chance to finish his first step. The lights went down and we carried him offstage. His eyes had disappeared and so had his pulse, and there was blood trailing from his right nostril (though that could've been from the fall).

Roger Syd Wines, Syd Lyserd to present galaxies, died ten minutes later, just before arriving at A&E. And we, destitute and orbiting stratified stratospheres, wound up down the local police station. Post-mortem: acute LSD overdose.

Considering that Louise, Maddy and I were foreigners, we were offered expulsion in exchange for release and, naturally, we accepted the blackmail: the prophet had freed himself of this mortal coil and we would have to seek other parishes to preach his mad gospel.

We searched for them in Amsterdam through ten mud-stained years: there, we crossed paths with a little monster called heroin and after getting acquainted with it and everything that implies, it tore almost all the wings off our psychedelic utopias: first the political and social, then the mystical and cultural, and finally the purely ethical and existential. But this is another, much more pathetic and twisted story and one which I've already said I have no desire to tell.

Anyway, the character that was Roger Lyserd, the very person who has led me to attempt to tell this tale that has marked me and everyone that knew him couldn't be told in even a thousand books. No doubt a couple of his songs would do the job better, but I don't believe there are any surviving recorded testaments that are even minimally listenable.

As way of a goodbye, I'm including the last text Syd wrote the same day as the disaster (Maddy and I dared to draw up the definitive version departing from the nine and a half drafts he'd worked through). The title, naturellement, is a reference to the chemical formula of lysergic acid.

C16 H16 N2 O2
Change is the
Capital letter of the
Coming language, of
Course, and our tiny little
Crafts are ready to
Certify it within the
Codes and the
Cyphers that'll build the
Cemeteries of this
Civilisation

calm your waters and their woods
carefully hoping for the light
caressing your inner eyes with
certain rites nobody but you
can physically
conceive.
House I know as
High as

Highness on its zenith.
Happy with my
Hearings and the beating of my
Hearts, I tenderly be-
hold my cosmophonic
Hands within the
Hopes of the falling
Humour of the falling hour
hunch or truth, I
have some decent
Heaven, in spite all flesh,
hunting, with my soul-guns, some
home inside god's inner
House.
No hinge can hang,
no human can
hon
our.

16-11-96

From: Alexandre Oscà, Cal Fumall, Malanyeu (Alt Berguedà)
To: Enric Costales, Editorial Albina (BCN)

Dear Enric,

I'm not sending you these lyrics (wow, writing is some good dope!) so that the 'project', as you like to call it, moves forward: it's moving, it's moving. I've since received a few more collaborations thanks to a couple of lost sheep postally recovered and relatives of deceased sheep postally willing, and the collection of great tragedies almost triples the volume of more or less fun-time stories. I'm already well aware that I'll have to make a pseudoassertive selection that falsifies the percentages, not merely regarding the tragic element (which would plunge the concept instantaneously into a cheap melodrama), but also the sordid element, which would otherwise impose upon the reader a logbook similar to so many others that have recorded the junkie crew ocean crossings of the second half of this most glorious century.

The crux of my letter: I often feel that I'm revealing things that don't belong to me, things that form part of a taboo I'm unable to describe rationally, despite perceiving it when I write. I often think this 'project' has a certain pornographic something to it. Not in a sexual way (if only!) but rather in the most morbid, macabre sense of the word. As if in order to maintain a certain fidelity to the presence of these memories I had to betray the very people who manufactured them, with or without me, in a defunct present.

Moving on: on sunny evenings in wintery Malanyeu an old ochre stretches out drunkenly on the horizon as though it had no intention of ever giving up its bed to the approaching maroons and sapphires. I get myself set up on the porch half an hour beforehand, well protected from the fog and wind and cold, to revise the pages or doubts from the late-night silent disquiet jotted down the following midmorning. Sometimes I laugh. More than not I laugh and cry at the same time. Almost always I return to the dilemma over whether I should give up or go on: 'What is nobler for the spirit?' And then the capitalised, plural night spreads through me like a kind cancer and the ideas return, obsessive and intellectually obscene, to dirty the pages without system or sentience.

Closing remark: out of this literary-leaning-cultural-chaos I've extracted (among other things) the three sequences enclosed with this letter. Do let me know what you think, Enric, my friend.

In the meantime,

Oscà, king of trees,
sends you his regards.

P.S. It'd be great if you could try and come up one weekend: we need to have a serious talk and I don't fancy telling you what I have to tell you if it's not up here surrounded by all this peacefulness.

STORM OVER POBLE NOU

There's a killer on the road,
His brain is squirming like a toad
'Riders on the Storm', THE DOORS

it's raining so hard that all of my concentration is on driving. when i get to bián's street i pseudopark on the corner carefully mounting two of the seat's wheels onto the curb. only afterwards do i spot the funfair of police outside his front door: three vans nine sirens a hundred clowns:

i forget all about what's falling from the sky and the foot of water racing down les rambles and head east again: obviously bián's got problems and that means fermín el bueno has too. no choice but to hunt elsewhere. then a bolt of lightning like the ones besieging barna flashes in my head and i remember a certain someone somewhere giving me the number to a different dopedive in the same neighbourhood used as a stash:

when i run out of rambla i take a left and park up. i see there's a police station just thirty metres away. today poble nou is planting storms everywhere:

i drive a hundred metres up carrer del taulat park up again and reach five orangutan fingers over to the glove compartment and grab the piece of animal hide i use to file my personal and professional papers: four wrinkled photos i keep meaning to throw away the eternal card collection from pubs clubs and cafébars i'll likely never step foot in again and a worn notepad full of codes and hieroglyphics. today's cock and bullshit phone number (someone called pearl) is under f for fabià where it shouldn't be of course:

i notice a bar twenty metres away but the downpour dampens my enthusiasm: clutch brake ignition with one smooth movement:

bar and car sidebyside: i harlemshuffle over to the passenger seat
one two leaps and inside looking goddam washed up and looking
for the goddam telephone:

i get the sudden idea there won't be one when i hear another
siren blaring down carrer del taulat. more police: not even tempests
scare the bastards (should slow them down a bit though). i spot
the phone in the corner by the bar when i realise i'm acting like
a fucking fool: what am i going to say if they pick up? that i'm
an old-time customer of bián's and i'll be popping over for a
dozen grams? those sons of bitches have more than likely got
the line under surveillance and all. i'll ask for pearl and if she's
there for her to come to the phone then if she knows where ruth
is: rational ruth from vic fabià's wife: but if it feels hot even just
a flicker of a flame i'll hang up and ride the storm out of there:

i'm deciding upon this strategy as i count my change and a
giant andalusian oaf serves me without a glass or manners the
beer bottle i ordered despite not planning on drinking even a
sip of it:

i dial the number and light a crooked cigarette to help me
bear the inevitably slow ringing: one... two... three... five...
seven... nine times. i hang up feeling washed up and weighed
down before dialling the number again: through the glass pane
of the cabin i see the storm swell with thunder and wind. the
awning above the fishmonger's opposite is hanging onto dear
life by a thread. i know the feeling pal. if no one picks up i don't
know what the fuck i'm going to do. but i'll do something:

while i'm weighing up the different options and outcomes of
la mina sant andreu or badalona a female voice says oh hi mín
not on the phone but behind my ear: i spin round and (who said
i never get the rub of the green?) i find myself face to face with
none other than rational ruth with red eyes wounded by salt and
a sadaddictsmile:

'ruth babe!' i say and we kiss on one two cheeks slightly beyond simple politeness. 'i was just…' and then i remember the still-ringing phone and clumsily hang up. 'where'd you come from? you want a drink?'

'this is where i normally have lunch…' she says biting her bottom lip and indicating a discreet door. 'give me a shorty, gustavo…'

it's incredible how a scene can change so rapidly when a certain character unexpectedly walks in! gustavo all smiles now brings her a shot of whiskey and asks me if i want one too. i tell him no thanks because despite feeling saved now i've found ruth i am of course sweating monkeys out of every pore. but gustavo now with the creepy bearing of a servile dwarf insists on inviting a friend of my dear ruth to a drink on the house. with a smile as big as it is fake i thank him for the shorty: a shot of whisky as small as it is revolting more than aware it's going to perforate my stomach like a firebomb:

luckily for me it's only a dozen more phrases until ruth a very sensitive person realises that i'm trembling and breaking out into dribbling yawns and dry-eyed tears and desperately trying to disguise the waves of nausea each time i inhale a bit of smoke or sip some whisky:

'but you're in a right state!' she blurts unexpectedly.

'a state of emergency.'

'why didn't you say something?'

i answer with a helpless hapless look somewhere between lost pride and the woeful feebleness of addiction. but she's already up on her feet and walking towards the door: come on she tells me and imitating a flamenco dancer's click-clacking lets gustavo know she'll be back later:

we get into the seat under a festival of warring winds but at least the rain seems to be stopping. we go six streets west and eight streets north: ruth gets out and opens a scrapmetaldoor to what i guess is a tiny garage: i park my hunkofjunk: we go up to the first floor and she sore eyes and sad smile cooks me up a shot of flu killer. but i still don't have the slightest fucking idea what the hell has happened to fabià:

after our respective jabs ruth rolls some rainydaywoman and begins narrating events with an almost domestic air:

'it was seven in the morning or thereabouts… i'd been asleep in the back bedroom for about three or four hours… suddenly i hear the boiler… bián's having a shower… at seven in the morning… i don't know if you know about his level of hydrophobia… it's not like any ordinary junkie, his is off the chart… but, hey, i thought, this damn heat's dragging on and everyone likes a cool shower from time to time… even fabià…

'… so i lit a cigarette and went into the kitchen for some cold coffee… but when i saw the moka pot steaming on the stove, i really began to worry… i poured myself half a cup and was sipping it slowly, with a bitter aftertaste in my soul… if you'll excuse the expression… just as he got out of the shower and went into the bedroom… i poured another right to the top with three spoonsful of sugar, just the way he likes it, and took it into the bedroom…

'… he was clean shaven, hair combed back, wearing the black jeans i got him for his birthday and was putting on his long-sleeved beige cotton shirt… the one with the wide pockets… next to his wet feet was a pair of sport socks and trainers… and well that was the straw that gave the camel the hump, you know what i mean?…

"where you going?" i asked, although i knew perfectly well. "don't start."

"i didn't marry you to end up a widow."

"don't make things worse. you knew who you were getting

involved with."

"and the kid?"

"the kid will have to smarten up the same as i did. same as you, if i can't. life's cruel. we both know that."

'… and that's all folks… that last comment he said with a wry smile and it even got one out of me and i wasn't exactly in the mood for jokes… i passed him the mug and we both drank our morning fix… then he prepared two doses and we shot up our second morning fix… he kissed me softly on the lips, picked up the sports bag i got him last christmas and left without a sound… inside the bag, as always, was his baseball cap and gun…'

BLOODY INTERLUDE

Angel of darkness is upon you
Stuck a needle in your arm
'That Smell', LYNYRD SKYNYRD

I open the garage and take out the moped. I close the door and get going without any hurry. I ask myself if I've got oil, if I've got petrol, if I've packed the cap, the plimsolls and the piece, if I remember everything I've been planning the last eight days. Damn I'd love a smoke. I look at my watch and it tells me it's past quarter past. In twenty minutes I'll park the moped thirty metres from the bar ('Amigos', I think it's called), in case I need a getawayhideaway. I'll walk casually into the bar, no bag no helmet, and demand an absinthespresso and a bun. I won't go to the toilet because I checked them out the day before yesterday. Then I'll head back to the moped and park it in the alley round the back. The rest will be a question of luck. But luck doesn't seem to be on my side today because the bar's closed due to bereavement so I'll have to choose another one at random (a hundred metres further up on the other side of the street) and also go to the toilet and check if the money bag will fit, if push comes to shove. I do it, as the saying goes, in two minutes flat, without raising the suspicions of the matriarch manning the miserable den. I must look like a tourist. Bun, coffee, cigarette, and shit some smack would be good right now, even half a line. If I'd come with the car… When I worked with Gaucho everything always went smoothly: an exceptional driver and a solid partner to boot. I could stop in another bar and smoke some foil, but no. I drop the pastry on the floor to not have to dry chew any more of it. I pick it up slowly and ask for the bill while muttering thank you. I walk decidedly towards the moped because

I've decided it's high time to get to work. But the alleyway I'd chosen behind the bank, too narrow for any car to drive down, is closed for some neighbourhood festivity and I have to leave the moped somewhere else. Long story short, I enter the bank at eight-twenty and everything looks to be more or less how I envisioned: a few customers, the same staff, the same inevitable security guard. I go up to the guard with the piece hidden in my hand, press it into his kidneys and whisper into his lughole my devastating intravenous veracities: unseen, he gives me his gun, not breathing a word, and walks over with me to the cash desk. Smooth as silk. I pronounce a few words to the ill-starred audience, keeping it short and sweet, and everyone appears to grasp that it's a polite stickup: done for money and with no desire for anyone to get hurt. The cash assistant, her breasts round like her spectacles, collaborates by quietly placing three million eight hundred thousand pessetes in the plastic bag inside the sports bag. Pure silk. As I'm walking out with the guard's piece in my pocket and mine doing threatening windmills, a voice shouts at me to stop. I turn and pull the trigger, naturally. As the individual lurches forwards and falls to the floor, I throw myself at the closed glass door, slamming into it: me, the bag and the gun, smashing the pane into a thousand shards. The impact leaves me lying on the ground with my senses at sixes and seventeens and when I finally get up onto all fours ready to flee, I hear a gunshot and feel the bullet burn in my left knee.

'If you so much as move an inch,' screams a wounded, traitorous voice as I fall to the floor, 'I swear on my kids' lives I'll put another one in your back!!'

Whoever he is, he's got me.

STORM OVER POBLE NOU: CONTINUATION

Children of misery and pain
TRIANA

it's raining it's pouring the old man went whoring:

the only other living creature i sometimes see sloshing in six inches of stomach-churning water is a black rat the size of a hare trying to climb up onto the bumper of a car that's about to float down the street like a tugboat. it's obvious that i can't move from here even if i wanted to. and i don't want to:

the fateful interruption (as told by ruth amid shots spliffs and rain showers) was a police chief on holiday who used to go for a stroll each morning with his non-service shooter strapped under his armpit like someone taking the dog out for a piss:

the man oh sad hero of capitalist paradoxes who'd gone into the bank to draw out thirty thousand pessetes and square up his accounts to the last fatal penny after the police came to take both cop and robber to hospital muttered son of a bitch and died:

son of a bitch is what bián would also be saying for a thousand months or more:

and i lacking any remorse will be in bed with his wife all afternoon and not for the first time if we recall the penultimate night of drugdriving on planet vic: oh ruth!:

before making my way back to pont de suert where no doubt lily and lex are waiting for me with tears in their eyes i'll buy sixteen grams of horse from her the colour of monkeynuts and strong enough to resuscitate king kong:

but what a fucking mess this story of the captain and fabià: the full vengeance of institutional capitalism is going to come down hard on him which means thirty years if all goes well. but we'll do everything we can for him with the little we have. i really mean it. and i know ruth does too:

meanwhile wrapped warmly in the sheets of sex and the duvet of drugs i'll wait for the storm to pass and the rats to return to the sewer. rats like me.

PERFECT LOVES, UTOPIC LOVES

From my hands you know you'll never be
More than twist in my sobriety
TANITA TIKARAM

I met canonical Susana on the Massana Art School patio one exquisite April afternoon amid criticisms and chronicles on Dadaism, with a joint as an excuse. She sat down on the bench opposite and had no doubt noticed me rolling because as soon as I lit up she was already approaching with a shy but complicit smile, pushing buggy and baby.

'I don't mean to be rude… but can I ask you for a drag?' she mumbled in absence of a greeting.

I must admit that my first impulse was to say no; and sixty-nine times out of a hundred I would, indeed, have said no, because I've always had a certain fear of meeting people at random: you never know for sure what the hell might come of it. But in this case, with half a how do you do smile, I told her sure no problem. She sat down and, after the ineluctable presentations ('I'm Susana'; 'Eulàlia'), we shared an amicable silence until she asked if I studied at the university. I answered by asking her how she'd guessed and she answered my question-answer by saying she'd seen me coming out of the library and, well, you know. I didn't tell her how many people spent the afternoon there, chatting and looking to hook up: naivety has always provoked a certain affection in me, if only in the erotic sense.

'I'm going to study information science next year. If I pass the access course exams in June.'

The comment made me smile. She spoke reasonably fluent Catalan but her grammar revealed she'd learnt it without books and used it rarely: judging by her appearance I'd have no doubt classified her as a trainee addict and/or prostitute, but she said she was preparing to study journalism. She didn't look anywhere near old enough to be doing an access course, even though it was clear the kid was hers. What's more, she wore a gold ring on finger number four. I passed her the joint: she'd smoked her fair share in life, that was clear enough, and as though reading my mind she told me she'd finished her bud the night before and wouldn't have any until that evening: that's why she'd taken the liberty to ask me for, well, you know. I repeated no problem and added that if she wanted, we could skin up another.

I'm forced to admit that my obsession with spying characters on the street to transform them later into literary creations lured me into playing a dirty trick but I had the crystalline vision, and almost genuine excitement, that chatting for just half an hour with that singular creature would teach me ten times more about the arts of fate and fortune than a hundred library afternoons.

At first, she refused out of common politeness but when I insisted she accepted with a wide, sincere smile and shake of her long hair. Though a little on the thin side, she was pretty much what your average man calls a 'bombshell': strong, supple legs, perky apple bum, slinky bumblebee waist, and two pitchers freshly filled at the fountain; the cherry on top was her feline face, with its Egyptian profile somewhere between Tzigane and the indecipherable: almonds eyes that were almost too big and wide set; a nose as round and smooth as her backside; prominent but soft cheekbones and jaw; and her mouth, What-a-Mouth, was simply sublime. Without that mouth she would've been if not ugly then at least a bit strange looking but her lips and teeth when she smiled were a well of light and expression. I looked at it in more detail while she sucked on the roach. I even attempted absurd mnemotechnics to retain the vivacity of her beauty when she smiled (thinking about it now makes me smile… but only faintly).

I studied her, she burnt chocolate, the kid slept in the buggy. Suddenly she handed back to me what I'd originally handed to her and stood up saying 'be back in a mo' before disappearing in the direction of Carrer de l'Hospital. There, under the arches, she caught up with some African guy with a cravat and braided goatee and they spoke for around ten seconds. Then she waved me goodbye before vanishing down the street with him and I was sure they'd just dumped the kid on me.

I twisted another cornetto and smoked it casually, trusting that none of the usual pigs who try, unsuccessfully, to avoid a proliferation of needles on the corner wouldn't come over to ask me the kipper's name. I was more or less halfway through the joint when sleeping beauty (it was dressed in blue so for the time being *it* was a *he*) woke up and started to cry. Cry, wail, scream, howl, scratch… I'm not a person who's used to dealing with babies. They charm me like any baby animal, especially mammals, and I cherish the intellectual miracle they carry imprinted on the DNA of their souls, but I never know what they want or what they need or what the fuck to do with them.

As I was beginning to genuinely worry about both kid and cops, Susana appeared via Carrer del Carme, tripping over herself with apologies. I passed her the problem, which I'd picked up in a useless attempt to calm it down, and the problem immediately fell silent. Probably because Susana had unbuttoned her blouse and shoved the nipple of her right breast into its mouth. The scene and the sight of her tit fascinated me: I had to make a conscious effort not to look directly at it because hidden desires of maternity and concupiscence rose up within me and I confess I'd have happily latched onto the other nipple to see if it's true that mother's milk is both warm and sour.

Needless to say, I wasn't going to ask any questions. I could perfectly guess where she'd gone and what she'd done in the nine nervous minutes that had crept past: the raspy voice, the muscular relaxation, above all to her face revealed a heroin fix, even if just a titbit. Her laugh, for example, was no longer the same, despite being slightly more charming, if only in the artistic sense because now, in addition to her natural beauty, there was an additional indecipherable artifice in the corner of her eyes and lips.

Needless to say, I wasn't going to ask any questions of any sort. But nor was I going to get up and go back to the library like a dunce (no way, José). I sensed she'd make me suffer in the long run but that woman was certainly (as certain as death itself) a rough and ready diamond; anyone with a pair of eyes in their head could see that, male or female. Waiting to see what excuse would come my way, I mixed and rolled the third and final joint while the baby sucked and she spoke about how the kid fed as she smiled and laughed and I filled more and more rolls of film with my photographing retina while simultaneously trying to disguise the aesthetic orgasm rising up in me.

The excuse for her surreptitious disappearance was honest enough: she told me the Gambian was someone she urgently needed to see and as compensation for not breathing another word about it, and for having forced ten minutes babysitting on me, she invited me for vermouth and more at a nearby bar. Naturally, I accepted. And, if I'm being honest, in spite of all the despites, I've never regretted it and nor do I plan to.

I guided the conversation in a way that she told me the truth about where she'd gone and she revealed everything with the smile of a cat with a full belly before offering me a 'bump'. Strictly speaking, I don't do hard drugs: cannabis and, if it's good grass, so much the better; a bit of soft alcohol to get through the week; and very occasionally half a tab. However, female perspicacity told me that if I accepted the invitation I'd have her, literally, in the palm of my hand.

'If you're sincerely offering and it honestly doesn't put you out,' I said as way of a preamble, 'I will happily accept a dab in exchange for lunch...' And after half a pause: 'Right here, if you fancy it...'

The bar, which over the last forty years had been everything from some sort of shop selling fabric or hats, an outlet for all manner of contraband, a night-time cafébar, and a disco drugs den, was one of those typical timeworn places in old exhausted Chinatown, specialising in fish and seafood because the owner was a wholesaler from La Barceloneta. You didn't need to be Sherlock Holmes to guess that the wholesaler/restaurateur was one of Her clients. And one of the good'uns, too.

She revealed all with half a dozen sentences inside the girls' room, having ordered a house salad and a selection of crustaceans and telling Joan, uncivil servant of the tables closest to the bar, to look after the rug rat. And don't worry about the bill, the brunette bombshell told me with a smile as sweet as it was naïf, half would be on the house whereas she'd pay for the wine and desserts. The fix she'd taken after buying had given her the words and desire to reveal more about herself and, after snorting the previously mentioned bumps, we – Eulàlia next to Susana, Susana next to Eulàlia – walked out of there like bosom buddies since birth, holding in the laughter over some utterly unrepeatable joke. It might seem contradictory but, generally speaking, I'm very reserved when making acquaintances, especially adventitious ones, but if one gives me a good feeling from the get-go then I throw myself into it without forethought or prejudice. And this was the case with Susana.

As we ate, I gave her the intro *comme il faut*: I studied History of Art at university because I wanted to be an artist and English off my own back because I wanted to go live in Edinburgh or

Dublin and, apart from writing, my secret passion was painting. She returned the confidence: she worked as night concierge in a hotel and that the baby, Jordi was his name, for the time being didn't have a dad. A year ago, one fine morning in March, he quick marched out of her life forever but it was a stroke of luck because he was one of those junkies who respects nothing and nobody: the number of times he'd abused, robbed and raped her, wounds fortunately already healed, would be enough to fill an entire Venezuelan soap opera.

'What about the kid? What do you do with him at night?'

'I live with my cousin. I pay the rent, she looks after the kid.'

'You live round here?'

'Five streets further up. What about you?'

'Three or four in the other direction. Plaça Padró.'

'Where's that?'

'You know Bar Americano?'

'Oh, sure… real nice. Do you have a view of the square?'

'A wonderful view,' I confessed, turning red from head to foot.

'You must be a rich girl.'

'Probably less than you.'

'Then you must be lucky.'

I didn't answer that because I concluded that she was most likely right. At least in comparison to her fortune.

I was wearing my Moroccan sandals but I'd slipped them off right from the outset, as if we (She and I and Barcelona) were deep in the dog days. I can neither confirm nor deny whether it was akin to the stray comma of a lackadaisical writer but the tip of my toe of my left foot risked an accidental brushstroke upon the soft canvas of her foot. Her pupils dove into mine with a pause of suspense, drip drip drip, as though lapping up the silent subtext before removing her shoe from her right foot and empathising the unspoken significance with swelling lips that erased all ambiguity.

'If you want I could show you the flat,' I mumbled on the edge of embarrassment.

'I'd like that a lot,' she said as her foot travelled up my leg and thigh.

'I'd love to draw you. Would you be my model for a fair price?' I asked, ever so slightly opening my legs, my smile, my literary punctuation.

'I'm slim with no clothes on. Big-breasted but slim.'

'That's just fine…'

Her foot caressed my crotch and my hands went under the table to help it find my pubis and press her heel firmly against my clitoris. Without warning she pulled it away, put her shoe on and stood up. For a split second I thought she'd been leading me on. But then she asked Joan for the key to the toilet and told him to look after the kid (sleeping like a tiny log again) and winked at me to follow her. Naturally, I accepted.

And in spite of all the despites, I've never once regretted it because those first love beginnings, brief and abrupt within the cramped cubicle, were already worth all the suffering that would inevitable come of them. Or almost. For a woman like Susana it was worth becoming a junkie and a whore, and that's exactly what I felt like learning, whatever the cost. But everyone has their limits. Even me.

JUDGE, VICTIM AND EXECUTIONER

The night I was born I swear
The moon turned a fire red
'Voodoo Child', JIMI HENDRIX

The suicide of J.A.V. (Jaume Argentina i Vidals), as sudden as it was unexpected, occurred on the last Saturday in October, just as dawn yawned behind a curtain of nocturnal drizzle. His still warm body was found by Leda (Leda Hostalets Marquey), his partner of six years, spread out on the sofa in such a way that on first sight Leda thought he was sleeping. When she turned towards the bathroom, however, she saw the needle stuck in the pit of his left arm.

More scared than anything, Leda went over to Jaume and touched his wrist, neck and temple, searching for a pulse, a sign of life, but there was none: his heart had stopped, his lungs were still, and his epidermis a turquoise colour. Seven minutes later the ambulance arrived. The paramedics confirmed J.A.V's death and called the police. The case fell into the hands of Lieutenant Amor under the jurisdiction of Judge Berluin.

On the coffee table next to a soup spoon and an empty cigarette paper was an A4 sheet at the top of which Jaume, in his usual albeit somewhat enlarged handwriting, had written: 'I can't find the words to express how sorry I am, Leda.' And next to it, the evening newspaper, open on the obituary page, as if he had been imagining his own eulogy.

Born in Móra la Nova, Jaume Argentina i Vidals' penultimate place of residence was the kingdom's capital where he had signed marriage papers (it lasted a year) with a law student from Tarragona doing her thesis in Madrid. Meanwhile, he was running a bar for local users and small time dealers. A short time after their separation, half-cured by a diet of propoxyphenes, benzodiazepines and a daily dose of willpower, he was back in Catalonia and living in a small town on the outskirts of Igualada. A couple of years later, already going steady with Leda, he settled down by buying a top-floor apartment. They didn't have any children, because Jaume didn't want to hear a single word on the subject, and their life was peaceful and harmonious.

He originally arrived in that small provincial town because of an admin job in an insurance agency that an old friend had secured him, but it was four years since he had gone out on his own by setting up his own office. Leda performed secretarial duties, meaning the only wage they had to pay was the cleaning lady's. In addition to the loft apartment, they had two new cars and a cottage in a cosy corner of the Port del Comte, already half paid for. They enjoyed winter sports and intercontinental holidays (they had set their sights on a whole month in Australia next year), for which they were happy to pay top dollar. But, contrary to appearances, they weren't your conventional couple: Leda was a trained teacher and had performed theatre in Vic, Terrassa and even Barcelona's *Teatre Lliure*, and Jaume, who had had the role of heroin addict for eight years and therefore little time to study, enrolled last year on an undergraduate degree at the school of philosophy.

Lieutenant Amor collated this information in six hours the very same Saturday and the following Monday, when reporting to the judge, summarised it in less than a dozen short sentences. The judge showed an interest in the deceased's addiction so the lieutenant outlined Jaume's police record for him: three minor charges for possession.

'It appears beyond question that the boy had straightened himself out and was living a peaceful second life,' he remarked.

'You mean to tell me,' asked the judge ironically while lighting another cigarette, 'that you didn't note the stench of *ganja* clinging to the walls of his flat?'

'Not only did I smell it, Your Honour, but I counted six roaches,' replied the policeman before glancing at the judge's ashtray overflowing with Lucky Strike butts. 'But heroin is one thing and cannabis is another.'

'Yet in spite of that it's the method he chose.'

'If you know what you're doing it's got to be a lot less painful than hanging yourself or throwing yourself off a bridge.'

'I see you're feeling rather liberal this morning, Lieutenant.'

'Someone who's managed to quit junk doesn't kill themselves over grass.'

'And you're certain he wasn't dealing either one of the two? Such a healthy financial situation…'

'…indicates that his business was going well and that he had no need to complicate life.'

'Sometimes ambition can…'

'He only dealt insurance policies,' ruled the policeman.

'Alright, alright…' the judge conceded with a sigh full of bronchitis, '… let's *suppose* you've convinced me. The motive wasn't drugs. So what was it?'

'That I *don't* know. And the way I see it, it's quite possible we never will.'

'What do you mean "never"? Haven't you already spoken to that tart of his? Haven't you found out who sold him the drugs?'

'That tart is called Leda and a tart is the last thing she is. She's a thousand times more in the dark than we are. And who sold him the drugs, well, only the dealer and the deceased know that and it's unlikely either of them will be popping in to tell us anytime soon. Anyway, I don't think the dealer would be much help, supposing we ever found him. They were a couple without financial problems, who never consumed anything more than the odd joint or the occasional whisky and in six years of living together Leda only saw Jaume snorting three or four times and not once with a needle. That's what she says and I believe her.'

'Now what do we do?'

'We don't do anything.'

'But what's this thing about AIDS? According to what I've read in the medical report, he was seropositive.'

'For eight years but every year he was getting better. One of those atypical cases who, God knows why, never develop the illness. Doctors and friends all agree that he was in such good shape that he'd all but forgotten about it. The last analysis, just two months ago, placed him on the same level as a non-carrier and there was no reason to fear any type of health crisis.'

'Is this girl of his infected too?'

Lieutenant Amor hesitated for a second, considering this sort of information irrelevant. Even so, if the judge really wanted to know he only had to request her medical report.

'No, she isn't. When they got together they were both aware of the situation.'

'Do me a personal favour, Lieutenant: solve this case for me.'

'It's suicide, Your Honour, and nothing more. The culprit and the victim are the same person.'

'I'm not talking about culpability; I'm talking about motive.'

Half on account of the judge's order, half owing to his own professional curiosity, the lieutenant used all proportional means available to him, and then a few extra. But the days passed and the investigation remained at a standstill. When it's a murder, thought the lieutenant, taking pity on himself, the motive is often so obvious it's impossible to miss. But suicides are a different beast, considering that the motive is at times only obvious in the deceased's own head. And just as he was beginning to despair at not having discovered a single lead, one bright morning a light suddenly switched on, a light that grew and grew the more he reflected on it: yes, if the hypothesis could be confirmed everything would begin to make sense.

He went to the library, requested the same Friday evening newspaper and read through the obituary page. It didn't take him two minutes to have the whole thing figured out. Despite already having found the confirmation he was hoping to find, after five or six phone calls a hospital confirmed that one T.B.N. had died the previous Wednesday of tuberculosis developed as a result of acquired immunodeficiency syndrome.

Lieutenant Amor remembered the report referencing a marriage certificate in the name of J.A.V. and T.B.N., registered nine years prior at a registry office in Madrid, the detail that put the finishing touch to his theory. Undoubtedly Leda had grasped it from the very beginning but had decided it was nobody's business. And now that he had finally worked it out, Lieutenant Amor had to admit that she was right. The dead, he thought, whether accidental or not, black, white or brown, also have the right to remain silent. Judge Berluin would just have to live with the mystery.

VISITING DAY

You know the night's magic seems to whisper and hush
You know the soft moonlight seems to shine in your blush
'Moondance', VAN MORRISON

The news is saying that autumn will end abruptly and that there will be heavy snowfall in the mountains above eight hundred metres. In preparation for the fine weather coming our way, I scraped twenty thousand pessetes together for a television, which I force myself to watch for a couple of hours a day so as to not lose contact with civilisation. It also helps me to combat moments of tedium after lunch, and one or two silent night stagnations after an excess of creative concentration. In any case, it's been lightly snowing in Malanyeu for an hour but there's a chance things won't go much further than a flurry because the wind's whipping itself up into an arctic frenzy. The pine wood I've placed on the fire to get the flames going begins to crackle just as the news confirms that where there's no snow there'll be heavy rain. 'May the gods bring rain and earth-shaking thunder and floods,' I mutter, fed up with so much autumnal isolation, 'until it drowns the Cercs power station!'

I force down the first advert and the last piece of bread and anchovy, and then ponder rolling some mothermary and fixing a short scotchespresso as I switch off the set. Unexpectedly, and against all forecasts, the mobile phone given to me by Dolors starts ringing out of reach, no doubt stranded in the Narnia of the living room cupboard. *Oh no, it isn't.* As though playing pantomime hide and seek, I finally locate it in the kitchen drawer, on top of the tea towels. When I pick it up and ponder what button I have to press, it cuts out. I check the device is working and switched on, and leave it on the side table with a sour look.

I pour a dash of yesterday's coffee and two or three more of fridge whisky into a large coffee shop mug and add a sprinkle of sugar that appears to have no intention of ever dissolving. As I'm walking out of the kitchen, mug held between both hands, the mobile phone rings again. I go back in and answer:

'Hello?'

'Hello, you freak. It's Lali.'

Holy shit! Eulàlia! I say to myself.

'Great to hear your voice!' I reply.

'Well, get your arse in gear because I'm leaving Barna in ten minutes and coming to yours for a cup of tea. I mean, if it's alright with you, of course…'

Shit, shit! Eulàlia!

'Suits me fine. I'll shower and talc my privates, just in case. As well as preparing a pot of tea, of course.'

'I know I should've given you a head's up beforehand…'

'You're kidding! There's nothing more welcome than a welcome surprise. Oh, by the way, if there's a lot of snow when you get to Berga – which I doubt, hey – call me and I'll come pick you up.'

'Don't worry. I'm prepared.'

'One more thing, Lali. If you can, I'd really appreciate a few specks of dust.'

'And you just had to ask me for it…' she replied, slightly peeved.

Shit, p'raps not, dammit! But, then again, chi lo sa?

'I didn't think it would matter anymore. It's been ten years,' I say. 'Listen, forget I said anything.'

'No, you're right. Look, I can't promise anything but I'll see what I can do.'

'Cheers. If you can, great. If not, no worries.'

And then goodbye-see-you-bye and the line cuts out. But

while I distractedly look over the chapter I gave life to late last night, four o'clock slips by, then five and six and She – Eulàlia Gonzálvez i Torres, aka *Lali* – still isn't here.

I go to the window for the twentieth time in a hundred minutes and see that the afternoon haze has aged into blackest night. It's been snowing heavily for forty-five minutes and I'm beginning to get anxious because a good few inches has already settled and the new highway is so seldom used that anything could happen, and because Eulàlia hasn't had her licence even a year and God knows what hunk of shit she's driving.

The kitchen clock says twenty-five past: I open the fridge to eat and drink something but close it again without the will to make a decision. Then I hear a top-of-the-range diesel pull onto the driveway and I go bounding towards the front door: it's Her. Or more precisely: Them. A cinnamon sculpture with cherry cheeks and a gymnast's body (responding to the name of Mònica, Lali's latest girlfriend) slips out of the passenger seat before beautiful Eulàlia, sweet Eulàlia, gets out the other side. We mark the reunion with hugs and kisses with lips, eyes and hands, while china white snowflakes the size of tennis balls and as sticky as velcro decorate our hair and clothes.

'You're a touch slimmer and two or three more attractive,' I tell her honestly, telepathically.

'Mònica, you already know Alexandre: Àlex, Alexa, Alexei, or simply Lex, according to the time and place. Àlex, be a good boy and give Mònica a kiss.'

We exchange a kiss on each cheek and Eulàlia grumbles, playfully, that two isn't one. I mumble a welcome and accompany the greeting with the hand movements and smiles demanded of all affable hosts while trying to disguise my (decidedly infantile) disappointment that Lali hadn't come alone. To say that I'm still in love with her would be an exaggeration but…

It's only when I close the door that I notice their lack of luggage.

'Oh, we didn't plan on sleeping here! That's why I didn't ask you if you had space. We wanted to swing by for a dinner date before spending the night at the infamous House of Torres with divine Cousin Joan and his reverent wife.'

'With the storm that's brewing? Forget about it. There's space here for ten people and I'm dying to chew the fat with ten times that… You have no idea how long this poor hermit hasn't seen such a pretty pair of three-dimensionals as you! You can't torture me by popping over and then disappearing two minutes later, like some game of mirrors. What's this: now you see us, now you don't?'

Without waiting for an opinion, I go towards the car – one of those Japanese amphibians capable of crossing the Himalayas – and start transporting bags and backpacks.

'Tomorrow, in the cold light of day, I'll let you decide if my humble hospitality was worth your staying or not.'

'But we'll only get in your hair. You've got writing to be getting on with.'

'Don't you worry about me. Even God rests once a week, Clea!' and immediately after pronouncing that name (it simply slipped out) I feel embarrassed and she goes red. 'Anyway, my only truly important work is surviving another day: a visit like yours is worth more than thirty pages of prose!'

We dump the bags in the large bedroom, already radiator warm, while I ponder whether it's polite to ask if they mind sharing a bed. A double bed, naturally. But I don't dare, firstly because I know sweet Eulàlia will only turn red again and secondly because I already know they'd be more than delighted to. Like every night.

Then all three of us settle down in front of the fire with cups of herbal tea in our hands and a plate of Danish biscuits on the coffee table. She said she was coming round for tea and when it comes to these sorts of things I'm very respectful, and at seven-o-eight the night begins to slowly blossom before us. There are two questions I'm itching to ask Eulàlia. Just as I settle on the more banal of the two, Mònica asks for the toilet and, when she's out of earshot, the most intimate coffers immediately spring open.

'Things going well between you?' I ask, hiding my envy behind a grin.

'Too well,' she replies, hiding her satisfaction behind a grin double the size.

'I'm jealous.'

'Here: drown your sorrows in this, then,' she says and passes me a piece of plastic converted into a baggy by the magic of fire. 'You owe me two thousand *peles*, by the way.'

I fish for the notes in my files next to the stereo and give them to her with the giggle of a naughty schoolboy.

'You two are going to help me, I hope.'

'Perhaps a dab as delivery charge.'

'Now or after dinner?'

'You fancy some now don't you?'

'How'd you guess?'

'Do one now and then we'll all do one together later.'

'Perhaps you'd prefer some virginmary instead?' I ask with a devious tone.

'How'd *you* guess..?' she replies with a sparkling smile.

I give her the weed box, set up my stall for a sample snort and drop the Big Question:

'Have you written anything?'

'You bet. More than you'd care to know. Apart from the pleasure of seeing each other, and it was about time too, what really spurred me on was my latest literary hallucination. I've conjured up a rural triptych, one part semi-autobiographic, one part pure invention, that lasts a million pages.'

'We'll have to make an encyclopaedia to go with it.'

'Now that you mention it, wasn't the novel meant to be titled *Contemporary Encyclopaedia*?'

'Enric suggested it. But I find it grandiose and pedantic.'

'What else do you have in mind?'

'*Floral Offerings for the Futilely Defunct.*'

'Too dark. And too obvious.'

'OK. *All Bums no Dharma.*'

'Nobody remembers Dharma anymore! Or Jack Kerouac for that matter!'

'I've been rereading it the last few days.'

'Sometimes you talk like you're the Last of the Hippies! But I know it's just one of your characters...' she says before a hesitant laugh. 'But the title: I'm sure you haven't told me the one you really like.'

'How does *Hey Jude* sound to you?'

'Not bad. But they'll charge you royalties.'

'Who?'

'The heirs of Lennon & McCartney.'

'You see? I'd hadn't even thought of that.'

And we laugh and we laugh: while I chop the material with an expired visa; while she lights her bush blend and goes to the bedroom to fetch her manuscript; while Mònica comes back and asks us, all innocence, what we're laughing about; while we, as way of an answer, laugh even more, until we finally infect her and end up laughing all three of us over nothing; while I think: 'this is how it always begins: laughing together at a private joke.'

'Don't pay any attention to us, Mònica,' says Eulàlia. 'There's been so much aiding and abetting over the years that just one look can lead us anywhere. Intellectually speaking, of course,' she clarifies, blushing once again.

'I thought I'd seen every single colour of horse going but now I see that I was mistaken,' I declare.

'I thought this stuff was always brown or white,' comments Mònica, spying the caesium powder on top of the book.

'Let's just say those are the best known varieties,' Eulàlia answers.

'Well, in addition to every shade of brown and white imaginable, I've seen pearl grey, green grey, meringue grey, green yellow, pistachio yellow, yellow yellow, beige, pink and some verging on red. But this ash blue is a new entry on my personal hit parade.'

I finish my intervention and, after a short pause and one fluid movement, snort the rail with my right nostril. Breaking the mould.

'You sure it's horse?' asks Eulàlia with a dubious frown.

I pass a finger over mission base and lick it.

'You betcha.'

Almost unconsciously, I sit down with Eulàlia's text in my hands and my eyes automatically follow the title downwards. I ask permission to be so rude as to settle down and read it, if it doesn't make them feel unattended to. Eulàlia replies that settling down to read her little piece of junk is the greatest compliment I could pay her, and Mònica sheepishly says, if it's not an abuse of my hospitality, that she'd very much like to take a shower because she didn't have time to pass by the flat after work. I get up to check the boiler before showing her the lights, soaps and bath salts. It's fair to say that the bathroom, with its huge oval tub, is the most celebrated attraction at Cal Fumall. She feebly protests that a quick shower will suffice but I sense that the space has seduced her and when I slip out she's already slipping off her shoes. Transporting towels, toiletries and smiles up the hallway, flows a sparkling, rippling Eulàlia.

I sit by the fireplace, stare coolly at my infusion and roll a fat fifty-fifty, as Mín would say, i.e. equal parts tobacco and ave-maria. I go into the kitchen and pour myself a shot of scotch. I go back to the fireplace, sip the malt and placidly light the joint. When I pick up the pages, Eulàlia comes in, blushing up to the whites of her eyes, sits on my lap and gives me a surprise kiss on the lips. But it's not an invitation, rather a type of prior apology.

'I've got two favours to ask you.'

'About time!'

'The first is that you let us take care of dinner. We've brought a few deli dishes with us that have to be eaten today.'

'More than a favour, it'd be a pleasure,' I admit, handing her the dutchie.

'The second is that you tell me, honestly, if you mind us taking a bath together.'

'It makes me a tad jealous, I have to say. Can I come and watch?'

'Maybe another day.'

'I'll hold you to that.'

'I said maybe.'

'I'll ask you again at twelve on the dot.'

We laugh and kiss, briefly, a second time, as I pass a furtive hand under her woollen skirt until trapping her crotch in the palm of my hand. She jumps back like a spring, full of giggles and coming out in a blush again, protesting I don't know what about her tights. I also laugh, mainly at my miserable depravity, telling her if the tights are the problem then I'm happy to help her out of a tight spot, just as I feel the horse begin to trot in my head. She also trots away, first to the bedroom to fetch the food and leave it in the kitchen and then towards the bathroom, but not without winking wickedly at me first.

'You know what I think, Lali? I think Mònica's too young and too pretty for you.'

Her only answer is a laugh that ripples up the hallway. And thus she departs, like a svelte Venus returning to the water, leaving me sitting on the shore with a great many urges and one tremendous doubt. I don't even get to focus on the first paragraph when the perfect excuse to go in, take a photo, do away with any doubts and, on top of that, make a good impression occurs to me. I knock back the scotch, feeling a warm spasm in my stomach, and go to the kitchen where I grab a bottle of cava and an ice bucket. I take three long glasses from the living room cabinet, open the bottle and pour myself one before going to the bathroom with the rest. As a result, I'm forced to knock on the door with my forehead.

'Little pigs, little pigs, may I come in?'

After a splash of water, a laughing Eulàlia says yes. Apologising, I walk in and snap the first Polaroid, while handing them the glasses and leaving the bucket on the footstool.

'Oh, what a sur*prise*, Lex!' quips Eulàlia. 'Avià simply *can't* compare!'

With the facial expressions of a butler but loading the film cartridge nonstop, I fill their glasses, place the bottle in the icy water of the bucket, and back out of the room with faux reverence (the imprint of their image in my retina and an erection saved in a dusty nerve cell). Then, playing a lively Brahms symphony in case they laugh or splash or groan, I sit down next to the fire ready to knock back Eulàlia's story in one go.

'Poke as much fun at him as you like, Làlia,' Mònica said, knocking back the first glass in one go, 'but Alexandre seems like a great guy to me. Bringing us champagne in the bath like that was amazing!'

'But don't you see he only did it to take a couple of photos of us and wank a hundred times over them?'

'What do you mean? He doesn't have anyone to…'

'Not for a thousand days or more.'

'Oh, poor thing! Shouldn't we let him in for a bit?'

'Whoa, whoa! Let's avoid putting the starved cat among the pigeons, shall we?!'

And that's how we went on and on, chatting and laughing about exquisite nothingness, while she perched her bum on the edge of the bath to roll a joint and I caressed and kissed her feet, calves, knees, thighs. Much more than just sex (but also that), it was a uniquely ludic and sensual session, both of us stimulated by the magic of the scene and the subconscious presence of the prohibited male (poor Alexa!). No doubt, deep down, this sensually immersive play, which begins with the first caress and ends with the last gaze of all humanity, is the best and most enduring component of this alchemic enigma called sex.

After one of those long half hours, I emerged wrapped in the blue moon dressing gown she'd bought for me and she emerged wrapped in the red sun dressing gown I'd bought for her and, carrying our clothes and shoes in our hands, we walked, barefoot and wet haired towards the living room, laughing like a couple of imbeciles at God knows what psychosadistic joke about enforced chastity. But in the living room our laughter suddenly froze over; our laughter and everything else, because the door was wide open and no one was there. I advanced on instinct when a man of around forty with a beard and gold-rimmed glasses approached, carrying a small suitcase and a large briefcase. He only escaped having his snout flattened against the door by a hair on his chinny chin.

'Hi!' he said, standing in the doorway looking even more shocked than us.

'Hi,' I replied without knowing exactly what to say.

'Are you a friend of Lex?' Mònica asked, the first to react.

Fortunately that's when Alexa walked in with a cardboard box in his hands and a huge smile stretched across his face.

'It's snowing like crazy!' he exclaimed before closing the door with his foot.

Suddenly, and with good reason too, he broke out into an insane asylum laugh. Mònica was the first to join in but the stranger and I struggled to see the funny side of the scene we'd been involuntarily cast in. In the end, though, we smiled and Alexa apologised and began introducing us.

'This is Enric the Editor: the madman who's entangled me in the mad plan that I've madly entangled you in. And this is someone I've spoken to you about a thousand times: sweet Eulàlia, beautiful Eulàlia, the fertile co-creator of our foetus. And this other young lady, no less sweet and no less beautiful, is Eulàlia's partner, Mònica.'

I went red to the roots of my hair and Mònica, who never blushes, to her eyebrows.

'And as luck would have it, after weeks without a single visit, all three of you have chosen this snowy day to come up here. It must be for a reason.'

'If it's bad timing, I can go sleep at Maçaners and we'll see each other tomorrow.'

'Come off it, Enric, this is your house! Sure, I live here and all this crap is mine… but the house is yours!'

'But that way I'd see the family…'

He looked down at the floorboards; we stood rooted to the spot, quietly giggling bedside the warmth of the resplendent fireplace. Alexa alternated between laughing wildly and holding it all in, like a child not knowing which new toy to play with first.

'Oh shut up you,' he said, placing the package carefully on the table and pushing Enric gently into the hallway.

'I insist. If I'm to stay then it will be upstairs. I won't make you change beds!'

'It's your bloody bed, Enric!'

'My bloody bed is in Barcelona and this one, until further notice, is yours. I'm going upstairs. Regardless, I find the west facing room most congenial.'

And transforming his words immediately into action, he began climbing the spiral staircase.

'He's a good guy, don't worry,' Alexa whispered to us before following him and Mònica fell into another fit of giggles.

'*Regardless, I find the west facing room most congenial!*' she copied quietly, emulating Enric's tone and intonation, and I quickly became an accomplice of her growing laughter, especially when she repeated the same sentence over and over again, each time with greater accuracy and exaggeration. When we could hardly breathe, Alexa came back down and (Christ knows why because he can't have known what was going on) he joined in. This Costales guy, I thought, is going to think we're three complete nutcases. Or druggies.

But it turned out to be a magnificent night. When we came out of the bedroom, comfortably dressed for a rural style supper, they were smoking grass in front of a nifty looking laptop: Alexa's face was that of a euphoric child while his friend had the air of a loving father, something I didn't comprehend until quite some time later.

Before sitting down for dinner on that long, unforgettable night, in addition to living and laughing, we did just about everything: 1) admire the new toy: a normally priced, normal laptop that Enric had got for Alexa because Monday was his birthday; 2) open one bottle of cava after another because 'our' birthday present, apart from dinner, was a humble box of brut nature; 3) roll innumerable joints with Alexa's grass and the hash Enric had brought over for Alexa, while Enric read my chaotic piece on the House of Torres and Alexa exhibited an incredible omnipresence with his new toy: now by the fire, bewildering Enric, now in the kitchen where we, already bewildered, were stretching snacks for three into dinner for four; and 4) laugh and chat and watch the snowflakes fall and snort a line per head of a fine, rose-tinted snow that Enric called dragonfly wing.

Afterwards, we'll sit down at the candlelit table and enjoy the meal and conversation. The lovely lesbians' banquet-gift will be smoked salmon, clams in special sauce and steamed king prawns. Very tasty but very snobby. We'll insist on cava and more cava (I also bought a box of the exact same producer and year), while listening to Beethoven sonatas and waltzes by Chopin. I'll light the conversational touchpaper by sincerely praising 'The Berga Ballads' I've just finished reading.

'You really think it's good? I was worried you'd find it off topic and too different from the others,' its author will doubt.

'What ever do you mean?'

'Well, only the second of the three stories has any relation to the world of drugs.'

'Yes, but the third story makes a clear enough reference to it,' Àlex will say, 'because it's easy to infer that Pere's suicide is fuelled by his son's addiction.'

'And the first one, the one about milk bread and the Berga blues, is the wellspring from which all the others pour,' I'll add. 'On the other hand, just because the general idea is to relate the drug experiences of a specific generation doesn't mean that every page has to be dripping with hash and hypodermics. One of the challenges of the project is portraying the protagonists in a natural, domestic way, in accordance with our national idiosyncrasies, if you'll pardon the phrase. In other words, how shit actually went down. How it's still going down now.'

'Now? Differently and less, I'd say,' Àlex will intervene, eclipsing me. 'For a few years you could find literally anything anywhere. I'm not saying that was a good thing, but there wasn't a single town in Catalonia of more than five hundred inhabitants that didn't have at least a couple of junkies.'

'Now they're all taking ecstasy, trips and coke,' Eulàlia will interject.

And I'll use her comment to pick up my thread again:

'What I meant to say is that the pleasure is precisely in achieving a register of 'normality', even of routine, to put it one way or another, so that the characters, in addition to being junkies, stoners and trippers, are people in a specific space and time.'

'Yes, of course,' Eulàlia will answer, pouring everyone more cava. 'In reality, it's merely a perversion of the same old endeavour: making the characters appear as three-dimensional humans with all their ineffectual coherences and indispensable contradictions.'

'Only, in this case,' Àlex will conclude, 'there's the added obstacle of relating experiences that can become terribly commonplace for those experiencing them day after day but that always sound extraordinary when heard by the uninitiated.'

'Exactly!' I'll respond.

Then there will be twenty seconds of genuine silence because the music will come to an end, emphasising the echoing fireplace.

'Not so loud, Mònica! You're giving me a headache!' Àlex will joke.

After the corresponding giggles, Mònica will say that if we do indeed want her non-expert opinion on the chapters she has read, twelve if we count the 'Ballads' as one, all of them are very believable. At times excessively autobiographical, according to her taste. The one that most moved her, she will add, if the present authors do pardon the offense, was Fermí in Poble Nou and, especially, Fabià's robbery. The problem, according to her perspective, isn't whether the characters' language is believable and accessible, chapter by chapter, but the overarching concept of the work as a whole.

'Bearing in mind it's only the opinion of a non-expert… my God!' Eulàlia will laugh while hiding a yawn.

'But if I haven't been deceived any more than usual,' I'll intervene, chuckling along with the music, 'Fermí and the Fabià of the robbery only exist in literary terms. They are Àlex's stylistic acrobatics. According to what he said to me, he struggled like a woman in labour to achieve the direct and informal forms of an agony-stricken Mín in the Poble Nou storm.'

'True,' he'll respond on his way back from the kitchen. 'And it's also true, as Mònica says, that the whole will continue to be the big question until we're finally able to engineer an agglutinating finale.'

'Even if the sensation of totality suffers slightly,' I'll defend, 'it's a price worth paying if the work has the strength and wealth of three or four different authors.'

'All I know is that strength and wealth are the least of what the present authors have,' he'll joke as he walks over with more cava. 'But we'll do what we can, right?'

And while Eulàlia goes to the kitchen to bring in a surprise chocolate cake that says 'Alexander the Great, fully 40,' Mònica will do the honours by grabbing the bottle out of Àlex's hand, deflowering it and proposing a toast to his, the authors' and all the collaborators' health: oh, elegant, enigmatic Mònica!

everything was a fairy tale; a fair is foul foul is fair fairy tale:

certainly Lex is an individual with two sides, to put it bluntly: he has a sense of humour perfectly developed for what they call emotional survival, and he lives at peace with himself because he's discovered that the only meaning in life – or at least his –

is to savour today without writing off the potential delights of tomorrow.

certainly his friend, Enric the Editor, is also a strange creature: we discover he's rich*super*rich from birth and that Albina is nothing but a grocery bill within a network of businesses as legal as they are lucrative, which includes a large Spanish-language publishing house, a line of five star nightclubs and another of six and seven star restaurants. the laptop he's given Lex, for example, will be tax deductible, VAT exempt, and God knows what else, and in reality it won't cost him a penny because it'll merely evaporate within company costs; a company that's subsidised to the hilt by all the right institutions.

and i'll think without daring to express how all this implies the looming shadow of fraud when he'll make me see it differently with the simplest of quips: 'what better way to promote literature than by obtaining the means and tools for an author without a market or resources?'

the big question, reflects Lex in his casually caustic tone, is whether the author in question deserves the questionable label of author: no doubt, he says, in many corners of the country there are more capable, more disciplined and more deserving people still working with typewriters.

then, a bit before or not long after, the philanthropist took advantage of his subliminal power to confess how he was dying to know (out of pure desire for knowledge and never idle morbidity) who had really written *Lluïsa: Exhibit 'A'* and the scenes about Clàudia attributed to Kiddo. Lex answered that during his time at the woodland lodge with his brother, the budding Buddhist who he hasn't heard from in two years, they spent long nights galaxy gazing and resuscitating a thousand dead anecdotes in stripped-down syntax, among which starred the aforementioned high mountain tragedy. the second part, in Orange, with the *femme fatale* fatally frozen at the height of summer, and the music and autosuggestion, was a metaphor for a real case that happened to another person he'd known. when it came to Lluïsa, however, he had three wonderful notebooks of hers, full of drawings and poems and ideas, even a few fragments of poetic prose, that her brother, Pepsic Pep, had most cordially posted him. and then, by allusion, the opening chapter emerged which, according to Lex, was sadly and strictly historic: that's why he'd been ruminating for days over how best to reword it.

i said that Lluïsa's first autobiographical exhibit had gone straight to my soul, despite its simplicity, causing Lex to puff out his chest like a proud old hen because – although the tone and a couple of scenes were taken directly from the notebooks – the words, dialogue and links were all his own doing.

and then Enric will mention 'Judge, victim and executioner' and i will have to make great efforts not to betray myself. and it's even more fortuitous that the forty candles we've placed around the living room will hide Làlia's blushes, who yawns before covering her cheeks with a revealing gesture. but luckily Lex, as if having guessed, will strike the symposium dead by saying it's high time to go for a walk, 'before Eulàlia completely falls asleep.' to rouse her (her and everyone else) he prepares three standard speedballs, that is: heroin and cocaine mixed approximately 30%-70% respectively while Enric, who despises heroin (he calls it literally 'the devil'), racks up two rails of dragonfly wing and a couple of compact, cocaine-laced cigarettes ('primos,' he called them). the reasons for his interest in narconarratives was becoming increasingly clear.

according to Lex, the speedball is our civilisation's single greatest invention after cheese on toast: 'the best and the worst of Asia and South America filtered through a depraved Europe,' he declares, before adding: 'sure, it's expensive, in terms of money and health, and it can't be abused for a second, but injected in these proportions, it's immortality.' even so, that doesn't mean he advises we try it, not today not ever. on the contrary. in fact he told us that he couldn't even remember the last time he did one. but no doubt he meant to say 'second to last' because his last time was right after finishing the sentence.

afterwards he'll begin tyrannically organising the adventure, advising us to equip hands, feet, head and torso against the cold because: 'don't even think about cars: the real fun is on foot.' six inches of crisp snow crystals serve as a carpet, and a slice of moon as a private lantern. fortunately, the silky veil and immaculate caster sugar tilled by the storm multiply its iridescence, without which we'd be falling on our faces every couple of steps.

in any case, in the excitement of the moment a kilometre in Lex's mouth would appear an acceptable amount to us. but by the time we've walked more than three halves, snow up to our ankles and overwhelmed by the silent spectacle, we still won't be anyplace. i mean, at *the* place. but not that it bothered anyone because the moment felt so unique.

a hundred and fifty metres further up our host Lex, as if awarding a prize, stops to breathe in the surroundings and slowly say:

'man is nothing, the work is everything.'

'that one's easy,' i say, grateful for the respite: 'Flaubert. although i believe he said it slightly differently.'

and we all return to our giddy laughter because it turns out the idea wasn't to guess the author but to enjoy the meaning. but the game ends up exciting them and we begin a round of quotations with the first person to guess the author winning a point. after fifty paces Lalàlia takes up the challenge:

'to use a man for his fortune, by God I'll never.'

as we take a break on account of our shallow city dweller lungs, first Lex, then I, begin to laugh, guessing the answer and the trap. but Enric will crawl right into it on all fours, confidently declaring:

'Lawrence Durrell.'

'Nessim caught in his own net!' he laughs.

'Nessim?'

'yep! Nessim. from now on I'm going to call you Nessim.'

'get bent! why, i'll bet my big toe that's from *Balthazar*. is it my turn now?'

'of course,' i'll then say. 'you've won the right!'

and we'll smile (but without laughing so not to cause offence) for another thirty yards until Enric, his gaze grazing the mountain peaks, synthesising language and the idyllic surroundings, will say:

'reality is, at best, an illusion between two lies.'

one barking dog, then a second, seemed to want to offer an answer as we approached a phantasmagorical farmhouse. stalling for time and to ease her stitch, Lalàlia asked him to repeat it and Enric, leaning languidly on the landscape once more, did so, thus giving everyone, both humans and canines, time to admire the moment.

but i'd be at a loss to describe that setting so saturated by shadows; shadows like spectres owing to the lunar glow bouncing off the snow: half dark spirit below, half white body above: 'reality is, at best, an illusion between two lies.'

on we'll walk, ruminating the whole while, until reaching the convergence of two narrow paths in some remote corner of the wood and Eulàlia will risk remarking that it has echoes of Pirandello, though it could be an old Zen adage.

'it's not a Zen adage, as far as i'm aware, and as much as Pirandello may have written something similar at some point, it isn't him.'

with a flash, the light penetrates my intellect:

'i've got it. oh, how easy! it's Lex. i bet my bottom dollar!'

after one of my long, dense silences, my emphasis and enthusiasm will surprise them all, especially Eulàlia. she'll ask me how i guessed it while Enric makes an utterly dispensable speech on my non-expert literary intuition and Lex's eyes fix on me through the veils of night, searching for i don't know what emerging glimmer of dawn. and then all of a sudden it seems we're coming to the place. and just as well because Lalàlia was already running on fumes.

but it's unquestionably a location more than worthy of our efforts: there's a wide wall of smooth stone, of three or more layers, stretching slenderly towards the sky, a dozen tall beech trees maypole dancing around it. but perhaps on that night, with the stunning snowfall and the water gushing into the pool below, it was more spectacular than ever. at least that's what Lex said as he cleared a section of the path with a folding spade he'd been carrying in his rucksack. out of the rucksack also come an isothermal blanket, which he'll spread open in case we want to sit down, and some square bars with the appearance of soap which, after five minutes traipsing amid the trees with a torch and a small axe, he's able to use to light the beginnings of a fire in the clearing next to the blanket.

the rest of us are also busy getting busy: Eulàlia positions a few candles around the blanket, which for the time being the post-storm calm respects, and sits down between my feet to roll a couple of joints; Enric is by my side preparing various lines of dragonfly wing while smoking one of his pre-prepared primos; and i, to avoid feeling at a loose end, grab the glasses and one of the two bottles from the rucksack. i don't think i've ever drank so much cava in one night, and i know i've never done so many drugs, but that doesn't mean i'm not enjoying it, for now.

then we'll snuggle up, all four of us, next to the full force of the flames, listening to the stream's impetuous laughter and the modulating silences of the wood, and Lex will whisper into my ear that i owe him a buck because the real author of the quote was Lluïsa Cabellera.

and everything will be just like a fairy tale; a fair is foul foul is fair fairy tale.

THE BERGA BALLADS

1. *A hundred years of milk bread and the beginnings of the Berga blues*

Under the oak we must reveal ourselves
before a winged demon arrives
SISA

For those of us born and bred in big Barna, having a cousin – or more accurately, grandparents, uncles, aunties and a cousin – in the heart of Berguedà is nothing short of a cultural heritage. First of all because of the *Patum* festival ('oh, ineffable secular miracle!'), but also because of the holidays there when we were small and the adventures when we were somewhat bigger.

My most vivid childhood memories – in both Stereo and Technicolor – are from my summers spent at the Torres manor, a fabulous farmhouse on the outskirts of the village of Avià. Nothing like those deplorable rural 'second homes' that only serve for feasting, fiestas and fornicating: the Torres farmhouse had three enormous fields with more potatoes, beans, onions and lettuces than they knew what to do with; two rippling seas of corn below the stables; a tended garden with fruit trees encircling a gurgling fountain; and all the land required by the animals: one hundred cows, one hundred rabbits, and more than a dozen each of pigs, ducks, hens and beehives. And that was in addition, naturally, to the corresponding human flock which in that Corpus Christi A.D. 1973 included: Grandpa and head of the family (Joan III, 70); Nana (Rosalia, 59); her younger sister (Aunt Dolors, 49); the first in line (Pere II, 40), his wife (Genoveva, 33) and their son (Joan V, 14); and, lastly, a bachelor shadier than a beech wood and as stubborn as a mule (Ramon, 29).

Patriarch Joan had had five children and still felt up to the challenge of more: first had come Joan IV, who died just short of his ninth birthday, victim of a stray bullet towards the end of the Civil War. Afterwards, in 1930, came Natàlia, whose birth the patriarch's first wife, Angelina (of the Grauxic household), would not survive. Not a year later (the day after the 1931 Catalan referendum), he married Rosalia (of the Perdiu household) and the following Christmas the boy destined to inherit it all was born: silent Uncle Pere (technically Pere II because Grandpa's father, also made legitimate heir after the death of the first born, had been called Pere). Then in 1940 came Montserrat (my mum) and finally, in 1944, owing to a natural birth control miscalculation (according to Nana's confession), secretive Uncle Ramon.

But that's enough lineages of the rural bourgeoisie. Let us return to the sublime dictation of childhood memory: one of the many wonders of this mythical house was milk bread. Everyone in the Torres household called it that, and the recipe was a bowl of cow's milk (heated real good so a thick skin formed on top) mixed with sugar, powdered cocoa and chunks of crusty bread. Even now, twenty years after giving up milk and sugar, I have visions of bowls of cow's milk, crusty milk skins, sugar, cocoa and hunks of bread! My metabolism wouldn't permit even two spoonsful of it but it's still the best thing I've ever tasted.

It might sound like 19th century folklore but even at the end of the '70s, Nana Rosalia would still take her cart and donkey – 'Buddy', she called him – into Avià and La Valldan at first light to deliver fresh milk in *petricons* (a measurement from an already disintegrated time and space equivalent, according to her, to one quarter of a standard table *porró*) come rain, shine or snow, three hundred and sixty-two days a year, not counting deaths, because for Nana Rosalia a year had but three holidays: Christmas Day, Good Friday and Sant Joan.

The patron saint of the farmhouse was John the Baptist

meaning that Sant Joan was always celebrated with large family gatherings and hours upon hours upon more hours sat at table eating and drinking and chatting and playing during which we nippers (in Berguedà they always called us that) would grow bored poking at our cannelloni or competing to see who could eat the most until finally slipping outside, with or without permission. Outside, of course, we were in charge because with only a bit of imagination all worlds were possible.

Just as, if not more, idealised as milk bread are the sweet sessions of sensual instruction with Cousin Joan, submerged under the waves of corn or shooting towards the stars from the giant oak on the hill, interpreting the uncertain roles of our flowering romance anywhere and everywhere but, above all, in the shed by the fountain – oh, the shed by the fountain! Apart from our proto-erotic secrets, the shed guarded another, very specific one that I've always suspected was generations old: at the farmhouse no one was permitted to a light a cigarette until they were eighteen and in steady employment, so we hid tobacco (or at least Gypsy's bacca) wrapped in plastic under one of the tiles. In my day, it was usually three and five. Or in other words: row number three, tile number five.

A different password, this one exclusively for older males, normally six and nine, indicated the tile where half a pack of condoms and a couple of French porno mags were stashed. In addition to Joan, this secret was known to all the bright sparks from the neighbouring houses over the age of twelve and on both sides of the gender divide, amounting to a dozen meat and veggies and four or five bean flowers, as we often referred to ourselves. One day, curiosity impelled me to take a solo trip to find out exactly what was lurking under six and nine and the person who caught me deep into my first masturbation (turning the pages with a stick because touching them grossed me out) was my dear beloved Joan. It left me mortified to such an extreme that I didn't want to give him another kiss on the lips ever again. It was bad luck for him because from what I gather he was counting on gently taking my virginity that very summer but it was also bad luck for me, too, because two days later at the *Patum* parade, the first time we were allowed to go to the central square alone, I ended up getting with a friend of his and it didn't go at all well. At least for me. I'm not suggesting the boy was worse than the majority but we were both completely drunk and completely inexpert – in other words, a disaster. It still pains me having chosen my first man and my first fuck so badly and that it hadn't been as I'd imagined, written and played out so many times! But as Uncle Pere always used to say: there's no point crying over spilt milk bread.

2. *The mayor's daughter*

When logic and proportion have fallen
I'll be there
'White Rabbit', JEFFERSON AIRPLANE

It wasn't easy redirecting Cousin Joan towards a platonic family relationship because his dear pal told him everything in a lewd conversation between males that ended in a punch up. That summer a gorge opened between us, out of shame on my part and a type of half enamoured resentment on his. At least that's what I think it was on account of, because we've never actually spoken about it. I spaced out my stays at the farmhouse but we always spent a few nights there at least two or three times a year. Much against his will, the patriarch of the family was aging at a vertiginous rate. Nana Rosalia died the day after they buried her Buddy. Uncle Pere was, with each passing day, more and more Silent.

Around 1979-80, the year of Anecdote No. 2, I spent two September weeks at the house and coincided with the Queralt Gala celebrations, the venerated virgin of the mountain that bears the same name. Joan, by now twenty years old and possessing a know-how that was frankly frightening, promised me an unimaginable experience. The official programme of events I'd picked up in some Berga bar was split into equal parts between religious acts (morning), institutional acts (afternoon), and kumbaya acts (evening) and, truth be told, I didn't see where the fun was to be had. But Joan knew much more about the secret traditions and rituals of the county's youth than the programme organisers did, and he paid his promise back in full.

I must say from the outset that he and his pal Guillem, aka *Ten*, had already taken a mid-afternoon mosey down to Manresa to fill the pantry: one gram of yellowy lead belly horse and fifty tabs of acid, codename: Volcano. They'd sell whatever they could and maybe even come out of it with a small profit (at least enough to cover our costs for the night). After a dinner of peas, bacon and black sausage in a bar along the way, they dropped a whole tab in the car park. I risked half, though I still believe I should have cut that half in half again.

Down by the church a group of boys were clowning around playing guitar and singing American folk ballads in clerical tones. By the third song I began to feel a rising anxiety, which is absolutely prohibited when it comes to acid. Then we went for a stroll in the mountains which were full of tents, sleeping bags, campfires, guitars, harmonicas, bongos... and teeming with animate shadows that came and went, laughing and singing, continually offering me joints, bongs and the occasional blowback, and I immediately found a blissful mental freeway free from crosstown traffic. I'm not exaggerating by numbering the tents at fifty or sixty and the people at four or five hundred. However, the most remarkable thing wasn't the number of people but the fact that at least seventy per cent of them were tripping on some sort of acid, while another twenty per cent were on even stronger subs- tances. After a pleasant labyrinth of twists and turns we ended up in a clearing where two of Ten's friends were enjoying a tiny campfire and a giant spliff. We laid out our few belongings and stretched out on the floor to size up the firmament. I liked Joan and Guillem's company because they were people who knew how to keep quiet – or more precisely, to dig the deep silence.

Who knows how long we lay there within the Tubular Bells, upon the fire's hieroglyphics, counting shooting stars and apparently immobile constellations! Joan, who had a passion for astronomy, told us that as much as mathematical probability pointed to other habitable worlds, the distances beyond our paltry solar system were so abysmal that even if we travelled at the speed of light it'd take us four years just to get to the nearest star – Proxima Centauri, if I'm not mistaken. And the entire incalculable conglomerate of our own galaxy adds up to little more than a standard molecule within the immense body of the universe, and that the distances between each molecule are so enormous that not even light can cover them, meaning that when astronomers look far, far into space they are essentially looking into the past. Needless to say, on a basic rational level I was unable to follow his thread but my intellectual instinct, exalted and highly charged on account of the acid, presented me with a whole new dimension of thought.

But suddenly a female whimper that had been humming away in the background broke out into a gut- wrenching scream of terrifying fear, and immediately there were more voices, more shouts and more screams. Truth be told, I was petrified: the change in 'vibes', as we called them back them, was abrupt and disturbing. Ten stood up and went over to the fire where the commotion continued, i.e. where the girl was groaning as though possessed and where his friend, Andreu, no longer knowing what to do, was desperately trying to calm her down by shaking and shouting at her. It was clear from a country mile that he was just as terrified. Between the two of them they got hold of the abject girl and began to carry her to where we were sitting but she kept escaping their clutches and running off in random directions. Needless to say, this was unspeakably dangerous: in her state she could easily throw herself off a cliff edge without knowing anything about it. After a whole load of caresses and tenderness, which are usually a lot more effective than threats and hysteria, we finally managed to persuade her to sit down.

Rattling off a couple of brief sentences, Andreu explained that they had eaten a bag of highly hallucinogenic mushrooms from the high Pyrenees and that everything had been chilled until she suddenly began freaking out: she wasn't listening to anyone, she couldn't hear anything and she was spacing out for long stretches. That was, of course, just as, if not more, dangerous than the cliff edges because there are people who've never been the same again after a bad trip, whether partially or totally, and we could all name a few: the individual's entire way of being shifts from one day to the next; sometimes it can be recuperated with time and good behaviour but other times they're gone forever. I can cite numerous cases, as real as they are dramatic, but I'll limit myself to the case of Toti, who I knew from secondary school in Sants (Barcelona). A kid like any other, perhaps slightly more shy and formal than the rest but who, after a few drags and a couple of tinnies, would get so incredibly high he'd be making contact with a constellation of gods, undergods and antigods, all cosmogonic in nature and whose names and genealogies grew and multiplied as far as the already mentioned edges of the known universe the more he continued to smoke and drink. At times he reminded me of Lovecraft's 'The Myth of Cthulhu', which I don't think he'd ever heard of. What I do recall is getting extremely angry one day with Xènia – *cruel* Xènia – after she deliberately got him stoned merely to record one of his freewheeling discourses.

While tonight's resident hallucinatory, Madeleine, daughter of a local mayor, relaxes for brief windows, the three males discuss the best line of action. I go and see what I can do to help and she hugs me all of a sudden, squeezing me to the point of doing me actual physical harm while whining amid tears and sobs that I must forgive her, that she didn't want to, that she knew I'd be mad… Christ, she thinks I'm her mum. I take advantage of the hallucination to lie her down and calm her, and she curls into my body like a baby seeking the protection of the womb. With a sense of surprise and shame, I realise the contact of her body is exciting me sexually, as if now were the right time.

'The best thing would be to take her straight to hospital,' Ten said.

'What, and let her dad kill me when he finds out!' protested Andreu, more scared than a yellow-bellied coward.

'Big deal! The only thing that matters right now is her!'

'There is another solution, I think…' Joan interrupted, dragging out each syllable.

'Well, go on then!' Andreu urged him.

'When I feel too high on acid, I do a line of something stronger.'

'What are you getting at?'

'Blow. Or even better… smack.'

'Are you fucking crazy?' shouted Andreu in an outburst. 'She might as well stay as she is!'

'Suit yourself. But I for one, to ward off the evil vibes, am going to do one right away.'

'I think Joan's right, Andreu. What are they going to do at the hospital except give her a tranquiliser?' added Ten, verbalising pretty much what I was already thinking.

'Yeah, but they know which one to give her and more importantly how much!'

'Andreu's right, Ten,' Joan butted in, turning the discussion on its head. 'Come on, let's get her to the hospital. It's the safest bet.'

There was silence: a long, heavy, surreal silence because poor Madeleine was still hallucinating and having delusions about a group of big-eared children Morris dancing by the pond where the moon lived: a moon in the shape of a mermaid: a mermaid in the shape of a centaur: a centaur in the shape of a spaceship, with winged rose-shaped pistachio-coloured jellyfish flying out of it, which she didn't like at all and which flung her into another crisis. Or an even worse crisis because by now she was heading towards a menacing paroxysm capable of carrying her off to a veritable inferno.

In the end, almost out of habit, my cousin's hypothesis was accepted and they began racking up donkey rides for everyone. The problem of how to administer it to Madeleine was yet to be resolved because nobody knew or wanted to know anything about needles (yet) and she wouldn't and couldn't snort a thing. But, yet again, it was solved by streetwise Joan who wrapped a conservative dose (to see what effect it had on her) in bit of cigarette paper: a bomb, he said it was called. The job of putting it in her mouth and getting her to swallow it was mine but luckily I'd gone back to being her mum again. After she'd dropped hers, I made mine a double, reasoning that if she had to get dragged into the rabbit hole then, come what may, I'd be going with her: oh, lesbian Beatrice! All things considered, I'd been having an intense trip of my own until the mayor's daughter and her boyfriend put a damper on things. But with a stubborn smile and a soft kiss on my ear aimed at my cunt, Joan told me not to worry, that in ten minutes the drama would be over. As far as

Madeleine was concerned, he was spot on: ten minutes exactly. The only thing we had to do was to make her swallow another bomb three or four hours later to keep her asleep. Meanwhile, Andreu got feet first into the tent with his head poking out and followed our underground-overground party, reactivated after the first lava flow had cooled by another shared volcano.

Drugs have between them a sort of official hierarchy that, despite not having any scientific basis, almost always works in practice: on the first level (always relative and subject to the idiosyncrasies of each individual) we find tobacco, tea, coffee and hashish; on the second, alcohol, marijuana, and a wide selection of pharmaceuticals; on the third, a range of barbiturates and amphetamines (some of which are perfectly legal), natural psychotropic substances, LSD, and other designer drugs, not to mention coca, opium, peyote, etcetera, in their natural plant state; on the fourth and final level we find all the substances crystallised in laboratories, such as mescaline, cocaine, morphine, heroin, etc. This is more or less what Joan explained to us the following morning after we had congratulated him on his successful management of wee Madeleine's crisis who, despite being exhausted, felt perfectly fine, or thereabouts.

Cosmological conversations to one side, my lasting memory of the night is the pantomime performance by a bunch of local *berguedans* convinced of their collective ability to fly: one after the other they leapt off a relatively high edge, spinning their arms like little windmills and smashing slapstick style in the spectacular darkness. A couple of them even threw themselves off three or four times and I'm amazed none of them broke as much as a finger. Naturally we watched and laughed without intervening until they finally got bored and went in search of another game to play.

The warm golden light spread over the old silver ash and

we removed blankets and jumpers as the sun grew in the sky. Joan then proposed the penultimate donkey ride which thrust us into a sweet, absolute Morpheus embrace. After that night and over the following days, bearing in mind that the effects of acid can spread subliminally beyond its high water mark, I conserve three or four short sketches that I will leave (with a certain shame deeply certain) as an unavailing lyrical complement:

an enormous empty sea of energy
a hundred billion oceans of solar systems
and me, solitary and sightless,
s   a   i   l   i   n   g
scum recycled
by fire
into visual poetry;
star
t
h
a
t

f
a
l
l
s
and dies

how will you tell
with phonemes,
short poem,
all the silences of the cosmos?

3. *The decline and fall of the House of Torres*

It's paradoxical to think that the decadence of the Torres manor, a property belonging to the family since 1849, began from within like a cancer at a time when the estate was undergoing expansion. After Grandpa Joan's embolism, Pere became the head of the family and the property was passed to him, as had been decreed by Rosalia. Though not a blood descendent, Rosalia was a flesh and bone symbol of the farmhouse's spirit but, taking the key of good sense and the lock of consensus with her to the grave, after that it seemed as if everyone had an axe or two to grind.

Patriarch Joan III, now mentally recuperated and feeling more in charge than ever, gradually developed a specific senility that led, transported and returned him to decisions that were not only highly capricious but grotesquely contradictory and which – whether owing to dearth or excess – only served to undermine the efforts of his silent successor, Pere II, to rationalise and modernise the estate. Subterraneously, because in theory I was the only one who knew about it, was Joan's Addiction. He had discovered there was nothing, in the West at least, that simulated nirvana as well as heroin and he was using it in quantities that suggested a serious illness that was paid for, needless to say, by the multiple generous teats of the House of Torres. One fine day, Ramon, who never explained anything, not even his silences, announced that he'd finally finished his philosophy degree after ten or twelve years of distance learning and that he was leaving for Rubí to work as a teacher while he put the finishing touches to his dissertation. Without even a remotely comprehensible reason, his father opposed it head on, rudely and threateningly, spouting gibberish about the inheritance and the farmhouse and its land (officially Pere's property) and his money and his other properties and that it was supposed to be split between all the children when he died. But Ramon merely stood up without uttering another word or raising an eyebrow and slipped off like a shadow to pack his bags. I was later informed that Pere, the Son and Heir, assigned him a generous figure as a farewell without telling the old man about it.

As much as the tractors and harvesters, fertiliser spreaders and automated milking machines maintained the farmhouse afloat, deep inside the decay had already set in. A year and a half later, on a cold November night in 1981, Pere II, aka *Pere the Silent*, cut a piece of rope in the garage and hanged himself from the oak tree that stood, and still stands, up on the hill. A veritable inquisition began both inside and outside the family and the home, in both senses of the word, with a thousand and one hypotheses that out of decency I'll refrain from mentioning. Only now, fifteen years later, do I realise that the combination of five or six uncontrollable elements, like a huge jackpot on a giant slot machine, would be necessary to guess even half of the dead man's dead truth. Suicide seems – to me, at least – a human being's most intimate act and it often leaves its sufferers and enforced spectators with a pile of futile questions of every imaginable mien.

Of course, despite the bewildering concurrent circumstances, the ceremony at the Catholically consecrated temple and grounds was attended by almost everyone, despite the ancestral prohibition on religion, and back at the house after the bitter cemetery rituals the psychological landscape was worthy of Shakespeare at his most tragicomic. Old Joan II, with eighty years, two wives and two successors on the scorecard, stared at Genoveva as if she'd pulled the knot tight with her own hands and had to be summarily sentenced to death at dawn. Genoveva, now matriarch of the household two times over (whether she liked it or not) contemplated the dark corners with the docile gaze of an imbecile, as if seeing shadows there worthy of tenderness. Black sheep Ramon, who'd been relishing his newfound independence, smiled to himself while assimilating the pluses and minuses of the scene and blocking his father's corrosive gaze with cynical silence. Apart from Nana Rosalia and Uncle Pere, among the absentees was my dad, definitively settled in Lisbon and separated from us, and the person who in theory had the role of sculpting future filigrees and guiding the congregation: Cousin Joan. But after discovering his father's body while trotting back from Pleasantville at eight in the morning and starting the unavoidable process by calling the family doctor, he'd vanished. Genoveva finally took refuge in her bedroom, accompanied by Mama Montserrat and me. Montserrat gave her another tranquiliser, even though we seemed more upset than her, and she fell asleep after asking me to go look for her son. I picked up the phone, looking to immediately embark on the mission, but no one knew where he was or at least didn't want to say. A friend of his from Berga (Ten had disappeared off the radar) came to pick me up and we did a tour of the county, passing by Joan's typical hangouts. But he wasn't in any of them and no one had seen him. However, when we got home a light suddenly went on in my perception: I sent the driver on his way with a heartfelt thank you and went immediately to the shed by the fountain. No more than two hundred metres from the house, half hidden in the foliage of a path seldom travelled, I found his metallic-blue Lancia. Approaching, I grew more and more frightened, perhaps because of the effects of the looming red winter evening. But my fears amounted to nothing because inside was Joan, spread out on the straw, up to his eyeballs in junk, but alive. Nothing or nobody was enough of a reason to convince him to go to the house and considering that all he could do was smile goofily and try to fondle and kiss me, as if that were the right time, I went back up to the house alone to save them all the heartache.

But at that precise moment no one was thinking about Joan the Younger because Grandpa had finally blown his top and, arming himself with the most course language he knew, was busy accusing Genoveva of being the root cause of all the calamities faced by the family, this latest one in particular. Ramon showed a strength of character and a perspicacity that none of us knew he had, at least me, and gave him a few home truths, beginning with: 'you're the least qualified to lecture anyone about adultery' and ending with: 'he who is without sin, let him shove the first stone up his arse.' As way of a response, Grandpa howled that he never wanted to see him again and that if he didn't leave the house right away he'd call the police. But Genoveva, who'd seemingly been asleep within an insubstantial spider web, suddenly stood up to clarify that the house, in accordance with the last will and testament of the deceased, belonged to her and her alone and that if anyone was going to be thrown out it certainly wasn't going to be Ramon. Grandpa shot up enraged, likely ready for physical combat, but after foaming at the mouth his eyes rolled back and he collapsed in a heap on the floor. He wasn't even half the towering, well-built man he'd been thirty years before. Aunt Natàlia's paediatrician husband put him in the car and took him straight to A&E in Berga: he'd suffered another embolism, worse than the previous one, and he'd avoided meeting his maker by minutes. But maybe it would have been for the best because afterwards all he did was sit like a cabbage in the corner for two long years before finally croaking.

It pains me to put pen to paper on this but if Joan had been a different soul then the estate would most likely have been saved because his mum was a good matriarch. But Joan was already a serious addict before the disastrous event and he turned into a totally unhinged one afterwards. I suppose the diagnosis – if we'd managed to convince him to go see a specialist – would have been a black dog depression and guilt complex as he alternated between periods of absolute apathy and bad attitude, and days of euphoria and a terrifying vitality. In addition to the great escape of drugs, he began to throw away money and health by the bucket load on cars, extravagant building works and conversions, and highly expensive astronomy devices. And that's without mentioning the bills sent by the private clinic where Dolors had rented a double room and established her living quarters, which left its own black hole. I should also add that my aunt revealed herself to be capable of tremendous spite by telling a thousand lies of differing magnitudes about the family members who'd stuck by Genoveva, though this was most likely provoked by her own sense of guilt. Aunt Natàlia and her husband, along with the children of Grandpa's dead siblings, took the side of blood by filing a complaint that called into question the validity of Pere's will, arguing that the end he'd chosen proved he wasn't of sound mind. But the real enemy, if I may put it in those terms, was within, and his name was Joan.

Fate bared its fangs the following Christmas when Uncle Ramon and Mama Montserrat persuaded Genoveva to put her cards firmly on the table and confront her son once and forever. Sat around the kitchen table with a bottle of cava that no one thought of finishing and a number of painstakingly prepared dishes were our four sad souls: it was hard to think that just two years before there were more than thirty of us singing and dancing and laughing in the large dining room! Sat like a yogi master, though I doubt she even knew what one was, Genoveva grabbed the problem by the horns.

'Listen, Joan,' she said firmly, establishing the tone from the start, 'it's been a while now that I've known about your drug problem.' (Calm pause). 'What I'd like to know is if you're willing to do something to overcome it... and if you think we can help.'

(Similar pause). 'I'm telling you, because at the end of the day...'

'At the end of the day,' Joan interrupted irritably, 'my problem isn't drugs... it's you! You can't leave me alone for five minutes! You add up and analyse every penny I spend as if I were fifteen years old. And you fill the house with your allies and plan to lock me up in the nuthouse and keep it all for yourselves!!'

It was a response unworthy of Joan V the Clever, and I exploded like gunpowder. He was sitting close to me, too close, and before he finished the insult I finished it for him with an open palm across his face. I immediately regretted it, fearing an even worse explosion on his behalf, and the scene stood in suspense as though there were nothing more to say. Joan stood up with a sadistic smile aimed at the soul of my sex, touched his lip Marlon Brando style (I realise now that he was, luckily, still in love with me), breathed deeply and said to his mum:

'You may well be the matriarch of the household but I'm the head of the estate. I want you all out of here by noon tomorrow. If not, I'll go live in town until you do leave.' And with that he launched himself towards the door to leave but not before yelling: 'Come back for my funeral if you want a good laugh!'

Genoveva began to sob quietly and for a long while. It's the only time I've ever seen her really cry, despite all the hardship she's been through. I opened another bottle of champagne, seeking to deceive the moment by sweetening the bitterness, and if I'd known where he kept it I would have snorted a fat line of Joan's smack. Uncle Ramon, who had refashioned himself to the point where he no longer seemed either shady or stubborn or even a bachelor made a sardonic quip about why God permits these terrible scenes between family members during the holidays: it was Christmastime and the Heavenly Father, naturally, was busy having dinner with His own family. The sheer cruelty of the joke made us all laugh as if laughter were the sodium bicarbonate to our tragedy. And that was when Genoveva surprised everyone by suddenly showing a side to her character that had hitherto remained hidden:

'The day before yesterday it was twenty-four years since I married silent Pere, may he rest in peace, wherever he is. If I have to leave this house so my son can ruin it in peace then we might as well leave now and spend Christmas someplace else.'

Half an hour later we were in Montserrat's car and on our way to Sants and the half-paid-for flat where mum and I lived. And there we spent Christmas, just the four of us, sad but calm, and Genoveva then stayed a while longer with us until she got set up. It must be said that after just three months she had already signed a lease on an eatery in the neighbourhood and rented a flat. But inside she was still wounded and it cost her whoknowshowmuch to recuperate from that backwards forwards step. Above all because the news that reached us from the manor was always bad and only got worse: the following August, amid a range of other lesser catastrophes, a wildfire consumed a third of the wood and half the fruit bearing trees. And – to put the finishing touch to the anecdote – the shed, too.

While Joan V's centennial Berguedà estate foundered in the flames, in contrast and despite the difficulty of the process, Genoveva rose up from the ashes reborn, successfully reinventing herself in Barcelona's service sector.

Uncle Ramon, more stoical with each passing day, would often say that nothing is ever so bad, no matter how grave it may at first appear, that nothing good can come from it. Despite the sorrow it implies, I'm tempted to apply his saying to the terrible accident Joan suffered in February 1985 while driving his brand new, four million pesseta BMW 750 csi. But that is the inflexion point between the fall and the resurgence of the House of Torres and doesn't enter into this particular slice of tragedy.

FISH OUT OF WATER

Between Two Waters
PACO DE LUCÍA

It's true when I say I'd gone a number of years without doing primetime material, except only very occasionally, and that my last experience of the daily mainline commute was in Madrid, back in the neighbourhood of Vallecas. Therefore it's also true that, after making the decision, I had a supply problem as I'd conscientiously let my little black book fade to black, and that comes with a price. But never in a million years would I have imagined that getting a couple of grams of heroin could be so complicated.

To begin with (out of pure habit rather than any real hopes of picking up any harry) I 'got lost' in the two wondrous labyrinths of the underground either side of the lower part of Les Rambles, nowadays almost completely refashioned by champagne socialism. But eight or ten years back I knew three or four holes where you could almost always get small amounts of any illegal drug, except crack perhaps as it was a fashion yet to be exported to our shores. The first place I looked up, or rather, looked for, was the flat of a certain Micky from Sabiñánigo, who spoke with a lisp and was someone I'd had a certain trade trust with back in the day. Not only could I not locate Micky but after half an hour of asking around over rounds (if you know how to play your cards right you can find out anything over beers, even where the Pope takes a dump), the answer came that the house I was looking for had been torn down three years ago. Next I went to check out another nearby bar (a shithole of a place as large as it was gloomy as it was empty that always reeked of piss and damp sawdust despite the toilet having being closed to the public since the dawn of time) only to confirm it no longer existed, especially as there was never more than five customers in there and all of them only ever drank small beers or cups of coffee. To my absolute surprise I found it exactly the same as before, with the same woman manning the bar and the same sad clientele. The obscure reason behind a 120 m2 bar just forty paces from Les Rambles remaining in that miserable 1950s tavern purgatory is, has and always will be, to me at least, a socioeconomic enigma of the highest order. If I didn't have other plans, I reckon I'd make them an offer and open a restaurant specialising in paellas.

Of course, the fact that I recognised owner and place didn't mean owner and place recognised me, and the only thing I came away with, on account of some old androgynous whore I randomly clocked going into the chemist's on the corner, was that Micky had died six months ago and Blackbeard (a small time pusher who looked like Rasputin and was normally in the area) had got caught in the act two years back and was in Can Brians doing a stretch three times that. But, if I wanted, he/she could get me whatever I was looking for… of course, I'd have to give him/her the money upfront. Aware I was breaking the most basic rules of the black market (for the record: never deal with touts and never pay for anything until you've got it in your hands), conscious I was doing what in Vallecas they call 'biting' (hook, line and sinker), I decided – in order to wrap up the adventure once and for all – to risk a thousand pessetes and go wait for an hour, having changed the Great Gloom for a fusion between wine cellar and delicatessen that didn't smell much better but at least had toilets. It goes without saying that a thousand pessetes wouldn't be enough but if it went smoothly then afterwards we'd see.

At around five-thirty (or seventeen thirty-eight, according to the Pepsi clock on the wall), forty-eight minutes after the agreed deadline, I pulled my arse up off an excessively warm bar stool and paid for the two gins and tonic with the seven one hundred coins I'd won on the fruit machine. Crossing Les Rambles on my way up to the northern labyrinth, I consoled myself by calculating the money I still had to play with, despite the dirty trick that dirty fag had pulled. But up top things were no different: no one I knew, or trusted in, in and around Plaça Reial. That is, none of the old-time African traders who set up the first flea market, or any of the Peruvian porters who sometimes helped them with moving the goods, or anyone in the basement boozers on the periphery or on the periphery of the basement boozers. And after sending a thousand *peles* down the drain I wasn't in the mood for pissing away anymore.

It wasn't even a quarter to seven in the evening but the November fog was flooding the minimetropolis with a thick nostalgia which in wintertime condenses the longing for summer. Then suddenly, unexpectedly, I felt like shooting up purely for the sake of it and to hell with all your stupid-ass asspirations and the rest of your so-called civilising conceits. It was donkey's years since I'd forgotten that vertiginous emptiness, that sweet *ennui*, as Bián called it, as lethal as it was morbid, but the quality of that sad perception of the world, and my world in particular, perfectly complemented the emotional memory of my junk years and the only thing I was missing was a good fix (in Catalan, 'fix' is pronounced 'fish', which is why over that absurd evening I kept calling myself a 'fish out of water').

I crossed Les Rambles again, collected the car from the Plaça Gardunya car park, and journeyed the few kilometres to the ferocious jungle that is Can Tunis, a place even the famous Doctor Livingstone would struggle to emerge from unscathed. After a glut of twists and turns, and doubts and fears over this street or that, this house or the next, this face or the one lurking behind, which no doubt raised the suspicions of the local security service (the police never went there), I finally scraped enough courage together to test the old arts of an old userdealer. With the ten five hundred notes folded under the sole of my foot (right shoe, as always), I wandered twenty metres up the street with a quick Camel as an excuse, without losing sight of the Golf in case the mosquitos were looking for fresh meat, instinctively putting my trust in a chance meeting that, otherwise, never materialised. Always the way: when you don't want to see certain people there's always a fly landing in your soup but when it's roles reversed no one's buzzing around. It's true that two or three individuals offered me heaven and hell for a few rotten greens but one was a trembling turkey dressed up as a gypsy king and the other, in addition to cold cravings and dubious gypsy royalty, was a cheap whore. It's terrible having to go down to the lowest rungs because of fucking addiction. I, Jaume Argentina i Vidals, also fell a fair few, even if it was on a different social ladder, during my hardest horse riding years. Never again. But let us leave both aspiration and its adjacent psychological terrain to one side: the universe was still the same universe, the sea still reeked of polluted sea, and the fires that the teenagers lit in the middle of the squares to illuminate their shady dealings still stank, as always, of dirty wood and greasy rags; of junk in flames, of dreams going up in smoke or coming true, for better or for worse, within the grotesque process of a common child delinquent's 'triumphal' transformation into an adult trafficker in the ranks of an organisation.

But socioeconomic theories are for those who earn a living from them: let us return to my particular emotional anguish because none of these profound reflections were going to get me a speck of dust. In that outright unrepeatable moment all the springs and rivers and seas and oceans were guiding the poor little fish towards the ineluctable hook. In the end, I decided to take a chance on a golden-haired gypsy girl with bright blue eyes who was leaning in the doorway of a miniscule cafébar. I went up to her and asked in Vallecas Spanish if she happened to know who might have a bit of you know what.

'Ha ha! Come off it, snout face!' she replied. 'Lose a few pounds first before you come sniffing around!'

It took me a moment to process the information correctly, giving her time to put the finishing touch to her meticulous description of my appearance.

'You've never shot up in your fucking life! You reek so much of bacon even the stoolies are shitting their pants.'

I was about to show her a few of the souvenirs I have for life on the epidermis of both forearms when a mixed couple stepping out and a male couple about to step in heard the last part and sent me packing towards the car with wild accordion laughter.

While I was wondering whether to go mad or simply go home, sick of playing splat the rat with a blindfold, two morons of mishap approached, who the fish – by now, well and truly, out of the water – hadn't detected on its radar. Let us just write it off as the price of the adventure because one thing is having been to war and quite another is returning to the front line ten or twenty years later. All things considered, I came out of it pretty well: the tiny, gaunt, hunchbacked one with the squirrel face positioned himself directly in my path with a bent Ducado between his lips and the eyes of a bragging murderer.

'Giv me all yeh moneh or me partneh ere is gonna stab yeh wiv aids.'

His marked accent awoke my dormant instinct, and after grabbing him by the shoulders and sending him flying into his 'partneh', i.e. the imbecile brandishing a needle in his right hand as though it were a Magnum, the kitchen sink drama was done and dusted before I'd even considered the consequences. The two pathetic stick up men were so meagre that they collapsed like a castle of toothpicks, interlocking limbs and squalor where they fell. And I, once again running on instinct, despite the little good it'd done me up until then, got going as calmly as possible under the circumstances towards the car to flee that waking nightmare. But just as I was drawing up to it, from a bar so nondescript that I hadn't noticed it when I'd parked up, came a voice, a flamenco spirit's delicious song that I knew well from gypsy Madrid: if that sonar tapestry wasn't a bulería by Enrique, aka *El Sardinita de San Lúcar*, then my name has never been *El Gaucho Catalán* (Oh, Vallecas and its million meccas!). The bodega, or whatever its licence listed it as, if it even had one, was a long, thin animal pen divided into three sections on different levels. Directly opposite the entrance was the bar; three steps down and to the right of the audience were half a dozen tables pushed up against the wall forming a stalls of sorts; and at the back, at the same height as the entrance, sat the paradisiac stage. But Enrique, Quique, El Sardinita wasn't on stage or among the tables but rather sat on the end of the bar top next to a wine barrel with a guitar swaying between his open legs.

'Gauchooo! Don't cry for me *Argentinaaaaaa!*' he sang, leaping from the bar and throwing his guitar into the air. 'Whereyabin?'

He was celebrating the fact that after twenty longs years of art and hard graft, he'd managed to record an album.

'Serious stuff, Gaucho,' he kept repeating, evoking an expression of mine that became famous at *Bailekas*, the 'establishment for the sale of alcoholic beverages' that I ran for those three years as worthy of Kafka as they were of Madrid.

He sincerely wanted to repay me the one hundred Prado-sized monkeys I'd coaxed off his back in exchange for a handful of private flamenco performances by buying me a glass of red wine to celebrate the album and then a spliff to commemorate the fact it would be a CD; in other words, eternal.

It's true that in that utterly unrepeatable moment, surrounded by El Sardinita's human warmth, in turn surrounded by his two dozen friends (men and women of all ages celebrating the fact that one day of life is life, even for the downbeat), yes, in that Moment I discovered some discursive sense to the whole stupid Kafkaesque adventure preceding it, and for a moment, just one, it led me to question my original decision. It was as though a jigsaw puzzle had entered into that particular afternoon or even into the entirety of existence in general and that this were the Piece, precise and exact, that gave meaning to all the previous fishes out of water. But it's also true that after a few wines, some fried fish, and more spliffs (*vinillos* and *pescaíllos* and *chinillos*, in Quique's idiom), followed by more proud singing by the boldest cocks and more ritual dancing by the sweetest chicks, I was finally able to corner Sardi and convince him, between rails and joints, that if he really wanted to prove his friendship he had to get me a few grams of '*ese asco*', or 'that filth', as he called it. But it's also true – as true as death itself – that I didn't tell him what I wanted it for. Fish in the ocean, fish out of the water, or in other words: night-night, sleep-tight.

30-12-96

From: Fabià Juncadella
To: Alexandre Oscà

Addressed to you, my dearly missed Alexandre,

is my last letter of the year. I am sad and stoned (much more than sad, much more than stoned).

Permit me from the outset to renounce, once and forever, your old-time Lex, just like I have renounced my stupid Bián (the less said about Robles the better), thus denoting on the onomastic plain the human transformation we at least appear to have undergone.

You will have to pardon my opioid handwriting. I hope it's not completely indecipherable. Permit me secondly to submerge myself, if merely for a moment, within the volcanic existential effervescence of my terror-stricken prison reality: my lawyer has told me that there are 'real possibilities' over the course of next year that the judge will grant me parole.

Permit me, as an appendage to the same point, to solemnly thank you and re-thank you for the supply of funds ('300,000 aces', as Ruth would have put it) that your priceless friend Enric provided. Look after him better than you look after yourself. Or at least as much. I am unable to put my finger on it but I suspect that these new hopes of a soon-to-be-signed early release, apart from my tally of years ('*many years, so many years, too many years*' as Raimon sings), has a subjacent connection to Enric's benevolent benefaction (1).

Naturally that depends on how you interpret the word soon: twelve months are the same as 8,760 hours or 525,600 minutes or 31,536,000 seconds but in comparison to the 131,400 hours or 7,884,000 minutes or 473,040,000 seconds constituting the fifteen years I have paid back, as far as I am concerned (if I can rationalise it and really believe in it), one year doesn't seem an excessively large obstacle to have to overcome. Above all because now there is an aim in sight, whereas before there was only pure speculation (my original sentence was thirty-nine years and one day). But I am doubtlessly killing you slowly with these 'scared parrot' (2) phobias and it wasn't this garbage I wanted to put down on paper. Naturally with a head full of junk I am amazed to have even made it this far.

Perhaps it surprises you (up until a point) that I am writing while galloping (like when time was still time) but it's the result of an event (a 'narrative' as you call it) to do with a genuine Wild Horse who the night before last was still sleeping next to me (in the other bed, you filthy-minded freak!).

He was called (what the fuck does it matter what he was called but to symbolise his martyrdom let's call him) Jesús and he is (or was) the junkie who had quit the habit most times (or thereabouts). Furthermore and then further and more, there was the additional distinction of his partner, (to maintain the metaphor let's call her) Maria, who gunned the same but wasn't to blame. They met very young (He, 18; She, 16) and got hooked (heavy-hooked) together, simultaneously, reciprocally (He, 20; She, 18). Two or three years later, because they really did love one another (truly, madly), they went hand-in-hand to get clean and later had their first child together (a girl I shall baptise Maria Magdalena). She was joined after twenty months of unbelievable and complete peace by another (Third Maria), who brought with her two more years of sweet joy tucked under her little arm. I hope you of all people understand that I am not referring to any sort of euphoria, whether emotional or social (and certainly not financial), but to a 'plain sailing' kind of groove made up of actions and hours with nothing to rock and roll the boat (despite my addiction I tasted broken shards of this humble nirvana when Ruth gave birth to my sorely missed cub). And Jesús, who from a young age had always earned his bread serving gravy (his older brother has been climbing the ranks of an international cartel for the last twenty years and always put some B-road traffic on a plate for him) had chosen to go good for good and was earning sourdough in a poultry slaughterhouse while Maria toiled at home with the two chicks but, despite the cascades of laughter, the cash flow was barely a trickle.

Then came the first cast iron hammer blow: all of a sudden Maria Magdalena (daughter no.1) turned anaemic and pale then yellow and hepatitic and ever weaker. She was diagnosed with I don't know what type of cancer and it ate through her in three months. Needless to say the whole thing derived from AIDS. It had never occurred to Jesús or Maria to take the corresponding tests. They had always kept it clean, they hadn't been hooked for many years and they almost always cooked up in their own kitchen, but after the unavoidable tests and the inevitable verifications all four were confirmed positive. Well, in reality, all three, because Maria Magdalena died right around that time.

Maria and Jesús were powerless to prevent a week of needle sorrow and just a few weeks later (arm-in-arm, hand-in-hand) they were hooked again. Hooked not so much in the physical sense (which of course is no joke) as in the psychological: hooked on the habit of using it and looking for it and buying it and not having to think about anything else, which in their case was the much lesser evil because Maria Magdalena's death made them feel something much more dreadful than guilt. And if it hadn't been for Third Maria they would have unquestionably opted (hand-in-hand as always) to slip silently and sweetly away.

But one day Maria's dad (who happens also to be my lawyer) warned them that he would request legal custody of 3rd Maria if they would not or could not take care of her, forcing them into another immense decision. After six months on a self-sufficient farm (hand-firmly-in-hand despite all the rules and regulations and recommendations against it), they overcame not just their physical and psychological addiction but also an obsessive guilt that was pure mental illness. The calm lasted almost three years.

Then, in the form of a cancer painfully similar to the preceding one, AIDS took their second daughter, and Jesús and Maria hid themselves away again in the bottomless pit of injected heroin until, about a year or so ago, outside a motorway service station, a thickly sliced fillet of full flavoured horse left them on the verge of an accidental overdose. However, a lorry driver who had just woken up spotted them and called the petrol station attendant who called the paramedics who called the pigs. The paramedics, in accordance with their job description, saved their lives (above all Maria, who had stopped breathing and already turned blue) and the pigs, in accordance with theirs, booked them both (above all Jesús, who they regarded as the main culprit) not just for the two grams of horse dotted around the car mats but the fifty grams of charlie in the glove compartment.

But, as you so often say, something good can always come of a shithole situation ('however faecal the treacle') and this new catastrophe prompted Jesús and Maria, Maria and Jesús to once again decide to get free of what are commonly known as hard drugs. And they did it simultaneously, reciprocally, more hand-in-hand than ever, in spite of the iron bars between body and soul, and in the process they recuperated the desire to live out together, when they finally could, whatever amount of life they had left. A newly resurrected Maria opened a hair salon (financed by her dad) and Jesús actually got somewhere on the detox programme despite the numpty of a psychologist we have now. As the old adage goes, experience is the begetter of wisdom, and even the worst habits and addictions have only been genuinely overcome once they have been overcome once and for all. The few of us that have had the 'fortune' of living and seeing it invariably end up regarding drugs as dangerous toys in the hands of adults with a deadly urge to spin the wheel.

But that's enough fast food philosophy because the narrative – implacable like our most ancient tragedies – continues beyond the third cast iron cannonball. After a year of bearing the weight the best they could and more or less happy despite the iron bars piercing heart and head, one fine morning, or rather, one terrible Tuesday two weeks ago, Maria – i.e. Maria who still lives in Jesús' sacred heart – didn't come to visiting day. His father-in-law (her dad, my lawyer) came instead and made out it was a bad case of flu but it didn't do any good: Jesús read it in his eyes that he would never see Maria again. No, I am mistaken: he requested and obtained a special permit to visit her in hospital where she awaited the end with resignation. That was five days ago on Christmas Day. The look on Jesús' face when he got back was enough for me to comprehend that the curtain would soon be coming down.

The following morning, with a couple of half-finished sentences and a stiff smile, he told me that he had signed the papers and given the order for them to switch off the machines maintaining her vital signs and that she most likely would not make it to New Year's. Adieu, Maria, adieu. But he had plans not to make it either. He would wait for her on the other shore, if indeed there was another shore for him to wait on. No, I didn't utter a single dissuasive word nor did I make the least attempt at condolence because the Drama of Jesús and Maria goes far beyond the pain and stoicism of mortals like me.

The night before last, making the most of the minor miracle of having the cell to ourselves, we said a first-class farewell with white nurse and a new needle (oh, divine luxury) and afterwards he lay down in his bed to inject his final passage. Even though I was more loaded than a spirit-seeing shaman I couldn't sleep or reach some approximation of it during the whole night and at wake up time I called the screws who carried him away (in his shirt pocket they found a letter to his father-in-law thanking him and apologising). They are burying him this afternoon in the same cemetery where they will bury Maria a few days from now, the same one where Maria Magdalena and Third Maria are already buried. At least now the four of them, who couldn't share a life together, will be able to share the same space in death.

They refused my application to attend, naturally. But thanks all the same. Farewell, Jesús. Farewell, sweet family.

And farewell, Jaume Argentina. I imagine you have already guessed the reason behind his decision but of course it must be nearly twenty years since I last saw him and who knows what became of him. In any event, too many suicides: so many dying to live, even for just one more day, and these two who still could…

And while we are at it, farewell to you too, sorely missed Alexandre! Permit me to snort this last line and pretend to sleep a while.

Fabià

P.S. (the following afternoon): I have two new cellmates already. One has stinky breath, the other has stinky feet. But apart from that they seem alright. Write to me soon because I am still sad but no longer so stoned.

(1) It's fun pursuing words in the dictionary after my readings of, what you call, the classics, the masters, the geniuses through the wide-open winter depths of these dull afternoons of routine

and then attempting to write them in my own words, as if I have always had them in my armoury. It's a lot of fun, almost as much as music, and it has a certain something, for which I also have you to thank, considering that my relationship with the world of the written word has changed – metamorphosed – thanks to the dozens of letters we have sent one another over the last four months. So, thanks once again.

(2): A 'parrot' according to the private slang I have developed with Jesús is someone who has been inside for more than ten years (because they know how to move better than anyone in such an enclosed space and because they always repeat the same set phrases). A 'scared parrot' is one of these veteran inmates faced with an imminent return to life on the outside.

TRANSPORTERS TRANSPORTED

'Born to Run', BRUCE SPRINGSTEEN

No matter where I've slept, no matter where I wake up, I'm out of bed at seven, into my scarlet xr3 and on my way to the Sant Joan Despí industrial estate. My one year temporary contract is as transporter for a company that manufactures and supplies all manner of electronic components for the chemical industry but in reality I'm a jumping jack of all trades, often giving Montse the secretary a hand – who gives it her all but just can't get the hang of it – and even helping out with basic tasks in the workshop when I get the call.

I always carry two or three joints with me in my packet of fags and at half nine, right after breakfast, I like to get one down in five long drags. Someday someone will grass me up to the boss but I can't say I care.

The best days are when I do the work as actually stipulated in my contract and have to go to Valencia, Jaen, Madrid or Bilbao, to name a few of the furthest destinations, while the trips I do in and around Catalonia are too numerous to count. Some mornings the boys in the workshop already have the van loaded up for when I clock in at eight and I head straight to Tarragona, Reus or Flix to be back in time for a second trip up to Girona, Olot or Manresa in the afternoon. And if I end up doing a couple of hours overtime I can even put a bit of bar time down on expenses.

Generally speaking, out on the road everything rolls along smoothly and as long as I keep more or less on schedule no one gives half a monkey's how I do things. And I can stop in whatever bar I feel like along the way (even if it means sacrificing my lunch break), choose which service station to stop in, or which is the most scenic route there and back. But when evening arrives – my pocket filled with bread but my body brutalised after so many hours of driving – my morbid spirit rebels against a certain malady peculiar to routine and all the bars, cafés, restaurants, pubs, clubs and concert halls, all the squares, boulevards and terraces in big Barcelona (from Mataró to Sitges and Granollers to Sabadell) aren't enough to quench my thirst. For alcohol and life in general. Being *really* good, and for *real*, is complicated for diehard junkies. And it was for this exact reason, in my hour of weakness, one ominous evening I decided to go see Mín.

It's ten past eight and the workshop is closed and empty. I open the door, leave the van inside and clock out. Then I get into my xr3 without bothering to change out of my work clothes and head to the apartment I'm sharing with Carles, one of the company's six partners. He pays the rent – or the company does, what do I care – and I live there the whole week and he only comes over on Tuesdays and Thursdays after an aphrodisiac dinner for his indispensable semi-weekly fuck. Today being Thursday, there's a ninety per cent chance that Mr Carles will arrive around eleven/eleven-thirty with his usual floozy. The one he's had for the last three months (Mr Carles is very loyal to his whores) goes by the name of Jenny. I tell you right now, I'd eat her up, strawberries, fig, apple and all, if it weren't for the fact I'm not accustomed to paying for it and the fact she must earn in one night what I do in a month. But, as Mín would say: her loss.

I get to the apartment (Provença, two hundred and some-thing, fifth floor, second flat), shower up and go out onto the balcony with a beer. I roll a couple of blunts, suitable for all audiences, and light another of blunt force while watching the unwavering traffic warden who everyday leaves a ticket on my car. Eleven months I've lived here and those little yellow and pink slips must add up to a hundred, but given the car is registered in

Manresa one more of this or that colour is all the same to me. I finish the beer and the blunt instrument, inhale the twilight slowly descending over Eixample, an urban landscape between tribal and metropolitan, and put on the first dry thing I find on the clotheshorse. I should really do a wash but I wouldn't hang it until who knows when and, anyway, tomorrow's Friday, and Saturday I'll do everything. I make sure the communal bathroom is tidy, even though the main bedroom has an en suite, and leave the flat jacketless. I have no fucking clue where Fermí *le fou* lives, bearing in mind he changes hidey-hole every few weeks, but I do know where he works. If what he does can be called work, that is.

My scarlet xr3 – christened Marlene in keeping with Lily's tradition of naming our dearly beloved vehicles – awaits me on the opposite kerb with a pink rectangle on the windscreen: 1,000 for each wheel, including the spare – you do the maths. I put her into gear and head up Aribau towards the city's private parts. I decide to pull into La Vila de Gràcia because it's still early and because I feel like a jet black jet from the barrel in the cosy right angle of some square. I settle on Plaça del Sol in case that sweet Venetian who works at *El Cafè* is about but the grizzly behind the bar tells me no one's heard from her since Monday. I order a pint of stout, head out onto the terrace and sit down next to two slim, long-legged Scandinavians, languid looking and looking lost. I sculpt a dovetail joint and erupt into an inner smile at the anticipated aftertaste of the Barcelona night as I sigh over the AWOL Venetian (Sonia, she said her name was).

I reconsider my non-intervention policy and accept my role of affable Mediterranean male and solve the Nordic nymphs' orientation problems with the help of their map. The livelier of the two suggests I forget about Fermí and play guide for a ride but an urgent desire makes me turn them down: I much prefer two rounds with Guzmán *El Malo* than four sordid snowhite breasts, however generous. Tonight, at least. So I pay, start her up and get going.

On the corner, ten metres down from the disco where big man earns his beans, is a Galician restaurant with the luxury of a small terrace and a large kitchen. I'm not feeling particularly hungry but I'll have a tapa of thinly sliced cured ham (always delicious) and a few beers. I arrive at nine thirty-seven and the club doesn't open until midnight but with a bit of luck one of his workmates will fly by to munch, like me, on something *galego*. Like clockwork: fifteen minutes later I spot giant Javi who works on the door and the little brunette from the cloakroom whose name I don't remember. While I'm chewing over how best to ask her without causing offense, a panther pink British convertible mounts two wheels onto the kerb next to the terrace. Out of the passenger door steps an exquisite ebony model and from the driver's seat: Mr Fermín Guzmán Rual, wearing tailored Italian shorts, a Scottish bonnet and Yankee sunglasses! And to think *that* is what accuses *me* of having no taste…

He hugs me, sits down, introduces me to Ghana, his black beauty, and invites the others to join our table. He takes my last slice of ham over to the telephone and the solitary table magically transforms into a banquet. Javi remembers me affectionately and the brunette, who's called – or says she's called – Noemí, smiles at me as if we'd slept together the previous night: you see, being a friend of Mín's can mean any number of things to any number of people. However, the African princess, by far and away the most interesting of the bunch, has gone inside, maybe to the toilet, maybe to the telephone.

The waiter appears with clams, prawns, octopus and more sliced ham, and leaves the plates on an empty table next to us. Then Fermí comes over and asks if I've had dinner but before I can respond he slips smilingly away. More telephone. Or more toilet. I finish my beer and when I call the waiter to bring me another he comes over with a bottle of Ribeiro. As we eat, Mín (the lovable bastard has sat his girl Ghana between the two of us) puts me through an exhausting examination.

'If you're after gear,' he fires at me, not mincing his words, 'Noemí should have some. I don't do it anymore, as you already know.'

To hear Fermín Guzmán say that, and say it happily, as if he didn't miss it in any way, fills me with hope because I often feel something is missing and it's terrifying.

'I wouldn't have come all the way here just to score smack, Mín.'

'Well you've caught me by pure fucking chance because this is my night off.'

'Great!'

He went inside to ask for the bill and sat back down, this time on my lap, while waving the piece of paper in front of my face and asking how I was for John Dough. My first thought was to let him fall on his arse and walk away, but instead I told him fine while swaying him coyly from side to side. He's got a strange way of doing things but the man's more legit than the Crown Court. At least with me.

'How d'you fancy three purples for dinner and a spot of cocaine for two? Or are you washing your hair tonight?'

'Give me one for dinner and keep the cocaine.'

We settled things just like that and got in the preposterous pink panther to roll back down the hill into the city centre. A few dirty raindrops helped to freshen up the atmosphere and deepen the green patina along Passeig de Gràcia. But I was only praying not to end up sloshing around in needles. Or maybe that's exactly what I was hoping for, I really can't tell.

I attempted a conversation in French with the divine model and just as we were getting onto Camus and Genet, Mín pulled over next to Plaça de Tetuan. She departed with a kiss for him and a huge smile for the both of us and I got in the front to discuss the Five Ws of the night ahead.

'Trust me,' he said, overflowing with anticipation, 'you're going to try something that will make you forget all about heroin.'

'Hah, hah, hah!!' I roared, between curiosity and disbelief.

We did a lap of inner Barcelona while squaring up I don't know what calculations on the buy and sell circuit with various stops at different banks (cash machines were the new vogue) to take out half my savings and godknowswhat else. He had a savings book and two cards, none of them in his name, but it didn't seem at all strange because Mín always lived that way when he could.

Then he took us back uptown to the snobby bars and made me wait in the car for twenty minutes. But of all the innumerable waits in cars he's put me through this was by far the sweetest. It was cinematically comfortable in the cosy Jaguar, smoking spliffs like there was no tomorrow, listening to an Eagles album at a sweet volume, waiting for Mr *Malo* to open Pandora's chest. Before long he is back with a happy-go-lucky half smile and two baggies full of pink capsules ('pink shuttles', according to the dealer) and three blocks later, after we're stopped by a spot of standard inner city traffic, we both down a shuttle with a swig of cold beer. From the looks of things, we've got a lot of work to do, in Figueres, in Girona, in Sitges, in…

It's ten fifty-three and we're heading straight on the Diagonal towards the AP-7. We've closed the roof and the tank is full. I roll and light another joint and we start chatting like old times. More accurately, he chats and I listen, just like old times, but now with more reason than ever because my experiences at the workshop can't compare with his adventures at the nightclub.

'So the whole scene starts when two nut jobs come in last

night, round half three. The taller of the two still knew where he was but his mate was up to his short arse in whisky and cocaine and it didn't paint a pretty picture. He starts hitting on Ghana, who was there with a friend of a friend and when this friend and then Tomàs – you know how he gets, always braver than a tiny tailor – start showing him who's boss the guy lands two punches on them so fucking big I reckon their heads are still spinning.

'In short: shit storm in the middle of the bar, Ghana's friend and fearless Tomàs on the floor, tables tipping over, glasses smashing and wild child's pal desperately trying to break up the bar brawling and get his mate out of there. Finally he gets him up the stairs and we break with custom and don't go outside to serve him his own arse on a plate because it really wasn't worth it. But just when it looks like the show's over we hear the unmistakable sound of a gun being fired.

'We go bounding up the stairs only to find the tall one on the floor with a circle of blood on his forehead, lying by Javi's feet who's got his arms stretched in the air like a windmill and clearly shitting himself. Wild child is three metres away holding one of those guns so heavy you've got to use both hands to blow someone away with it. Then he stares at us, one by one, in silence.

'I swear to you I thought he was going to kill someone else, and Javi was odds on because he was first in line and he's a big target, too. Ignacio, me and Tomàs, in that order, were stood behind him, frozen, when the dude hails a cab, cool as you like, puts the piece in his pocket and gets in like nothing's happened. Memorise the license plate, memorise the license plate! was all I kept thinking.'

'You're pulling my leg…' I protest unconvincingly.

'Not likely! You'll read about it tomorrow in La Vanguardia because Enric, one of the owners, knows someone who works there. Or go ask them down at the police station on the square.

They're the ones that turned up and are running the investigation.'

'Man, what a trip! They come in for a drink and one ends up shooting the other dead!'

'Wouldn't surprise me if we ended up the same.'

'Good thing we don't carry guns on us.'

'On us, no. But in the car...'

Needless to say we were just kidding around so when he opens the glove compartment and I see a gun inside a holder, my smile turns rigid. I don't tend to get rattled over just anything but a gun is a gun is a gun, right? And I doubt it was there just to be admired.

'It's loaded. Are you scared?' he laughs, reading apprehension in my silence.

'What do you want me to say? The tool in itself doesn't scare me. The reason why you're carrying it, perhaps. But that's what adventures are made of...'

'In other words, you came to see me because you needed a good time.'

'Like a hole in the head.'

And we laugh and laugh when I suddenly realise that something is going on inside of me while the motorway zips by at two hundred km/h. A new, strange sensation that I can't define spreads up my spine towards the medulla oblongata and from there into my head and back through my entire body.

'Anyway, if I am to believe a word of what you're telling me, at least tell me how it ends.'

'Well, if you didn't believe the beginning I don't know how you're going to take the end because it turns out that murderer and murdered...'

'Don't tell me... were cops.'

'Very *good*, Alex the Great. Very clever indeed! Drug squad lieutenants no less.'

'Who just happened to pop in by chance…'

'Ah, well that's not clear yet. According to the police they were off duty.'

'And you believe that?'

'Mate, that guy wasn't in a state to police anything or anyone. He wasn't too far off snorting one last line and dropping dead on the mirror like Tomàs' older brother.'

'What? Ginger Dan? He fell on the mirror?'

'Perforated his skull and an air bubble got into his brain. Collapsed right on top of the mirror with the tube still in his nose.'

'Holy shit!!' – and then a pus-filled pause in memory of Dead Dan – 'Going back to what we were saying, I'd be on red alert for a few days. I'm sure down at the station they know perfectly well what goes on at the club.'

'Why d'you suppose we're on the Road to Nowhere as usual?'

And we laugh, and laugh some more, and I feel whatever it was rise up my spinal cord once again – a tender warmth that flows up my back, into my brain, and back out to everywhere. No doubt he feels the same or more and is only waiting for me to mention it first.

'These little pink pills seem like fun. I think I'll drop another one.'

'Whoa, easy boy! Skin up and wait half an hour.'

'But I'm starting to feel it coming up. Whatever *it* is.'

'Roll another one before we roll into Girona. We've got a spot of bizniz there.'

'But spliffs only make me thirsty and we're out of beers.'

'What a pair, you and your thirst!' he laughs while opening the glove compartment again.

'You're not going to shoot me to help me get rid of it, are you?'

'It's probably the only effective method! But, no, I'll wait. Next to the gun there's a small bottle with a black label: do me a flavour, would you dearie?'

'You see? Now that I do like. Even the gun loses its bad vibes next to a bottle of single malt.'

'Damn right. Makes the movie sweeter.'

'And gives it colour. Six irons are always scarier in black and white.'

'Damn right.'

I take a swig like a boss just as the Springsteen tape finishes and pick out another by King Crimson, 'cos I know Mín idolises them, and then get busy rolling one with two papers. We're touching two hundred but the British chassis is steadier than a French train. A few drops of rain begin to fall and we enjoy a long silence during the infinite minutes of 'Larks' Tongues in Aspic, Part One'. Though Mín's tapes never have any more than the group's name on them, if that, I know what record it is because I annihilated three copies of the very same one ten years ago at Woodstock's through overuse and abuse.

'It's sort of like acid,' I seem to mumble out loud.

'Yeah, but only for short moments.'

'Ah, now I get what you mean! Right now it's got this sort of extra sweet gallop.'

'You get it?'

'I *feel* it.'

And now nothing but the silence of the motorway impregnated with thunderous Crimson.

'You like it?'

'The music or the ecstasy?'

'Two tricks, same magic.'

'True, true. Honestly, I love it. I don't think I can finish this joint though…'

'About time.'

'Mate, I'm high as a kite.'

'Hah, hah!! About time for that as well…!'

He laughs while my head goes shooting upwards to one of the many stratospheres beyond the mundane. I finish the most disgusting blunt of my life, convinced that dear Fermí, the apple of my eye, has poisoned me.

'But you're having a good time, I trust?' he asks.

'Yeah but I'm a bit scared.'

'Hah, hah, hah! Scared! Live a little, you filthy junkie. You ain't gonna die 'cos of one little ecstasy!'

'I hope not. But I'm seriously high.'

'Let yourself fly a little. When you're back, you'll be in the pink.'

'In the pink pill.'

'Aye, just a wee pinkie.'

And he was right, just for a damn change, because he knew what he was talking about from experience. I've got to say those pinkies are one of the most glorious substances I've ever tried. In fact, the night, the car and the company catapulted my virgin flight to the zenith of what we called a Night Out of this World. The rhythm rose and fell and went serenely from one colour to another, occasionally imprinting the supraintellectual depth of LSD only to change direction towards a peaceful hilarity or measured euphoric ebb or ecstatic general relaxation that went upwards, always upwards, without ever losing itself. They were reactions that could be attributable at different times to cocaine, heroin, speed and who knows what unknown etceteras: it seemed a very special sort of cocktail. Special and spatial because, if you put your mind to it, you could make sense of any type of intelligent idea however complicated. But at the same time – and this was the most surprising thing of all – it had a sociable vibe to it that meant we could stop in any service station like it was nothing and refresh our aristocratic appellation, as Mín put it, with a few proletarian beers, and above all to make a couple of calls.

'Everything's sweet,' he purred as he put the receiver down.

'Sweet as a nut,' I winked back at him while raising my beer bottle, despite feeling both there and inside an unreal dream bubble.

'You wanna drive?'

'Aren't we running late? I can't go at two hundred like you.'

'Late? Late for what? You got to be back before midnight, Cindy?'

'Oh, right, no, of course not. I'm putting the cart before the horsepower.'

And then the inevitable reprise of laughter.

'Relax. You want to drive until Girona?'

'Much appreciated.'

And we laugh and laugh and pay and leave and then it's more motorway (twenty minutes, according to him) and more music and ecstasy and silence at full volume. Inside my head: inside the totality of my being.

'You're number one, Mín. I'll be grateful for tonight for as long as I live.'

'Careful, Lex, don't make promises you can't keep. Anyway, we're only now just getting into the knickers of the night.'

'Yeah, but I'm visualising a whole range of new concepts…'

'…that you will have forgotten tomorrow afternoon when you're showering off the night.'

'I don't think so. I'm pretty stubborn when it comes to ideas. You know that.'

Lex knows how to do everything except make money. He doesn't let himself go with life's impulses, which is a ride you have to take without baggage or predetermined destinations, always prepared to reach the end of the line, any place, any time.

His problem (and I know him as if I'd given birth to the kid)

is that he still believes one day he'll understand what he calls...
ssshh!... *human existence*. Hah, hah, hah and *hah*! Hooman
eczistans! I'm no one to be quoting the prophets but what Christ
said about the birds comes to mind: 'if God provides food for
the birds all year round, why do we, being bigger and smarter,
have to worry about anything?'

In any case (as he always says), it's great the little birdie flew
past tonight of all nights and that he's accompanying me on this
voyage: we'll make an unforgettable night of it, just you wait.

'We had a hundred of these ecstasies reserved and they have
to be paid for and off our hands *tonight*.'

'A hundred?!'

'No more, no less. Half for Figueres-Girona, and fifteen or
twenty will stay in Sitges.'

'And you lot do home delivery?'

'Here's the theme of the scheme: they were s'posed to come
down to the club and pick them up *tonight* but the ways things
have gone we opted for a chartered flight.'

'And that's why Tomàs lent you the pink panther.'

'The idiot broke his wrist last night getting his arse kicked
by that midget.'

'Answer me something, Mín. How is it that Tomàs can
afford a king's car on a lower league barman's wage?'

'That's a story chocker-block with an array of risks, my dear
boy. I doubt your yellow belly would be able to stomach it.'

'Oh, no, I was only asking in the abstract sense!'

'Dealing night and day in anything with a price tag: drugs,
guns, women, cars, jewellery, credit cards. Even antiques and
paintings.'

'But when we dealt we earned just enough to survive.'

'What you're forgetting is that we were very experienced
users but complete dealer apprentices.' After a minimal pause

of, let's just call it 'nostalgia' and be done with it, I pick up the thread. 'There are ways and then there are ways. And in between there's a whole hierarchy. Whatever the case – and mark my words sonny Jim – Tomàs takes too many risks and needs to start watching his step.'

'If he knew you like I do he'd listen, for Fermí is true to his Word and his Word is true.'

'I'm forever saying to him: "Ground Control to Major Tom! Ground Control to Major Tom! You're circuit's dead, there's something wrong." But does he listen? Like fuck, he does.'

When we enter the city Lex asks if I want to take the car but I tell him no and begin giving him directions.

'Drop me off on the corner. Park up somewhere and wait for me in that bar over there, okay?'

'Okay.'

I love this boy to bits because you can take him anywhere. And you can always trust him, straight down the line. Yeah, he's got his hang-ups and, sure, he's a bit wet behind the ears but the kid's more kosher than a straight judge. Bingo-balling to one side, when they checked me into the Hotel I was lucky to have him and Lily.

I walk the twenty metres to the designated door and buzz the flat in question. An interphonic voice mumbles 'who?' and I answer 'Tomàs.' The door opens almost in tandem, I stride over to the lift and then it's up two floors, up to the flat. While the girl sets me up with an almost cold beer, the guy starts telling me forty. Or even fifty – if I can give him ten now, pay later.

The guy ordered thirty and now he wants fifty. I take a polite swig of beer and light a cigarette as I prepare my best sub-smile (Harry Lime style): oh, well, it goes without saying how oh-so-sorry I am, but this product you see here is in high demand and this is all the stock we currently have. An order's been placed, I assure you, and we're expecting a delivery, so maybe we'll have more next week. The problem now is that the price has gone up slightly and we left ourselves a tad short this time round.

I improvise all that off-the-cuff guff 'cos it's clear the guy has figured out these pink shuttles are the fucking A-bomb and wants to get his mitts on as many as he can for when they do run out. Cheeky bastard. But we're one step ahead, as usual, and this is exactly how we played it.

We go over some other business and I manage to get twenty thousand *peles* out of him that were more than overdue, which will put me in Tomàs' good books. In return I give him three E's of a different type, not quite on the same level (but watcha gonna do?), and half the half gram of high grade green pea coke crystals which, strictly speaking, belong to Tomàs, but oh well.

I take the freshly rolled ready to light dutchie from the ashtray with a second and final sub-smile at the girl, only half as generous as the first, and remind the guy that the club is under surveillance and that phones are a no-no until further no-notice. Then I hand him back the Flemish flute in order not to attract any unwanted attention on street level and leave.

Once I'm back in the lift, I hide the notes in a secret pouch in my beret and secure the velcro (routines of the trade).

Lex is stood outside the bar sipping a Guinness and chewing over two sweetlittlesixteens with a carnivorous gaze but when he sees me arrive he chucks me the keys and tells me where the car is. I head over to it with a silent nod and he goes inside to pay for his beer and buy another one for me.

'Fuck, it's a shame we gotta to go to Sitges 'cos both Girona and Figueres are worthy of a night,' I mutter as we circulate between people and cars, through what they call 'atmosphere', towards the city's medieval centre where we're to meet Olaf who's come down from Figueres so we don't have to go up there.

'On a Thursday?'

'Any night of the week. At least during the six months of summer.'

'You're casting the net wider, I see.'

'As wide as I can.'

'Let's do it next week.'

'You're on.'

I head directly towards the bar where we've agreed to meet and already clock Olaf waiting on the terrace before we get there. I pull up on the corner, shout over to him (the open top in the city has its advantages) and he gets up quick – too quick, in fact – and reaches the car with three supersonic steps. My kid partner frees up the front by getting in the back.

I improvise a five minute route, mindful not to go too far, too fast, selecting the right streets, while Olaf and Lex exchange items, money and pleasantries. Olaf – even Olaf – assures me he can take a few more if credit is available and such is my disappointment – oh Olaf, you of all people! – that I dump him on the next corner without another word and without doing the fat one I was planning on offering him. My partner and I will draw ourselves a couple of continuous lines to follow onto the highway of our lives.

The first thing I ask Fermí after that shadow Olof has slipped away is if he knows who he's risking his money with. It was obvious Olaf was on the horse, no doubt gunning it, and it was equally obvious that he was dragging a hefty monkey behind him. Bed bugs are a strange sort of brotherhood and they, ahem, we, recognise each other, loaded or sick, with just a couple of glances. But Mín was in a good mood and labelled me a fascist. 'We've been just as hooked as him. And, when we were, that was precisely when we needed to deal more than ever. Am I right or am I right?'

Of course he was right. It wasn't thirty months since he'd quit horse riding but he could still give me the occasional kick up the arse. And I was always quick to get on the defensive and turn my nose up at my... *unfortunate comrades in misfortune.*

Without wasting any more time Fermí pulls onto the motorway and immediately pulls into the first service station to fix two good golly miss molly lines of blow the colour of shamrockandroll (in the toilet, one in-one out, of course). I snorted mine without thinking much about it because my mind and soul were so very far away: they were sauntering like libertines amid the gloomy colours from a much too certain past towards the uncertain colours of an inferred future over an iridescent but ephemeral bridge in the present... It might seem ridiculous but that day – that night – in Girona and, later on, I had the impression I could laugh and enjoy myself again after so long of not daring to; that I could be and feel after so long of not knowing how. Me. Without heroin... perhaps without any hard drugs. In other words, recovering the joy of living one day, one evening, one hour; of bearing the weight of my own existence, whatever its worth, from the present moment until the definitive end.

From that wondrous reunion, in essence the prologue to our second stint together, I could outline many more details, post-mortems and etceteras but the most spectacular is un-doubtedly our Neapolitan adventure. But from that particular night, beyond the aforementioned flash of existential awareness, alongside the private, untranslatable sensation of omnipresent, perpetual well-being, I remember a surreal episode in a Sitges side street amid a queue of angry cars behind a dustbin lorry and the two of us laughing and getting out of the Jag to ask the other drivers why the rush to get somewhere when right here, inhaling the night, they could be perfectly happy! Needless to say, they weren't amused, not by a long shot, and the fact there were two of us was what most likely saved us from a beating. But we, or rather, our superfluous generation floating between Utopia and No Future has always been misunderstood.

In one final attempt to complete an impossible kaleidoscope, I'll risk a quick sketch of our last splash at dawn down on the Sitges sand.

'You're such an ass,' said Fermí.

'You are too then, because knowing it you still take me out for a walk.'

'But at least I always have a girl,' he said in his defence before cupping the right breast of his latest catch snared with two whiskies and one line at the penultimate club of our lives.

'Yeah, because unlike me, you're an ass that pushes *and* pulls.'

We both fucked her, one after the other, or perhaps at the same time, because Mín had made it a question of honour, or maybe she was the one that fucked us, separately or simultaneously, because instinctively I understood, however real it was in the ephemeral present, that the following day it would be a dream. I don't know what her name was, nor do I care, and as far as I'm aware, the only connection we have is that bizarre, sordid scene.

Often I'd like to forget all my names and beings and be something else: a mountain, a tree… a pebble far from any path.

SOMETHING FOR EVERYONE AND EVERYONE ON SOMETHING

1. *Intro: Strictly sober*

I'll keep on singing,
until the sun comes up!
LONE STAR

I honestly didn't think it was a good idea, but whatcha gonna do? I'm not suggesting it was entirely his fault, of course not, because me, what a piece a work, right? It's just that Lex and I are like two flammable gases stable when kept apart but which explode of out of sheer compatibility the moment they come into contact. For that very reason, one of my personal prison promises back in Lleida during the whole of '82 and the first third of '83 was to maintain a safe distance. No jealousies, no hard feelings. Just a healthy bit of fear, nothing more. But the kid was bored out of his numskull with the van and the workshop, and after hooking up with Noemí, the brunette from the cloakroom who sold smack, he started going out with us after we closed, half the time going to work without having been home. To be completely honest, I still don't know how he didn't cause a pile up on the road. In short: they set Tomàs up at the big new bandstand in Poble Nou (a neighbourhood fast becoming fashionable in light of the hypothetical Olympic Games) and by the time I took over the club Lex had already spoken to Enric and signed a contract.

Four months have gone past (if I've got my maths right that makes today New Year's Eve) and as things stand we've stayed strictly sober. In terms of tar, that is. And that's despite Noemí usually having some and the temptation being both in and on the house. Naturally, we pay the price with every other substance going: cocaine, ecstasy, whisky, amps and, Lex being Lex, industrial amounts of spliffs of all sizes and ingredients. If there were such a thing as an all-you-can-smoke buffet, Lex would put them out of business because at any hour of any day or night, in any situation and high on anything, even when he's no longer even able to stand, he's always ready to skin up. I give it a wide berth, personally; quality bud, maybe, but hash only makes me feel tired, dirty and bored.

Alongside work, dealing and drugs we also share an apartment (since I left my old man's almost fifteen years ago he must be the person I've spent most nights with under the same roof). I would've preferred to avoid it, in all honesty, but Lex had an amazing flat slap bang in the middle of Eixample that a partner from the company passed over to him before going to work overseas and I had little option because Tomàs' place had been too crowded for too long. I'm aware it's very practical from a bizniz perspective because we have everything to hand, and when it comes to Yma (who, by the way, we don't and will never share) three quarters the same because she needs a place to eat and sleep like a normal person. At least until we get home after our post-bar bar drinks. There are days we still aren't home when she leaves at seven-thirty but most mornings I'm back between six and seven to wake her up with a lovin' spoonful. Maybe it's because I'm getting on in years, after all, I'll be thirty-one in sixteen days, but for the first time in my life I can actually picture myself working on my wrinkles next to a woman: oh, Yma, my saintly sex bomb!

2. *New Year's Eve chronicle for choir and soloists*

Welcome, come on in, come on in
and we'll turn our sadness to smoke.
'Any Night the Sun Can Come Out', SISA

I told them to work it out themselves because, New Year's or
no New Year's, I had to work and I wouldn't have time to buy
anything until the evening. I'm still waiting to see just what
they're planning on doing exactly because it's seven already
and all we have in the fridge are dates, cucumbers, asparagus,
tomatoes, cheese and a couple of pots of pâté and caviar. I'm
guessing they're the starters that Pere the painter and Leo the
ceramist are in charge of.

I better take a shower now before the house begins filling up
with people and it wouldn't be a bad idea to lie down for a bit, too,
before the end of year begins. Hang on... if they've already brought
the starters over, then where on earth *are* Leonor and Pere?

'Do me a favour, Leo, and open the door.'

'You've got the keys.'

'I gave them to you in the shop. They're in your purse.'

'What are you talking about? You've got them in your pocket.'

But, of course, they aren't in my pocket or in her purse and
there's me, frozen dessert in my frozen fingers, wondering if I
should put it down on the floor, pass it to her, or chuck it over
the side of the staircase.

'Ring the bell, Leo. Maybe someone's in.'

Leo holds the bell down for a long while. Silence. I put the
cake down on the floor and Leo tries again: two long rings with
one impatient pause in between. More silence as I grab her bag
and rifle through it myself. Leo insists with a series of short

rings, topped off by an interminable one. I leave her bag on the floor and check – carefully, conscientiously – all of my pockets. Meanwhile she has her finger held on the bell for another three long rings, after which we hear Yma snap back:

'Al*right*, al*right*! I'm *coming*!!'

And then a further thirty seconds wait as we argue over whose responsibility it is to go back to the patisserie three blocks away and look for the cocksucking keys. But when she bends over to pick up the cake, I hear a jingle jangle so I thrust my hand into her anorak pocket and (what do you know?) I pull out the cluster of keys Mínos gave us. And right on cue Yma, a thick dressing gown wrapped around her, a wet towel on her head, opens the door.

'I'm so sorry, Yma,' is all she can think to say. 'We couldn't find the keys.'

'*You* couldn't find the keys! The bloody keys were in your bloody pocket!'

'And you'll be reminding me of it all bloody night!'

'Until next year, at least.'

'Could you do the favour of coming in? I'm *bloody* freezing!' interrupts Yma. And then half to herself: 'God, you're like an old married couple!'

We go in and leave the things on the table, and Leo says that's *exactly* what we are but I choose to bite my tongue because this has been going on too long already and it's high time we ended it. Then Leo goes over to the sink and starts rinsing the vegetables while I, from the kitchen doorway, contemplate Yma's reflection in the wardrobe mirror as she slips into the bra and knickers wet dreams are made of. If it weren't for *bloody* Leo I'd go straight into the bedroom and make her a couple of offers she couldn't refuse. Mín, at the end of the daydream, doesn't deserve her and won't be able to hold onto her for long.

The phone rings and Yma comes rushing out of the bedroom and towards the living room wearing only her underwear and a pair of pink espadrilles. She perches on the arm of the sofa nearest to the door and I see her, legs apart, balancing one pink shoe on the end of her big toe, her erect nipples visible under the claret-coloured silk. She looks in my direction and smiles. But not at me, rather at her invisible interlocutor, a person I only know by name, some girl called Lluïsa.

All things considered: I don't know why the fuck we said yes. Quite what Àngel and I would be missing by not being there among all those strangers, I do not know. One thing is having dinner, Mín and Lex and me, without any partners... But New Year's Eve, and all the madness that word implies, should never be risked in a mixed environment. If it weren't for the fact they had it all organised and that it would seem rude, instead of see you at ten I would've said see you next year.

But then again, Àngel and I would've only seen it in at home, at most going down to the pub on the corner for a whisky, so at least Lex and Mín will make me laugh all night long. And boy am I in need of some laughter. But it also makes me feel bored. Bored beyond belief. Like almost everything does these days.

But I'll have to lighten up a little unless I want to rain on everyone's parade, which I don't. Good job I still have half a gram of that smooth-trotting Thai horse. In addition to Mín and Lex (oh my dear Lex, recovered after three whole years!), who alone justify the risk of the party, there will also be Yma and Tomàs (who I met only recently after bumping into Mín one lazy Sunday afternoon in El Born), a painter and his ceramicist other half, and some stranger (whose job is being a millionaire) called Enric Costales.

'Hello? It's Enric.'

'Where are you? The line's terrible.'

'*I'm* terrible. I'm at Madrid Airport. You've got to do me a favour, Aurora.'

'What's wrong now? You know we're rushed off our feet here.'

'Grab a box and a half of that *nature* we have on offer, half of sparkling wine, and another half of white Rioja for the seafood, and have it sent to the following address. If no one can go now, call a cab.'

'Gotcha…'

'Oh, and add a few bottles of rosé and two or three of a good red, in case anyone's fussy. Make a note of it under my name and we'll sort it out later.'

'Gotcha…' repeats Aurora, manager of the most famous of Enric's three Barcelona restaurants. 'Am I not invited to this alcoholic orgy?' she asks after confirming order and address.

'Of course! If you feel like it…'

'Will anyone I know be there?'

'Yes, actually. Painter Pere, Maria Leonor… and your dear Tomàs.'

Luckily I only have to take care of the coke and they've had it put aside for me for days: exactly half an ounce of a sparkly-scaled substance such an occasion calls for. They wouldn't sell it this clean and uncut even for ten thousand pessetes a gram! I hope the others know how to appreciate it and chip in because I still owe for it. But best not to think about that right now.

With any luck I'll earn one hundred thousand pessetes net at the bar tonight, both over and under the counter. If all goes well, maybe even one hundred and fifty. And then I'll get the whole lot of them off my back in one swoop because the bottom line is if things don't add up then before you know it ten years have flown by and you're dealing on desolation row.

Luckily, Enric will keep five or six grams and pay upfront, and Pere p'raps two or three if he doesn't have any. No, yes, more or less – normally they all behave as they should, apart from that dick Fermí, who has it in his head that the merch grows on trees just because we've done a few hook ups together. But Mín is Mín and there ain't nothing you can do about it.

Luckily, everyone is already there when I ring the doorbell at ten past ten (we're only waiting on Enric who phoned from the shower saying he was on his way ASAP) and they've delegated tasks: Fermí is making sure the wine and cava sent by Enric are all at optimum temperature; Yma and Leonor are in the kitchen putting the finishing touches to the seafood and the starters; Pere is in the living room with a carving knife preparing a dozen lines; and next to him is some guy, cocktail shaker in hand, who I recognise from El Born and who Pere tells me is 'some friend of Lluïsa called Àngel.'

What the *fuck* am I doing here? I don't like the fact she takes drugs, not one little bit, because it's clear they're killing her but if you love her then... patience, Àngel, patience. But why the *hell* did I allow myself to be duped into spending New Year's with this group of coked up snobs?

If she fancied an all-out orgy with her old allies, then perfect. I would have arranged to spend the evening at my parents' or my brother's and no hard feelings. Or just the two of us, alone and peaceful at home; our pretty little house at the bottom of Tibidabo, which will never be pretty and will never be ours because instead of living there she overshadows it. But if I must resign myself to the truth, I would have been awfully frightened not coming with her, wondering what she was up to and with whom the whole night. The entire silent night sweating blood until who knows what time tomorrow.

I serve the dry martinis I've just finished preparing, starting with the kitchen, just like my mother showed me. But I bet they don't know how to appreciate a good martini or good manners. The brunette erogeneity is Yma, with a 'y', God knows y, and the one with blonde hair, big tits and long legs is – despite looking like the exact opposite of a virgin – called Maria and/or Leonor.

This affected little thing who came with that Lluïsa girl is trying to force a drink into my hands just as I'm carrying two plates of starters over to the dining table. The interphone buzzes but my hands are full. Tomàs is busy doing a bump and Pere gives me a look as though carrying plates and opening doors were the essence of my existence. I place the platters on the table and go over to the blow mirror when the interphone buzzes again. 'Can't you hear somebody's ringing?' says Pere, slowly pronouncing each sarcastic syllable.

'I'm deaf. You go. You've got two legs like the rest of us.'

He gets up with an ironic glance and goes over to answer the interphone while I clear my nose, pick up Tomàs' silver tube and snort my line. As dear Lex often says (who's gone missing in action with ghost girl Lluïsa, by the way), either we all get high or the dealer gets it.

Fermí comes out of the kitchen with three bottles of cava just as I catch a glimpse of a giant, glowing cherry on the balcony and the shadows of a man and a woman heavy kissing. It goes without saying that I couldn't care less what they get up to but, just for the record, it's Lluïsa and Lex.

'Maria's looking,' I giggle quietly.

'And who's this Maria? The carpenter's wife?'

'Hah, nearly! The painter made an honest woman of her.'

'What a customer, that Pere! He's one of those that undress you with their eyes.'

'I did the same. As soon as I saw you.'

'You're a different type of monster. But don't get soppy on me now. You know a bit of celebratory lip service on a night like this doesn't mean a thing. Come on, let's go back inside.'

We go back inside just as Enric appears and now that we're all here we raise our martini glasses, shaken not stirred, and excellently prepared according to my taste. But I go and stick my foot in it for the second (or third) time by congratulating Àngel, who offers me more with the coldness of an English butler and the stare of a Roman conspirator. I pass the ticket booth, hit a bump of candy like there's no tomorrow and light a primo freshly prepared by Tomàs. Afterwards I greet Enric with a heartfelt kiss on each cheek and we all take our places around the table.

I have lily Lluïsa's right knee agonisingly close to my left one and I'm aware, too aware, of the contacts, involuntary or premeditated, brief or persistent. This woman has a power over me that has nothing to do with simple sexual attraction. And to make things worse it doesn't wane, regardless of how many years go by.

The seafood platters are splendid and the succulent starters out of this world. The coke Tomàs has brought with him is handonheartofhearts among the best I've ever tried, and the cava and wine are more than worthy of their supporting role. In other words, if I don't lose my head over Lily and the gift of a healthy half kiss amid an exultant evening, the night will be, as Mín would say, unforgettable.

3. *New Year's Eve chronicle for choir and soloists: Continuation*

Morning has broken
Like the first morning
CAT STEVENS

After the monstrous boredom of Christmas Day, Boxing Day and all that, the New Year's Eve party was an unforgettable night: one of those that will live in the annals of infamy. At any rate, the first anecdote of the year came courtesy of Andy the Jerkoff, one our main suppliers, who phoned at twenty-two minutes to twelve asking if we still wanted the box of cava we'd ordered: cava being fifty of those pink E's we hadn't seen for almost three months. You betcha we wanted the box! We'll be right over!

So at three minutes to a quarter to midnight, we got in Lex's Marlene and after a couple of steps on the gas and a few more turns of the wheel were outside Andy's, which luckily wasn't far from the flat. The shutter was already halfway down so it was a question of going inside, leaving the money and grabbing the cava.

We get back in the car at six minutes to midnight and Lex, who must have been coke euphoric, burns the first set of lights. When we get to the second, his smile spreads all the way up to his earlobes and he accelerates even more while hitting the horn with short beeps.

'Are you fucking crazy?'

'Stick that rag out the window and make it look like you're having an attack?'

'I *am* about to have an attack!

'Oh, *relaaax*, the pigs aren't flying tonight.'

'Jesus, if the cops catch us now…!'

'I already told you, there aren't any pigs about.'

He jumped a total of seventeen consecutive red lights before parking up in front of the house. He said he'd learnt it from Sandro. Yeah, I can believe that: I've seen first-hand how Sandro would skip traffic and traffic rules, even in the city centre. We didn't come across a single car or pedestrian, at least at the lights. And out of pure luck, no flying pigs, either.

We stepped out of the lift just as the second bell was chiming and they were starting the stupid ritual of eating a grape for each chime. Five minutes later I was explaining to them the utter dementedness of the incident with the traffic lights but no one believed it, except Lily perhaps. The ecstasies went down a treat and everyone took one except for Àngel, who didn't even smoke, and Tomàs, who after dropping one slipped two into his pocket, as always.

In short: we'd made it to Next Year, I mean, 1986. I took advantage of a moment of widespread chaos to lead Yma into the bedroom and give her the ring I'd bought for her. She put it on and started crying but on whether we'd be getting married and when, not a word. Perhaps Lex was right when he told me that if I really wanted to make good with Yma, I'd have to quit drugs and find a different line of work. I always thought he'd said it out of jealousy (Lex always falls in love with my girls) but maybe he was right this time: she was made of finer stuff, was Yma.

The boy loves me, that's for sure, but he's got a screw loose: if those in the middle are bona fide diamonds then the ring must have cost him at least two hundred thousand pessetes! But a ring doesn't buy a marriage: there are much more important things than symbols, however expensive and appreciated they might be.

Just the thought of going out there to play the part of ecstatic-girlfriend-showing-off-her-jewel feels nauseatingly dull but there's nothing I can do about it: Lex is staring at it like he's having visions, Maria Leonor looks slightly jealous, Lluïsa looks more surprised than envious and is staring less at the ring and more at Fermí, Enric winks and gives me a knowing look, whereas Tomàs and Àngel can only see its material value. The last to say his piece – affectionately as only he knows how – is Pere.

'If you leave it with me for a week I could get a great painting out of it,' I announce.

'Yeah, flogging it to Tomàs for cocaine!' protests the loved-up big-spender.

From what it seems, Mínos is deadly serious about Yma: and there I was thinking of kidnapping her just this afternoon! But if it's marriage she's after then he's welcome to her. I've tried that gig already: twice in thirty years, in fact, and both times I've had my fingers burnt. As far as experience shows me, as soon as a man and woman go 'steady' they rapidly develop an unhealthy fungus of possessiveness and auto-affirmation that only has two possible outcomes: one of the two succumbs and lives life for the other, or a continual battle comes down to preserve private territories and initiatives. And the older we get the more weighed down with complexes we become. And I am no exception.

We consume more cava, more pearl, more time. At two on the dot, Màs, Mín and Lex tell us that they really ought to be dressed like penguins behind their respective bars. Tomàs, poor guy, goes off alone to Poble Nou while the rest of us, after tidying up the tiny chaos, will head down to Àlex and Mínos' joint, if only because we'll get in for free and drink on the house. To Enric's health, of course! He is the boss, after all.

I don't know why exactly (out of all the many possible reasons) but I'm horny as fuck, so I signal to Leo from the corridor with my eyebrows. She comes over, full of merrymaking, and I nod towards the bathroom door. She goes in, switches on the light and winks at me. I go in, turn the light off and lock the door behind me. We kiss with open mouths while she takes off her knickers and pulls down my boxers. Luckily, she loves this sort of frivolous fun and sexually speaking we're two peas in a pod; or rather, two dirty minds that think alike.

I see the New Year in with a good fuck from behind, lustful and hard, my mouth tightly closed and my eyes wide open, picturing that girl Lluïsa.

That New Year's night was my last fun night, my last night of genuine debauchery and, definitively, my last big night out. The ecstasy (given I don't touch sniff, even for Sant Joan) gave me a deep intellectual vibe that thrust me outwards and, once I'd convinced Àngel to go home and not wait up for me, the connection and communication with the others was magnificent.

Before heading to the club, Enric took us on a cava-crawl, all five of us crammed into his small Mercedes, the two men up front and the three women in the back, raising and downing our glasses of cava and looking for wine bars where we could buy more.

Pere and Maria Leonor seemed much happier with one another now and were in charge of finding suitable subjects to chat and laugh about. Affable, astute Yma contributed to the conversation with the specialised opinion of a high-ranking civil servant. Maybe she was just eager for us all to acknowledge the importance of her day job in the office of I don't know which parliament front bencher but she was sardonic in the extreme and, whether a mask or not, it paired perfectly with the acerbic, aristocratic humour of our driver, Enric, the one whose job is being a millionaire owner of restaurants, clubs, publishers and whoknowswhatelse.

It must have been half four when we finally arrived at the club, hopping with as much festive excitement as frogs in the rain and, I have to say, despite not knowing them and not being particularly in the mood, I ripped it up like in the old days. After a few discreet nasal rounds – the boys in the office making more racket than a rat-arsed army, me in the toilet wrapped in the privacy of my habit – we regrouped on a sofa next to the dance floor. There were half a dozen glasses and two bottles of cava on the table that Enric had paid for but when I told him to let me pay for at least one, he replied, smiling, that he hadn't paid for them either, at least nowhere near retail price. At the end of the day and night, the club was split straight down the middle between his brother-in-law and him: the evasive Enric Costales Grausec.

Needless to say, she's not my type, but this Lluïsa Cabellera i Enbosc is a classy woman. She has a touch of aloofness, a certain mystery, and it's no surprise that Àlex is so obsessed with her. Such a shame (unless I'm wildly mistaken) that she's still in the saddle. At least tonight. Although I must admit she does carry it beautifully. But there's an inflection in the corner of her mouth, an instinctive tendency to lightly scratch her eyebrows and cheeks… I've never tasted it and I doubt I ever will, not in this incarnation, but I recognise the symptoms almost as well as they do. Out of pure curiosity, I ask Fermí and he answers with one of his vague yet affirmative smiles.

The person who really has problems but doesn't realise is Tomàs. I bought three grams from him just so he didn't find out that I can buy it directly from the same people and at a better price. But he owes them half a kilo and if he doesn't wake up soon they're going to wake him up when he least expects it. I know Bald Eagle and Feliu and one thing Eagle and Liu don't do is feel sorry for the hard-up or hooked. And as far as Àlex and Fermí are concerned, if they don't stop dealing behind the bar they'll have to find another one. I'm laid-back but enough is enough!

One thing is being no saint and doing a few lines once in a while, but another is doing nothing but snorting and selling snow the whole cacophonous night. And they don't deal in order to save money but purely to damage their health!

Never mind, tonight is a party so we'll order more good cava while we still can, but I can't help worrying over Tomás as I refill everyone's glass. Lluïsa, like the sweet sage she seems, asks if something's the matter.

'I was just thinking about a friend…' I say, following my usual policy of never revealing the truth without lying, '… a friend who is happy today but who could well be crying tomorrow.'

'That can happen to any one of us on any given day,' she smiles knowingly yet sadly. 'Is it Tomás?'

No, this isn't the happiest night of my life, even if everything is going perfectly: perhaps everything's going perfectly 'cos of the good vibes of the ecstasy keeping a lid on the excess of coke and cava but, no, it's definitely not the happiest night of my life because Liu and Big Man came in for a menacing whisky and as soon as I saw them, before a single word was spoken, I got the message: Eagle wants to settle my tab. I promised them two hundred thousand slugs tomorrow afternoon – what else could I do! – and they told me they'd be round the flat at two p.m. to pick it up. If I had it, maybe Eagle would be willing to talk about the rest, and if I didn't, the time for talking would be over. It was just a little joke, of course, but I know that big son of a bitch: he's more than capable of sharing a laugh with me today and tomorrow be smashing my ribcage to pieces and then I won't be laughing for another year. They left, trailing their funereal music and swarm of junkie whores, and I got busy like never before translating everything I own into cash, even making a few offers in an attempt to raise more liquid capital. I can make it to two hundred thousand *peles*; I can make it, even if it means asking Richie and Mínos for money. The problem is the deadline. And the fact I already owe Rich Enric a hundred and thirty thousand.

This is the internal discourse, more insistent than I'd like it to be, that pursues me as I serve rum and cokes, cava and beers, and God knows how many whiskies, gins, vodkas and brandies, straight or mixed with all types of fizzy drinks and juices; or as I go to the office or the toilet, grabbing or passing or charging a gram or two of pearl or packs of ten or twenty pills on the way; or as I shove notes of all colour and value into my pockets while adding up the takings, adding up and taking away. By the time night has turned to day and the crowd has begun to thin out, I calculate I'm only short by fifty.

Then I hear the distant echo of an ethylic voice obsessively calling behind me and when I finally turn around, I spot at the end of the bar a dishevelled and unsteady man who keeps shouting 'hhap new year, Tomàsh! hhap new year...!'

I can't believe my eyes. It's only that scarecrow who was with Lluïsa, that uptown snob called...

'Àngel! Dont youu member me? We ssselebrated (hiccup) new yearz togeff juss half hour ago and youu dont member me?? (hiccup) Gimme a wishsky pliz... Yor still open, I hop...'

'Yeah, we're still open,' he smiled back with poorly concealed pity before pouring a trickle of whisky over half the Arctic Circle.

'No, wait... open me a bottle ov the bess cava you got (hiccup). Cava dont get you drunk. At least not like (hiccup) wishhhsky.'

'Where are the others?'

'Youu tell me. I've been... sssent pa-acking. New Year, new LIF! (double hiccup) One less wooman, one more friend. 'Cosh yor my friend, aint ya, Tomàsh.'

'Sure!'

'Well if yor my friend, git me a bottle of cava, I dont wan anymore wish-key!'

I don't remember if it was at that point or later on that I showed him the wad of cash, nor can I be all that sure who told me, like someone chastising a child, to do whatever the hell I wanted as long as I *would just stop crying*. I can't be sure because, at the over-ripe age of thirty-eight, this was my first and last great alcoholic intoxication and at an undetermined moment everything turns fragmentary and nebulous. On the other hand, despite the twenty thousand pessetes I spent at the bar and the fifty thousand I lent Tomàs (and which I will subsequently never see again), from the range of ridiculous ways in which I publicly humiliated myself, the only incident I recall with genuine hurt is the look of embarrassment on the faces of rich Enric, Pere-that-paints and the anti-virgin Maria (or was it Leonor?).

Enric and Pere go straight into the office with Màs and I get dumped with that bottle of cava on legs called Àngel. Mythological little angel guzzling more wine than Dionysus! Pathetic Icarus with wings of hot air asking over his private Eva, rib… snake.

'I think Lluïsa got a taxi,' I make up to pass the time.

'Buwhere'da fuck shego!'

How do I know where the fuck she went! But what I can guess is that she went with her fuck, along with someone else and their fuck, to wherever the fuckity-fuck it is they went together…! But you already know that, don't you, my little angel? You've known ever since we left the flat, perhaps since you got there, and who knows, maybe even before that! I certainly realised what was going on and it has nothing to do with me.

But I'm not going to say another word: I drink another glass of his cava and light one of Pere's primos. The airy fairy has far fewer airs about him, now that alcohol and misery have crumpled his one button suit and the dirty underwear of his soul, now that he's fallen almost to the level of a mere mortal. He looks at me with all the energy of his deplorable state and tries to read what I'm thinking: if the alcohol doesn't prevent him from doing so with a thick black shawl, he'll spend a full quarter turn of the minute hand visualising Lluïsa making love to Lex, aka *Alexander the Gratefully Undead*.

I'm not going to pretend I didn't get my hopes up when I saw them arrive without Àngel, and by 'them' I mean Lluïsa, of course. But within the swelling mayhem, overwhelmed by work and euphoria, we hardly had time to share a dozen words with one another.

'You don't by any chance have a dab of devil for me, do you?' I said as an excuse.

'Devil?'

'Yeah, that's what Enric calls it.'

'I thought you'd quit.'

'It'll be three years in April.'

'What? Not injected, not smoked, not snorted, nothing?'

'Not once. Three whole years.'

'But if you do it now you'll fall short.'

'I'm not scared of it. Not anymore.'

'Then you're in luck because I do happen to have some. I'll fix you a bomb if you like.'

'Wait for me until we close. It's no fun doing it alone.'

'Oh, yeah? Since when?'

When Pere and Maria Leonor slipped off with Enric to make a last-orders call on Tomàs, Lluïsa stayed at Yma's table smoking some Colombian herb. When we were finally able to return to the world of light, we were greeted by a morning dressed up in springtime drag. We decided to stop off for waffles and chocolate, which I wasn't particularly in the mood for, and after getting some from the wagon that's stationed on the corner all year round we went up to the flat, which was waiting for us clean, ventilated and cold because they'd left the balcony open. But the golden barley sun had already reached the rail and would soon be warming up the living room.

During the drive and the brief breakfast, they continued to share stories about New Year's, and the party in general, while Mín and I continued with ours about the club, and dealing in particular. Maybe no one knew how or dared to start a conversation, however banal, between the four of us.

When Lluïsa went to the bathroom I followed her with the excuse of a shower which, up to a certain point, was true. We consumed our verbally agreed lines of devil and despite her being fully dressed, I lured her over to the bathtub and we laughed and splashed and masturbated like little children.

Image: waking up in the living room in the warmth of a new-born year, immersed in the vinyl concert of classical music that She had given me ten years before in Ibiza, our naked bodies bursting with life under the black blanket.

Sensation: the ecstasy giving our skin a fourth dimension and our spirit an extreme voluptuousness far beyond the grasp of mere lust. But, yet again, equal to or even more powerful than the drugs was the company. Because for me, Lluïsa Cabellera was unique. Immediately after the first line, our first kiss felt as though it lasted a week! And our first embrace, despite She being fully dressed, had a depth of intimacy and passion that lasted months. Because for me, Lily Lluïsa was unique.

Logic: the condoms as proof of her life sentence, considering the fact we couldn't entertain the idea of unprotected sex because she was HIV positive. I feebly suggest that possibly I was too but she tells me that I'd do well to get myself checked and that she won't fuck without a condom.

But none of that could break even half of the enthralling utopia of our reunion. We devoured the solid and the ephemeral together – Lluïsa and Alexandre – amid condoms, demons, cava and lashings of Rachmaninov magic, sleeping and making love and sleeping and making love until late on the third day. But none of that implied anything concerning the fourth day because Lluïsa had a concept of life that benign Angels and grateful Alexanders had no command over.

(As an epilogue to the happy nothingness of that absurd yet delightful end of year ritual, I'm leaving a libertine sonnet salvaged from one of her notebooks).

NEW YEAR'S DAY ONE (SONNTAGSONNET)

When he came in I was urinating in the bowl,
my skirt hitched up around my bare stomach,
my panties stretched between my open legs.
In the dark, he slowly took off his black jeans,
his shoes, his shirt, his shorts, now nothing left
But his nakedness. He says: "I need a shower"
as I wiped my vulva and pulled up my pants.
Far from his splish-splash I cut and prepared
the holy fixes that served as our excuse.
He was wet like the wide open ocean
so I brought him the mirror, I fitted the tube:
left nostril, some things never change.
I stripped down and slipped into the bath,
and he whispered: "I still dream of you".

(Lluca, BCN, 18.1.86)

MULES, ASSES AND GENERAL BEASTS OF BURDEN

And suddenly a shot
rang out like a cannon
'Pedro Navaja', RUBÉN BLADES

It was a more or less normal day within the bestial routine of
'88, after sweet Lali had already given me my marching orders,
and Mín and I, junkies to the core once more, were running
the routes up to Andorra. We bought in Sabadell, Badalona,
Barcelona or Tarragona, and sometimes in Valencia, Seville and
Madrid, and then went up to the border with the co-Principality
via Manresa or Igualada, alternating the route Berga-Bagà-Puig-
cerdà with Cardona-Solsona-La Seu. We made a minimum of
two trips a week, moving a minimum of ten grams each trip; ten
that could end up being twenty or thirty, according to market
liquidity and the profit margins on the menu. After all, that's
what we were in it for.

If I'm not mistaken, that particular day began the preceding
noon when we woke up in the latest B&B (Sant Julià de Lòria)
and decided to save ourselves the price of a night: we'd soon be
out of marzipan so we'd have to go to market either way. While
I packed our bags, Fermí cooked up a war-whooping fix so we
wouldn't have to think about slamming for a good while: Andorra,
as everyone knows, is no laughing matter. After a shower 'n'
shave and a lunch of whiskyespresso and half a croissant, we
headed back to our one true home: my masterly, much-loved
Marlene, the red Ford xr3i I bought five years before when first
starting out as a (legal) courier.

To cut a longish story short: we tore through the afternoon –
mountain high, valley deep – dealing to your typical immigrant
labourers, then supper in Les Escales and coffee and cognacs

in La Vella, before setting up orders for the following day with your not-so-typical counterculture Andorrans. Because in this wide world, even though you wouldn't always think it, there really is a bit of everything everywhere. It was Wednesday (or at least a day that seemed a lot like it) and Andorra doesn't promise much in terms of night liveliness beyond chic bars full of silent couples and deserted discos longing for the winter season when they'll be crammed with horny adolescent skiers. But in La Seu d'Urgell we were able to knock back four or five hours of the sort of good times that we like, beginning with bourbon on the boulevard, then a couple of fixes and a spot of bizniz at the home of a concupiscent regular customer, finishing with the penultimate doubles in one of those bars that open on the outskirts to take advantage of the disaffected youth from Andorra and surrounding counties until they receive the inevitable police order. The aforementioned regular customer and her best buddy for the night both had the following day off (according to them, at least) and were up for whatever adventure we might have in mind. It was four a.m. so we still had three hours to spare because two hours was plenty to get from La Seu to El Prat, and because Carmela the gypsy woman didn't serve anyone before nine o'clock, not even the Pope, and that's despite having his portrait hanging in the living room.

'Anyway,' smiled Mín, weighing up the wild geese, 'it's been ages since we last had an octopus.'

'Octopus?'

'Eight arms and legs, and no head.'

We left La Seu with cold beers in the glove box and a fresh bottle of Four Roses between the regular customer's feet. She was sat upfront with Mín while I was spread out in the back with her friend, and by the time we got to their flat on the outskirts of Puigcerdà she'd made me cum twice, something that's not without merit considering how horsehigh I was. It's a damn shame I lost track of that little wonder (as young as she was licentious) who went by the nom de guerre of June. Such a shame, because she did it like no one else. And that's bearing in mind that I've never been a great lover – Susie not included – of professionals. But, of course, when they charge something other than money it's a whole different cock-and-ball game.

Beyond the orgiastic nebulosity of sex, needles and further four-way childishness, what really left its mark from those hours in that puny Puigcerdà apartment was my conversation with Mín on their tiny balcony as the sun came up and the two girls slept arm in arm on the sofa like two deflated sex dolls. I will endeavour to transcribe not only the words but the ideas they contained:

I began by telling him how I'd had enough of sailing so damn near to the wind, how I needed to dock on some island for fourteen days, or fourteen years, get off the trade route, find a new direction, a new line of work, relearn how to walk without the help-hindrance of hard drugs. His only reply was silence. But it's possible he wasn't even listening.

But I insisted: I was fed up of running up and down like a frantic mosquito, risking my life thrice daily out of the ephemeral excitement of possessing it fully every single second. Surely there were less suicidal ways of holding on to and enjoying it, if not existence, then at least one's own life. But his only reply was the metallic sound of our provisions case, which meant only one thing: he was about to fry up a hearty fix for breakfast. Right then, in that moment, I saw everything clearly, and while he injected me, and also later on once we were on the road again (the two tamed geese catnapping in the back like dormice), I continued to push the notion that we'd been at it too long, that the party was and is and would always be unending and that by pushing the pedal of our non-transcendent existence to the floor like madmen, we wouldn't ever be able to synthesise the slim slice of truth we were chasing, not if we were unable to visualise the moment to slow down and stop.

'Slowing down and stopping are two different things,' he muttered.

'You don't want to understand me.'

'Perhaps it's not even necessary. You're free to live your life and I'm free to live mine. We weren't born joined at the hip thank God.'

'You're not wrong there.'

'You've been blinded by sweet Lali's sweet snatch. Personally I think you're mistaken. We're like the eternal beach upon which the snatches lap like the waves.'

'Mín, you're a rotten poet to your rotten core,' I answered while thinking about but not daring to mention Yma.

But he was right, as usual, at least in part because the catalyst for my decision to attempt to alter the Plotline for the second time was Lali of course. Oh, Eulàlia…! If Lluïsa, owing to her emotional carnality, deserved the name Justine, then Eulàlia had the elegant spirituality of a Clea. She only drank cava or wine, she didn't smoke tobacco, she almost never used hard drugs, but that didn't stop her – with just a sprinkle of tea or chocolate – from being the most attractive intellectual this half of the galaxy: novelist, poet and painter, as if it were the most natural thing in the world.

Despite the year and a half of our self-imposed heaven/hell cohabitation, Eulàlia wasn't made to be my long-term partner, nor was I prepared to go back to living without heroin if not substituting it with scandalous, bacchanal amounts of whisky (and company). Nevertheless, in some dark recess of my soul, I'm aware that my experience with Eulàlia helped me when I eventually met Micalea.

The journey flashed by at a good rhythm and at eight-thirty we left the girls in some nearby layby, ate something quick, and at five past nine were parking up thirty metres from Carmela's block. If Mín had gone up nothing would've happened. But as rotten luck would have it, I said I'd go.

I step out of the car, my stomach bulging with the sixty five thousand pesseta notes that I will exchange for twenty grams of high-grade horse at fifteen thousand a gram (it's an expensive deal but Mín has a theory that says buying quality pays off in the long run and if I play my cards right, twenty grams, money upfront, no doubt a gram on the house will fall my way) and walk the thirty metres from door to door wondering how there can be so much yellow glow in the sky even with Mín's Ray-Bans on. I go in and up the stairs to the third floor. I ring the doorbell (two short and one long, as always), they ask who it is and I respond Andorran Àlex (the same tacitly accepted password, as always). After twenty seconds of murmurs and silence, one of Carmela's innumerable nephews opens the door. They've made me wait – I know their customs – so that when I enter the customer before me can leave (and it's only six minutes past nine). When I go into the tiny entrance hall my blood runs violently cold because I already recognise the Canary Islands accent before I see the face and hump. I cover my face with my left hand when we cross paths and fake a yawn of junk sickness but I've already taken my sunglasses off on the stairs and he's clocked me for sure. He didn't give himself away, oh no, but he recognised me and will be waiting halfway down the stairway with a switchblade. I bet my neck on it.

My whole neck – from ear to ear – because I owe him half a kilo from those distant days in Lo Pont de Suert and because I know he'd slice two necks for less. At least enough to call in the debt. I can't help feeling angry because, deep down, I know he's in the right: I owe him money and I've got to pay up. On the other hand, even if I gave him everything on me, which is only 50% mine, it still might not be enough to save me from the cleaver. My guess is his plan is to wring as much out of me as he can and then sink the blade in as deeply as he can. No, can't risk it. In other words: no other choice but to put my cards on the table. Gypsy Carmela, who I've known for years, pulls a face and tells me Humpty is an even older customer than me and that if I owe him it's my problem. But I manage to get her to see that the confrontation will end in blood and, as much as it pains me to be the cause of it, that will only have negative repercussions for her business.

Then the doorbell rings, making me shudder. Carmela asks the morning's third caller if she's seen anyone on the stairs and the girl – a toothpick dressed up as Lily Marlene who hasn't had a minute more sleep than me – answers, yes, now you mention it, there *was* a strange shadow at the end of the hall. The gypsy sends her nephew downstairs to convince my creditor that her patch isn't the right patch before ushering me into the kitchen to look over the merchandise. I get permission to draw myself a sample and while Carmela serves the scarecrow her three grams I prepare a line from the ounce that's sitting on the mirror. After snorting it I go over to the kitchen window that provides a view of the left part of the square, just in time to see the giant nephew accompanying Lanzarote to his brown Seat 131. He gets in and drives away, passing right by Marlene, which thankfully he doesn't recognise and which thankfully is empty because Mín is in the bar opposite, opposite his third whiskyespresso. The giant waits a while and watches the car turn the corner before calmly signalling towards the window and slowly walking back.

The gypsy, softened by the smell of fresh greens, gives me the twenty grams as agreed and, as expected, a bonus track on the house, wrapped separately. According to her, the encore is for Fermí because it's clear I've been a naughty boy. Despite her obsession with dressing in black whatever the weather, I've always liked that sexy, switched-on gypsy woman and widow of thirty years, and I reckon it's on account of (as folkloric as it may seem) the totally natural way she spoke Catalan. Oh, and that tight little tush of hers, of course.

With the big packet and my tiny tail between my legs, I head straight for the car, desperately thinking about how to flee without ever coming back. At least until I have the nuts, or the peanuts, to face Lanzarote. After twenty minutes wait in the bar, Fermí doesn't take twenty seconds to reach the car, and by the time he has one foot inside I'm ready to drive awayaway.

'What happened?' he asks, his worry wrapped in weariness.

'A piece of bad arse luck,' I blurt back.

I trace the usual route to the usual abandoned plot outside of town while pulling the cylindrical package out of my trousers and passing it to Mín who puts it the oil can. As usual. When we pull up, I open the bonnet and change the can, as usual, and he cooks up a healthy hit from the bonus track that will leave us listening to the silence for a good while. The practice is as old as it is timeworn: one time the bad guys caught us but we came out of it unscathed by playing the martyrs and sacrificing the small package.

Now it's goddam obvious that with twenty grams on us and Lanzarote roaming the area we should have galloped thirty kilometres in the opposite direction before stopping anywhere. But habit is like that and it can come at a high price. And none was higher than that day when we were caught not by the bad guys but by the worst son of a bitch among a sea of bastards: Don Javier Peyes Pozos, aka *Humpty*, aka *Lanzarote*, who had waited for us God knows where and followed us God knows how. Just as we were shooting up he arrived in his 131 like a runaway train. Even though I regularly see it at night in my dreams and moments of insomnia, I'm not entirely sure I'm capable of describing exactly how events unfolded:

Lanzarote had gone mad and looked hell bent on slitting my throat straight away without wasting the spit on a conversation about payments. Mín appeared on the verge of a mental meltdown owing to the shocking change in vibrations but held up the attacker the best he could by grabbing the arm and wrist of the hand clutching the blade. And I… well, I honestly didn't know where to hide. Amid the yells and death threats, I offered him a down payment there and then if he could just give me some breathing space to negotiate the rest, but he wasn't interested in listening. That was when my partner all of a sudden got real mad and after a final tug of war they both ended up on their arses: Mín against one of Marlene's open doors and the attacker on the dusty ground. But Lanzarote was fast back onto his feet and launched himself at me like a demon, as though instead of half a kilo I owed him the moon and the tide.

A couple of seconds later, just as I was having the first frightful visions of the steel blade tearing through my stomach, liver and heart, I heard an explosion that sounded very much like a gunshot. I leapt away as if a thousand springs had simultaneously launched me into the air and saw Lanzarote with a bleeding hole in his back and Mín already behind the wheel: he'd hit the bull's eye with the .38 we'd procured for the pimp in Bourg-Madame and here was one little canary bird who wouldn't be singing anymore.

I knew Fermí would be having problems for the next thousand minutes so I pushed him over to the passenger seat, turned the ignition and put her in first: we had to go very far with the minimum number of stops and without making the tyres screech.

Nevertheless, this adventure flows directly into another, still irrelevant at this point. When it comes to June and the lascivious regular buyer, as far as I know, ten years later, they are still waiting for us in the same service station in El Prat de Llobregat, where, needless to say, I'll never step foot in again, not in this life or the next.

JOAN'S ACCIDENT, OR HOW A BRUSH WITH DEATH CAN REBUILD AN ENTIRE LIFE
1. *Hospital Clínic as a second home*

'The House of the Rising Sun', THE ANIMALS

According to the report filed by road police, Joan Torres i Guixers, resident of Avià, travelling on the C-1411, direction Manresa, lost control of his vehicle, a dark blue BMW 750 csi, Andorran licence plate, at Puig-reig on 18/02/85 at approximately 23:15, crossed the central reservation, crashed through the opposite barrier and rolled down the hillside. There were no other cars or individuals involved other than the aforementioned J.T.G and no eyewitnesses.

According to the medical report submitted by the intensive care unit at Manresa Hospital, Joan Torres i Guixers was admitted on 18/02/85 at 23:37 in a coma and with various bone traumas: two to the left knee, one to the right elbow, however the most serious ones were to the second and third lumbar vertebrae. The initial prognosis was very poor, and it was doubtful he would even wake up from the coma.

When reception staff telephoned the Torres home to deliver the latest dismal news they only found a vegetating Aunt Dolors, who'd brought along a private nurse and moved in with the young patriarch a few days after Genoveva had left. My poor aunt didn't know Genoveva's phone number; she only just about knew Manresa. Amid tears and sobs she managed to phone Mama Montserrat, who informed Genoveva and Ramon on one side, Natàlia on the other.

Montserrat, Genoveva and Ramon picked me up from my house at ten past one in the morning and twenty-eight minutes later we were at the hospital. But the receptionist at A&E told us she was deeply sorry but Mr Torres had already left us: after some basic treatment he'd been flown by helicopter to Hospital Clínic in Barcelona. So we did a U-turn and headed back to Barna. When we arrived at Hospital Clínic, where so many long days and agonies awaited us, Joan was in the operating theatre and at the mercy of science and his own human biology. At seven in the morning, after five hours and forty minutes of surgery, when we no longer knew what to say, where to sit or pace, or how to stop chewing things over and over, we saw two doctors coming over to us looking as drained and hollow as prisoners of war.

'Are you the mother?' uttered a bearded man of around forty years with sweat pouring down him.

'No, I'm his aunt. Genoveva…'

But Genoveva, after four hours of sitting immobile, quietly weighing up the silence, took her time in getting up.

'Permit me to get straight to the point. Are you aware that your son is an addict?'

'Yes.'

'And do you know if he has HIV?'

'No.'

I felt an almighty sucker punch to the stomach, like a surprise kick from Pegasus.

'Pardon me for being so intrusive but it's very important that we know.'

'I'm sorry,' Genoveva sighed breathlessly.

'How is he? Is he alive?' interrupted Montserrat.

'Oh, I'm sorry! Yes, he's alive and we trust he'll pull through but for the time being he's in a coma.' After that he appeared to recuperate the regulatory countenance that he had momentarily misplaced: 'During the primary intervention we drained the encephalic haematoma and stabilised the vertebrae fractures. He's in ICU but we will have to wait forty-eight hours while we continue to monitor his evolution. His age is our greatest hope.'

He said it in one go, without hesitation, as if he'd learnt the speech by memory. He then moved his neck back and forth and from side to side, and began massaging his temples, while seemingly searching for the ideal moment to make a decision.

'Once again I do apologise for my intrusiveness and insistence… but there has been an accident and a nurse has pricked herself with…'

'I really don't think there's anything that we can do about that, Doctor,' I intervened rather bluntly. 'Apart from sincerely offering our greatest sympathies, of course.'

He interrupted his circular massages and nodded.

'Right, well, thank you. And my apologies once again.'

Whether it was professional tact or it'd merely slipped his mind, he didn't wish us a good day. The doctor in question was called Gonçal Camps Cifuente and he was already deemed an eminence in three or four specialities. Over the thirty-three days that crept by before Joan came out of his coma, we had time to admire him with greater ponderance, not just as a doctor but as a person. And later, owing to his conjugal relationship with Genoveva, we were able to admire him further and with increased intimacy. All of us are convinced that if Joan is alive today it's thanks to Doctor Camps making him a personal cause from day one.

And as much as it pains me to do so, I must note that the corresponding test for human immunodeficiency virus came back positive for Joan, as it did for the unfortunate nurse. Even Doctor Camps was left dumbstruck but, according to his reasoning, exceptional events form a fundamental part of statistics whereas the suffering of medical staff, relatives or whoever it may be belongs to a wholly different discipline.

From a distant dream during those first few weeks of round-the-clock hospital visits, either to relieve Genoveva or to be by her side, I recall Uncle Ramon whispering in a festive voice that one must always be prepared for death. Afterwards, Genoveva – who I couldn't see because she was sat behind me – agreed with an echoing voice: 'yes, prepared for our grandparents' death, prepared for our parents' death, prepared for our spouse's, our siblings' but, above all, every Lent, for our Son's.' Then Joan, naked and bearing a thick rope in his hands, entered the virtual room dressed like Jesus Christ from the Passion, which had since become a confluence of the kitchen at the farmhouse and an imagined operating theatre, telling us not to worry, that he was fine, that we must go in peace. But then Gonçal, arising from the void wearing a white coat and gloves by pure oneiric artifice, began to explain, much like a paedophile teacher before an infantile auditorium, how one must look life full in the face while always being conscious of the arbitrary ticking of the pendulum clock. In his left hand he held out a beating heart and in his right a giant pocket watch that dripped like pizza.

On the 2nd of April, I was finally able to see Cousin Joan: he was laid flat out on a bed in a ward for twenty, hidden under bandages, counterweights, tubes and machines. He could move his eyelids and pupils, and occasionally clench his fists, but he was paralysed from the waist down and still being fed artificially. However, bearing in mind his point of departure, the outlook was encouraging. What was needed now, not just on his part but from his surrounding satellites as well, was a universe of patience. That day, the prodigal son in the making managed to push out two words, the first of which was 'roses.' This was on account of the bouquet of twenty-five I'd placed by his bed the day after the accident to commemorate his birthday: they had all since withered and died but they were still there by the head of Joan's bed, wrapped in the original cellophane thanks to Gonçal. After more patience and a colossal effort, just when the nurse was already giving me the 'sling-your-hook' look, I made out a second word: 'music.' This desire was somewhat more difficult for me to satisfy because ensuring that he had a fresh rose every day was merely a question of putting our minds to it. I must admit it provokes a not inconsiderable amount of personal pride to say that the idea of the rose was so well received that some evenings there were two or three by his bedside, and the following day the same again.

But Joan's valiant mentality deserved this and many more sacrifices. I mean dedication because for me, for *us*, satisfying his needs didn't imply the slightest sacrifice. Before anyone, because she had more than demonstrated her devotion, was Genoveva; then there was my mum, Ramon and me (Joan had always been the brother I never had); and finally Aunt Dolors who, after almost going out of her mind with loneliness and isolation at the farmhouse, at seventy years of age was now living in the home of her old enemy, Genoveva, in the heart of Hospitalet, helping with both patient and business. It was just like Ramon so often said: no matter how well you think things are going you can never tell who you might have to rely on when tragedy strikes. Even Natàlia's side of the family appeared on occasions before finally fading away again, as did other offshoots of the very same branch that only four years before had legally contested Uncle Pere's will.

Joan's recoveries and convalescences were so numerous and lengthy that they spread over many other exterior events that don't fit into this preamble. And I say preamble because all these tricks and twists and sleights of destiny's hand, to a greater or lesser extent melodramatic and/or implausible, are nothing but the anecdote that frames the miracle, whether secular or sacred, performed minute by minute, hour by hour, over five hundred days by the broken, stricken Joan Torres i Guixers.

2. *Diary of a hyperpatient (fragments)*

To cure you they must kill you
LOU REED

If I had to explain my first recollection, it would be the smell of roses. But this could be an accidental image from my subconscious. Or a previous life.

If I had to explain my first idea, it would be having died two or three times while they transported me from hillside to ambulance, ambulance to operating theatre, operating theatre to heaven. However, as Gonçal would later tell me, the scientific explanation for my sensation of that slice of happy heaven could be the coma sealing me in a purgatorial amnion suspended between life and death. But what really makes me reflect, and more with each passing day, is the fact I was clinically dead at least twice during that night.

I behaved very badly, from what they tell me. I tried to escape from God knows what or who and would claw, continuously, callously, at the tubes working to keep me alive. Such an extreme might even signify a subconscious desire to die. Now that I am more aware of my situation they will take off these undignified gloves and stop strapping me to my sarcophagus. I hope.

Today is Sant Jordi. I know because I have been patiently waiting for it for days. In keeping with tradition, they will each come with a rose and a book. Except for Eulàlia, who will perhaps bring me two roses and two books and two cassettes. Music and reading, reading and music: as immobile as I am inside this frozen igloo, now that they have taken the cast off my arm and are gradually granting me permission to exist a little, these will be the two crutches that I will spiritually walk and survive upon.

It's ten to seven but dawn doesn't know where to begin breaking the tubercular horizon that I picture behind closed eyes despite the resonant reality around me. The patient in the neighbouring bed urinates loudly into the bedpan before the nurse's blank apathy when I realise, with certain embarrassment, that I also have the urge.

> *Night time rain*
> *like so many Aprils*
> *feeling the pain*
> *deep in the marrow.*
> *Night time in bed*
> *broken but awake*
> *savouring the rain.*

(I have since left intensive care and live like a normal patient in a twin room. Oh, and it has also been a week since they unplugged me and that I have started eating boiled fish and soup).

In my depositary of nutritious ideas, I have a stockpile of reasons to be cheerful and, even though I can't go so far as saying I am totally happy, I am certainly happier today (18th May) than two months ago, before my last spin of the wheel. Firstly, I am starting to get my head straight, at least in terms of motor coordination, which was horrendous to begin with. Secondly, and of no less importance, I have Gonçal, who is no longer my physician but a type of Doctor Frankenstein with the additional role of scientific father figure in psychoemotional terms. He has informed me that the most promising thing of all is that I am physically free of every single one of my old destructive addictions, from tobacco and coffee to acid, cocaine and heroin. If I knew for sure that I will be able to assimilate it spiritually, emotionally and rationally, I would hop, skip and jump like a child in spite of my paralysis. But one thing I do have clear in my mind is that this long clinical agony has to be the foetal state for the development and metamorphosis of a new being able to confront this thing they call – for want of a better word – the world.

It's three in the morning on the night of Sant Joan and I am awake savouring the sound of firecrackers, spirited shouts in the street below and the nurses' giggles, all of whom are even more presumptuous than usual, which only seems normal to me on a night like this. It has been a very special day for me. Just before midnight and after having already been dozing for an hour in front of a fatally flawed film, Mama Genoveva, Doctor Gonçal, Cousin Eulàlia and Uncle Ramon (the 'Four Souls of the Resurrection', as I call them) came in with a bottle of cava and one of those cream cakes I like so much. I am guessing they were allowed in because they had brought another bottle for the nurses (in fact, Genoveva and Eulàlia already know them all by their baptismal names and ask about their families as though they were old friends). Then Eulàlia gave me a kiss on the mouth, her lips still wet with cava, and I still recall the sharp taste on my tongue and the scent in my nostrils. I would love to masturbate right now and refresh my memory of the primary essence of pleasure, but I am afraid this body don't boogie like before.

The doctors say they will operate on my vertebrae next week for the third and final time and that from then on the improvement will be notable. But they have been telling me that for the last three weeks already.

Yesterday was All Saints and, to celebrate it, last night I had an inspired dream:

I was in a Borgesian cemetery with cypresses on both sides

that stretched towards the glaring sun, stairs twisting into nothingness or intertwining with other twisting stairs, and inaccessible crypts elevated like circus tent domes.

I was carrying a dozen black roses while Rosa, one of the sexier nurses at the hospital, trotted like a puppy by my side as she held forth a bedpan and asked me who they were for. We were in an ample room with no ceiling housing a hundred horizontal tombs where, instead of graves, crosses or niches, there were translucent, ash blue pyramids: one hundred pyramids distributed into four blocks, twenty-five to a block and each of them one metre by one metre by one metre, and at the foot of each façade was a tailor-made epitaph.

I took Rosa by the hand, embarrassed by the fact that she refused to hide the bedpan as I had requested, and one after the other we checked the different states of decomposition of Papa Pere, Grandpa Joan, Aunt Dolors and a few cadavers not of blood relation but equally mourned, if not more. Meanwhile, we looked for the necromide (I have no idea where I got this word from but that is how it came to me) where I, according to the inner logic of the dreamscape grammar, had to place the bouquet. When we eventually found it, it turned out to be my own.

'I didn't know you had a twin brother,' Rosa turns and says to me. 'When did he die?'

'He's not my twin brother. He's a sublimation of my own person.'

'But there's no way you can be inside the necromide and talking to me at the same time. And another thing: how come you're able to walk today?'

'Apparently it's a miracle. Anyway, I've always had exceedingly good legs.'

Then Genoveva appears with a wheelchair, telling me over and over again to be a good boy and sit down, but I run away pretending not to have heard her and try to lose her in the wire meshing that both divides and connects the four blocks. But along the next passageway I'm met by Eulàlia, and on the following one by Aunt Dolors, and then Dad on the third, and on the fourth by Aunt Montserrat, and then Grandpa and Doctor Camps, even Ten, who I have not seen or heard from in ten months; every single one of them with a bullshit wheelchair, telling me to stop being a scoundrel and come and sit down.

At that point the dream turned into the typical nightmare of persecutory anxiety until, completely surrounded by family and friends and empty chairs, I screamed a long, deep 'no' that crossed the frontiers of sleep and woke me up, my body soaked in sweat but my mouth bone dry. My scream also woke up Genoveva, thanks (or not) to the intercom connecting my room to hers upstairs. When she came down to sooth my terrors, I downed a glass of water in one gulp. End of nightmarish report. Full stop. New paragraph.

Pause.

I spent the summer in and out of hospital, where the interventions on my vertebrae now form part of institutional folklore. If I am not miscounting, we are up to six. But, wait, because tomorrow we are 'back in'. Apparently, I lack calcium, my bones are like water, and there is no way of welding the buggers back together. I have already told them that if the problem is water then I will happily wash myself with milk and go back to quenching my thirst with wine, beer and whisky, delicacies I now only have an abstract knowledge of. But they are convinced they know better and aren't willing to at least give it a try.

The truth is I am coping with life after hard drugs very well and I don't miss a thing; nothing that doesn't mean leaving hospitals and surgery behind and going back to walking and living a more or less normal life, of course.

I am writing this entry from 'home', which for Joan and Genoveva is now at Gonçal's house on the coast. At first I wasn't happy about Mum closing the business in Hospitalet to move up to Premià de Mar with the doctor, not because I thought it was a bad idea, after all she is still young and has the right to live like anyone else, but the fact I was in this shattered state, a shard of glass lodged deep in their hearts, I felt that I was forcing her into decisions that she otherwise wouldn't have made.

Nevertheless, here we are, sharing joys and pains: Mum, who has invented a day job cooking from home so her role as my slave isn't so obvious; the doctor-host, who sleeps here on Tuesdays, Thursdays, and three weekends a month; and yours superfluously who, once propped in his chair (wheelchair, naturally) with catheter and additional accessories, now enjoys a certain autonomy within the house thanks to a number of in-dispensable but wildly expensive architectonic improvements: from the bedroom to the living room and from the living room to either the kitchen or the garden (where I am writing these November reflections despite the wind). I often cry-baby brood over the deep autumnal tones of the trees at the farmhouse. Ah, the Torres farmhouse… what broken Joan wouldn't give to be back living there so that the House of Torres may prosper once more! Patience, as they say, is a virtue.

Pause.

End of reality.

Over and out.

My neighbour died in his neighbouring bed last night, without a word of protest or a kiss goodbye. They carried him quietly away as if committing an awful act. I was awake but made it look as though I were sleeping to mask my heavy, silent, selfish tears that reflected my own self-pity rather than any genuine sadness for the departed.

My neighbour was called Jimmy and he was from Reus. No one apart from a Christian poet ever visited him. He never told me his legal birth name but everyone called him Jimmy. He was born in Reus but had lived for many years in Castelló. He was homosexual, or at least bisexual, and had been in a motorcycle accident on a coastal road in El Garraf. His boyfriend had been upfront and died instantly, but Jimmy escaped with two broken legs and a fortnight in a coma. I will have to ask Gonçal how, after only a few broken bones and having already woken up from his coma, he ended up in a box. I will also ask him what I have to do so that the stranger comes to pay me the odd visit. He used to read Jimmy passages from the Gospels and poetry by Maragall, Carner, Rilke and Blake.

We said mass for my neighbour in the chapel. I went there in my chair, with Eulàlia playing nurse. Apart from us and the priest, there were half a dozen nuns (who always begin their morning shift with mass), the aforementioned Christian poet, and six or seven people playing the role of friends and relatives. Well, relative friendliness, because in the six weeks that we shared a room not one of them came to see him. I took advantage of the occasion to ask the volunteer (whose name is Pere like Dad's) if he might come and read to me one day and he accepted with a beaming smile. The burial ritual relaxed and contented me, and the sadness I felt during the ceremony was this time genuinely dedicated to the departed.

My neighbour died in his neighbouring bed last night, without a word of protest or a kiss goodbye. Nevertheless, what really strikes me as remarkable is that in this week between Christmas and New Year's I will have gone to mass more times than in my entire previous life. And that is no laughing matter.

I am not in the mood for anything. I am not in the mood for reading. I am not in the mood for continuing to struggle. Today is Valentine's Day and from inside the ward, because I am not in the mood for going outside, I can see the spring sun illuminating the blue Mediterranean tangent. It's most likely a radiant day, a splendid day, or at least a beautiful one, for most human beings. But I am not in the mood for talking. Or thinking. Or existing. I especially don't feel like remembering that we are 'back in' in six days (this time my knee, which refuses to make the minimum movements expected from a minimally respectable one). I must say though that this spine we have running up the middle of our back appears to evolve of its own accord and, however farfetched it might sound, I am beginning to regain a certain amount of movement in my three lower extremities. But the muscular atrophy, accentuated by the problems with my kneecap, often feels insurmountable.

I am not quite sure why I am thinking so much about courtly love this 14th of February. Being the good Catalan that I naturally am, I have always celebrated the concept on the 23rd of April. Well, I say I am not sure why, but I have an inkling: my longing for an emotional, not to mention sexual, life beyond this circle of familiar mirrors ravages my spiritual reserves.

At random I open the Book to the Gospel according to Luke (5:10) and the printed Word tells me that Jesus says unto me: 'Fear not; from henceforth thou shalt catch men.' Word of God? Who knows. In my case, leaving Everything behind like the disciples did would be a lot less difficult than following Him because I am unable to walk ten steps on these crutches without the inevitable Fall. While I wonder whether to flick through the TV channels or sob through the intimate channels of my being, I let the Book fall open at random again and now it's according to John (4:48) and the printed Word tells me that Jesus now says unto me: 'Except ye see signs and wonders, ye will not believe.' And with it a cascade of light fills the womb of ideas: how often we experience miracles and yet still scorn them as insufficient! It's akin to winning the lottery and grumbling that the jackpot isn't as large as other weeks. And here I recognise comparisons with my situation: I am alive, I have my limbs, my five senses and my reason all practically intact and yet I whine and blubber like a baby over a stiff knee instead of singing a symphony of praise to the immensity of the sum that I possess. I have decided henceforth to be more positive and, smiling serenely, I open the Book and trust in Fate to present me with another tiny miracle.

PARALLEL ADVENTURES
1. *Intro: Natural curves in the road*

You who are on the road
Must have a code that you can live by
'Teach Your Children', GRAHAM NASH

When it comes to family, the relationship between Genoveva and Gonçal, nurtured by a shared interest in fine dining and classical music, grew and grew to the point where she spent more nights at the doctor's flat than her own; and afterwards, when Joan began his long and winding ambulatory therapy, they ended up moving permanently into Gonçal's holiday home in Premià. Dolors, poor thing, as though taking it as a personal affront, died last winter, 1984, of a cirrhosis as corrosive as it was undeserved. Uncle Ramon showed up one day with a girlfriend ten years his junior and was the envy of all. But the truth is, with Susana living with me, I was more than served and satisfied. Mama Montserrat was the only one not to have found love, possibly because her professional successes in the extravagant world of television were already enough of a reward for her.

In addition to Cousin Joan's jaw-dropping gymkhana and other anecdotal family developments, there are two or three private scenes from those years that are worthy of narrating.

2. *A fly in the ointment*

Tell me why, tell me why, tell me why
SADE

Susana and her son, Jordi, had been living with me in the loft apart on Plaça Padró for about a year. If I am not mistaken, the following scene is from one Sunday in August 1985, all heat and humidity, while the little one was napping and we were digesting our late lunch of black rice and squid and weighing up whether to go down to the breakwater or up to the outdoor pool on Montjuïc. Normally, we'd have chosen the pool because Su and I had a concentrated pile of concupiscent pacts, including underwater underhandedness, sizing up the most fanciable females with our expert eye and exciting the gaze of overheated muscular males, all of which allowed us to recharge our morbid batteries in tandem.

The doorbell rang (unfortunately the door to the building was sometimes left open during the daytime) and I got up and walked over to the door. When I asked who was there, a deep but timid voice replied in Spanish:

'Er… Hello… Is María in?'

María with a Spanish 'í' was Susana's baptismal name, so I mumbled 'Su, it's for you' while opening the door with sweaty apathy. Immediately, the door crashed first into my body then against my head at an incomprehensible speed. The first blow thrust me into motion, whereas the second I received with my back against the wall. Then I slumped to the ground, confused and almost out for the count.

My narration inevitably slows down a scene that was as swift as a tornado. The fireball in male form that had sent me flying into the wall now blew through the entrance hall and into the living room. Blinded by burning rage, he yelled:

'Oi, slut!! Where's my son?'

She, i.e. María, Susana, Slut, shot up instinctively in the direction of the bedroom screaming a single terrifying phoneme. But he, the muscular male hurricane, seized her in the style of a film noir thug before giving her two lip-splitting slaps and launching her into the table causing a crashing of crockery. Woken by the violent melee, the kid had curled up in the doorway and was crying out of fear. I was crying too, out of shock and pain. And so was María-Susana-Slut, but out of searing resentment. The only person laughing, if he could be called a person, was that deplorable creature. However, just as I was getting to my feet, baying for his blood, Su bounced back up from the table as though she had springs in her stomach and threw herself at that nonperson in a long embrace. He abruptly altered his posture and facial expression with cinematic surprise.

'Oops… I slipped…' she purred before they both sank slowly to the floor.

According to the posterior medical reports, the fork Su stuck in his groin had perforated both testicles: two holes in each, just to balance it out. We called an ambulance and the police while he lay on the floor coddling his poached eggs and howling threats of impending death and torture. I took the kid to the neighbour's and the heroin up to the roof: there wasn't even two grams of brown but no doubt the wounded cock, when he was able to crow again, would dedicate a couple of revealing numbers to us.

Instead of the beach or the pool, we spent the afternoon down the local police station making statements and receiving congratulations from the officers: an arrest warrant had been out for M.N.O. over three robberies and one murder for two years. Unfortunately, there was no cash reward.

The case didn't go any further because the judge ruled that she'd acted in self-defence, while any fears of future retribution remained strangled to death by a wire in cell 6, wing 1 just ten days after the skewered ex-husband checked into La Model. Despite having been disowned by her honourable gypsy family from Tarragona, María had, as is so often the case, a brother-in-law who had a brother-in-law.

I must make it clear that she didn't ask or pay for it. M.N.O.'s violence towards his browbeaten wife already amounted to three criminal complaints and five hospital visits, so after she explained the latest violent spectacle to her sister, the aforementioned brother-in-law decided enough was enough. Despite the masses of utterly unhinged cocks, thankfully there are still men in this world with a pair of well-balanced balls between their legs.

3. *New old friendships*

Nights of white satin
Never reaching the end
THE MOODY BLUES

The second scene, occurring just two or three months after the first, starts at 07:33 as I was lying in my wide, empty bed. All of a sudden, I heard the key enter the lock, the lock click, and a few inferred whispers. The radio alarm clock had to get me up for 08:22 because the art gallery I worked in was only a five-minute walk away but for too many nights already I'd only been sleeping in fragmented blocks: that's her... no, it's only the neighbour; that must be her now... no... yes... but she's not alone...

I couldn't stake a claim because from day one Su had confessed or, more accurately, confirmed that she worked as an escort and sold smack on the side, and by the time she moved into my apartment my blind passion for her sex, her son and, above all, her 'pathos' made me accept these basic elements. No, I couldn't stake a claim to anything; at most I could only complain. Some nights were interlaced with an excess of sex and drugs when I attempted to learn how to savour it and let myself completely go until losing all consciousness of who I was and who I was with, as she often told me. But even if the results were remarkable owing to the drugs, sexually speaking they were often an absurd farce.

While I asked around for a waitress job for a girl with a pretty face – and there were more than a few paying a pretty enough penny – she suggested we started specialising in triangles and quadrangles, firstly because they were more profitable and, secondly, because she told me nothing excited her more than seeing me being penetrated, or at the peak of an orgasm, in the arms of another. Rather than perturbing me, I was fascinated, and no doubt she instinctively felt the same morbid curiosity. What I mean is that Su, in stark contrast to me, didn't get her ideas from some overly contrived book or conceited film.

The whispers transformed into classic music in the living room and then a stream of water from the showerhead. I turned over for the fifth time knowing perfectly well I was done sleeping. This was, above all, owing to the unmistakeable double panting of an erect heterocopulation that gradually grew above the sound of the jet of water. When I realised, a knot formed in my throat and I thrust a hand between my thighs and began a compulsive masturbation. I stopped almost immediately because, although the thought of her fucking someone else physically excited me, unlike her I needed the emotional presence of a body. But there was nothing I could do about it. And handed the choice between weeping my same old silent whimper and weeping the same but deriving some sort of pleasure from it, I decided to follow my impulse and masturbate unreservedly.

They lasted more or less the same amount of time in the shower as I did, that is to say, not long, and just as I finished my teary-eyed wank, the pulsating water fell silent and I heard Su laugh and gleefully say:

'Now, Àlex, *you* come with me. This we'll both enjoy.'

By the sound of things, whoever had been in the shower with her hadn't left her very satisfied.

Above my soft weeping and wet orgasm, I heard damp,

naked, masculine steps tread from the bathroom to the sitting room followed by a few deep monosyllables and similar steps going up the landing towards the back bedroom. Then I heard the naked, light skips of Su's aphrodisiac feet head over to the second stranger in the living room. At first, he refused her offer with a chuckle and two or three indecipherable monosyllables. Few men say no to Susan, especially when it's free, I thought, curling up foetus-like. Though not even five minutes had passed since wanking, my body was already boiling with desire again and my mind simmering with images as voluptuously fantastic as they were gratuitously innocent. I decided (at 07:53 according to the digital reveille) that a long cold shower was what I needed and so I went, as naked as the day I was born, into the living room and towards the bathroom.

To say she was giving him head would be practically a euphemism because what Su was busy giving that cute blonde stranger, his shirt undone and naked from the waist down, was a genuine professional blowjob. Professional [comma] and what's more [comma] done with desire [full stop]

'Hi,' I said sheepishly.

'Hi,' he answered with a timid smile sprinkled with overt desire.

'Can I play, too?' I asked, captivated yet decisive.

'Fine by me!' he answered eagerly despite his uncertainty.

I walked over to them slowly, while caressing my breasts with my left hand and sucking my right thumb from top to bottom. When I was next to them, *among* them, I first greeted Susana Slut's buttocks and thighs, before placing my mouth close to his open mouth and sucking and licking his lips, at times his tongue, too. During this prologue, my wet thumb searched, found and entered Su's anus who, not the least bit distracted from her task, returned the favour by caressing my vaginal lips with the fingers of her free hand. While Su pursued her own sordid task, the Man and I went from mouth-to-mouth to mouth-to-breasts and, shortly afterwards, mouth-to-cunt. I have to admit I was having a killer whale of a time, despite crying like a child, because in addition to feeling him I could admire and masturbate her. Afterwards, he moved backwards slightly, slipped a hand towards my clitoris and his mouth towards my anus. If I hadn't been so aroused I may well have frozen because up to that point I'd only ever received that sort of treatment at the hands of Su and it could be counted on one hand.

While he was preparing me (now it's obvious but at the time I didn't realise), he rose her head up, probably so not to ejaculate too soon, and I began giving his testicles a vigorous massage, which Su had told me was good for maintaining the tension. All the while, she (perfect Susana, Susana the whore) and I kissed, clawed at and masturbated one another as much as we could, and then some. When he swivelled me around and positioned himself to sodomise me, at first I made him stop: beyond Su's tongue and fingers, or some small domestic instrument randomly to hand, my anus was still virgin, but if I said no, in addition to missing the culmination of the scene, I'd have to watch him penetrate her because it was clear he wouldn't think twice about it. So I consented and I don't regret it in the slightest because (perhaps owing to the fact the fruit had ripened on the tree) it was an experience that transformed my understanding of and feelings towards sex, and the world in general.

If this sequence seems excessively cinematic and explicit, which is not my usual aesthetic approach, then I promise it isn't out of vanity or pure pornographic catharsis, but rather because of the events that unpredictable and improvised threesome gave rise to. Perhaps I am committing the sin of excess by seeing – with the soul's eye, admittedly – a grand metaphor in it for the interweaving of our personal destinies, at least in the short term.

In any event, under the hot shower, my legs still trembling, while Su made coffee and toast, and the male stranger (Lexalexalexandre) prepared a few well-mixed lines of horse and pony, it was as clear as the newly breaking day that for María Susana and I, Lali Eulàlia and Her, there would be no more rising suns.

I hope that nobody hopes to find in all of this the macho myth of the Phallus that Turns Lesbians: what I wanted, what I needed, was a certain intimacy, security, fidelity. And from the very first moment, Alexa showed me an exceptional amount of tenderness and capacity for love. Proof of this is that there were barely six months between the day I told my idolised goddess, Susana Slut, to look for somewhere else to live because I needed to go back to single life and my studies and the day when Alexa dismantled my plans by moving in with me. Within that time I gifted and permitted myself a good number of heterosexual experiences, with both Him and others, to contrast different situations and sensations, and to reconstruct the reality of only having slept with one man half a dozen times since that distant deflowering during the Patum of '73 and exclusively during my circus performances with Susana. Horses for courses: as far as I was concerned, playing the whore wasn't enough for me. But loving One with intellect, body and soul, despite it being the only authentic object of my passionate love, would have ended up rotting my water lily heart in no time.

4. *From bad to worse to breaking the curse*

Those days are over, you don't have
To sell your body to the night
'Roxanne', THE POLICE

And thus my level-headed plans of singleness and chastity

remained precisely that: plans. My sexual baggage, owing to my age and the life I led, was that of a shy Lolita.

Needless to say, my relationship with Alexa was, generally speaking, less frenetic, less sweet and less sexually and emotionally ambitious. But at the same rate the petals were being torn off everything else around us, so our little love turned sour, selfish, past it shelf life. If Alexa had moved into the flat above the square it was, for more than any other reason, because Fermí (the stranger in the shower the day of our threesome) was getting married to Yma and they needed more privacy. Quite why Alexa had to move out when it was his name on the contract was beyond me, and the normal thing would have been for the happy couple to go look for a new love nest. But I figured they'd work it out between them without considering how it could affect me.

And then one dreadful day, when the couple had already had the apartment to themselves for a few months, Fermí turned up at mine looking like a train wreck (it remains the only time I've ever seen him cry and rage) and explained with three or four grunts that Yma had gone to live at her sister's and left him for good. The strangest thing of all was that Fermí didn't give any reason for the sudden breakup and, coming from such a switched-on soul as Yma, there had to be a cast iron one. But there was one, of course, and it spelt trouble for us, too: AIDS.

But one thing at a time: the official version, I mean, the one they both told us separately, was that she didn't want to know anything about unprotected sex or proposed pregnancies (Fermí the Lunatic had got the idea into his head that a baby would put him on the straight and narrow) if he didn't first get tested whereas he, out of pure panic or fear, didn't want to hear another word about it. It was tempting to speculate that he'd already got tested and come out positive, but this was Fermí we were talking about so it was by no means certain. The controversy, in any case, prompted Alexa and me to seriously pose ourselves the question. And we both had pretty short odds, albeit for different reasons.

But a further caveat is required because after the first test, I came out positive: I had it and he didn't. After a few days of horror, sadness and a lot more information, I was convinced that if he didn't have it then I most likely didn't either. We repeated the tests and, lo and behold, this time it was roles reversed: Lex yes, Lali no. Naturally, he told me he preferred it that way because if one of us had put their life on the line for the thrill of living – and from a young age – it was him, and he said he was more than aware that the existential groove his sub-generation had chosen implied a highly intense and often brief life. Despite not saying so himself, it was clear that he was more than willing to play the martyr. So we did a third test, and a fourth, followed by I don't know how many more, because in that past present we didn't have much time for condoms. He was right when he said we were still learning to use the damn things because the spontaneous sex of our adolescence hadn't had any particular need for them. Until now, that is.

Whatever the reason, two things were clear: Yma had left the Eixample apartment and Fermí was spending more nights in my back bedroom than at his own place. The icing on the cake was when the police ordered the closure of the club where they both worked, leaving them to earn a living on the hop between random bar tops and dealing day and night in whatever they could. When I was on the verge of having a serious chat with Alexa regarding his pal, Fermí disappeared up to La Seu d'Urgell having secured work as a waiter in a high-class restaurant. It was as though he'd read my mind.

Things quickly began to flow nicely for them again, economically speaking at least. Alexa was in charge of transport up to La Seu and Fermí took care of distribution throughout a zone that, according to him, was as mountainous as it was rich and as rich as it was depraved. But they blew the easy money they earned dealing as if there were a never-ending flow from the source. At least Su, when she pushed poppy or did overtime with a special client, usually put something aside for Jordi's future or her own utopic university enrolment. Or for some domestic improvement like the day she bought me a new washing machine to replace the old one we had dying on the balcony. But this sort of behaviour in what we might call the world of small-to-mid-range dealers is normally the exception to the rule: the vast majority of those that I've known, unfortunately a considerable number, push the boat out when the going's good only to find themselves cut adrift, living life at such a rate of knots that it ends up ravaging both health and bank balance.

Fermí had established a solid roll call of contacts and this, combined with his own habit, didn't leave him much margin for a forty-hour working week as a waiter and so he jacked the job in after just seven or eight months. Sometime around Christmas, if I am not mistaken. And as though he'd instinctively understood that I wouldn't be welcoming him back with open arms, he pulled a girlfriend out of the bag: a certain Lídia who shared a house on Carrer de les Acàcies with an entire female squadron of university friends. Alexa was working down in Sitges, where he had more meetings than a cabinet minister, and my guess is that Fermí was in charge of transportation.

Only they know what agreements they had in place and how they shared the profits, but I must make it clear they were as thick as thieves, those two, and I never once saw them argue over money, not even in their lowest moments. To risk over-egging the pudding, I should say that their relationship as both friends and partners was closer than that of many brothers and most lovers. So, on they roared, earning money and deepening their desire and need to live pedal to the metal. I recall how on many an evening, especially after they'd promised to atone for their smack sins and leave junk be, we'd go into bars and directly order a bottle of whisky. Really. If they had company, or sometimes when it was just the two of them, they'd buy a whole bottle to help the minutes creep by. And then another bar, and another bottle if necessary.

One night I said to Alexa, purely with his best interests at heart:

'If kicking heroin means becoming an alcoholic then you've got a problem.'

I honestly don't think he was trying to be clever or evasive but he didn't offer a single word of protest. Instead he just murmured that I likely didn't know how right I was.

The savage shock of Lluïsa's death was a turning point, and from that moment onwards things got worse by the day. I only met her once (they called her Lily, short for lily pad, which was a dumb joke about her flat chest) down at the beach after we'd phoned her to come have lunch with us. It must have been shortly before she… Anyway, the five of us (Fermí had brought Lídia along), and Lluïsa more than anyone, chose to play down her poor health and general appearance because it was clear for everyone to see that she could count the weeks she had left to live on half a hand.

I'd say it was that day, having witnessed the unequivocal reality of her impending death, when Alexa entered a vortex of horror and pessimism that he could only alleviate with shot after shot of whisky and/or heroin; what he called the 'pit' when he wept. Even when you experience something like this first-hand it's very complicated to identify the personal reasons behind each individual case. But just as Fermí began abusing junk again after Yma's goodbye, Alexa only fell from his taut high wire after Lluïsa's collapse. There is also the possibility that he'd been incubating private thoughts about what the fuck being a certified carrier of HIV/AIDS actually meant for his short and long-term reality, and it made him capable of doing anything. Melodramatically capable, when seen with the benefit of hindsight. I am no psychologist, nor does the idea attract me, but if I had to risk it I'd be inclined to diagnose poor Alexa with a guilt complex so deeply rooted that he accepted the tragedy of the virus as penitence for his sins.

The day of Lluïsa's funeral – when we force fed ourselves a dune of monstrous heat only to suffer the spectacle with her brother for dessert, whose desire to slap us silly outside the cemetery left me with gravel rash on my thigh as a fine memory – Alexa still had his stuff at my place but it'd already been a while since we'd agreed to put our impassioned cohabitation on hold until he'd kicked hard drugs. He was honourable and generous as ever, shouldering the blame and promising to get clean so as not to lose me for good. Junkie or no junkie, the boy really did love me. Many times I have asked myself to what extent I loved him but still I don't have a clear answer. But what is certain is that *he* loved *me* very much, even if he wasn't able to keep his end of the bargain. Perhaps it all stemmed from the void that Lluïsa had left in the heart of his soul, because Alexa had always worshipped her like the sun. Just as I had with Su. Ah, utopic loves, perfect loves. How I'd love to end this chapter on this bittersweet note but unfortunately there was another event hurtling towards us through space and time that only served to make a bad situation worse.

It was midweek in mid-September. I know this for sure because I'd only just got back from Mum's apartment in Cadaqués and was working at the gallery again. It was a humid, hazy, drizzly sort of morning and I was busy falling asleep in front of some avant-garde neo-realist painting that didn't say shit to me. My twenty-minute break wasn't due until ten o'clock but when Alexa came bursting into the room, as white as a corpse and stuttering histrionically, I asked Mr Germán for permission to briefly step outside and we raced out the door. Fermí was waiting for us in the bar on the corner. Well, more precisely, in the toilet. After a few gulps of milky coffee and a noticeable lack of detail to his responses, I gathered that Alexa wanted: 1) the keys to the apartment in Cadaqués for two or three days; 2) that I went and got them from Mum this lunchtime and took them to Carrer de les Acàcies without stopping by Plaça Padró; and, above all, 3) if anyone asked after them to say I hadn't had a sniff of them in days.

Everything he asked could be easily granted because I still had the keys to the apartment on my key ring and I sincerely hadn't seen a hair on either of their heads for a week or more. A slightly different story, however, was getting Mum's permission (it was her place, after all) and finding out exactly what had happened to them. But Alexa's only answer was the less I knew the better it'd be for everyone, before getting up to fetch Mín from the toilet. When Mín finally came out he was as soaked as a sponge and wearing a neurotic smile as a mask. With a couple of cropped but coherent sentences, he told me he'd murdered, sorry, killed in self-defence, some dealer called Lanzarote.

I called Mum and floated a watertight lie before handing them the goddam keys to the apartment. But in that very moment I decided that once we'd all squeezed out of this tight spot I'd have to lose sight of both of them if I didn't wish to get further entangled in their net. It wasn't a question or selfishness or a lack of solidarity but merely facing up to the fact that sharing certain paths with certain people can ruin the lives of everyone involved. In any case, I wasn't cut out to be a dealer or to live with one. And if I'm being totally honest, my crash course in heterosexual emotions and practices was already coming to an end. I suppose what I'm referring to here is passion because I've always loved that idiot but when it comes to actually being 'in love' (to use words everyone can understand) that only lasted nine or ten months.

But given – as Uncle Ramon says – that nothing is ever so bad, no matter how grave, that nothing good can come of it the bloody reunion with Lanzarote made them disappear as if by magic and, although Alexa still had half his life at my apartment, after that manic morning in the bar we didn't see one another again for a whole year. Alexa, I mean, because I never saw Fermí again. And if I'm being brutally honest, I've only ever missed him in an abstract sense.

TO BE OR NOT TO BE
1. *Intro: Frets to forget*

Why do we suffer each race to believe
That no race has been grander
'Time Table', GENESIS

In all our years rolling through this world, both together and separately, Fermín *El Malo* and I, Alexandre the Grateful, have witnessed, participated in and caused a thousand feuds. In almost all the cafés, bars, clubs and pubs we've worked in, some day or other, things have ended up coming to *les quatre cent coups*. I could write an entire encyclopaedia exclusively with entries documenting scenes of violence I've seen or heard of, but no doubt that would be callous, not to mention dull.

Nevertheless, owing to both its implications and ramifications, I can't resist recounting the one that happened to me at Friends & Co. one distant summer in Sitges, when four thugs of dubious nationality speaking drunken English (though they could easily have been Dutch or German or Scandinavian) began to insult, among themselves but with increasingly louder voices, a black guy called George who'd been coming in now and again over the preceding month with his girlfriend. The girl in question, a Venusian nymph of Catalan and Danish descent named Inge, was both the excuse and reason for the envious provocation: in all likelihood they couldn't accept the fact that a beautiful, blonde white woman preferred a 5'3 half bald black man to them.

George and his girlfriend got up and came over to the bar to pay, having decided to leave and thus avoid any trouble, but I (left to my own devices because the others weren't in until later) told them to keep their money and see you tomorrow. But the

Nordic numbskulls, having already started a raucous game of pool, insisted with all sorts of 'witty' insults: the drinks must be on the house because I was fucking his girl, and that if I was fucking her and nigger boy was too, then they'd have to show her what a pure-blooded white stallion was like.

And that's when George did something surprising: he told Inge to go look for a policeman and, after she'd reluctantly left, walked slowly over to the pool table, stood face to face with the last one to have spoken and nonchalantly informed him in fault-less film noir English that if he so much as breathed another word about him or his girlfriend he'd kill him on the spot. His supreme sense of security shocked me, so much so that if I were his adversary I'd have certainly thought twice about it. But a punch up was precisely what they were looking for and considering the fact it was four vs. one, two if I got involved, they weren't the least bit concerned. Also, in spite of the flourishing beer guts, they were all well-built and at least 6 ft. Not that it did them any good. And so, after a brief chorus of indolent laughter, as if they'd just been threatened by a mouse, the guy stared squarely at George and said: 'You're a fucking black bastard and I'm going to fuck your tart's tight Aryan arse right after I've finished smashing your dirty mug in.' Or something like that because he said it in an almost unintelligible slang or cockney, or whatever the fuck those lot use to speak to one another. Either way, he barely had time to finish his sentence because, in the blink of an eye, George's right hand made contact with his left temple and he plummeted to the floor like a sack of shit. There was no magical artifice, no martial arts involved, he'd merely struck him with one of the billiard balls. The black ball, to be exact.

Dumbstruck, the other three took a second and a half to react. The first to move was a paunchy, sunburnt goon who'd been lurking at the back and who charged at George while wildly swinging his pool cue. Fortunately, or unfortunately, George was on the ball: he avoided the blow by crouching down and, after aligning his energy, rose up and thrust the cue he'd grabbed from the one out cold on the floor two centimetres underneath his navel: two centimetres underneath and, thanks to the force of the coming together, three and three quarters inside. I'd since positioned myself next to George to help him but I wasn't able to do much other than hold up one of the two remaining hooligans by hitting him across the head with a barstool. And right on cue, just as our grisly get-together had reached a tacit conclusion, Inge walked in trailing two coppers and all six of us were officially given the right to remain silent.

In short: the two unharmed provocateurs (my brief opponent ended up with only a grazed cheek while the other didn't have time to get his arse kicked) got off with a night in a police cell and an infantile fine. The one who'd been stabbed with the cue was discharged from hospital a week later and was neither arrested nor fined, most likely because Thug No. 1, the one who'd been decked by the eight ball, had died of a brain haemorrhage two days after the incident. And George, naturally, was charged with murder and denied bail. My statement and the one by a local couple who'd been propping up the bar didn't help a jot: 'There's a dead body that has to be answered for!' is all the judge kept saying, over and over again. With a judge like that if, in addition to being black and African, George had been poor, he would've been done for. But that wasn't the case with old Georgie boy, oh no, and when I finally got to see him a few days later he wasn't giving the incident the slightest shred of importance: his father was a wealthy, influential politician and he, despite having a Zambian passport, was a professor at a Dutch university. The problem, he told me, his soul overflowing with tears, wasn't the murder charge: not at all. The problem was the murder in itself, which made him guilty of a disproportionately violent act, for in that instant his spirit had been flooded with pride and rage, demonstrating to both Inge and himself the full extent of his racial sensitivity. He was utterly dismayed at his own behaviour and convinced that Inge would never trust him again.

The end of the story was Inge's farewell, as sad as a withered flower, and George's release on bail a month later. Temporarily free from exterior bars but forever captive to remorse, he passed by the pub to say cheers and all the best, a plane ticket in his pocket and sadly repeating what he'd already told me at the police station: Inge, as he had predicted, had seen how he wasn't worthy of her (a different story was whether I'd ever understand her decision).

I've permitted myself the luxury of this prosaic introduction because it wasn't until Mín shot Lanzarote in the back below the low-flying aeroplanes in order to save my life that I was finally able to comprehend what George meant and how Inge had felt.

2. *Continuation: Frets to forget*

When the night wind cries
On the blood red feather
PETE BROWN, COLOSSEUM

In all our years rolling through this world of scumbags and shitheads, Lex and I, either together or separately, have been up to our necks in at least a thousand fights, more or less all of them ending in bloodshed and more or less serious injury.

But if I had to choose only one madcap fable to relate it would be from Lo Pont de Suert when stupid Manel tried to get smart with a ski instructor from Vielha called Ramon Maria who was going out with Manel's cousin, Gemma, hands down the sexiest and sweetest girl in the county. Despite having attempted a career as a boxer and still believing himself to be a dab hand, Manel was really just a strong, simpleminded fella who earned his beans doing bread and butter labour and, as long as he wasn't coked up or with the wrong crowd, was a good egg. If he ever got worked up his loud bark tended to be a lot worse than any genuine threat of a bite.

Amid shouts, shoves and smashing glasses, Lex and I, along with a few volunteers, manage to push the problem out onto the patio only for Manel, who's tied high to the cocaine mast with a head full of rum, to aim a hook at his adversary's pearly whites. However, in a display of enviable reflexes, Ramon Maria takes one step back, makes an opening and replies with a jab to the solar plexus that sits the immense Manel on his backside. The entire bar spills outside, around thirty or forty people in total, and makes a circle around them as though it were Fight Night. I grab Gemma by the arm and take her back inside before picking up my boxwood cane should anyone be called on to reinstate peace and love. Then I tell Lily to lock both doors and phone the fuzz, just in case.

Outside, the combat continues as before: Manel is throwing blind hooks, as energetic as they are ineffective, while Ramon Maria, who clearly knows a great deal more on the subject, either dodges or blocks them and is able to get close enough to punish his rival with a series of short, sharp jabs. After taking half a dozen of the type that leave a mark, Manel tries his luck with his legs, then his head, even attempting to bear hug his adversary, who unexpectedly drives a knee into his stomach, leaving Manel bent double.

'What? Had enough?' pants Ramon Maria.

'Enough, and then some,' I say, stepping into the circle ready to call time.

But someone shoves me hard in the back while simultaneously kicking my ankle and I'm sent sprawling over to the other side of the makeshift ring amid general laughter. Meanwhile, Manel has taken opportunity of the distraction to get back to his feet and launch himself unseen at the other. 'He's got a knife!' screams Lex, before stepping forwards to block him. The crowd instinctively takes a step backwards and the visitor from Vielha flings himself over at me. When we both get up again, he's holding my cane and shouting:

'Out of the way! This idiot needs a lesson!'

We shouldn't have listened to him, of course not, but the situation was so intimidating that we all instinctively moved backwards.

'I'm warning you both!' I hollered in an attempt to scare them. 'The police are on their way!'

But Ramon Maria had seen red, and with good reason, too: he was bopping from side to side, passing the cane from one hand to the other and waiting for his far less intelligent rival to attack. But his opponent, still hunched over his own stomach and following the heavy stick with a hypnotised stare, couldn't find a way in. With one lightning quick movement, Ramon Maria struck Manel on the elbow, disarming him, before striking him behind the knee. As the big man was falling to the ground, he landed a fist directly in the middle of his forehead prompting Lex and I to run like whippets into the middle of the circle because another punch could have been fatal. When Lex had him restrained by both arms and under control, I took the cane out of his hands and put an end to the war.

'Those of you who want to go back inside, now's your chance, and those who don't, it's home time! Show's over! And you two…' I added, pointing the cane at Manel's pals, one of whom had sent me tumbling to the ground while the other passed him the blade '…I don't *ever* want to see you here again. You hear? Never!!'

But then Ramon Maria screams out in pain and Lex begins raining insults down on Manel and his entire family while kicking and punching him like a raging windmill. I'd never seen Lex so angry. But immediately I realised why and, I have to admit, it was fully justified: as we were all filing back inside, that idiot Manel had got up, grabbed the knife and stuck it in the ski instructor's back. Now that the other was immobilised, Manel's two friends made a move to get involved but a couple of stinging strikes of the cane made them change their minds. And right then the police arrived, late as always, and radioed for an ambulance.

Lily kept the bar open with the help of a couple of volunteers because closing suddenly at eleven p.m. would only have served to magnify events and while Ramon Maria, Gemma and fucktard Manel went up the hospital, Lex and I ended down the police station. After our (im)pertinent statements and their fun-time threats about the day they'd catch us with our pockets full of hard candy, we were able to go to the hospital.

'It's our fault,' groaned Lex when we finally got access to his room.

'It's nothing. Just a prick,' Ramon Maria whispered magnanimously.

'But if it'd been just two centimetres nearer the centre…' I ventured, because a nurse had explained godknowswhat about his spine before she let us in.

'Forget about it,' said Gemma, who hadn't moved an inch from the top of the bed. 'It's my cousin's fault. And that bastard got off with a broken rib and couple of scratches to his stupid mug. But if I'm being completely honest, it's my fault too…'

'No, no, it's ours, it's ours,' insisted Lex, 'if we hadn't got involved…'

'Then I would've smashed his skull to pieces and been safe and sound in a cell on a murder charge. I'll be out in a couple of days and we'll have a few drinks to celebrate you two saving me from something infinitely worse.'

'But what I don't get,' I said, 'even though Gemma is the prettiest girl from here to Bordeaux, is Manel's bad blood.'

'We'd already come to blows in Vielha a few months ago and he was out for revenge.'

'Let's hope he's had his fill.'

'Don't worry,' said Gemma, looking deep within herself. 'I know how to end it Once and for All.'

When they came to Barcadia a few days later to say thank you and give us an update, Gemma let us in on a little family secret by explaining how the whole sordid story had begun and how it was finally put to bed, something that not even Ramon Maria knew the full extent of.

Five or six years earlier, when Gemma was seventeen and the two of them were on their way to Barcelona, strong Manel tried to force himself upon her sexually (fortunately unsuccessfully) and from then on he had systematically hounded friends and lovers out of pure disdain. It was certainly childish, and also rather tragic, bearing in mind that Manel was almost thirty, but I suppose God put a little something of everything in the world, if only for His own amusement.

In the end, Gemma's solution for that old problem called Manel had nothing to do with cops or courts but to instead explain the situation to her dad who, despite being the most peace-loving man in town, was a giant in a family of oaks. Mr Manolo, uncle and godfather to a degenerate fuckwit, took ten minutes to load his shotgun and drive over to the building site where his nephew laboured. Standing by the cement mixer,

Manel saw him step out of the car with the gun over his shoulder and ran as fast as his legs would carry him towards an empty neighbouring plot. Mr Manolo promptly got his gun into position and emptied two cartridges into his back. Having accompanied her dad there just in case, Gemma had witnessed it first hand and was now relating events with wild eyes and bacchantic laughter.

'His workmates were frozen with shock,' she howled, 'just like you two are now! But when they saw my idiot cousin holding his arse and howling they realised they were salt shells and started roaring with laughter.' Continuing to giggle wickedly, she added: 'My dad then put the shotgun down and walked calmly over to where Manel was moaning in pain. He grabs him by the ear and starts slapping him, telling him this time he got off with a child's punishment, because that's what he was, but if he ever went near me again he'd swap salt for lead. Then he asked him ten times or more if he understood while continuing to slap him and pull his ear! And that huge man, normally so full of himself, was on his knees, hot tears streaming down his face, repeating: *yes, yes! I understand! Never again, Uncle! I swear…!*'

I still retain the exuberant image of Gemma on that dazzling day etched onto my retina: she radiated not only physical beauty but a happiness that came from deep within now that she'd finally removed the thorn embedded in her skin for so long. She was, quite simply, divine and I regretted not having made the most of my opportunity the previous summer one late early morning down on the riverbank.

In short: a whole load of frets to forget.

3. *Chaos and plans*

I've seen the future, brother
It is murder
LEONARD COHEN

In all our years rolling through this world, both together and separately, Mín and I have interrupted, received and given an array of beatings and we would've sworn we'd seen it all but, of course, up until that point neither of us had ever killed a person and the vertigo, shock and shot of adrenaline left us trembling and disorientated.

'Listen, in the movies they take the rod apart and throw away each piece separately,' I muttered after a minute of silence, driving as discreetly as possible.

'What rod?'

'The gun, man!'

'What gun?'

His face was that of a moron so I pulled over and stopped the car.

'Oi, wake up!' I shouted while shaking him. 'Where's the goddam gun?!'

'I don't have a gun!' he replied. 'I must have dropped it…'

I rummaged through his pockets and searched the car before getting back behind the wheel, pulling a U-turn with pedal and handbrake, and following the same road back.

'What the hell are you doing?!' he shouted at me. 'Are you crazy?!'

'We've got to go look for the gun, Mín!!'

'You *are* crazy!!'

'If they find the gun we're screwed. Don't you realise they've got our prints?'

'But what if somebody's already found it?'

'Then they've got our arses, as well.'

Fulfilling the premise that murderers always return to the scene of the crime, we raced all guns blazing back to the shady spot where Lanzarote's car was parked. I pulled up by the side of the road, grabbed a rag from inside the car, and got out to collect the gun. The body was just a few metres up ahead but I didn't look at it, only unwillingly out of the corner of my eye: there was no question he was dead.

'Is he dead?' I asked while wiping a glop of vomit off my trousers.

Lex didn't answer. But it's possible he didn't hear me because he'd already hidden the rod (wrapped in a rag inside a bag) under his seat and was now fully concentrated on getting away quickly without causing a scene.

I've got to say he did a real fine job right from the get-go with the headache over the gun up until the migraine of the next couple of days when we set our trafficking trip to Naples in motion. Truth be told, I was incapable of thinking or making any type of decision until the following day, apart from gunning shot after shot, of course. But I did manage to make the occasional contribution like, for example, after it occurred to Lex that almost as dangerous as the gun (we wrapped the separate pieces in plastic bags and threw them one by one out of the car window each time we crossed a bridge) was the car: yep, his beaten up but beloved scarlet xr3, aka *Marlene*.

'I've got it!' I shouted. 'Forget Cadaqués. Let's go to Dixi's place instead!! We'll be able to hole up there and change cars…'

We'd already reached the top of Avinguda Meridiana on our way out of Barcelona so changing direction for Manresa was as simple as flicking the indicator and turning the wheel. Twenty-five minutes later, being careful not to speed but still trembling, above all the three times we crossed paths with a patrolling squad car, we were pulling up outside the garage that Cousin Alberto, aka *Dixi*, had opened on the outskirts of Olesa. Alberto (who nobody knew as Dixi anymore except for a few surviving war veterans) welcomed us with open arms: no doubt as soon as he set eyes on us he saw that if he played his cards right there was money to be had. Ever since he'd drawn a line under speed, the only thing he got his rocks off over, apart from his woman and all the others, were a few fast bucks.

My first reaction was that Dixi had changed. A lot. He was now the proud owner of a spectacular garage and a no less spectacular beer belly and, what's more, he was clean shaven and with a number 2 all over. If I'd bumped into him on the street I doubt I would've recognised him. When it came to our own personal trials and tribulations, Mín played his hand very well and after we sketched out the situation (telling him we'd left someone in a bad way with a blade, without mentioning anything about debts or guns) Dixi took care of everything. After driving away in my car he was back an hour later with a black vehicle with leopard print seat covers (oh Marlene, poor baby! No doubt she ended up in the cruel hands of a poundland pimp). But I'm getting ahead of myself because first a shower and a spot of rest while Gràcia, his wife, put the finishing touches to a paella. As everyone knows, in Catalonia, Thursday is paella day and their homesweethome was no exception.

The house was above the garage and had two floors and a loft. Dixi, Gràcia and their three-year-old son lived on the second floor, which was connected to the converted loft by a staircase. The first floor, as Dixi explained to me as we went upstairs, had been rented out for the first few years as a source of quick and easy money but in the end he got fed up of the tenants always being privy to his comings and goings. Now he used it as a temporary storage space, at least until the kid started school and his wife went back to work and he'd be able to set up a shop selling parts and accessories: everything from radios and shock absorbers to gloves and sunglasses.

While we were showering, shooting up, and floating differing hypotheses and theories on how to vanish off the map for a long while, Fermí told me that half the house had been earned dealing in cars and the other half in drugs. Dixi's motto was that drugs had to return him all the money they'd cost him, and it certainly looked like it was working out for him. I bumped into him outside the bathroom, almost as if he'd been waiting there expressly for me, and he invited me out on to the balcony for a couple of cold beers. It wasn't until the second sip that I thought to offer him a line and he immediately replied okay without me having to insist.

Afterwards we all sat down and paid our respects to the paella. In truth, none of us said very much on the subject, despite it being delicious, firstly because Dixi and Gràcia had been hit hard by the smack they'd snorted and secondly because Mín and I had been hit even harder by the murder. But it was self-defence, right? Technically speaking, yes – if we accept the proposition that A kills B to avoid B killing C. But it's still murder at the end of the day. I admit it's as stupid as hell but what made me feel especially guilty was knowing that everything had happened because I owed Lanzarote an amount I'd no longer be able to pay him. And now it's on account of that first debt that I had a second one with Fermí, which I also wouldn't be able to settle in my lifetime.

Thankfully, at fifteen hundred hours local time, when we finally managed to speak to Sandro at his Neapolitan *trattoria*, the chaotic fog lifted and we began to make proper plans.

Savouring the coffee and accompanying fixes, we begin making a list of bright buttons to press:

1) The issue of the car will remain in the hands of dear Dixi, who this very afternoon will find us one that runs and tomorrow register it in our names. The document will be provisional, of course, but after paying insurance, taxes and whoknowswhatelse we'll be able to go wherever we want without worrying. About the car, at least.

2) The merchandise Sandro is most interested in, when all is said and done, is blow, and quality blow at that. We'll have to translate all the horse we have into liquid dough and pay a visit to either Pere or Bald Eagle. The head of the household will help us with the first transaction and take five or six grams off our hands at a good price to sell in town. The rest we'll share between the girls on Acàcies and María Susana, because we can't risk the usual routes.

3) We'll have to phone Lali at the gallery to let her know we haven't gone to Cadaqués and that we'll bring her the keys, then dot the i's with Susan, before crossing the t's with Lídia so she brings me the one hundred thousand pessetes I have hidden in a pack of condoms and come pick up whatever merch she wants. What we certainly can't do is go anywhere near the flat because if that gyppo has mentioned Lex and they're looking for him then no doubt they're also looking for me, if only to ask me where he is. Anyway, Lídia isn't a problem because we're sure to find her at Manyo's with her four o'clock coffee.

4) We'll need a car to go to Barna tonight and get the ball rolling. Dixi won't lend us his car but he will act as taxi driver and that at least means someone will be able to show their face in the open if needs be.

5) Finally, we will have to invent a ruse that allows us to cross two international customs with good old Charlie boy on-board

without us fretting too much about it. I've got an idea that's a stretch more civilised than the oil can: this afternoon my sensual cousin-in-law, graceful Gràcia, who the undeserving Dixi has no right to, will buy me a pot of glue, a few nails and a chessboard and that way, while Lex and Dixi are in Barcelona, we'll have something to keep our hands occupied.

I remember a great many things from that trip with Dixi, too many, in fact, for my intellectual stomach to digest, beginning with his incessant chatter because he seemed to view me as a free psychiatrist. I was made privy to the ins and outs of all the material triumphs and spiritual disappointments of his adult life: the ifs, buts, and cons of being faithful (or not) to one's wife, whether or not to hit the boy when he wets the bed, or to screw over one's employees according to the waxing of the moon, and a long, twisted etcetera which I, out of pure personal interest, didn't dare interrupt, despite having a belly full of my own, much more convoluted complications. Thankfully, just before we entered Barcelona, he stopped to fill up the tank and, after a thick rail, let me get behind the wheel of his long-serving green Citroën, repeating for the tenth time that the reverse gear was different. But everything from that point onwards was full steam ahead.

Mín had arranged for Lídia to meet us at nine on the dot in a billiards bar near Plaça Maragall where we usually hung out in the evenings. Along with Lídia there was Isolda, Neus and Mercè. Christ, the only thing left to do was invite cousins and aunties, too! But in actual fact, it was a pretty good cover because those young, beautiful things always looked stunning, even when they were junk sick.

Neus, Isolda, Mercè and Dixi went for an opportune game of doubles while Lídia and I discussed three invoices and the terms of two further transactions. I informed her that Fermí would call her tomorrow at four at Manyo's; that she could give me the cash stash now, but if she wanted more marzipan she'd have to pay upfront; and that no, she needn't worry, there'd been a little mishap but, having said that, I really shouldn't be in a bar at night in central Barcelona. I tell Dixi to pay for the drinks and finish up the game fast before taking Lídia to the car, parked a couple of streets away, to close the deal. She was short but voluptuous and had a certain *something* about her… above all in her oceanic eyes and juicy lips… and while she was handing me the notes and accepting a few paper pouches in return, I thought how I should've paid that flaming spirit more attention because Mín didn't love or deserve her.

But right then a smiling Dixi arrived with the three girls and off we shot to exquisite Su's place. I must confess that going with Dixi and not Mín suited me down to the ground because I was secretly hoping – time permitting – to give her the farewell fuck I never got to give Lali. Sioux had already reminded me ten times or more amid smiles and laughs that we'd never made love, and ever since Eulàlia had dismissed me she reminded me of it every chance she got.

I left the motor in a nearby car park and gave Dixi a pouch so he wouldn't get bored.

'Snort it in a cubicle,' I told him, 'but make sure you're in the bar on the corner by ten-thirty. I might be a wee while… I have a bit a work to do.' Then I added with a conspiratorial wink: 'But there's a sea of terraces and an ocean of pretty little things here to keep you busy.'

Su was living with another friend close to Passeig del Born in a loft apartment much larger than Eulàlia's and with almost as much natural light. This friend (a certain Flor, who I never met) had taken the kid to the cinema around half nine because Sioux had had the exact same idea as me: now was the moment and if it wouldn't come about by magical randomness, as it had been on the cusp of so many times, we'd have to organise it ourselves. While I cooked up a couple of standard shots, she began an overture of caresses and squeezes, kisses and bites to ear lobes, armpits, nipples and thighs. I shot up as she continued to undress me and when it was her turn I stripped her naked and returned her the small percentage of oral sex she'd given me. She enjoyed it immensely, perhaps more for its emotional significance than its purely sexual sensation, but I can't be entirely sure because soon we were fully focused on fucking, which is precisely what we'd never tried together, and the appetisers were placed on the back burner.

The evening was as gratifying and vivacious as her skin, as deep and fragrant as our sex, and in the shadow of the balcony (where we ended up naked and smoking a 'skagfag', as she called it) a cloud of longing already began to form around me.

When I got up to take a shower and leave, she told me that she'd always liked me and that she hadn't felt what she'd just felt with me – both during and after sex – with any man since meeting her monster of an ex-husband eight years ago. I listened to her velvety voice while drying my hair (which I always let grow long in those days) and before we knew it we were in each other's arms again.

'Do you know what I think?' I told her as we smoked one last gun together. 'What really attracts you to me is that I never look at you, or fuck you, thinking you're a whore but instead thinking, *knowing*, you're a woman and, what's more, a wonderful, gorgeous woman like few others. Having said that, if I were to fall in love with you, which I'm not planning on doing, I couldn't ever be your partner, not if you didn't change profession. I'm too emotionally unstable to deal with it. The same thing happened to Eulàlia, if you don't mind my saying. Now that girl really *did* love you!'

This honest but improper, perhaps even jealous, comment inevitably dispelled the magic of the moment and she began a tearless sob while offering me seventy thousand *peles* from a sock in exchange for a postcard now and again. I accepted the money with a kiss on the lips and a guilt-ridden sigh. Here I was, creating another emotional debt I'd never be able to pay back. If I'd suspected she was in love with me, for want of a better word, I would've done things differently. Or maybe I'd already sensed it and all I did was take advantage of it. This often happens in the minds of humans: we dress up and disguise the most perverse actions with the garb of innocence, even kindness. I can only assume it's some sort of psychological self-defence mechanism to not have to face up to the cruel reality of our own self-centredness.

I had time to meditate on this at the bar (while waiting for the hamburger I didn't eat) because, despite not getting there until gone eleven, that slacker Dixi was nowhere to be seen. On the terrace my only company was a couple cuddling in the corner and I got down to daydreaming about Susana and Eulàlia, and who knows how many thousand and one three-dimensional nights… But I couldn't avoid looking at my watch every five minutes and by eleven forty-five I was sweating blood and guts. I didn't know whether to phone Olesa, leg it to the car, take a tour of the local bars, or wait it out where we'd agreed to meet, which is always the most difficult but, ultimately, the most sensible option.

Dixi finally arrived, a complete nervous wreck and laughing at everything, and we went straight to Painter Pere's apartment. On the way there he explained how he'd ducked into a telephone cabin to hoover up some dust because toilets made him feel claustrophobic but that on this occasion, out of pure rotten luck, a policeman had spotted him. As he wasn't carrying any more drugs on him and only his I.D., they carted him back to the station to mess him around for an hour or more before taking a statement and telling him to be a good boy.

He knew perfectly well they couldn't do anything but he was worried about me. And he didn't dare ring the house in case we, you know, Mín and I...

ALL-INCLUSIVE HOLIDAY
1. *Touristic snapshots*

When I was younger I changed
name at every border
JOAQUÍN SABINA

When it comes to Naples I have a number of memories, all of them more or less vivid, but the one that will never leave me for as long as I live (I know it's a cliché) is the incredible traffic madness. I've driven in Barcelona, Valencia, Madrid, Paris, Amsterdam... but I'd never seen anything like it.

Being as exhausted as we were and without knowing the layout of the secret structures of that insanity, getting to an actual address seemed such a dangerous undertaking that we preferred the unpredictability of a random parking space. We set off on foot before Lex decided it would be better if one of us kept an eye on the car from the bar on the corner while the other took a taxi to the restaurant. I was feeling feverish and tiger tired so I offered myself as lookout while he ventured into the jungle with only a city map and a couple of phrases of macaronic Italian.

When it comes to Naples, I have a number of memories, good and excellent, bad or worse, but undoubtedly the one I will never forget for as long as I live is walking into *Trattoria da Ischia*. I was informed that Sandro wasn't there by a golden-haired beauty with a turquoise gaze who, I'm embarrassed but nevertheless obliged to say, I mistook for a boy. Most likely it was because she had her back to me and her short hair hidden under a black leather cap. Blushing like a little boy because I was helpless to break the spell of her Adriatic eyes and smiling, suggestive cherry lips, I managed to order a beer and light a cigarette to combat the fatigue. She told me her name was Micalea and that she was Sandro's little sister. After serving my beer she went to make a phone call and assured me that *il sue fratello* would be no more than twenty minutes. We began a conversation via her rusty Buenos Aires Spanish because my best attempts at Italian only made her giggle. But soon we discovered that in English (she'd worked as a hostess and I'd served tourists the length of the Catalan coastline) we got our message across just fine.

In Italy, and Naples in particular, I learnt a couple of important (and interesting) things very quickly. The first being that not all Italian women are brunette bombshells with baroque hips and cinematic breasts. Leading on from and into stories I was only marginally able to understand owing to the language barrier and the difficulty of concentrating on anything that wasn't her (her charm, her intelligence, her delightful affability), that fairy at the bottom of the garden told me that her whole *famiglia* heralded from Ischia, where they still had roots, trunks and branches of grandparents, aunts, uncles, cousins and nephews (first, second, even three-times removed), the vast majority of them blonde with blue eyes. If I understood everything correctly, at the turn of the century or thereabouts, there was a significant immigration of *tedeschi* (or Germans to you and me) and from that point onwards the genetic makeup of the island had drastically changed. But from what I could tell, it'd only affected their physical features because there was nothing Teutonic about either hers or Sandro's character.

The second thing I learnt, accompanied by red-faced embarrassment, was that the majority of cafés, restaurants and pizza parlours, especially the more down-to-earth ones, don't have customer toilets. But Micalea, displaying all the hospitality that a guest of her brother's deserved, handed me a key and pointed to a door at the back.

The third one is that the residents of Naples and the surrounding area are obsequious to the point of boorishness and gregarious to the point of impoliteness. Micalea never went that far but she did officially present me to each and every customer that came in, whether young or old, male or female, during the seventy plus minutes I had to wait for her brother. When he finally turned up, there were six of us sat at table together, commenting on holidays to Mallorca, Salou and Torremolinos as though we were childhood friends.

And last but not of any less importance, the fourth and final thing I learnt was time, because Neapolitan minutes are not like those in the rest of the world. In all honestly, it's hard to even call them minutes.

The bells chime eight p.m. and I'm fed up of watered down beer and waiting awake and upright in the same chair. I'd almost be glad if someone did try to force or steal the motor. Or if any one of these kamikazes accelerating through the red lights swerved and slammed straight into it. Then I start to worry about my partner and begin having visions of him riddled with bullets on some Neapolitan street corner in broad daylight for his wristwatch and scratched Ray-Bans when I'm roused by an insistent car horn and waving hands. Sitting in an Italian sports car with the top down is Sandro with Lex by his side and two girls in the back as attractive as they are different from one another. Sandro introduces the brunette to me as Olga, his *fidanzata*, a sculpted bacchante with long hair flowing down the length of her back. But of course, Sandro's immense humanity needed a woman like that, and many more things besides. The other is a blonde, stylish sylph who on first sight, perhaps because of her short barley hair and black cap, I took for a guy: Sandro's sister, Micalea. Then Micalea goes with Lex to our white VW and I get in Sandro's wonderful yellow Alfa-Romeo. If I wasn't so dead on my feet, I'd no doubt have enjoyed the journey like any normal tourist.

The drive was an exquisite symphony of the senses that lasted barely twenty minutes but the fragrances from that unique universe and moment as we hugged the bay on our way up north and the vivid, intense aromas when we turned onto the country roads linking the coastal towns (despite the accumulated tension of my tiredness) were twenty 'truly Neapolitan' minutes. As exaggerated as it might sound, if I really let myself go I'd be tempted to say they are still on-going. Naturally, next to me, as we swerved past a thousand obstacles and dangers with beeps of the horn and impromptu slams on the brakes, laughing and talking like the shimmering waves, was luminous Micalea.

2. *Inner voice in voce: Invoices and receipts*

'Dealer', TRAFFIC

Sandro's place was a small villa overlooking the quay in the village of Pozzuoli. Before we got there I had already begun to note a strange odour, like rotten eggs or bad farts, but they informed me amid friendly laughter that it was only the *solfatara* and that the following day I'd hardly notice it. But the following day the smell was still there, even if it didn't seem quite as bad as before: it formed part of the landscape and the magic of that strange all-inclusive holiday.

After showering and shooting up (much called for after stomaching twenty-four hours of open road on only one pack of rigged cigs and a couple of lines), we shut ourselves away in the garage with Sandro to look over our invoices and receipts. He loved the idea of the chessboard glued around the edges but hollow in the middle where we'd stashed the merchandise. Needless to say, we had to saw out the bottom to get to the juicy filling, but that was precisely the fun. We racked up lines and dabbed cigarettes in the powder and began the process of scrutinising its smell, colour, texture, taste and subsequent effects on both a physical and psychic level, and fifteen minutes later we were all convinced of its quality. In any case, it was a white crystal that Pere had called '3P' i.e. *pure premier league product* and, what's more, it was uncut and would go far. [At two a.m., having added up projected sales and takings, calculated the cost of a round trip, made the corresponding reserves for the car, and with Dixi drowsy drunk and slumped in the corner of a third-rate bar, Lex bought sixty grams of crystal at five thousand five hundred pessetes a unit. Knowing Pere, it was a good deal, too]. But the price and amount agreed on with Sandro over the phone (using cava as a code word) was forty grams at thirteen thousand. Therefore, according to the way he saw it, sixty had to come at a lower unit price. We discussed how many percentage points the price should be honourably lowered by to compensate for the increase in quantity before finally shaking on twelve thousand five hundred pessetes. He told us he'd have five hundred and twenty thousand ready on Monday but that the remaining two hundred and thirty thousand would have to wait a couple of weeks: he was going to the USA on Tuesday until the end of the month. I assured him we weren't in a rush just as his sister knocked on the door to tell us dinner would be served in two minutes. When we were breathing the final dot-to-dots and bringing events to a syntactic close, Sandro made a rapid mental calculation regarding the commission we'd have to pay if we wanted to charge half the amount in dollars; a service we had to accept, whether we liked it or not, because the last thing we wanted was to descend into the millionaires' inferno, even if it was only Italian lira.

3. *Inner voice in voce: Love and loss*

Te voglio bene assaje
NAPLES GRAFFITI

We nourished that first, delicious night with *tagliatelle alle von-gole* (Olga's speciality) and later with whisky and *caffè freddo* while ambling amid the volcanic eruption of kiosks, cafés and cocktail bars in and around Naples. I was suddenly flooded with the same intoxicating longing that I'd sensed on Siouxsie's balcony, possibly because I'd already comprehended that these people, regardless of how much cocaine was or wasn't involved, lived in a placidly human dimension. They lived life, as they say, in the slow lane: now it's time to eat, now it's time to go out, now it's time to sleep or swim or stroll or work or cry, even. Each notion seemed to demand and find its own specific spacetime in a spontaneous yet measured way in spite of, or owing to, the special inner workings of its clock.

After my first long break in '83 (which experienced its first cracks New Year's '85 over three days with Lluïsa before continuing to widen on account of Noemí's home cooking), it was almost three years that I'd been sporadically getting back in the saddle but the last few months, owing to Lluïsa's death, the despondency of AIDS and my separation from Eulàlia, the wild beast had begun to gallop again. But then Micalea's fresh giggles, Olga's happy chuckling and Sandro's deep, generous laughter appeared, resuscitating the desire in my veins to live without horse. For donkey's years I'd entertained the idea that one could live just as happy being a junkie as long as one had the means to buy gear whenever and in whatever quantity was needed but now I was beginning to understand, based on my own experience, that the emotiveness of and relationship with your immediate surroundings, including your most elemental mood rhythms, were altered by daily heroin use. And if, on top of that, you begin to feel captive to it – as happened to me on more than one occasion – then the labyrinths and traumas are multiplied by nine.

Consequently, the first love that I experienced in Naples was for myself because the humans around me were alive and I wanted to feel that way again, too. Hand on heart, I can honestly say that their passion for the lived moment and their ability to prepare, feel and enjoy it with serenity and a beautifully balanced sense of time exorcised me once and for all of the tyranny of heroin, even if I was still lacking a section of small details and two or three weighty concepts.

My second love was more ordinary yet completely extraordinary and it was, of course, Micalea. To this day I'm convinced that, as much as I fell in love with her, I also fell in love with what she personified for me: that is, the freedom to live fully and with all its consequences without destroying the future and a good part of the present. Once again, the ominous, omnipresent maxim was confirmed that states that between two lovers there is always one that loves and one that lets his or herself be loved and, as always, I had the sterile second role. Nevertheless, it's important to say that ours was a sure example of what often gets called 'love at first sight', a straightforward arrow fired by baby Cupid that pierced *anema e core* the moment we laid eyes on one another: Saturday, 18:35, Trattoria da Ischia. And I say 'we' because the first time we made love the following Monday (contemplating the evening from a hire boat three hundred metres from the Pozzuoli quay), she confessed the same thing had happened to her: a smack of white heat that penetrates, floods, and transports you from the first look. Barely fifty hours had passed since Saturday afternoon but as far as we, and our intimacy, were concerned each hour represented a week. And even though all the signs had been telling me that she felt it too, I found her so wonderful and it felt so glorious being with her that I refused to believe in it until it was an indisputable fact.

When Sandro departed for the States on Tuesday afternoon, Mín and I got a room in a B&B he'd found in the *centro storico* near the *duomo*, but I didn't even step foot in it because by then I'd set myself up with Micalea in Vomero at the house of some friends of hers who were away on holiday. We spent a week of unparalleled harmony when wrong place, wrong time, I had the great notion to call Eulàlia at the gallery. It must've been around eight o'clock in the evening.

'There are people in the shop right now but we need to talk. Give me your number and I'll ring you back in an hour.'

Her voice sounded different, sort of shaky, and I was on the verge of hanging up.

'They've been asking after me.'

'No, no! Nothing like that but we really do need to talk.'

'You're telling me they haven't been sniffing around?'

'Yes that's what I'm telling you! Hey! What do you take me for?'

'Alright. I'll call you back at nine on the nose.'

At nine I spoke to Eulàlia for exactly twenty-seven minutes. When we both hung up, Micalea had already taken a shower, got dressed, done her hair and makeup and put on perfume, ready to go for dinner and she was beginning to get restless.

Given she was on holiday we slept until whenever and had lunch at home in the late afternoon with Mín. Then we'd do a spot of tourism, either alone or with him, and in the evening we'd go for a slap up meal, just the two of us. Each night she took me to one of her favourite places, some, according to her, that even her brother didn't know, and he knew everywhere. I have to say that, in addition to serving the most exceptional meals, they were all beautiful and intimate, aesthetic and romantic, as though built expressly to frame a Neapolitan love film. And that's precisely how the preceding nights had been (in Marechiaro, in Posillipo, in Ercolano, in Postiano, in Amalfi). That is, full of waves and candles, tenderness and passion, of present ecstasy and love for the future. Each of those places deserves ten pages of lyrical description and any one of those nights would provide the perfect post-romantic screenplay. But that particular evening I had the conversation with Eulàlia in the forefront of my mind and Micalea noticed my anguish before the drinks had even arrived.

'She's your girlfriend.'

'Was.'

'But you still love her.'

'Yes. But that's not why I'm sad. You've wiped from my flesh the love I felt for her. The problem is a different one, much deeper, much more tragic, and a lot more difficult to solve. Let's change the subject or it will end up tearing the evening limb from limb.'

We were in a restaurant by the quay of I don't know what village on the southern bay that had tables on a wide wooden platform two or three metres above the sea. The moon shone with tones of Arabian jade that splashed and frolicked with Micalea's pupils. She took me by the hand in an attempt to brighten my mood but when the waiter brought us our *gnocchi* I turned away so he wouldn't see me crying.

'Don't worry about him,' she whispered softly and smiled. 'He'll think it's a lovers' tiff. When it comes to questions of the heart, men here are a bunch of... *piagnucoloni!*'

Despite recalling more and more Argentine with each passing day, that word she said in Italian. After a round of laughter, because the word sounded so silly to me, I deduced that it meant 'cry babies'. It must have been a premonition because I blubbed through the whole damn dinner and night; a night that was painful like few others.

Before I go on narrating the pleasure-pain of that particular night, in order to better outline events and each character's 'momentum', I must mention that the four grams of heroin we'd taken along for ourselves, hidden next to the coke, had run out by Thursday morning. That same evening Mín locked himself in his B&B room with two bags of meds, a pack of cigarettes and half a box of whisky, whereas I spent the best withdrawal of my life using and abusing codeine and Micalea. And truth be told, I barely missed it at all though perhaps it wasn't all that surprising bearing in mind I'd only been hitting half a quarter gram a day for the last five or six months. Of course, in large part it was down to the magic of the moment, Micalea's charming spell and the help of the painkillers. But, as is to be expected during junk withdrawal, my emotional organism had been affected and tears of tedium and fear, of joy, longing and regret flowed out of me with much greater ease.

If it hadn't been for Micalea no doubt I'd have gone running to Mín, convinced him to postpone our plans of redemption, and we'd have thrown ourselves headfirst into the adventure of scoring a bag in Naples. Of course, that was something I could do anytime I wanted by giving Micalea a more or less credible excuse but I didn't want to see Mín or do the rounds of dopedives, dopedealers and dopeheads. In that tragic yet sublime moment, I had no wish to hide myself in the belly of the horse. What I did do, however, before proceeding to explain my life story to delicate Micalea, was order more whisky and ask her where we could pick up some herb. After a round of walnuts, we went to buy three hundred thousand lira of Libyan in Forcella, a thoroughbred neighbourhood in central Naples that Micalea told me was best not to enter if you didn't know where you were going. Fortunately for me, she did.

We bought a bottle of single malt and ten metres of cigarette paper, and began a circuit of squares, searching for some cool corner where we could sit (which in Naples in the summer, because of the stone, is everywhere) and smoke a spliff and sip scotch. But then you stroll to the next square, buy a beer on the way, and keep on circling until your head is doing circles and the squares are circling within you and everything is spinning and circling around you. As the party that night had something of the *viacrucis* about it, I apologised between stations along the Way for not having told her I was HIV positive but her only reproach was to suggest a toast to condoms. Smoking, drinking, laughing and crying uncontrollably, I told her all about Lluïsa, already dead and buried by then, and how it could well have been me that infected her or vice versa, and then my conversation with Eulàlia who'd told, assured and sworn to me that Yma, Mín's ex, had tested positive in each of her last five tests. Christ, Yma as well! Naturally, Fermí would have to be informed so he could take the necessary precautions, whatever they were and, naturally, it was my job to play pall bearer. I'd have sooner chopped my own arm off. At a quarter to who cares, long after we'd stopped counting the spliffs and shots, the squares and sobs, Micalea decided that the best thing would be to leave the city for a few days, and the sooner the better. It was all the same to me whether we left or continued to follow the spinning circle within the infinite wheel. But she was right: if we were going to leave, first we'd have to solve a little problem called Fermín Guzmán.

'You've got to go and tell him. If not right now, then first thing in the morning.'

'You're right. But it's not that simple. He's doing cold turkey and is probably in a bad way, so I can't just give it to him like that.'

'If what you're trying to tell me is you need a bit of sugar, I can find you some. But get one thing straight: this is the first and last time.'

And so it was.

I will refrain from describing the scene with Fermí out of psychological shame and an assortment of other personal reasons. Ten years of love and loss had caught up with us amid the panic over the taboo of AIDS and the anguish of watching our friends and hopes die. On the surface he barely even reacted to this latest blow dealt to us by the epidemic and to our latest attempts to get clean. In my rage at the shattering circumstances, I cooked myself a fix and then left him what remained of the gram of brown (Brown Sugar, as The Stones had called it when we were just small) that Micalea had managed to pick up God knows how and where at five in the morning. While I silently collected the little I had to collect, we uttered a muted farewell.

'Look after the car. Naples is alive with thieves.'

'You're leaving with Micalea.'

I answered with deafening silence.

'You're going to have big problems with Sandro.'

'Out of all the problems I have right now that's the one that worries me the least.'

'Where are you going? (long pause) When will you be back?'

'Next week (long pause) See you later.'

I left the B&B for the first and last time at six in the morning. I know because the bells of three or four neighbouring churches were chiming with dodecaphonic rhythm. Micalea was waiting for me with her bags and fears in a café on the corner that opened from dawn to dusk and afterwards I followed the echoing bells down to the quay, my bags and regrets on my back. But the dirty grey city dawn erupted into blues, greens, yellows and reds lathered with foaming whites the moment we set sail for Procida.

Oh, Procida! Oh, the island! If, ten years later, just hearing any name associated with that region makes me break out in goose bumps then Procida is the key that opens a chest brimming with fragrances of suffering, need, desire and hope!

Without doubt Procida is the third love from those melodramatic all-inclusive holidays! I'd describe it as Ibiza with the attitude of Formentera, but in many ways it was even less touristic than Formentera because not even Neapolitans went there on holiday. As Micalea explained, the Neapolitans that could afford it went to Ischia or Capri and the ones that couldn't didn't go anywhere because no one in Naples knew you could go anywhere else.

Whatever the case, there were only two cafébars and one *trattoria* on the quintessential island square set inevitably next to the harbour, and the bus that took us inland was the only one operating on the whole of Procida and it spent the day doing back-and-forth trips from the aforementioned square to an even smaller, simpler one on the island's western tip. I felt sick and dirty, more dead than alive, so I would've happily stayed in either of the two hostels on the square that overlooked the harbour. But when we walked through the door to the hostel that Micalea had reserved, high up on the island summit, we were welcomed by a lemon orchard and a ceiling full of fruits that, owing to their sheer size, looked like melons. Yet if the Lewis Carroll imagery was an A then the fresh citric aftertastes and ripe September sweetness deserved an A+. There were two-seated benches strategically positioned in three or four places and in the centre was a natural stone fountain that must've been millennial at least two or three times over.

'It's like a dream,' I seem to recall muttering despite the weight of my fatigue and the hypnotic effect of the place.

'You've not seen nothing yet…' she responded with smiling eyes that I've carried etched onto my soul forever since.

We ambled towards the bottom of the overflowing orchard, tended in the extreme (at least in comparison to incandescent Naples), and after passing reception Micalea opened an iron door with pride of place below an arch that also seemed millenary. With her sweet tango accent, she quietly intoned:

'Close the eyes and give me the hand…'

Ignoring the obvious grammatical error with the buds of a gleeful smile on my lips, I blindly obeyed and breathed in deeply. Suddenly the lemon aroma transformed into a livelier, deeper, much wilder scent: the sea. The garden was right on the edge of the island's southern tip and beyond the arch there was only a semi-circular lookout with a couple of old stone benches above a formidable cliff face that plunged almost vertically into the foamy water.

'*Incredibile! Semplicemente fantástico*!!' I gasped, immediately displacing the anxieties and impotence drowning my soul, as though I'd suddenly been transformed into Vittorio Gassman.

Micalea had wanted Room 2 because of its sliver of balcony jutting out over the cliff face, but it was occupied all week. However, we were told that Room 1 had an even bigger and better positioned balcony, and that it had been vacated that very morning. It goes without saying that it was more expensive but then it also goes without saying that after our trafficking trip money was about the only thing going well for me. Money and my newfound company, of course.

We showered, unpacked and went down for breakfast before stretching out on the bed to sleep awhile. The room was simple yet stylish and the views out to sea made it the most magnificent place to make love that I'd ever seen. To make love or commit suicide, because one courageous leap and you'd crack your coconut against the rocky waves two hundred metres below. It must've been the first night, as we were digesting our pasta and seafood with lemon sauce, that I mentioned it to Micalea and she replied that it was without doubt the perfect place to film a suicide scene for a movie but wholly impractical to commit one because there was the chance of breaking every bone in your body and surviving. At least, that's what happened to a Canadian tourist who tried it a few years ago.

'He jumped from here and *lived*?'

'Ask anyone here. They were even thinking of officially declaring it a miracle. But luckily Procida doesn't go in for that sort of publicity.'

'But a miracle is *exactly* what it is!'

'A strong *scirocco* was blowing and it pushed him back against the rockface. He fell thirty or forty metres onto the first ledge and got tied up in the bushes.' She paused for a swig and a drag before passing me the *cannone*. 'When it comes to suicide, I'm more classical: a good hot bath and a bottle of barbiturates if you don't want to muddy the waters.' Swig, drag, swig. 'Although I must admit, the idea of the knife cutting my veins and the cold blade contrasting with the boiling water excites me a lot.'

'Must be your Roman senator's blood.'

'Ah ha! Joke as much as you like but my granddad used to tell anyone who'd listen that he was a descendent of Cato the Younger.'

'Who?'

'A stoic philosopher from Julius Caesar's time.'

'Is it true?'

'Well, that's anyone's guess. But he got so obsessed with the idea that he started wearing a tunic and speaking in classical Latin. He's been wasting away in an old people's home for the last two or three years reciting satirical verses against tyranny.'

'Is there a home for senile young people, too?'

'I don't think so but I'm sure it could be arranged.'

'You talk as if we've been married for ten years, as though you were chained to my chains.'

'Aren't I?'

'I hope not. That's all we need!'

A barn owl marked the rhythmic silence hanging over the celestial, half-lunar lookout as I peered over the side and listened to the lapping waves.

'In a couple of weeks I'll be taking my private hells back to Catalonia and you'll continue living your serene Neapolitan life. Apart from the heroin labyrinth and its many morbid moons that have led me astray all these years, I also have my fair share of embolisms between essence and existence that urgently need treating.'

'And wouldn't I be of any help?'

'Sure! But I don't want you getting mixed up in this mess because one never can tell where these things can end up. I know myself that much at least.'

'I'm not sure you do.'

'But here you've got a good job. And a rich playfellow, am I right? Surely you don't want to leave all that behind and just… disappear.'

'The question is what *I* want to do. Jobs aren't important, and money even less so. What's important are people: their feelings and emotions.'

The comment left me speechless. I couldn't tell if it was merely naivety in liquid state, which is what inevitably floats all romantic ideals, or the sublime synthesis of two thousand years of philosophy her granddaddy claimed to have coursing through his veins. In any case, the whole thing sounded like dyed-in-the-wool stoicism, and much more than just Naples dreaming if it really had been motivated by love.

'How about you teach me how to make love with a condom

and we leave all that for another day?' I smiled sadly just to cut a line of conversation that would've only lowered me further into what for many years I referred to, when speaking to myself, as the 'pit'.

It's possible that the actions, images and conversations from the eight days that our Procida paradise lasted are blending together because they were, generally speaking, a slow, sumptuous succession of impressionist picture postcards and emotional gardens. We left our doubts dangling over an abyss, postponed painful decisions for our departure, and although we always spoke sincerely we devoted little time to taboo topics. Amid the gaiety, giggling and irregular sexual results was the testimony of the condoms, a tyranny that even today, with forty years under my belt, I haven't got completely used to. However, as Micalea rightfully said, in addition to fucking there were ten thousand tomes full of other sensual pleasures and that the most important element of any emotional-sexual relationship (which also serves to achieve heightened pleasure-performance levels) is each individual's non-transferable desire to materialise itself in the hunting and possession of the other's. This reflection was originally Sioux's, who knows more about sex on a philosophical-existential level (or any other level, for that matter) than anyone I've certainly ever met.

I vividly remember another evening strolling along the edge of the island after a downpour had left us as drenched as ducks. We'd just had *maccheroni all'arabbiata* for dinner at the *trattoria* by the harbour and that meal, one of the best of my life, was also spent with tears running down my face (bitter ones because I was 'aware' that our dream was ending, one moment at a time, and joyful ones because I wasn't at all used to chilli peppers). That night we set up camp on the seafront with cold noodles and sardines on plastic plates and a bottle of Chianti chilling in the lapping water.

Although it was prohibited, we brought food and drink. Although it was prohibited, we lit a fire upon the skin of the sand and laid our sleeping bags out by the blood of the sea. And although it was most definitely prohibited, we lay down to make love and elicit the moon and galaxies. I recall traces of a dialogue as we watched an aeroplane fly south above our heads.

'I don't know how many times,' I whispered while choking back my tears, 'I've seen a plane and wanted to be an anonymous passenger, heading for an unknown scenario but with an exact objective, totally different to my soporific, spent scenarios. But in this unrepeatable moment I wouldn't switch seats with anyone. Not even if they were flying to the bosom of the moon.'

'You should turn that idea into a poem,' she giggled. 'Sorry to bring you crashing back down to earth but I worked as an air hostess for six months, covering for a friend, and it's a lot less mystical than that: the majority of passengers are rude and have smelly feet.'

'Fortunately we only smell of weed, sardines and white wine.'

'And sex. Everywhere we go, my love, we leave a trail of animal odour that a blind person could follow.'

'As long as their nose was always in heat.'

'Well said, Fred! A red-hot nose!!'

After listening and digesting the graces and silences, both inside and out, both beautiful and bloody, we read a number of poems, aloud and caressing each syllable, as Lluïsa had taught me to do a thousand years ago on the secret beaches of Formentera. I particularly remember a short one by a certain Ungaretti that she recited with her voice transfigured by the night:

Chiuso tra cose mortali,
anche le stele finiranno,

The sixteen days that our fire had been burning was a unique, highly instructive experience that taught me a whole load of home truths about myself, ones I'd hid for years. Like acknowledging that having heroin and nothing but heroin meant there'd never ever be enough heroin. Like how after ten or twelve years of seafaring with Fermí it was time to dock and turn my gaze inland.

But then, like the bitter fruit falling into the pure stillness of the fountain, Sandro came crashing into our romantic neo-realist love film without any love lost, and our elliptic reality was instantly transformed into a resoundingly violent one. If I'm not mistaken, he turned up at the hostel on Friday afternoon and the cherry on the cake was that he caught us in bed enjoying a nap – condom and anal sex included. Thank God the door was locked.

'*Qui c'è?*' asked Micalea, stopping us dead in the act, but the only answer was harder, more persistent knocking. '*Qui c'cè?! Si prega non disturbare!*'

'*Sono Sandro,*' he yelled. '*Apri la porta!*'

'*Vaffanculo, Sandro! Questa è la mia vita!!*'

'*Tu ancora non sai che cose è la vita! Apri la porta!*'

He began thumping on the door again as I hurriedly put on my jeans and she put on a t-shirt.

'What the *fuck* do you want?' I asked him through a ten centimetre gap in the door.

'I want to speak to my sister.'

'Wait for us in the bar. Five minutes.'

'Bullshit, five minutes!' he spat back before kicking the door and pushing me out of the way with a surprisingly strong forearm. 'You're crazy! If your illness forces you to jump in bed with every Spanish tourist that washes up in Naples you could at least be more discreet! You could've gone to Venice or Hong-fucking-Kong instead of passing through every romantic spot in the province! What's Paolo going to say, huh?! And stooping so low as to go to Forcella to buy sugar for your daddy…!'

While I was desperately trying to figure out how to avoid a serious physical confrontation, he'd already taken a few steps forwards and grabbed her tightly by the wrist.

'Show me your arms!'

'Don't be ridiculous, Sandro,' uttered Micalea with a frightened smile. 'You're showing yourself up!'

'If you hurt her I'll give it to you!' I threatened, picking up the bronze candelabrum from the dressing table and raising it above my head.

He threw Micalea onto the bed and she fell revealing her pubis and navel. Then he pointed a forefinger at me as if it were the barrel of a gun.

'Do yourself a favour and shut your mouth. If you weren't a friend of Mín's you'd have already gone headfirst over the balcony.'

Micalea got off the bed and calmly took the candelabrum out of my hand.

'You're creating a Neapolitan scene, Sandro, and you know full well it doesn't suit you.'

She uttered it with a huge dose of humour and the beginnings of a fearless laugh. I thought Sandro would explode and start swinging left, right and centre but fortunately he just exhaled like a raging bull and paced towards the door. It was precisely at that point when I suddenly realised that Micalea did whatever she pleased with her brother.

'I've got work to do tonight but I want to see you back in Mezzocannone tomorrow at eleven a.m. Alone!! Make the most of the time you have left to screw to your heart's content because this – whatever *this* is – has finished.'

I was about to answer him back with an insult, a groan, a finger, anything, but Micalea's hand stopped me. He slammed the door behind him with a formidable crash and Micalea burst into hysterical, disdainful laughter.

Throughout my short but intense existence as an adult human being, I've made a number of hasty decisions, some of great consequence, but this one was by far the riskiest. But, in hindsight, also one of the best. I'd already made the firm decision to phone Eulàlia, Lídia, even Mum and, if they still hadn't received any ominous visits, to return to Catalonia. Micalea, on the other hand, had decided to go with me, if that was what I wanted. So, in order not to compromise myself any further, I suggested that we leave immediately for Naples, collect the car (if we could find it) and head north where we still might be able to permit ourselves the luxury of a little more tourism. We finished the tender fuck that had been so rudely interrupted and at ten past six we boarded the 17:55 *aliscafo* back to the mainland.

Not just etched onto but alive in my memory is part two of my farewell with Fermí, this time in the bar below the B&B, on account of my premonition (false, like on so many other occasions) that it'd be the last time I ever saw him.

'Where are you going? (pause) Can I come?'

'Nowhere in particular (pause) Come if you want.'

But he was only asking out of habit and I hoped as much. Selfishness? Damn right, but if Mín had come all the dreams I was creating alongside Micalea would've evaporated in an instant. The kid was adamant on splitting Sandro's second payment 50-50, even though he'd paid the lion's share of the car I was about to drive away in. But I accepted the money, if only to not have to discuss it any further.

'When will you be going back?' I ask.

'Dunno. P'raps never,' he mumbles.

'Call Sioux if you change address.'

'Sure.'

'Bye, Mín.'

'Goodbye, Lex.'

Micalea and I fled Naples like two fugitives and by seven-thirty we were racing along the motorway towards Rome to catch dinner in any random town on the metropolis' ancient outskirts and then do a lap of the city centre with whisky and *caffè freddo*. I would've liked to have stayed in the Eternal City for a few days but, by the time we were back on the motorway, Micalea had already decided that we'd be breakfasting in Florence. We spent two days in Florence and four in Venice: the experiences, emotions, doubts, fears and tears lived through over that week are as private as they are ineffable yet, nevertheless, in order to guide this *tarantella* to its conclusion I must, despite my embarrassment, resurrect a couple of moments that Mín would usually describe as 'unforgettable'.

The first one, melodramatic whichever way you look at it, was Micalea's confession while we ate dinner outside Rome that there was *some* truth to what her brother had said. She loved and fell in love like anyone else but, when it came to sex, she did have a bit of a problem with excess, something that men often disparagingly labelled 'nymphomania'. I took it as a joke and between giggles reasoned that almost all men suffer from that, and proudly too, the only difference being we're never fully able to satisfy it. Not without paying, at least. As far as I was concerned, it stank of a disorder invented by tin-pot male psychologists and that's exactly what I told her. She furrowed her brow and told me she was aware of the theory and believed in it up to a point. Unfortunately, it was something that defied simple analysis.

'Let's make a pact and, what's more, try and keep to it…!'

I playfully proposed. 'I won't cheat on you with horse and you won't cheat on me with other stallions.'

'Hmm, that's a difficult pact for both riders. I think it should include that you don't cheat on me with other fillies or mares, either.'

'Proposal accepted. I have no desire to be with anyone but you anyway.'

Another day, this time in Venice, we had the sudden idea to get married (a civil service, obviously) and if it hadn't been for the paperwork, certificates, deposits, witnesses and personal documents, no doubt we'd have gone ahead with it, too. The whole thing happened in the *Caffè di San Marco* where we'd gone to waste thirty thousand lira on two *cappuccini* and one croissant when all of a sudden I was overcome by uncontrollable laughter. The attack was so strong that I was forced to seek refuge in the toilet, leaving Micalea full of both wonder and vicarious embarrassment. When I got back and floated her the idea, or what's generally termed a 'proposal', it was her turn to choke on her own giggles and guffaws, so much so that she had to go hide in the toilet. When she returned to our table we'd already long been the centre of the other customers' increasingly reproachful gazes but each time we looked at one another our laughing fits returned. In the end we decided to leave the famous *Caffè* before they threw us out.

As a succinct conclusion to this rather long story, I'll add that in spite of the weight of our circumstances, Micalea and I spent four years and three months together in the most fruitful harmony. There were a few infidelities along the way on both sides, but we always preferred to view them as exceptions and to live and let live.

12-6-97

From: Fabià Juncadella (La Model, Barcelona)
To: Alexandre Oscà (Cal Fumall, Malanyeu)

Listen up, Alexandre, listen up,

for the topic is of unparalleled import: in thirty, no, twenty-eight days, I'll be free of this box! After fifteen years, eight months and six days, I can finally say that in less than a month I'll be leaving this universe behind to embark on another. I don't know if it's any better but hey ho here we go! If I'm being completely honest with you, notwithstanding a general exaltation somewhat analogous to euphoria, I note a tremendous anxiety resembling panic (remember all that stuff about 'scared parrots'?). The city, people, their lifestyle, clothes, everything must have changed so much that I can't help worrying I'll feel like an extraterrestrial.

It is honestly my least intention to force you to do anything you don't want to do but if there is any chance you might be able to help in whatever small way, then please allow me to take the liberty of reminding you that I will need a bit of work and somewhere to rest my head. No doubt it will reek of cowardice, bearing in mind how we used to move from one place to another without worrying, always finding somewhere to sleep and something to eat, but the subject is causing me considerable stress. I don't know whether it's some form of perverse morality but I desperately don't want to go near any sort of illegal activity beyond smoking a few joints now and again. Honestly, who's going to hand a job to a washed up musician about to turn fifty who looks sixty-five and has spent fifteen years inside for six hold ups and a homicide? Who's going to rent an ex-con a room if he's got no way of paying for it?

If only Glòria, the splendid psychiatrist who resuscitated me intellectually and emotionally a hundred years ago, were still here it would be a different story but, alas, she's now a paid up congresswoman in the capital of the empire. The one currently running things is a boundless imbecile with an Apollo face, a Francoist mentality and is fresh out of school, and I wouldn't share as much as a wet fart with him.

Laura, my beloved Parisian aunt, has already sent me money in order for me to catch the first available high-speed train to hers. But the truth is I can't face all that. Not yet, anyway.

If it's not too much to ask I would really love to spend a few days with you in Alt Berguedà amid the beauty of the trees and the purity of the air. It's your fault, anyway! The descriptions you've left between the lines of your letters are to blame. But if it's not convenient, don't worry: we'll work something out.

Your friend,
Fabià R. Juncadella

Postscript: (the following morning just before sending the letter): over the last few days there are times when my laughter mixes with my tears.

7-7-97

Cal Fumall, Malanyeu, Alt Berguedà
Alexandre Oscà i Punyol to Enric Costales Grausec.

I have enough good news and bad news, oh Richy,

my rich friend, that I could give 'em away for free. The good news, which I know should always be left for last, is to do with Fabià and literature.

First things first, as you already know, Fabià is getting out on the tenth and, needless to say, you will have to go pick him up. I think he could help you a lot with the hypothetical conclusion to the novel. Also, I need you to do everything you can to set him up with something. I am asking you as if it were for myself, Enric, and I know you wouldn't turn me down.

Secondly, between Sweet Eulàlia, who I know will forgive me, and yours truly, Alexandre the Grateful, who has never deserved the friends he has, we have managed to prepare some sumptuous snacks relating to the second half of the eighties, which according to you didn't have enough filling, and to also fry up the following episodes regarding the first marvellous and monstrous Italian spread. Furthermore, saved on the laptop is one last document that struggles in vain to sketch the framework of those twilight years that, depending on how I look at them, are either full... or full of nothingness. Therefore, when She, or You Both, manage to pull a chapter-summary out of the oven to sublimate the melodramatic inflexion of my death and take the edge off any overly sharp concluding points the great feast will be ready to serve.

I really hope you don't end up putting arse and elbow on the line over this, not because of the money, because I know that isn't a concern of yours, but rather because of the effort and hope of all those who have dared write it. And above all because of the implicit homage to the various victims: the dead rebels who failed, rotting without Dharma or memory (to stir up personal citations), and all those still living in victimhood. There goes the good news.

The bad news is once again to do with the hospital. I have lost two more kilos (I now weigh 62.4 kg, that is, 12.6 kg less than four months ago) and the same thing is happening to me that I saw happen to my old man: I eat for three yet have nothing to show for it. Apart from tuberculosis and hepatitis, as you already know. I was always sure it would be my lungs but, what d'ya know, in the end it's my liver. Tomorrow (Monday) I was due to be admitted for goodness knows what tests or revisions but they will have to go ahead without me. Yes, you have understood correctly. I won't be going, not tomorrow, not the day after, not any other day. The misery and pain is finally over, once and forever.

So there it is: whether it's good news or bad, I have decided nobly, serenely, thoughtfully, to cull the long list of anxieties, deficiencies and suffering by performing the only truly free act that remains: when I finish this letter I will get into your stunning oval bathtub, full to the brim with hot water, gun my last fix just to drug myself a little more, take hold of the breadknife and, with a flick of the wrist to each wrist, off to sleep (and who knows, perchance to dream I have been reincarnated as a wild horse). But if not, then to sleep and slowly decompose in my translucent, blue quartz necromide. I trust you will forgive this last abuse of our friendship and that my choice of end doesn't break the charm of our Home, the greatest among millions.

In short (as Mín always said): the most difficult anxiety to relinquish has been precisely our intimate literary creation which, in my opinion, if it ever grows into a real, independent being, should be christened the Deadbeat Generation. Good news: beyond the title, I reiterate in writing that I am leaving you total freedom over the correction and layout of each story, epigraph, appendix and their great mama in the sky. However, please confer with Eulàlia and Fabià regarding all hypothetical tasks and decisions of a creative nature. Bad news: in addition to this scarce literary testament, I have no other option but to name you as the general executor of, if not my assets, then at least what are known as Last Wishes.

Speaking of assets, firstly allow me to thank you for your generosity and altruism. Now with one foot in the tomb I can suck up as much as I please. If the most minimal profit should come of these written words, make sure you get your many repeated investments back. Thank you, Enric, from the bottom of my heart. If after settling your investments and whatever interest you see fit there should be by some crazy or secular miracle even one pesseta left over, forty cents are for Eulàlia and twenty for Fabià. Please divide the forty cents that constitute my share between Micalea, who for some reason is/was my wife, and Dolors, who for some reason is/was my sister.

Onto more practical things: after my body has been dried of water and blood, please burn it until I am nothing but ash, which I ask you to spread at the Font de les Travesses any morning at first light. And so you don't get bored the night before as you keep vigil over these atoms, eat, drink and be merry with what I am leaving you in the pantry. In addition to me, I beg you to also raise a Toast to Lluïsa and Another to Fermí. If you wish, feel free to raise one for each of the one hundred and forty-four characters in this so-called novel and that way you will end up as stinking drunk as skunks. In other words, see me off with a good old-fashioned knees-up.

The problem of who will find me and when has been solved (I don't like the idea of being reincarnated as a bath sponge, not one little bit) thanks to a letter already sent to the Guardiola town hall: at some point tomorrow a secretary will notify a councillor that a suicide has chosen them as undertakers and the councillor will have no other option but to notify the police or fire brigade who will have no other option but to come up to Cal Fumall to check if a suicide has indeed been committed.

Do you want to hear one last second-to-last secret? Writing about one's own death as though one already formed part of the past is an experience nothing short of sublime, as succulent as a ripe cherry.

So, Enric, my FriendtotheEnd, here I finish my letter. Hi ho, hi ho, it's off to bed we go.

Yours always,
Alexagod

Postscript: Only one last thing remains for me to say: I am so blind, stupid and insensitive that I probably would never have realised if not for Mònica, but in the end I have understood and processed the fact that for some time you have had deeper feelings for me beyond our close friendship. I have never known, nor would I ever know, how to return them in any way other than I already have. But I want you to know that far from an insult I take it as a compliment.

Now I realise that in all of these lived experiences I can't include a single genuine homosexual relationship. But I guess everyone has to follow their own personal instinct; at least that is what I have done in my own very special way. But on that subject, and all the others, I have already said all there is to say.

I truly hope from the bottom of my heart that Làlia forgives me from the bottom of hers and that she lives happily ever after with exotic Mònica forever and ever. Amen.

ONE CIVIL PARTNERSHIP

Tenimmoce accussì anema e core
SALVE D'ESPOSITO, TITO MANLIO

I finally managed to overcome the fatal attractions of horse around Christmas '92, paradoxically when Micalea decided to leave me and return to Italy. And I say paradoxically because Micalea was both the motor and motivation driving my efforts to stay clean during the years that we were together.

By then it was four years since we'd arrived from Procida via Venice, and three and a half since we'd married in a Tarragona registry office with Dolors and Sandro as witnesses and a dozen much loved guests around the table: on my side there was Kiddo, still full of Dharma and playing the Bum, my sister Dolors (previously known as Loleta), who'd graduated in journalism and married a botanist, along with a six-month-old koala they'd produced together called Diana. There was also Yma, Leonor, now definitively separated from Pere (who was living in Berlin), and Enric and his partner, who everyone called Freddie because he was the dead spit of Mercury. I didn't invite Eulàlia and Susana out of pure cowardice. On Micalea's side there was Sandro, who we'd patched things up with, and Olga, his eternal *fidanzata*, even though I'd certainly never heard either of them ever talk about getting married.

Micalea was somewhat melancholy because her parents hadn't been able to make the trip for health reasons and because her childhood friend, the one who'd lent us the apartment in Vomera where we'd spent our first week together, had fed her some insipid excuse about her son being in hospital with appendicitis. As was fully expected, my mum also found an ailment so she wouldn't have to come but, in all honesty, it was all the same to me whether it was real or invented. I was perfectly happy having Diana, Loleta and Kiddo with me. And above all, Micalea.

Perhaps it will seem laughable, considering that I'd already crossed the frontier into my thirties and was lugging a large amount of existential baggage, but I had the (genuine) feeling of having touched heaven with my fingertips; of having crossed the immense vastness of hell in slow motion to finally recover, in terms of both mise en scène and plot, a final framing of Paradise. It wasn't something that I thought in words, no, but rather in accordance with the instinct of events and I envisioned one of those marriages that last forty years or until one of the two simply perishes. Obviously, no one can say from the outset how long one will last. A life, I mean. And, of course, I had two daggers dangling perilously over my head: the first threatens every living being owing merely to the business of being alive, but the second – HIV/AIDS – could slice me in two any day. And that's not to mention that I'd been a junkie for a thousand years and, as Mín often said, had covered so many miles, in such a hurry, along such a tortuous highway, so high on crank, that my crankshaft must be shafted good and proper. But my biorhythms were high and my desire to live forced the virus into hibernation, to put it poetically.

On the whole things were looking bright for us. Enric had set us up in a hotel in Vilaseca where Micalea worked as a receptionist and Alexandre as head barman. We earned little and saved a lot, and after the wedding, supported by both Enric and Sandro's financial injections, Micalea was finally able to realise her dream of opening a *trattoria* in Barcelona. Well, not quite Barcelona as technically it was in Hospitalet, at the place Làlia's aunt (Genoveva) had bought eight or ten years prior. It cost us more sacrifices than I could fit into a full page of prose but it paid off. She worked as cook and I had the role of maître and waiter, and we seemed like any other normal, urban couple. By then, Italian cuisine was fashionable in Barcelona and we soon found ourselves with a clientele that wanted better wines at higher prices. Not even Fermí and his horse cart of wretchedness was able to break the spell, so instead he just crashed it straight into us. Typical fucking Mín.

TWO LESS THAN CIVIL DIVORCES

'With Or Without You', U2

It hadn't even been a year since we'd opened the *trattoria*, christened 'La Procitana', and we were just about getting our heads above water on the back of hard work and saving when, one fine day, or rather, one horrendous evening, Sandro called from Mezzocannone to give us one final warning regarding Mín: either we came to look for him now or there'd be nothing left of him to look for. He told us he'd seen him on the off-chance the night before looking like death, a walking write-off, both physically and mentally, and that if we didn't find a solution the boy would be in a box before too long.

Given that Micalea and I hadn't had time or money for anything even remotely resembling a honeymoon and what's more it was the backend of July, we decided to close for two weeks and head to Naples, perhaps even Procida, and visit her family and look to rescue Fermí. No doubt we deceived ourselves with our intimate memories of the island, both of us believing that a moment frozen in time was awaiting us in the same place we'd left it three years ago but, either way, she wanted to visit home and I felt indebted to Fermí. At least enough to try.

Keeping with tradition, we used the trip to export an ounce of snow, this time hidden – despite my deep concerns – above a trimmed tampon in Micalea's vagina, taking advantage of the fact that she had her period. We flew to Fiumicino on a charter flight full of students because it was both cheaper and more discreet and Sandro met us the other end in his brand new convertible. When we arrived, the sun was high in the sky and the August afternoon was already hotter than a camel's backside.

Less than an hour later we stopped at an outrageously

expensive restaurant in some horrendously miserable town to savour an authentic Italian lunch in honour of Micalea's return, as if we didn't eat pasta every day in Barna, before breaking with tradition and each taking a pinch of sugar with our coffee. Afterwards, we burnt two hundred kilometres of hot motorway with the top up, the air con on full blast and the speedometer pushing 220 km/h. The prow of our speeding ship was pointed towards Pozzuoli where we were to spend the night. It was just like the first time, only Fermí wasn't there and Micalea and I would be allowed to sleep together.

After a shower and a night time pizza, we went for a lap of hard core Naples to see if we might bump into that piece of junk from Manresa who for some time had been of 'no fixed abode', to use official terminology. Another celebratory lunch was planned for the following day with *tutta la santa famiglia* in Ischia where things would be even more exaggerated in more ways than one. Sandro told me about it while the girls unpacked and the boys went for seconds on the coke, which he deemed to be of good quality, without any evidence of brother-in-law's tampering or sister's tampon, for which he paid me in full even though we still owed him money for the *trattoria*. But, according to him, one business deal didn't have anything to do with the other. And, really, that was Sandro all over: if he knew you and loved you, he was an old softy at heart.

We didn't find Mín anywhere that night and no one had seen or heard from him in days. We were told he had two or three places to crash, all free of charge, but where exactly he spent the night depended on the motivation and meaning of the moment. However, the most frequent of the three was a squatted factory to the east of the city which fashioned an even more aggressive scenography than any of those I'd seen, either close up or at a distance, in all the down-and-out alleys of Barcelona and Tarragona: on a dead-end street decapitated by a motorway lay a dark domino line of derelict factories and warehouses, all as looming as they were grotesque, all exhaling deep nocturnal despair. There were lines of whores of all three sexes beside the motorway access ramp and yet more countercultural offers near the velodrome opposite that labyrinth of industrial decay. No doubt during daylight hours it was slightly less gloomy but I swear I wouldn't have dared go anywhere near the place if not in the company of Sandro and Claudio, an ex-junkie pal of his who played the role of Charon. No doubt sobriety was starting to soften my underbelly but then the shadows overseas always appear deeper, denser, more dangerous. When you're an addict and you need your drug, you don't see or consider the peril you're walking into. Not that you care, of course, because in that moment there's only one concept that has any value: getting what you need and getting it quick. But on that particular trip to Italy, having gone there with a couple of years of almost total abstinence as perspective, when I looked into the eyes of all those sad addicts, so abandoned to themselves in both essence and existence, I was incapable of recognising myself in their image, not even in the past. I remember telling Claudio the same and he understood me perfectly because after six years of not touching the stuff he still sometimes had the same absurd sensation. I thought a lot about it over the following days, believing the affirmation to be the result of a paradox until finally realising it wasn't, because the only true reality is the present.

The next day we went for lunch in Ischia with the entire family enterprise where I was finally able to meet father, mother, grandparents, uncles, aunts, cousins, sons and daughters of cousins, etc., etc. I'd always believed Catalan families to be the closest thing to a Jewish tribe until I met one half of Micalea's, which came to approximately one hundred people. But they treated me much better than I thought they would, concerned at first that the older generation might have a bone to pick with me over us not having been married by a priest. But perhaps their warmth towards me was really just relief that someone had finally managed to soften the harpy's fury or, to put it bluntly, satisfy the nymph's appetite.

On the journey over on the *aliscafo*, Sandro gave me a crash course in what truths could and very much could not be uttered on the subject of religion. Basically, it was a question of making sure to mention that I came from a traditional Catholic family and hiding whether I was agnostic, atheist or a Communist. All other faults, be it adultery, rape, robbery or murder, could be forgiven as they were sins of the flesh, but doubting the existence of God or the infallibility of the Pope were incurable spiritual maladies that must be avoided at all cost. At least in the presence of *famiglia*.

Though the man was frankly repulsive, I remember with special delight my father-in-law's bishop half-brother who spent most of the afternoon listing in a preaching and vain manner the innumerable advantages of certifying our marriage ecclesiastically. By the time I'd had my fill, aware that the following day we'd both follow our own goddam destiny and never set eyes on one another again, I broke with Sandro's commandments. Making sure we were far enough away from the crowd not to be overheard, I whispered into the man's ear that he was living proof that God didn't exist because no God, even minimally perfect, would have accepted him as a minister. Maybe I went too far, but when he finally understood, despite the limitations of my mediocre Italian, his puffy eyes and alcoholic nose suffered a spasm of perfect contrition that, while not causing him to reach for the hair shirt, certainly gave him an excuse to park religion and get as pissed as a newt. Which was what I also did that night, albeit for different reasons and wholly without enthusiasm. And despite the questionable worth of the anecdote, it was the first time in my life that I was in bed by midnight, just as the younger among us were getting ready to go out.

I have no idea where Micalea disappeared to because I've always believed that what you don't want to know don't ask but she got home at seven-seventeen with her skin marinated in sea salt and her hair peppered with sand. I pretended to be half asleep while caressing her and seeking her sex, and after a half-hearted no and a few hesitations she opened herself up to me. During our lovemaking I sensed what I now know for certain: she wasn't with me or thinking of me. And so the old Marxist thesis was confirmed. The first time I experienced this unique 'emotional situation' (Lluïsa, fifteen years ago, Formentera lighthouse) it was a veritable tragedy but now, second time around, it was merely a pathetic farce and, although Sandro despaired at my docility, it was a physical divorce that we'd already reconciled ourselves to: from time to time she chose 'another' for two nights or twelve, whereupon we'd spend half a month of conjugal distance, re-charge our impulse towards sexual possession and thus conjure up a new period of equilibrium. Nevertheless, it still saddened me when she decided to stay in Ischia the following day instead of returning to Naples to look for Mín. It's true that she barely knew him and that Naples in August was a ghost town but if I'd found the moment and the words I would've begged her on my hands and knees to not make a cuckold of me so openly in front of her family. But I'm aware that could also have just been masculine pride heightened by my surroundings. As reward for my suffering, that night at three-thirty in the morning, we caught sight of a swaying spectre, ghostly to the point of translucence, answering to the name of Fermí.

'Good thing you two showed up…!' he exclaimed in place

of a hello. 'If not, I'd still be trying to shake these two Arabs!'

As Sandro and I pulled up outside a bar on Piazza Garibaldi, he was busy disputing a complaint by two Algerians who'd bought a gram from him and, from the looks of things, wanted their money back. For reasons unbeknown, our appearance put an immediate end to the argument and we moved onto the corresponding laughter and embraces. He'd undoubtedly changed physically (he seemed taller, thinner and transparent blue, like a Dracula understudy) but was wearing the same simple black clothes (70's Milan style) with his usual grungy elegance of the heart throb of the underworld. And he still knew how to trace one of those tough asymmetric smiles that would've found him fame in any James Dean style movie.

We bought beers and headed back to the car, which is where, summer or winter, Neapolitans spend half the time when they're not at home. After a few pleasantries, Sandro slipped away, as subtle as a stranger, telling me that he still had a few things to do before giving us the keys to his latest convertible and the villa in Pozzuoli. He dedicated Mín a timid *arrivederci* and I remember him smiling at me and asking if I'd be able to make it back alone. I told him perhaps I wouldn't but certainly the car would but, the truth is, if it hadn't been for Fermí I'd have ended up sleeping godknowswhere. But then again, if it hadn't been for Fermí I wouldn't have ended up with a head full of junk which, after months and months of good behaviour, made me sleep and vomit, sleep and *heeere we go again*, with the sloppiness of those unaccustomed to a hearty horse bite.

We shot the first scene of the night by the sea in a godforsaken corner of a gigantic, seemingly abandoned railway yard where I couldn't muster one crazy reason not to board the locomotive with him (even if it did mean, counter-custom, sharing a needle: not the first time but it would be the last). But he merely remarked, smiling with the tip of one eyebrow: 'If you don't want to get burnt don't dip your finger in the gravy.' And, as usual, he was right. Afterwards we sped the splendid *macchina* through the horrifying hieroglyphics with Mín directing me late or incorrectly or not at all on our way to the aforementioned velodrome to pay a debt and buy more diesel. I was convinced they'd steal the Porsche out from under us, piece by piece.

'If you drove in here on your own with this motor, chances are neither of you would make it out again. But if you come here with someone who knows where to go and can provide a name then you're automatically protected by the local mafia and no one can touch a hair on your head. As long as you don't outstay your welcome, of course…'

While he got down to business I stayed in the car with his pistol (in Naples, without a handgun to hand even a moron will mug you) and a smoking gun of my own, lapping up that inimitable stage, chatting to pushers and peddlers, and whores of every sex, who buzzed around me like mosquitos until I mentioned Mín's current moniker.

'I'm a friend of *El Catalano*. I'm waiting for him.'

The third act we performed in a theatre I seemed to vaguely recognise because we went directly from the factory to deliver five grams to a contact in Forcella (perhaps the same who'd hooked Micalea up the night of our tremendous nocturnal circuit). Whatever the case, we shot up for the second time at this fella's place while they chatted and chatted (with cheeks and lips, and eyes and eyebrows, and shoulders and arms, and hands and fingers!) and Mín showered, changed his clothes and laundered his dirty ones, the whole time spitting words and shooting horse and chasing tiger. He said the car was also insured against all risk thanks to the neighbourhood law but I used the excuse of savouring the summer night air to go sit on the balcony with a beer and keep an eye on it. When we finally got back in the miraculously intact car with Fermí behind wheel (owing to the circumstances), he allowed himself the liberty of laughing at me and saying that if they'd wanted to take the car apart I wouldn't have found a single piece because I'd been asleep on the balcony for two whole hours snoring like a pig! But the night turned out to be nothing but a brief epilogue when the sun met us, high and tormenting, and the final farewell with Fermí figures more factually during the following day's events at Sandro's villa, who only phoned once to make sure that everything 'was under control.'

At some point in the afternoon, I was woken by female screams cascading through the balcony door which I'd left wide open despite the punishing sun. I turned over onto my side as I'd already done four or five times, trusting that sleep would deliver me from at least the most hungover part of the hangover. But the wailing went on, penetrating me deeper, and the memory of Mín running loose in Sandro's domain made me fear goodknowswhat and more. Making an enormous effort, first with eyelids, then with legs (which wanted nothing to do with my earthly worries), I managed to make it over to the balcony: a heavy-hipped woman of around forty was scolding two fifteen-year-old boys who, instead of being troubled by it, merely yelled back at her even louder. Afterwards another woman, younger but similarly shaped, came out onto the neighbouring balcony with an empty plant pot in her hands and threatened the teenagers who merely pretended to urinate in her direction while continuing to laugh at and insult them both. In addition to not understanding them, I didn't want to hear them and so I got in the shower only to realise I was still half dressed. I was giving off the typical corporeal pestilence of having used heroin, which always gives your perspiration a special facet, and I hummed a stronger tune than ever because, after sleeping clothed in August, I'd sweated so much I could've wrung the mattress out.

I grabbed a t-shirt and a pair of shorts from my rucksack and searched the house only to find it utterly empty. On the kitchen stove was a note written in Mín's almost indecipherable handwriting: 'i've taken the porsch for a few lapsch but i'll be right backsch so dont stress outsch.' Don't stress out! It didn't bear thinking what Sandro would do if he spotted Fermí driving around Pozzuoli alone in his convertible. I began to tremble uncontrollably, but that could've just been the aftereffects of the previous night's chaos. Next to the note there was a pouch containing a touch of turkish but the mere thought of it made me nauseous. I coughed and spat some sticky, filthy phlegm into the kitchen sink where Olga did her cooking and promised to sterilise the house from top to bottom before leaving (but owing to the inevitable scramble to leave, it was a promise I was unable to keep. Like so many others).

The digital stove clock was telling me it was sixteen-ten as I turned to take a jug of water from the fridge and drag my sorry arse over to the main balcony, the jug in one hand and a normal cigarette in the other. When I was halfway through one and at the end of the other, the Porsche poked its nose onto the driveway. Christ, at least he hasn't sold it. Then the starman himself greets me with a beep, as though everything were hunky dory, parks up and leaps out of the car without opening the door: like a young Jean-Paul Belmondo.

'You want me to close the top? Or is it better to leave it in the garage?' he smiled in full Neapolitan character.

'Don't worry. Leave it to me.'

'What? Like last night…?'

He closed the top and locked the doors anyway, all the while rapping storylines with little rhyme and no reason before opening the front door with his set of keys and joining me on the balcony.

'I trust you found the note.'

'Yeah.'

'But you didn't touch the pouch.'

'I got high just looking at it! I almost spewed!'

'Are you feeling hungry?'

'No way…! I've still got the bile here,' I answered, pointing to my throat.

'I hope Sandro doesn't mind if I take some cheese and a beer from the fridge…'

'I doubt it,' I muttered. 'The Porsche, maybe. But I doubt he'll mind a bit of cheese and beer.'

'We could make an omelette…' he proposed while weighing up the contents of the fridge.

'Knock yourself out.'

'You don't want any?'

'Half an egg, maybe.'

'You used to love them.'

'I still do. But my liver's on holiday.'

He made an omelette with four eggs, onion, potato, bell pepper and three different types of cured meat. Not only was it delicious but it was very decorative, too.

'You should do this for a living.'

'I used to for a while, in a pizza joint in the *centro storico*. Until your dear brother-in-law came in and told them all I was a no good junkie sonovabitch.'

'I don't believe you.'

'Suit yourself.'

He shot me one of his sly smiles that mock death and those who mourn because of it while I laughed for the both of us. But whichever way you looked at it, there we were, the two of us, eating stolen omelette on a borrowed balcony without knowing what else to say to one another. And I, having set up the whole expedition, realised how woefully naive I'd been, acting as though we were still children and someone had to come protect us from the dangers of life! But we'd been adults for years already in every imaginable way, and we'd always invented the most serious dangers ourselves.

'You could do it with us at the *trattoria*.'

'Ha, ha! Now that would be unforgettable! (pause) Have you asked Micalea?'

'Relax. That won't be a problem.'

'No one goes to an Italian restaurant to eat omelette. Anyway, everyone and their grandma knows how to make them in Catalonia and makes them at home.'

'I really mean it, Mínos. Why don't you come back?'

'Don't tell me you made this whole fucking trip just to save my soul?'

'Your soul, no. Just your heart.'

'Leave the sweet talk alone. It's my life and if I need God I know where to find him. In Naples there are more churches than junkies!'

'You'll come round one day.'

'Don't start with the pseudo-patriarchal redemptions, you lovable bastard. We've known each other too long for that.'

'Or not.'

I remember (I *confess*) right then having the genuine feeling that, deep down in the heart of the matter, we hardly knew each other at all: our external lives had merely coincided in time within the Deadbeat Generation's suicidal race but in our hearts, in our souls, we were strangers in space with few structures in common beyond those days lived out together. More out of pity than nostalgia, I saw it (or at least *tried* to see it) as having been nothing but a sort of pathologically prolonged adolescence, as utopic as it was buried, whereas he'd chosen to remain in character for as long as the show went on.

'Hasn't the life you're living given you enough already?' I blurted.

'It's a whole lot better than wasting away behind a counter selling macaroni with a part-time whore for a boss,' he counterattacked.

I stared him in the face, feeling my top lip curl. But there was no resentment because, deep down, I could see the funny side, however masochistic. But two seconds later my silence had defeated him.

'I'm sorry. That came out badly.'

'Let's get back to what we were talking about. Don't you want to quit horse?'

'Don't be ridiculous. You know better than anyone that no one *quits* horse. Once you get in the saddle, you're in it for life.'

'I'm surprised to hear you of all people try to sell me that stupid lie. That's what the fascists told us in school about all drugs just so we didn't try any. But *I* know and *you* know it's nothing but a gargantuan fib.'

'Alright then. Give me names. How many people do you know that have gone deep and come up again?'

'Me, for example. I've used six times in two years.'

'Including last night?'

'OK. Seven.'

'Or twelve or twenty or double that.'

'I'm telling you! I'm clean! For fuck's sake, Mín, you got off it for a couple of years, right?'

'Yeah. Stuffed full of coke and soaked in whisky.'

'Well, I get by on a few joints and a couple of beers.'

'And that's enough for you? Weekends, too?'

'I swear to you.'

'I don't believe you.'

'Suit yourself, as you put it. Keep heading straight towards the shit.'

'I'm in it already.'

'And don't you want to get out of it?'

'No. It's fine once you recognise the smell and get used to the taste.'

'Up to you.'

'Up to me, *dooown* to the ground. I like smack, I like the v-i-b-e.' And then after thirty freeze frames of silence: 'I don't want to change my life. I want to savour it to the full.'

Right then I should've asked him how his health was and told him about the great shape Lídia, Eulàlia and Susana were in, and how Yma hadn't been so lucky. But he didn't mention anyone except Dixi and his wife.

'They separated. Dixi got hooked on fool's gold like a fucking idiot. He didn't touch needles but he was snorting two grams a day.'

'You're kidding me! Two grams? I only slam that much smack at Christmas!'

'He sat crying in the restaurant as he told me everything.'

'And the garage?'

'From what I gather, graceful Gràcia, who has a bigger pair than Elliot Ness, has kept the lot.'

With a maximum economy of words I told him how Dixi had laid two or three heavy hands on her when he was junk sick and she wouldn't give him money from the shop, and how she then rang her brothers who came down that very night from Olesa and threw him out of the house.

'Out on my arse, Dixi kept saying over and over again without believing what had happened.'

'Out on my arse! Out on my arse!' Mín repeated, each time laughing more and more.

'I thought you'd feel sad for him.'

'*Aaagh*! Mark my words. That bum's not worth a penny. But Gràcia… she's a million dollars.'

'Of course she is. Gràcia is a woman.'

'And a gorgeous one at that.'

'Well now's your chance. She's single and all alone because Dixi has been a guest at the Hotel for the last six months.'

'La Model?'

'No. He went looking for wool in Madrid and they sheered his arse in Carabanchel.'

He went back to laughing as if it were the funniest thing in the world, and I went back to thinking how we really didn't know one another. His complete lack of solidarity was an expression of cynicism and resentment that I'd never indulge myself in, not even as a joke.

'What I don't get is how you manage to fund your habit.'

'Same old. Dealing, swindling, conning. Stealing when I've got no other choice.'

'You'll end up inside.'

'I'll ask them for a transfer to Madrid and share a cell with my dear cousin! We'll have a ball!'

'You're strung out.'

'By the red thread between nothingness and eternity.'

'Where'd you get that from?'

'The back cover of a Mahavishnu Orchestra album. I do DJ sets at weekends for food and tequila.'

'Tequila? A whisky lover like you? Now *that's* an attack on nature.'

'Now you see… the times they really *are* a-changing. As a-always.'

'Well, long live countercultural back covers and counterattacking disk jockeys!'

And then we laugh and laugh despite knowing, in our heart of hearts, that our shared laughter was being extinguished with each dying moment. But I was still trying my best to deceive myself, so much so that when Sandro phoned I asked him if we could take the car to go eat in Formia.

'Go eat wherever you like. But keep an eye on that partner of yours.'

'Relax.'

We went to Formia for dinner and to sell small amounts of marzipan on the maze of backstreets Mín knew like the back of his hand. Then we did a lap of cafébars on foot, dealing the whole time, and in the wee hours ended up in the same Forcella flat where we spent the previous night, equally as strung out. But at least we didn't go back to the squatted factory. In fact, everything was as fun and flowing as fifteen years ago when I was working at the Hard Rock in Manresa and he offered me my first line of smack to counter the acid I hadn't dropped.

Stories to not get bored. Anecdotes to help pass the time. Bottles of balsamic vinegar to dress life up and sacks of salt to ensure the wounds sting. I won't describe the second hangover because it was far too similar to the first, except for the note that Mín left me and which I found when woke I up: 'Take care you son of a bitch. See you in hell, boy.'

Nor will I describe the rest of the 'holiday' because when I phoned Ischia to try and get my beloved other half back, she'd gone with some friends on a cruise along the Amalfi Coast. Her mama told me in great detail how Micalea had been looking for me everywhere on the eve of the trip because she'd wanted me to come along, so instead of blaming her I should in fact be apologising. But beyond what we did or didn't say over the wire, we both knew what we knew: from Justine to Justine and it's my turn to roll the dice. Perhaps, deep down, when all is said and done, that's what I enjoy: them giving it to me hard up the emotional arse. In short, the cruise lasted five days and I spent every single one of them in Pozzuoli under Sandro's hospitable wing, who I think felt guilty and embarrassed over the whole affair, and there I penned stories similar to this one in the daytime and filled up on cocaine and whisky at night. But with my role of cuckold as an excuse, I didn't have to feel guilty about a thing.

I chose to not go looking for Mín again and it proved to be the last time I ever saw him. I often think that when Sandro phoned months later to tell me he'd been found riddled with bullets in some rail yard on the city's southern limits, it represented much more than just losing Fermí. It meant losing tiny pieces of everything we'd shared, tiny pieces that had been my story, however brutish and short; my own non-transferable story had evaporated into the eternal mists of time: Sílvia, Dixi and Gràcia; Ruth and Fabià; Eulàlia and Susana; Tomàs, Pere, Yma and Lídia; other co-protagonists such as Noemí, Lanzarote, Gemma, Marc Tejida and Max; and obviously, above all else, Her, The One and Only: Lluïsa Cabellera.

When they buried Fermí and Lluïsa, in a way they buried me, too, if not in the present, then in the past and the future. Though I'm still not rationally able to comprehend it, emotionally and sentimentally I perceived it there and then.

THREE DESERT CROSSINGS
DESERT N°1: *Introduction*

'Amazing Journey', THE WHO

The desert crossing of the title refers in a sadly sarcastic way to my sex life and emotional existence after Micalea's goodbye in the lead up to Christmas '92. I stuck a 'To Let' sign on the door of La Procida on the 22nd and went on a drinking spree that lasted until the second week of January. I only went home to the apartment above the restaurant, still impregnated with Micalea, to shower and sleep a short while every thirty or forty hours. I also retain a foggy image of the straw mattress at a police station filthier than most stables and no less sweet-smelling. When they picked me up for sleeping on a bench on Les Rambles, fortunately I'd already shot up everything that I'd bought, so the only thing they could do was leave me to scratch and snore until kindly showing me the door. Around the 9th or 10th of January, when I finally awoke from that long hangover, I went to see Enric to tell him my woes.

'Think of a fair price and the business is yours. It's the quickest way to get back what we still owe you. But do it now while the place still has a good reputation and customers because in two or three months it'll be worth nowt.'

'Okay, we'll work something out. I've got too much cash blowing around anyway, which I need to do something about. Let me look at the numbers.'

Enric gave me a good price but once the loans, rents, taxes, stamp duties and a myriad of other charges were paid only one million eight hundred thousand pessetes was left over, half of which I sent to Sandro to give to Micalea. Sandro called and tried to convince me to invest half in 'champagne' (cocaine, of course) and organise a wholesale export. But I really wasn't in the mood for more drug trafficking and even less so for returning to Naples: too many memories, even if Mín was dead and Micalea had gone to live in Miami.

Miami? Why the fuck has she gone to Miami, I remember thinking. *And who with*? But, as I've already said, if you don't want to know… It wasn't all that surprising, though; she herself told me before leaving that she was going, more than anything because she was bored: bored of the customers, of the *trattoria*, of the neighbourhood, bored even of pizzas and pasta. She was perfectly aware that the world had plenty more lives to offer her, all of them wider and richer in every sense of the word, and that now was the time to live them. On the other hand, I had no idea what I was going to do with my life apart from watching it slide wide open again and having it all to myself every single morning.

In the world of normal people, the idea of a boundless freedom of choice and movement is often mythologised but getting up every morning able to do anything you like with no limits other than those imposed by your own mood or means provides no guarantees of going to bed content. Or satisfied. Or any closer to having a purpose regarding the following day. In short, after thirty days of bumming around without reason or remorse, I went to see Kiddo, who was running a mountain refuge tucked away in the heart of the Aragonese portion of the Pyrenees with picture postcard views of Monte Perdido to the north-west. I'd even go as far as saying that the snow, stars, solitude and silence were the ideal ointment for the many wounds I was dragging between my legs and ears.

My conversations with Dalai Kid (as I called him due to his obsession with Buddhism) were congenial but scarce so in order to not completely forget about personal relations, that winter I threw myself into the inscrutable vice of literature. I admit it was a little like writing pornographic stories for the pleasure of autoeroticism but, as everyone knows, when reality is in short supply the intellect (just like sex) needs fiction more than ever. There was nothing spectacular about my work at the refuge, and my social life was limited to the few oddballs that spent the odd night there, normally at weekends, before attempting to scale some summit, more often than not Monte Perdido. An act that between November and March, except for truly first-rate mountaineers, was practically impractical. In other words, I had so much free time on my hands that I even relearnt how to play chess. At first I couldn't understand Kiddo's newfound enthusiasm for the game; we'd only played as kids because we lived opposite the chess club. And it was little league stuff at best.

DESERT N°2: *Li, or sublimation*

Soldier, your eyes, they shine like the sun
NEIL YOUNG

It must have been mid-March when one evening in the pub in
the village, I saw an odd-looking person giving the doctor the
beating of his life, the only old boy who seemed to know a thing
or two about it. Chess, I mean. I say 'odd' because I'd need a
long line of adjectives to get anywhere close to describing the
individual. For starters, he was from Cambodia, he had distinctly
Asian features and everyone called him Li. He owned a house
on the edge of the village and came up whenever he wanted,
whether for a couple of days or a couple of months. I sat down
to play, knowing full well I'd get a whipping, but I was eager to
strike up conversation with him and frankly desperate to hear
a different voice. But all of my expectations were surpassed as
soon as I told him I was Kiddo's brother.

'Oooh! Kiddo's brother! He speaks very much about you!'

To win a few brownie points I mumbled that he could only
be saying that out of politeness because my brother, if indeed
we were talking about the same person, seldom speaks about
anyone or anything.

'Sometimes one sentence is enough. I know he loves you
dearly and has worried very much about you.'

Though his Catalan was fluent, he'd occasionally insert the
odd word in Spanish, French or Khmer. He also knew English,
Arabic, Cantonese and a whole load of other languages and
dialects from India and south-east Asia. He usually spoke so
directly that it often left me speechless. That night I lost the first
two games but I managed to win the third and fourth, perhaps
because whereas I'd limited myself to two whiskies on the rocks

he'd knocked back five cognacs and three beers. The bar closed but I wasn't in the mood for driving forty-five minutes and then walking for twenty more minutes up the steep mountainside with our provisions on my back and snow up to my ankles, and I would've happily stayed at his house had he offered. But he didn't. And I now know he didn't precisely so I stopped being lazy and honoured my responsibility.

I've already said that he was an odd character but he possessed a profundity and a perspective that still return to me in rich ruminations, as though I were never completely certain of having exhausted all possible readings. Indeed, he himself said it was impossible to know any message perfectly because all messages change constantly, beyond people, through time, space and context, and even the message itself, which inevitably, after so much repetition, dies and demands a reformulation, even if it's only to express the same content.

'The first time you say "I love you" to someone,' he often used as an example, 'has nothing to do with the thousandth time you say "I love you", regardless of whether it's to the same person or not.'

In other words, he immediately solved one mystery for me (why my brother was so infatuated with chess) only to gradually replace it with a hundred more.

Li owned a martial arts gym in Vielha, another in Monzón, and two more in Zaragoza, and soon he'd be opening a small chain of south-east Asian restaurants in more or less the same area. My brother, Dalai Kid, met him in none other than Kathmandu where the two of them had gone, for distinctly different reasons, to purify themselves. Of what, exactly? Here you have two enigmas for the price of one. After a few weeks of sharing their many spiritual aches and pains, they became intimate friends and Kiddo told him that with a few bucks and a good teacher there was money to be made in Catalonia in martial arts. And so Li, by his own admission on the verge of choosing death over life out of sheer boredom, decided to dedicate himself a while longer to earthly pursuits.

The day after meeting him in the pub, he turned up at our hut in the late morning with three fresh lobsters and three or four bottles of wine and cognac in his backpack. He spent the rest of the morning cooking while Kiddo and I laboured out back so as not to get in his way. After eating grilled lobster prepared with nothing but pepper, vodka and lemon juice, served with brown rice, we began a never-ending chess triangle over coffee and cognac. I've never had much time for chess and, what's more, I sensed that the two men sitting with me, in reach of my voice, my hands, knew a dimension of this life and planetary existence that I'd never ever reach, and I would've liked to hang out, hear their stories of unprecedented adventure and fill my mental notebook of literary psychodramas. Kiddo and I were making our way silently through a quiet game when Li filled his glass, inhaled its fragrance and suddenly delivered his judgement:

'You don't concentrate on the game because you think the conversation and laughter will benefit as a result. On the other hand, you play very well because you instinctively understand everything that's being said amid the silence.'

'I'm sorry, I don't follow you.'

'That's a lie. Listen between the lines.'

He said it in French but I was no longer paying any attention because right then I decided to win the game. It wasn't difficult: my brother has never had much imagination and after a few more fortuitous moves I was able to take his rook, whereupon Kiddo threw in the towel claiming he was tired and hitting the sack. Then Li surprised us both by asking permission to give me a brief demonstration. Well, it surprised me, at least, because my brother's only external expression was to sit back down, smile and offer up the palms of his open hands which, in Dalai Kid language, means: *proceed with whatever you believe to be befitting.* Li then picked up a log the width of my wrist and the length of my arm.

'Do you think I can break this log with only one hand?'

I looked at it and told him no. Now I was starting to enjoy myself.

'Hold it,' he told me and placed it in my hands.

I should have smelt the trap because my brother allowed a kernel of laughter to pass his lips but I was in the mood for some fun and didn't reflect on it. I pressed my biceps firmly against my ribs and my hands against the log but the force of Li's chop made my left leg tremble and I toppled. Kiddo let out half of a whole laugh and poured himself more wine (he had only drunk water and wine for some five or six years) and said that if I'd stood my ground I could easily have broken my elbow or kneecap. I had a graze on each palm, almost a cut in fact, but Li said he could never hurt me because that wasn't his intention. At that point I felt slightly peeved and I reminded him that the log was on the floor still in one piece. Li nodded and asked Kiddo (who looked like a goddam kid at the funfair) to kindly step forwards and he got himself into position, more or less like I had, but with the benefit of foreknowledge.

'Ready?' Li asked him.

'Yep,' replied Kiddo.

With a movement twice as rapid, Li brought the side of his hand down against the log and broke it clean in two. I admit that I was wildly impressed. But I was even more impressed when, late one early morning, while playing chess at his place, he lifted his gaze above our black and white battle and announced:

'Do not fear death. Do you not remember that you will be

reincarnated as a wild horse?'

He said it as if it were the most natural thing in the world, in fluent French, but I made him repeat it three more times in three more languages, just to be sure I'd understood correctly. He merely let out more radiant laughter and replied:

'If you don't understand it's because you don't know and if you don't know it's because you're not there yet.'

I could share many more anecdotes and adventures regarding Li, many more than I've told or could tell about myself, and I would if it weren't so painful. As a result, I will only risk a summary of what I remember of his biography and sketch a few scenes that we shared down in the village (that I shall not name) and up in our remote refuge by Monte Perdido.

Li, real name Lon Siem, was born into a Khmer family on the southern shore of the Great Lake in 1947, the same year as Prince Sihanouk's first constitution, if memory serves me correctly, and he was the son of a public servant of relative political importance. In 1966, his father already a member of Sihanouk's parliament and the U.S. having just completed its great deployment of troops to South Vietnam, young Li – aware of his ancestry and a fervent follower of the Maoist praxis spreading throughout the region – ran away from home to join the Communist guerrillas in their struggle to overthrow the pro-USA military regime and to reunify the country under socialism. He participated in numerous renowned offensives and witnessed and survived a few of the Yankee bombings that now form an integral part of both 20th Century history and cinema. In September 1973, after seven years of apocalypse in the here and now, a grenade wounded him in the lung and he was later taken captive by Saigon mercenaries. However, in December 1974, having more or less fully recovered from his injuries, he managed to steal an automatic rifle from a new recruit and neutralise (murder, in military jargon) the eleven men and two women guarding him before releasing his six comrades imprisoned along with him in the hospital. Needless to say, his superiors deemed it an act of heroism and helped him through the posterior pain and anguish by awarding him the corresponding medals, but the fact of the matter was that of the six men he liberated five died in the wild and the sixth perished shortly before South Vietnam's surrender. Amid the euphoric disorder of reunification he found a place to rest and reflect on how he'd just made history but in March 1977 an unexpected conversation with his father turned his life on its head. And, according to him, it was about time, too.

I'm able to invent a conversation between Li – a thirty-year-old Vietcong hero and ex-prisoner of war busily organising his country's uprising – and his father – incarcerated for three years by the regime that overthrew the prince in 1970, who was fifty-eight but looked seventy, and had just been released from prison into an unhealthy, homeless reality. I'm able to invent it from cuttings of conversation with him amid chess moves and drug taking, from shreds of the past pulled from Dalai Kid like wisdom teeth and sounds and sentences without simultaneous translation from a dream I had the night I smoked opium with Li at his house. His father, as thin as a bulrush, opens the scene in a tough but tubercular tone.

'Your only mistake is not reflecting on your mistakes.'

'Perfection is by no means easy to attain. But it's important to strive for it.'

'Only with appropriate means. I know of an honourable man who has been ruined, persecuted and imprisoned because of violence. He's never fired a gun or wielded a sabre, and the only physical aggression he has committed against another human being, may Buddha forgive him, was to give you a slap on the backside when you were six because you were trying to get a kitten to befriend you against its wishes to the point of using cruelty.'

'But, father...'

'Vietnam has been reunified at an unfathomably bloody price, and now Cambodia is full of foreigners and fellow countrymen clamouring for immediate fortunes. You boys fought well but with perverse means, and evil and corruption have found a thousand paths along which to spread. Physical violence can only ever play into the hands of those that possess a violent spirit.'

'But without violence there wouldn't have been a revolution and we'd still be living under the yoke of feudalism!'

'That's not true. There have been many revolutions – and thankfully there will be many more – that have had nothing to do with violence. Take India and the figure of Gandhi as two cases close to us in time and space.'

'But much blood was spilt to achieve India's independence!'

'Yes, my son, much blood. But by the *others*. What is it that you can't or don't want to understand, oh malleable mind of the renewed and recently reinstated Workers' Party of the Socialist Republic of Vietnam? One may die for an idea, any idea, if one deems it just and worthy of one's death. But what one must never do, never ever, is kill for an idea, even if it's the same one.'

'Why not? It's only logical that if an idea is worthy of giving your own life for then it also justifies taking another's.'

'But it does not.'

'Why not?'

'The answer is easy, my boy. But if I tell you with words you most likely won't ever comprehend.'

'Tell me however you please. If indeed you really do know.'

'Of course I know and I'm surprised that you doubt me. All I ask is that you renounce your political position and privileges and go, as naked as possible, to live for a year in Kathmandu.'

But Li didn't pay any heed to his father's plea until a couple of years later when the old man was already dead and the Socialist Republic of Vietnam no longer seemed to have any need for heroic sacrifices. So, in January 1980, he liquidated all of his assets, both political and material, bought a cart and six horses, rented a guide and a hand, and embarked on a merchant journey west. He planned to pass by the Great Lake to pay his respects to his family but the political situation didn't permit it. In March 1980, he arrived in Calcutta without cargo, cart, horses, guide, hand, or sandals, and the following summer he made it to Kathmandu. Once he'd permanently established himself there, he began cultivating his past and his peace by studying a version of Taoism founded by Lao Tse and started a project that would span five lifetimes. In the summer of 1985, he met Dalai Kid, aka *Silent Kiddo*, who'd already been living there for a couple of years, and twelve months later, once again breaking with the norms and tedium of contemplative existence, they both flew to Barcelona.

'*Fly Air India!*' is what Li used to say with disgust. 'If I'd stopped to think about it too long I'd have come on foot!'

The funniest thing of all is that when he said such a thing it was because he actually meant it, and Li must be the only human being I've met capable of walking here all the way from Kathmandu without turning it into a product or writing a book about it. By association of ideas, I remember him telling me that of the three things that Westerners believe they have to do before dying (have a child, write a book, plant a tree) only the third would seem authentic in the East. There, books are left to those who earn a living from them, whereas procreating is looked down upon, if not completely prohibited.

Our maundering mass of meals, late nights and chess games

at the refuge, village pub and his house, along with the ineluctable cosmic conversations, as deep as they were unadorned, lasted fifteen to twenty months, give or take, because Li not only cultivated his widening business interests but also spent six weeks in Egypt, nine or ten by Lake Victoria and more or less the same amount of time in Vietnam and Cambodia. Only later did we realise that the last trip had been a final farewell. Like so many other tremendous surprises from my wayward existence, alive in my memory will always be the day he walked into the hut, his backpack full of seafood and alcohol, and told us he'd come to say goodbye.

'Where are you going?' I asked like an imbecile, thinking about his intercontinental trips.

'I don't know. But I won't be coming back.'

'Never? What about the gyms and the restaurants?'

'Shut up, Alexandre,' Kiddo muttered.

He stared tenderly and deeply into Li's eyes and, lightly touching his elbow, accompanied him to the kitchen to unpack the provisions and help him prepare the feast. And suddenly, in a flash, I understood: much like someone moving house or migrating to another country, he'd decided to leave for the land of the dead. And now that he'd confided in us, all we could do was to respect his choice.

Someone with much greater talent could prise a series of exemplary novels out of that sprawling night but after lunch the smoke and spirits began to flow, my memory begins to swim and, despite recalling certain sequences frame by frame, the general script gets lost amid the swirling waters. As usual, goddammit.

I do remember one pre-lunch sequence while we were playing chess with the Made in Taiwan digital clock he'd bought me for my thirty-seventh birthday set to five minutes. I had almost two full minutes remaining and was one bishop and two pawns up but I froze and ended up losing from a clear winning position due to the time rule.

'Chess is like life. It's a battle against yourself. Contrary to what people think, the challenge isn't your adversary but your ability to delve into your own being. Or to put it in Western terms, into your own psychology.'

Kiddo was knelt by the fireplace preparing the grill and he embarked on one of the longest speeches I've ever heard him make:

'Humans are capable of almost anything when we know how to concentrate our energy on a single objective. The only thing required is a deep knowledge of oneself and the ability to compartmentalise the rest.'

I placed the prawns on the grill and they left their chess game forever more to go for one last stroll together. It was the 25th of August and even up there in that lost corner of the world the night would be pleasant. Now I'm sure they took advantage of that brief moment of intimacy to make love for the last time but back then, if I'm being totally honest, I didn't suspect a thing and I'd have laughed in the face of anyone who might've suggested as much.

I had dinner just about ready when they got back and as we ate Li spoke with a cosmic glow in his eyes on the benevolence and evil of humans, on the coherences and discrepancies between East and West regarding what he called 'the utopic generation of the second half of the 20th Century', and on the perversion that praxis implacably causes within any social, cultural or political doctrine.

'In reality,' he said, 'I possess an optimistic spirit and I'm convinced that civilisation is constantly advancing. Pessimism, or more accurately, the (dis)illusion, comes from witnessing how slowly it moves. Meanwhile, millions of humans are born and die without a shred of light, and other animal and plant species are absurdly exterminated by ours.

'I'm optimistic enough to believe that when humanity is finally wiped off the face of the Earth many other less destructive life forms will remain to follow their own evolutionary path. Who knows if they will reach another life form, not necessarily intelligent, for many already exist, but capable of the artistic impulse and scientific thought that is, fortunately or unfortunately, all that truly separates us from other large mammals. The (dis)illusion, and also a certain perplexity, stems from the thought that our supposed global civilisation lived in much greater harmony with its 'home' two thousand years ago than it does today. It's as if progress, which in theory should be the tool that liberates the meek, had become the planet's death sentence owing to the blindness of the strongest. But, according to my teacher in Kathmandu, who was a hundred years old but looked seventy, this would be a Manichaean analysis and therefore contrary to the essence of the Idea. Our only consolation is accepting that the strongest, i.e. man, has imposed this awful law of survival upon the environment to the point of gorging on everything, just like the bird anxious to grow at whatever cost that first eats the nest, then the eggs of its siblings, then its parents and finally, when there's nothing left, slowly devours itself.

'Either way, I'm unmistakably optimistic when I behold the universe and see so many stars susceptible to warming worlds full of life. If the laws of probability make any sense up there then humanity is insignificant. And if they don't and we really are alone then we are even more meaningless. The chimeric illusion, in any case, is the result of our species' pride: of thinking, of knowing that if reason and honour were able to control and channel the technological advances of the 20th Century and balance the Blue Garden's resources and inhabitants, perhaps one day a few centuries from now, Paradise would just about be an earthly reality. Achieving the fair distribution of wealth and knowledge around the planet so that everyone has the genuine opportunity to be educated to the point of boredom and bored to the point of choosing suicide is the only objective truly worthy of humanity.

'Yes, I'm optimistic because my old Tao teacher, who possessed unparalleled wisdom, revealed to me that in the next life I will be reincarnated as a female falcon and flying has always fascinated me. But the painful chimera in this case stems from believing, even though it's so painful, that there's nothing as wonderful as being conscious of one's successes and failures and of meditating upon diverse philosophies and, alas, these are heights falcons are incapable of reaching.'

With fewer words yet more content, he made his final great speech as we stretched out together on the northern hillside to contemplate the sliver of purple moon kissing the stony nipple of Monte Perdido. In an utterly indeterminate moment, as though he were going to fetch something to drink or to take a leak, he stood up and said it was time.

'See you,' muttered Kiddo without moving.

'See you,' I managed to repeat, my throat tied up in knots of tears.

'If you wish to cry then cry,' he smiled softly at me. 'But please don't worry. Mine is a freely taken, deeply meditated act that isn't forcing me into anything except liberation itself.'

Then he turned and walked away towards the black mountainside. I began to weep amid Kiddo's silence, and I don't know whether it was over losing Li or because I didn't understand.

'Be calm, little brother. Life and death are the same splendour and the same shit.'

'At least tell me how he's going to do it,' I begged between sobs.

'He'll sit under the tree that has been waiting for him all his life and contemplate the hours without eating or drinking until his twilight comes eight or nine days from now.'

'When will we go and get him?'

'Never. Who knows where his tree is.'

Despite his Mitsubishi remaining in the car park at the bottom of the hill with its papers in Kiddo's name, as far as I knew he could still be alive. His death was never certified, his body was never found, nobody ever reported him missing. His earthly assets had been put in order before his departure and a week later I had the honour of attending a pseudo-Buddhist ceremony officiated by Dalai Kid in front of seventy or eighty people (all from Cambodia, all of them refugees in Vietnam until Li saved them) who'd come to pay tribute to their benefactor's passage. Thanks to Kiddo's last speech before leaving for Kathmandu, I discovered that Li's reason for coming to Catalonia had been to move what remained of his family – decimated and dispersed due to political upheavals – to a place where they'd never again experience fear or famine. And after seven and a half years of hard work and dedication he'd practically achieved it when the old desire to hand himself over to total non-action returned and was finally triumphant.

In his next incarnation, Li would be a female falcon.

DESERT Nº3: *Gràcia, or temptation*

I've heard that one day
Everything comes to him who waits
RORY GALLAGHER

Kiddo sold the Mitsubishi and bought a one-way passage to Kathmandu. I drove him to the port in Tarragona with what was left of the VW Polo that Dixi had sold us six years ago between the nightmare with Lanzarote and the adventure in Naples. When we said goodbye he confirmed what I'd already feared for days:

'Say goodbye to Loleta and Mum for me.'

'Don't make me do it, Kiddo. Send Mum a letter.'

'See you, Alexandre, little bro.'

'See you, Kiddo, big bro.'

I couldn't stay at the refuge with a couple of ghosts like them on the mantelpiece and anyway, I was itching to return to the earthly riot. Sweet Eulàlia had a year's contract at the University of Edinburgh and she kindly lent me her flat on Plaça Padró, so I gifted myself a couple of months holiday and chaos during which I became reacquainted with my old userdealer habits, if only in an experimental capacity. Life was wide open once again every morning and once again I chose to live the hours according to the hands of a manic clock and hide my anxieties over the void and my many poorly processed memories. Lily, Mín and the rest of the gang could now count on two more spectacular supporting characters: Li and Kiddo who, dead or alive, I'd never see again.

Using and abusing Enric's contacts and my brother-in-law's money, I scraped together a tremendous amount of courage and opened a pub (the last) in the posh area of Martorell, if indeed there is such a thing. But I admit that both the business and my ways had changed to the point that they were no longer compatible. I didn't want to serve cans of soda and sweets, and even less so bow to the tyranny of the pounding techno fashionable at the time. The few select customers that passed by after dinner didn't provide me with enough income or satisfaction and, almost without realising, I began dealing and using on the side, if only to pay the bills and make it through the winter.

One Sunday in March, on my way back from Manresa after Dolors had given birth to another ray of sunshine (called Dawn), the VW gave out. It was five o'clock in the evening and raining like never before. I dedicated a fat line to Roxy Music, keeping me company on the cassette player, and waited ten minutes for the rain to ease off before grabbing my skeletal umbrella, throwing myself headfirst into the storm and trotting the nine hundred and ninety-nine metres to the Olesa petrol station. I prescribed myself a whiskyespresso and called the nearest garage, but when I told the woman on the other end my name (over something to do with the car's insurance) she laughed loudly and told me it was Gràcia. *Gràcia*…? *Gràcia*…? Oh, *Gràcia*, of course! Dixi's ex! The one Mín had said was one in a million.

'Order me a coffee and a large rum and I'll be with you in five.'

She arrived with the tow truck and a mechanic before the coffee even had time to get cold. We hadn't seen each other since…

'September '88, if my memory serves me correctly.'

'It does, it does. How weird that I didn't remember after everything that happened to me, and yet you…'

'I have more reasons than one. First of all because my ex started using heroin big time after buying from you… everyday a little more until he was up to his neck in drugs again.'

The second reason was much more of a surprise: while her ex and I were away on our little alchemist trip to Barcelona, turning marzipan into snow, she and Fermí fucked amid paintbrushes and glue pots and she ended getting pregnant. She didn't tell me the surprising second part at the petrol station while her mechanic was loading my piece of junk onto the truck, but rather some weeks later during one of our many subsequent dinners in the most exclusive restaurants in the zone. Needless to say, I was left dumbstruck and after remembering how her boy, a little monkey of five or six, already knew how to drive everyone mad with his obscene questions, I asked:

'David?'

'David,' she confirmed while taking a photo out of her purse. 'What do you think?'

'No doubt about it. His mouth, the thickness of his lips, the dimple in his chin.'

'Exactly.'

'His eyes are big and black like yours.'

'Mine are dark brown.'

'They look black to me.'

'Colours, like feelings, are arbitrary and subjective.'

All of a sudden two or three Big Ideas popped into my head. The first, impregnated with nostalgia, told me that if Fermí had known about it, or rather, if I'd been able to tell him four years ago when we said our goodbyes in Pozzuoli perhaps he'd have come back to try and occupy the vacant position left by his cousin. He knew about cars and had always had a head for business. Anyway, it was too late now. The second, impregnated with panic, hounded me over the very real possibility that Gràcia had been infected; Gràcia and David, of course.

Knowing the first idea could only hurt her, I kept it inside, softening as far as possible the melodramatic finale of the kid's father. Regarding the second, after gulping down my fears, I tacitly kept to a few indirect questions, all of which received frank, direct answers:

'I got lucky.'

'Being a one-off and all…'

'You can't rely on that. I've got a friend that caught it after just one night.'

'Well, I guess it's possible, but then neither have I ever met a woman who got pregnant after a one-night stand.'

'Because they don't go around talking about it. My big sister, for example, got pregnant the first time she had sex, in the very act of losing her virginity.'

'Now that's what you call bad luck.'

'Tell me about it! It's a funny story, too.'

I got the impression she didn't want to go into detail about the other subject, so I listened instead to the amusing anecdote of two hippy teenagers who run away from home in the early seventies to live together in Ibiza and after the aforementioned nocturnal union in a public park are thrown off the island by the police just hours after arriving on the ferry, charged with vagrancy and public indecency. What's more, they were also made to pay for the return fare out of their own pocket. That night, after finding courage in the whisky we'd ordered along with our coffees (the same brand I found in the glove compartment of the pink panther the night of the transported transporters) and asked her the burning question:

'You don't want to sleep with me because I'm seropositive, right?'

'Wrong. But I'll be frank. I feel good around you and I like going out with you but I'm just not in love with you. Sure, if it weren't for this demon disease, perhaps I would have already let it happen, some night or other, to see if I like you just as much in bed. But I have two kids who don't have a dad and I can't take these sorts of risks.'

I could see where she was coming from but that didn't mean I agreed with her. I pointed towards safe sex and that intercourse isn't everything and in the end, wholly unexpectedly, I convinced her to come to mine for a line and a penultimate whisky. The preambles went smoothly and the night was a pleasant one but sexually we hardly got off the ground: I off-loaded a hefty amount of pent up desire (the type that vulgarly gets called 'wham bam, thank you, ma'am) i.e. two ejaculations with my cock as floppy as a burst balloon, while she only got a mediocre masturbation and some finger fucking out of it because she wouldn't let me do anything else.

The following day I understood what she meant by not taking risks. For us to be real lovers we'd require numerous training sessions because of the obstacles and apprehensions in our way, and time was what we had least of, bearing in mind how I was still haunted by Eulàlia's ghost and she, I believe, by Fermí's shadow. However, as with most things when it comes to Gràcia, this is nothing but guesswork because she never revealed anything to me on the subject. Nor did I ever really know for sure whether or not she was HIV positive because she had a certain way of reacting that made me suspect that the 'friend' who'd caught it after one passionate night was actually her and that by keeping it a secret (out of respect for her children) she multiplied her fears and anxieties tenfold.

I was tempted to renounce my burdensome independence, move in with her and help her with bringing up the boys and making the business grow. After all, one son was Dixi's (who she told me was eking out a living as a farmhand in remotest Galicia on a property belonging to a drug lord), and the other was Mín's (lying forgotten in a common grave in Naples), so the situation seemed to demand, if only in a literary sense, a stepfather like Lex. But literature isn't real life: I was no longer that Lex and the person who had to decide, Gràcia, had already made their mind up.

Financially speaking things were more than okay for her. She'd opened a car dealership next to the garage and shop in Olesa and another garage in Martorell, while I was sinking and drowning in that pub that always smelt clean. Too clean. I say sinking and drowning because I'd decorated it with a ship's wheel and a few portholes and called it 'Titanic'. Another fuck up to file with the rest. It was around that time when I was tempted to get hooked again or commit suicide in some other way because I was incapable of picturing any trace of a future that appeared even remotely satisfying.

The second and last temptation with Gràcia wasn't much better than the first, in all likelihood because of the repression that some sort of super ego exercised over our bodily instinct because, at least from my end, there was desire in abundance. Our dinners ended without us ever having achieved a breakfast together and Gràcia continued full steam ahead with her business whereas I sold Titanic to a local coke dealer for three million pessetes. One more wreck on the seabed.

ONE FINAL DESERT: *Epilogue to a present*

Oh, how I want to be free
Freddie Mercury, QUEEN

I moved into Enric's place in Masnou and dedicated myself to doing sweet F.A. for an entire month. Well, not quite, because I did do something: I'd get up at two or three in the afternoon, eat breakfast, write solidly until nine or ten, eat again and head out for drinks in Barcelona where, more often than not, I felt like a castaway because almost no one from the old roll call of friends and friends of friends remained. I hadn't heard anything from Pere the Painter for almost five years; Leonormaria had married a totally bald, totally conventional shoe manufacturer and flown south to Valencia; Tomàs had finally understood that coke comes at too high a price in the long run and escaped the grip of bars and bizniz to seek the open arms of psychiatrists and medication. He was the first person I knew to have to seek professional help to overcome his addiction to blow, but I'm sure he won't be the last because the most pernicious thing about powder is abusing it for years on end. I know of more than one marriage destroyed by the mania and the confusion it creates, not to mention the financial disarray. And I know more than one friend of a friend, and good people, too, who've raised a hand to their partner in the same way Dixi did to Gràcia because of smack.

But onwards and upwards: Susana had also found herself a partner; a professional photographer fifteen years her senior who'd been determined to bring her in from the cold despite she never having been a street walker. They were living in Valldoreix in the hills above Barcelona in a detached house on a middle-class estate that had been left half finished. Jordi was twelve, remarkably tall for his age, and attended a well-to-do school in Sant Cugat where he was top of the class in mathematics, believe it or not. Siouxsie did modelling work when she could get it, and to combat the inevitable boredom of domestic life she'd finally realised her dream of going to university.

'Journalism', I said to her.

'Information Science,' she corrected me.

And as far as I'm aware, she's scrupulously faithful to her husband. Eulàlia came back from Edinburgh with a caramel-coloured lover of Polynesian descent called Mònica (Mònica Armand), making her the envy of males and females everywhere. Though not quite as spectacular, she did make me think of that bombshell Fermí had introduced me to one summer's evening (oh, what was her name... *Ghana*?) Anyway, mulatto Mònica made me think of Ghana, who I've never again had the good fortune to see. 'If not for Eulàlia I'd sit you down right now to study the Kama Sutra together, one verse at a time' is what I thought when I first laid eyes on her. But that's only a figure of speech, of course, because after my dismal experience with Gràcia, and one or two depraved disappointments during the sinking of the Titanic (either because I pushed too hard or stayed anchored too long), I'd lost my touch and when I baited the hook all I caught were worms. This isn't some attempt at lyricism but it was as though somewhere between the moon and the night I'd lost the spontaneity of seduction: I'd sit chewing over my approach, over whether to explain my life story or to chop it into bite-size pieces, or instead wait for an intimate signal on the opposite shore, while the water ran through my fingers. Most likely I contributed to it ninety per cent of the time because of my own withholding or omission.

Onwards: Yma had managed to overcome a terrible case of tuberculosis that had her teetering over the edge of the end and was now working in none other than the mayor's office. She was unmarried, if we don't count her job, but she was at least alive: '*More alive than ever!*' as city hall's latest omnipotent slogan put it. And last but never least, Enric Costales, aka the altruistic plutocrat, had got involved in a business network down in South America and built himself a villa in Buenos Aires. Officially, the whole thing had something to do with a hotel and two publishers (or the other way around, I forget) but I suspect suitcases lined with coca paste arrived with him each time he flew back (that's a joke because Enric always made it clear that having money meant not having to take risks to earn more: there were plenty of others willing to do it for a price).

He came back for three or four weeks every three or four months and on one of these occasions he invited a friend I didn't know over for dinner. He did mention from the outset that he was a psychologist but I didn't put two and two together. Nevertheless, when we were having coffee they brought up the topic of addiction in such a premeditated way that it bordered on behaviourism and before I knew it he was trying to sell me a methadone programme.

'Listen, I know you only have my best interests at heart. And I'm grateful, I really am. But I don't need a substitute. Fifteen years ago I would've found it great but I'm no longer addicted or anything remotely resembling it. I just like to cross statistical lines now and again and snort a line of my own.'

'You don't inject it?' the psychologist asked without a shred of tact.

'Never,' I lied, telling myself that he had fuck all to do with it.

'Okay, you know best. No one is forcing you to do anything you don't want to.'

'Well, that's a relief…!'

That was the catalyst for an immediate change of topic and the psychologist evaporated like a shadow ten minutes later. And that was when Enric, determined to set me up and have me doing something worthwhile before leaving, proposed plan B, and so I went to live at Cal Fumall, where I've now been for two years and hope never to leave. The clauses of the contract that we shook on – verbal but binding – were more or less as follows:

1) He was leaving me Cal Fumall (Malanyeu) free from rent and any type of charges, fully furnished and equipped, on a one year lease to be renewed yearly.

2) He was granting me rights to the three vegetable gardens below the house and free use of the woodland beside the property. Whatever products and subsequent profit I might derive from the land and the sale of firewood were mine to keep.

3) I was committing to maintain the house and property in good condition, and to work no less than thirty hours a week on the rambling narratives that form the origins of this novel.

4) I was also committing to cut a minimum of twenty trees a month during the summer and half that during the winter.

5) The tools needed to begin working (for the record: a car suitable for the mountains, a large chainsaw, a small laptop) were my responsibility.

6) Food and maintenance costs, in addition to anything unrelated to the property's structure or services, were also my responsibility.

7) I was morally obliged to extend my stay until having developed or finished the novel, or something similar.

DESERT MIRAGE: *MÒNICA, OR IMPOTENCE*

At the bottom of La Rambla
I came across a black flower
RADIO FUTURA

When it comes to Mònica, though we'd seen each other a few times when I visited and we all went out with Lali, I didn't really get to know her until the night of the great snowstorm and our surprise reunion at Cal Fumall when we celebrated my last ever birthday. Two weeks later, with a skiing trip to Andorra as an excuse, she turned up alone in Malanyeu determined to sever my tragic chastity. I don't know and I'll never know if she was ever even minimally in love with me: maybe she felt sorry for me or had mythologised me and my literary labour within the wintery wilderness; maybe her relationship with Lali didn't completely satisfy her, as much as she told me the opposite; or maybe she simply enjoyed overstepping a few lines now and again. Whatever the truth, she did the enormous favour of enabling me to be myself again, as much as we had to take the necessary precautions, if not in a sentimental sense then at least in a sexual one. Therefore, the impotencies that I experienced with Mònica, from the very first night and over a dozen more during three or four months, were psychoemotional rather than physical, because we always enjoyed our time together (I felt the same as when I was eighteen and first met Lluïsa). But I never discovered the way to transfer my past onto our present, a past so puzzling and disparate that it deserves to be referred to in the plural. I don't know why it was so important to me, bearing in mind how distant I felt from those pasts, a distance that only increased in her presence, but it could be owing to an intimate desire to exteriorise the sins I'd theoretically overcome and to finally reach a sweet absolution free from adjectives. Nor was I ever able to feel that she belonged to me on a spiritual frequency. What I mean is I didn't sense that she was in love with me and didn't fill me with passion, at least not in the same way as Lluïsa and Eulàlia. But once more with nuance: I was in love with her, and very much so, and I still am, but perhaps I intuited that she'd be the last *dolcezza* on my loving list, and it was owing to these tiny abysms separating our intellects that we felt far too often like two strangers. Nevertheless, it was this situation that, sub-consciously and paradoxically, formed one of the most vigorous and stimulating aspects of our relationship.

FINAL FAREWELLS

And if there's one thing could do for you,
You'd be a wing in heaven blue
PATTI SMITH

When I was a little girl I once saw a film that said the 25th hour was for survivors and, despite not remembering the plot beyond the profile of a heroic martyr played by Anthony Quinn, the idea of roaming through an apocalypse and coming out of it alive, more or less affected but more or less unhurt, is what has inspired me to write this final farewell, which naturally must reference the posthumous tribute to the ashes of (not burial of) the deceased,

Alexandre Oscà i Punyol,

who one week ago chose to embark on his own private passage towards the stars:

'from the cosmos I have come and to the cosmos I will return, and I now understand that in reality I have been but a cosmic experiment,'

is what he left written amid the stacks of documents, files and pages, both manual and electronic, that constitute the bulk of his weightless literary testament which, notwithstanding its significance, cannot compare with his human testament, despite my opinion in my capacity as his past and last lover over the last few months (as festive within his new intellect as they were decadent within his old body) being subjective, biased and undoubtedly in love, and as much as I savoured the painful joy of witnessing how he prepared himself, as tender as a new shoot of mint, for death:

'while I've made it to and passed the age of forty, so many others much greater than I, have mouldered long before since the eve of time: poets, musicians, philosophers, scientists and prophets, heroes, kings and emperors of all three sexes have perished before reaching the age that I, with my hand forced, or not, or slightly, have chosen to disappear (which leads me to reflect on all the infants that vanish without the chance to ever develop as human beings and how it's like Li said: achieving a genuine adult education for all those born from a woman is the only objective worthy of humanity),'

is what he told me during my last (sadly platonic) visit to Malanyeu before the spreading of his ashes, of course; because the day we joyfully spread his remains we were all there, or thereabouts, at least at the meal Làlia was determined to put on at the Torres farmhouse (the family home in Avià that her cousin, finally recuperated from a terrible but terribly lucky car accident, had managed to revive), most likely to divide the attendees of the Farewell Meal as she called it from the Deflowering of the Ashes, as I called it:

the farewell spread was attended by Dolors (ex-Loleta), who came with her husband and two daughters, Dawn (two years) and Diana (eight), who got along very well with Gràcia's son, David, who had just turned the same age two weeks before, a week after his brother, Albert, had turned twelve, who felt more comfortable in the company of Jordi, Susana's son, who was thirteen and a half but looked sixteen:

'Susana came to see me and she had the tact to bring Jordi with her, as though he and I had an emotional tie (I no longer say family tie because blood doesn't always imply the best company: for years I've considered it better to make your own family from the people you pick up along the way and for these adopted relatives to choose you) and the gesture delighted me because the boy is like a beanstalk and intellectually even taller,'

is what he wrote to me in his penultimate letter from

hospital, in which he also added that:

'Conversing with Jordi in his capacity as the personification of the future of humanity, despite having been here barely five minutes, has made me accept that knowledge belongs to us neither in a personal, private way (because it belongs to the sum of civilisation) nor can its mystery – which we're continually searching for and losing as though it were made of mere seconds – ever be comprehended or possessed: it comes to us for a fleeting moment to give existence a minimum amount of coherence before passing onto our fellow man: we are what we touch and what we love, assuming we know how to love,'

he concluded, while ensuring me that he was saying it smiling and content, between swigs of prohibited beer and drags of illegal pot, or rather, just like we did during lunch due to the presence of Joan, owner of the farmhouse and sworn enemy of all types of drugs in his second life among the living and, despite the presence of his wife, Sandra, who was and still is a Jehovah's Witness but nevertheless 'the most sensitive, loving, wonderful human being I've ever met,' as described by Làlia that very evening at around nine o'clock when dusk summoned us and we got into our cars to drive up to Malanyeu:

the journey had a very special intensity: half an hour of the most beautiful Leonard Cohen reflected against the twilight horizons, a semiotic, symbolic, significant silence inside the vehicle that I was sharing with Susana, Jordi, and Gràcia, who'd left the kids at the farmhouse to go up there alone, I don't know why, perhaps because of us in general or someone in particular (e.g. Fabià) had attracted her to that unique ceremony...

although the ceremony itself (within the atemporal universality of the Place and the precise unfolding of the Night) was bursting with genuine memorial silences and laughter, words and gestures as transcendent as cypresses, what Alexandre really wanted, I'm sure, was a reunion of the living,

and I, in a very particular way, have him to thank for my inclusion on the list as he was the only person that even remotely knew me from that incredible group and only he could give me the opportunity to meet them, even if only superficially, given that the very act of meeting people (I don't want to say normal but from the outside world) was exactly what I most needed to overcome the trauma(s) of my imprisonment

(F I F T E E N Y E A R S
N I N E M O N T H S A N D
O N E D A Y)

and if not for that reunion and subsequent friendship with those people, I'd probably have ended up condemned to another sentence upon my release, possibly even more severe, as if it weren't for Alexandre, Eulàlia wouldn't have come to pick me up when I rang from the first yellowbellybar I found a phone in (eighty hours before the prearranged date, the exact same day he chose to kill himself), and they wouldn't have invited me up here like another member of the group – and an important one at that – given that from the outset they've considered and treated me as a true friend of the deceased (sure, but in reality only a penfriend) and as a true co-author of the utopic novel that they're truly trying to conjure up and/or distil down between the Sweet One, the Exotic One and the Rich One, who told me I could stay at Cal Fumall for as long as I wanted, for him it posed no problem, which lead Mònica and Eulàlia to decide to stay as well and see if they might be able to bring a bit of order and sense (while it was still fresh) to the universe of notes, sketches, projects, letters, pages, fragments, chapters, poems, quotations, dreams, epigraphs and a perplexing but prodigious etcetera that had us reading and contrasting, rereading and revising, for more than three fruitful weeks; and I felt good in Malanyeu, and at Cal Fumall I breathed the aroma of a serene and profound experience (unrepeatable and communal in the extreme) so utterly present that all the objects and the entire house were still impregnated with it; which is why Enric, also planning to take some holiday to collaborate with the conception and begetting of the Deadbeats (as we called ourselves), had to go back to Barcelona with Tomàs and his partner because...

here and now, now and after, a hundred times one hundred times, the immediate, precise feeling of hearing, seeing, sensing Alex, from the kitchen or when entering the bathroom or going up the stairs or in front of the fire, was so three-dimensional that it frightened me: it was as though he really had transformed into a ghost and were trying to speak to me through the thin veil separating nothingness from eternity; in fact, Eulàlia said...

eternity is all that remains for us to share, dear Alexa (despite the constant mutation and progressive disappearance of the mirages of memory, both private and collective, as it murmurs 'Farewell, Mirror'), the eternity of a silence woven with echoes of inorganic life that honours and accompanies you to the land of the

w   i   l   d   h   o   r   s   e   s